WITH THE CHILDREN

HENRY WEBB

outskirtspress

DENVER, COLORADO

Outskirts Press, Inc.
http://www.outskirtspress.com

ISBN: 978-1-4787-4659-1

Outskirts Press and the "OP" logo are trademarks belonging to Outskirts Press, Inc.

PRINTED IN THE UNITED STATES OF AMERICA

Please note that nothing in this novel is intended to be critical of teachers. It is the author's opinion that as a group teachers are a little better than the rest of us. He also believes that the U.F.T. is a worthy and necessary organization that would not exist if taxpayers were willing to provide the funds needed for public education without argument.

"I was always with the children, only with the children…
It was not that I taught them… they can teach us." Prince
Myshkin, Dostoevsky's idiot.

Contents

Part Three: Parents' Night 1969

Part Four: The Days Grow Shorter 1969

Part One:

School Starts 1969

Chapter 1:

We Gonna Be Bad

In a schoolyard: in south Harlem on a warm September morning was not the last place on earth Neil Riley wanted to be. That would be a Vietnam jungle dripping defoliant and body parts. Less unsavory, though by no means desirable, would be a youth hostel in Ontario, with Canadian migrant status and a work visa. Call that his emergency exit. Right now his choice was to stand trying to ignore the slow whirlpool of black and brown children swirling around him, looking him up and down, moving on; a slow chain of wary eyes and turned up noses and from a husky black kid a friendly smile, which Neil assumed to be a con.

Most of the children in the yard were gathered in loose clumps in front of adults of various ages, predominantly women, adults who were, like Neil, strung along the fence that separated the yard from the school. Neil knew that the adults were classroom teachers and that he was pretending to be one of them. Adult. Teacher. No way.

Not all the children were standing in front of the adults. Some hung out off to the sides or back from the others. And a few wandered from group to group. To his left he noticed three girls. One was a lean beauty in a black skirt and a neatly tucked-in white blouse; another was a pink-cheeked chubby girl in a blue skirt who wore her blouse out around her hips, *to hide her stomach,* Neil thought, knowing women. The third, doing all the talking, had a hard, straight body. She, too, wore a black skirt and white tucked-in blouse, though it was spilling out around the back. Her friends had long straight black hair pulled back neatly by those bright rainbow-colored plastic things, you know, barrettes, but her hair was wiry, barely reached below her neck and seemed to be working to throw off those barrettes struggling to contain it. As the other two listened the girl with the wiry hair turned at one point to stare at Neil, her expression revealing nothing. Then she turned back and with hands held up to the sky in supplication said something that got giggles from her friends, giggles they both hid quickly behind ladylike hands to their cheeks.

Neil was certain the girl had made an unflattering remark about him. *What's so funny about being sentenced to nine interminable months with a bunch of sniggering little girls like you?* he wondered.

The teachers, that would include Neil, stood along a freshly painted white line. Each teacher held a sign aloft that bore the numbers of her/his class. Neil's read "6-306" in his labored black print.

The high wire fence behind the teachers ran the entire perimeter of the yard. A gate opened into the rear entrance of the school. Another opened onto the sidewalk that ran along the front of the school. Neil had learned more than he wanted to know about this fence and those gates during his three days of orientation. When school was not in session these gates were locked. There was an asphalt walkway between the school and the fence and that walkway too had gates at either end that were unlocked at the beginning of each school day and locked again when the day ended. The school itself was opened at precisely seven each morning and locked down at precisely four-thirty every afternoon. No problem there. The last bell rang at three. He'd be gone by five after three.

Outside the fence on the sidewalk where Neil longed to be a number of women and two men stood staring quietly in at the children. Once upon a time the women's faded dresses might have been bright and colorful; they weren't now. One woman clutched the fence with an outstretched hand; another leaned her forehead in wearily between arms crooked at the elbow. The others simply stood and watched. If they spoke to each other it was too softly to be heard from over here. Black and brown women. Mothers, grandmothers.

The two men standing side by side wore identical shiny black suits and black bowties. Waiters? One had his arms folded over his chest, rocking. The other stood slumped forward, arms dangling, craning to keep his head up.

With trance-like clarity Neil picked up the tangle of suspicion and hope this crowd felt offering up their children to these well-dressed mostly white authorities. It was not a viewpoint he felt any particular need to explore. His attention wandered instead to a young woman about his age, a sweet swish of motion in a yellow dress, walking by this stew as if it didn't exist. Truly. It wasn't as if she had to work to ignore those people, the schoolyard, the children, any of it. As far as he could see, for her they just weren't there, none of them. She just walked on by.

A variable breeze raised the dusty smell of concrete, reminding him that just about now he should be swinging into Washington Square Park on his way to join Roger at the fountain, in jeans, not these pressed khakis; and certainly not in this starched white shirt and blazer, a tie strung around his neck, Florsheims locked around his feet. Neil and Roger would check out the young mothers, then head off to class, where he was supposed to be, in class, in his final year at NYU Law.

A whistle blew, followed by a whale-like snort from loudspeakers placed at the four corners of the fence. Neil straightened up, alerted. But his eyes still lingered on the young woman, a blur of yellow crossing the street way over there, moving out of sight. He sensed that the two teachers near him had turned toward the whistle and he forced himself to turn too, toward a short bleached blonde, in her late forties or early fifties, standing at the microphone next to the gate opening into the back doors of the school. Mrs. Bane, the principal.

She blew her whistle again. And again. Her exasperated voice came booming from all sides. "WHEN THE WHISTLE BLOWS

YOU STOP WHAT YOU'RE DOING AND RAISE YOUR RIGHT HAND! YOU ALL KNOW THAT! TEACHERS, HELP US PLEASE!"

Neil wanted to yell at her with the same insulted exasperation that he didn't KNOW ALL THAT! That wasn't the setup, however. The setup was, she yelled, he hopped to. It wasn't a deal he liked, but it was the deal. Or else. He focused on the children standing in his general vicinity. Some had their hands up, some did not. Three boys gathered about twenty feet off were oblivious to these distractions. They were engaged in some complicated game involving swiftly thrown fingers.

"You boys back there," Neil said in a polite voice, but loud enough to be heard.

He got no response. He took a deep, indecisive breath, stepped forward, then was saved for the moment from any further uncertainty by a man standing just to his right.

"Hey, you!" the man, obviously a teacher, shouted. "Didn't you hear the whistle? Raise those hands! Now!"

This bold *uber*teacher was nearly half-a-head shorter than Neil. Though he seemed to be still in his twenties he had a budding bald spot and an emerging pot-belly. At his command one of the boys, a small natty fellow in a striped shirt and a snap-on bowtie, whipped his head around, looking startled. He wiggled his raised hand, surprised anyone had wanted his attention, but fully intent on cooperating—he wanted you to know that. The tallest of the three boys, very black, stood staring back at the teacher, his hands folded on his chest. The third, a thin boy in a white tee shirt that had been greyed in the wash, put his hand to a very large ear, smiling, and called back, "What'd you say, Mr. Um?... What'd you say?"

"Mr. Knight! What's your name? I know you!" the teacher shouted. "John! Clyde!" He pointed at the boy with the folded arms.

"I know you, too! Get those hands up if you know what's good for you!"

"Oh. Mr. Knight," the boy with the large ears said. With a snappy stiffening of his body, his arm shot into the air. The boy who had folded his arms now moved the right one out so that his upper arm was stretched parallel to the ground and his forearm was dangling from his elbow. Then seemingly without his knowledge or intent his forearm raised itself slowly up, palm open.

The only teacher on Neil's left, a black woman with a stiff straight back, had quieted several children around her by snapping her fingers and glancing at them sharply. The grey in her hair suggested she was older than he would have judged from the smooth skin of her face. He should have remembered her name, but he didn't.

For a brief moment there was silence.

Mrs. Bane glared at her domain. "When you hear that whistle you stop what you're doing and raise your right hands. You all know that."

A small black girl with a round pretty face planted herself in front of Neil and craned her neck up at him, exaggerating their difference in height. "You my teacher?" She pronounced it 'tea-cha.'

"I don't know," Neil said.

"Then whatcha holdin' that for?" she said in disgust, jerking a finger at his sign.

"There's talking," an incredulous Mrs. Bane boomed over the loud speaker.

"Shhhhh." Neil leaned down and put a finger to his lips.

"I was just askin'," the girl wailed.

"You be quiet!" Mr. Knight told the girl.

"I didn't do nothin'," the girl said, indignant. She rendered *nothing* as *nut-in* and managed to douse both syllables with a deep resentment. She turned away from the two men and folded her arms and stuck her lower lip out, a rich red bloom.

The children standing in front of Neil had watched this incident closely.

"You may put your hands down now." And as everyone complied she said, "But don't talk. Your teachers are all holding signs. Hold them up, please, teachers. You know which class you're supposed to be in, children, so go to it and line up in front of your teacher. Two lines, please, teachers, girls on your left, boys on your right."

Just at that moment two girls, one of them much larger and better developed than Neil would have thought an elementary school child should be, entered the yard. They kept pushing each other and laughing. The game they played was a simple one. You push me, I push you back. With each shove they made long backward journeys, their laughter loud and forced. The big girl moved forward by sliding her legs as if she were skating. The other girl, the thinner one without discernible breasts, watched, head to one side, not certain she could or should follow this frolic.

"You girls there!" This was again the incredulous Mrs. Bane. "Arlene! You be quiet!"

"Oh, gaw," the skater said, looking now at the spectacle of all those children. She had a round chin that she lowered and left pressed to her neck, so startled was she by the strange scene she had just discovered. The other girl stopped dead in her tracks and brought her hands together at her stomach as if to place them on a desk. If this was meant as an ironic impertinence, she didn't quite bring it off. She looked like a felon trapped in an alley offering her hands for the cuffs. The skater, on the other hand, took this opportunity to do another glide forward, arms outstretched, ta da!

"Arlene!" Mrs. Bane's voice was laden with threats.

This gave the skater pause. "Gaw! Just in the gate and they already callin' my name," she said to the world at large.

"Arlene!"

"Gaw!" She stamped her foot, then stood glaring across the

schoolyard at Mrs. Bane, who glared back, hands on hips. "Gaw," but this was a 'gaw' tempered with a hint of compromise. Her eyes narrowed, searching for a way to step out of the spotlight.

And apparently Mrs. Bane was willing to let her go. "Get to your proper classes, please," she said as if Arlene had been successfully dealt with. "Quietly. Quickly now."

Despite the warnings, with much chatter, children drifted to their lines. A measure of Neil's inability to be in this place was that he only now realized this loose group in front of him might be his class.

"If you belong in Mrs. Robin's class, 6-308, you should go to the very end of the yard over there. Next is Mr. Riley, 6-306..."

He squared his shoulders. *You have to do this*, he told himself. But did he? He could do the gutsy thing. Take off, leave everything behind. He pressed his sign a little higher in the air.

"After Mr. Riley is Mr. Knight, 6-305. Then Miss Travers, 6-307..."

Neil didn't hear who followed Miss Travers because of a voice shouting right under his nose. "Clyde! John! Over here!" from Bowtie, who was gazing off in the direction of a clump of children beyond Knight's line.

"Be quiet, please," Neil told him.

A request that won Neil a squinty face clearly intended to stop his annoying meddling. The boy turned to call again, "Hey! Clyde! John!"

Neil's primary reason for not pushing Bowtie's jaw into the roof of his mouth was, of course, that he wouldn't get away with it. But further down there was another, more disturbing reason; he liked the kid. Could that be true? It wasn't just his fashion sense, though that was certainly part of it. Along with his bowtie he sported a pressed striped shirt. And instead of the jeans of most of the other boys, he wore pressed dark-grey trousers. In step with this outfit, but certainly out of step with the ubiquitous black high-tops of his peers, he paraded a pair of shiny black loafers. Neil knew that this fancy little fellow had beamed himself into place right under his nose just to play him, driven to it like a mosquito seeking blood.

It was a game Neil understood. He leaned down so that his face was close to Bowtie's. "If you don't shut up," he said softly, "I'M GOING TO BURST YOUR EAR DRUMS!" he shouted into the boy's ear.

Bowtie stood up straight, surprised, wide-eyed, for the moment subdued. Neil sensed, however, that this dialogue had just begun.

The whistle blew again. "Hands up!" from Mrs. Bane. "Hands up!" the teachers repeated up and down the lines. "Be quiet!" a shrill female voice insisted. Then, "You boys, where do you belong?"

This was Miss Travers, of 6-307. Neil glanced over at her, relieved that he was uninvolved. In fact, his lines were fairly orderly and just at this moment no one was talking. They, this motley crew, were quietly watching him and Bowtie, who was facing forward, looking down at his feet.

"Well get over there!" Miss Travers ordered.

It all happened at once. The two boys, Clyde! John! sulking, got on the back of Neil's boys' line and a skipped heartbeat later the two girls who had just made their noisy entrance through the gate joined his girls' line. The small girl who stood first in the girls' line with her arms folded, the one who had asked if Neil were her teacher, now raised her chin and took a bead on his dismay.

Mr. Knight pointed to Clyde and John. "Watch those two," he said in a loud voice. "They're a couple of bums."

At that moment Neil's 'bums' and the two girls formed a loose group behind the line, laughing and moaning, an unruly chorus.

"You in this class?" They sang the question like a glory choir. "I can't believe you in this class!" And a line of laughter to keep the beat, "Ha ha ha, ha ha ha, you in this class?" Then their ominous refrain, "We gonna be baaad. Oh, man, are we gonna be baaad."

"Oh, gaw, that poor teacha," from the girl Mrs. Bane had called Arlene.

"He be big, though," from John.

"That ain't nothin'," from Clyde.

And from Arlene the call, "Oh, lawd, we gonna be baaad."

And from the others, the refrain, "Oh, man, are we gonna be baaad."

Neil stood very still, looking at each one of them carefully. Then he walked to the back of the line, dangling his sign in his left hand, and stepped right in the middle of the four of them. "Would you please be quiet?"

He stepped toward each one, leaning down to make eye contact. When he did this to the boy named John and to the thin girl with scared brown eyes they each stepped back. Arlene and the boy named Clyde stood their ground. Neil had thought of Clyde as the tall boy, but facing him, he realized Clyde, too, was small, a child. They were, all of them, children, and not one of them, not even Clyde, was poised to block the pops he wanted to give them. How's that for a way to end your teaching career? Whack each one of the little shits, hard, very hard, meant to hurt. See the surprise on their smug little faces.

"What you gonna do if we ain't?" Arlene asked.

Neil breathed in deeply, let it out and told her the truth. "I don't know," he said, moving so close to her that if she hadn't stepped back he would have knocked her back. "I'm working on it." He pulled up to his full height and turned away from them, pausing long enough to invite an attack. To his disappointment, it didn't come. He walked to the front of the line, ignoring their snickers.

Why did it seem like such a revelation that he wasn't ready for this? Hadn't he known it all along? The whistle blew its shrill warning, deepening his confusion.

"Didn't you hear the whistle?" Mr. Knight fumed at Neil's class.

"Get those hands up. All of you."

And, by God, the children in Neil's two lines all raised their hands, making a V with their fingers. And by some miracle they had formed a girls' line and a boys' line.

Knight warned him, just before the whistle blew yet again, "Don't let that bunch get away from you."

Neil stood motionless, unable to react, to Knight, to the whistle, to any of it. That bunch had already gotten away from him. He didn't know what to do. His head began to throb.

"Your right hand should be up and your mouths closed," Mrs. Bane told them. And then, "That's better," she cooed. It was the same person speaking, but the tone of voice was so dramatically different that Neil glanced over the heads of the other teachers to see if someone else had taken her place. "Good morning, boys and girls, and teachers."

"Good morning, Mrs. Bane," everyone chanted back. Everyone, including Neil, who quickly caught on, and Arlene, who seemed to enjoy the moment. Everyone except Clyde. As the tallest he stood at the end of the boys' line, silent, staring off to one side.

"I want to make this brief because I know all of you are anxious to get started after the long summer months. I know you've all had a wonderful vacation. But now that it's over and school has begun, admit it, aren't you glad? Of course you are. As I look out at all those beautiful, smiling faces I know deep down you've missed us just as much as we've missed you." She did this "we're all so happy to be back" in several different ways before she finally wrapped it up with, "Now let's all have a good day and a good year."

After a hesitant silence clapping began, first from the teacher to Neil's left, Mrs. Robin, who leaned forward toward her class, nodding and demonstrating how they were to follow suit, and then from all the teachers and a smattering of children, then everyone, with some boys, like Bowtie on Neil's line, competing to see if they could clap the loudest.

No, not everyone clapped. Clyde didn't. He was looking off at the street. For that matter, Neil didn't either. He slapped his sign from one hand to the other, beating out his own silent protest: *I'm not happy to be here and I never will be.*

Mrs. Bane blew her whistle, but the clapping didn't stop, so she blew it again; and again, stepping forward toward the lines, looking at the clappers until they all went quiet.

Neil's attention drifted to the street beyond the fence, to an image of himself sitting in the booth of the deli on Broadway and 93rd with *The Times* spread around a buttered roll and coffee.

"Hey, Mr. Really, they going." This from the quiet, stocky black boy near the back of his boys' line.

The mispronunciation of Neil's name got a loud guffaw from the tall boy in the rear. That kid, Clyde.

"You hush up," Neil snapped at the stocky boy. "You, too," he barked at the tall one.

But, in fact, Mrs. Robin's class was beginning to march away.

"Let's go!" Neil ordered, and turned toward the gate.

When: "Fight! Fight!"

Knight's class broke ranks and rushed by him and his peeled off with them, all of the children forming a massive semicircle of backs pressing toward the fence.

For Neil time became a slow urgent place in which he could respond to whatever happened without hesitation. He tossed that stupid sign at the fence, gathering to himself the mood he needed. *Yeah. Who gives a shit.* He had often been one of the sluggers in the middle of the crowd, at least until it became apparent that no matter how big you were if you got him today you'd have to get him again tomorrow. Only now he was the grownup and it was his job to stop the mayhem. *Still, it's a kickass world.* He knew exactly where to go.

The exposed neck of the first small girl he had to move to get inside reminded him that he must be careful; he could really hurt someone. From the corner of his eye he saw Mrs. Robin also wading slowly into the mass of children. Both of them were hampered by the fact that when the children sensed intruders at their backs they pressed tighter to keep the violence going. Neil longed to just wade through, tossing the bloodthirsty little freaks left and right, really using his elbows, really bruising ribs. He didn't. And though he didn't have time to think about it, he knew he was now involved in some incredible internal turmoil. Because instead of lashing out, he moved carefully, pressing, squeezing, edging by the small, mostly waist-high bodies he encountered. This was a violation of something essential in his nature and the beginning of something new. *Be careful, don't hurt anyone.* It was in a weird way thrilling.

Forget that. A loud "ouuuu" informed him someone had gotten in a good one. Some kids were screaming, pressing forward to get closer. Others stood silent and were easily moved aside. At last he reached the protagonists, Arlene and a screaming boy, the big-eared boy, John. Arlene had him by the hair and by the cheek and was pushing his face into the fence, which shook and rang when she shoved. John's eye, the one against the fence, was in serious danger.

"Get back, get back," Neil growled over his shoulder.

Improbably, that tall sullen boy from the back of Neil's boys' line, Clyde, was there, pushing the crowd back. "He said get back." Clyde?

Neil grabbed the hand Arlene had on John's cheek first and pulled it loose and taking her forearm wrenched her arm behind her back. Then he pulled at the hand with which she gripped the boy's head. Her strength was impressive. The three of them stood locked together, Neil and the girl straining for the advantage; then Neil leaned in and said calmly, "If you don't let go, I'm going to pull your arm out of its socket," which he might have to do to save John's eye. He yanked at her arm enough to cause her pain.

"Ouwww. Get off me!" Arlene cried, but she let go of John's head, taking away a small patch of woolly hair in her clenched fist.

Mrs. Robin suddenly stepped between John and the frozen knot of Arlene and Neil.

And just as suddenly Mr. Bernbach, the assistant principal, was there, in Arlene's face, snarling, "I warned you, Arlene. I warned you. Now what's it going to be? School or corrections? School or corrections? It's up to you."

Neil felt her body slump.

"He said sumpin'," she muttered. She was near tears.

Neil squeezed her arms sympathetically, then warily let her go. He had nothing to fear. She stood leaning forward, beaten. Bernbach had whacked the fight out of her.

"Go to my office." Bernbach told her. "Straight to my office. You better be there when I get there." Then without any change in tone, he said to Neil, "Get your class in line and take them upstairs."

But instead Neil stepped closer and said, "Who are these kids? You know who I mean."

Bernbach looked stunned, but managed an icy, "Please get your class together and take them to your room."

Neil moved to within inches of Bernbach's face. Any man would know he was being challenged. "I *said*, who are these kids?"

Bernbach, with a smile, became the easygoing assistant principal who had hired Neil last May. If he was angry or afraid, he didn't show it. He put a hand on Neil's arm and said, "I'll explain later. I promise. But right now..." and he rolled his eyes at the crowd of children. "This is not the place."

"6-306!" Neil called, stepping away. "Line up, please. Girls on my left, please. Boys on my right."

He didn't seriously believe any of this would happen, but what the hell, school or Canada, school or Canada, it was up to him.

And, by God, they did it! Girls on his left, boys on his right! Of course, it wasn't in the tight neat lines of Mrs. Robin's class, which was now silently filing by. She had John in the front with her, her arm on his shoulder. "I'll have the nurse look at him," she said in a hurry, and from farther away, turning back, "I may keep him. I don't think they should be in the same class."

Why not take Arlene? Neil wanted to yell back. Meanwhile, Knight's class was slowly drifting toward the back gate. And where was...?

Knight was standing with his sign at the gate, snapping his fingers sharply as the children began to line up in front of him.

Turning his attention to his own class, Neil noticed the stocky boy he had told to hush, it now seemed ages ago. He had rescued that godawful sign and was holding it up to Neil.

"Thanks." Neil took it, nodding, and was shaken by such inner turmoil he had the insane notion the sign was attacking him. The rush of gratitude he felt for this boy's gratuitous kindness came wrapped in remorse, like a bouquet tied with barbed wire. After all this was the boy he had snarled at only moments ago for trying to be helpful. Now here he was again, sweet smiling obliging child, giving Neil back this sign he had never wanted to see again, this emblem of his charade, which he now held against his leg like a burning rebuke. Neil somehow knew, perhaps because it was so terribly unsettling, that versions of this moment—less than a second really—emotionally charged, wrenching, would be repeated again and again over the course of the day, *the weeks*, should he last that long, *the months* to come. *No matter*, he told himself, *keep moving*.

"What's your name?" Neil asked the boy.

"Morris. You Mr. Riley."

"Really," the tall boy, Clyde, said, to titters.

Neil glanced back at him with a look imitating that sassy look he had gotten from Miss Lower Lip and Mr. Bowtie, that all-purpose 'don't you start with me' warning, and for his efforts got a snicker from Mr. Bowtie, who understood exactly what he was doing.

"Listen, Morris, I'm sorry about yelling at you. I was wrong," Neil said. He looked back again at Clyde, meaning to thank him for the help during the fight. But the nasty look Clyde gave him, with a shake of his head, his lips pushed together, squelched that.

And Neil was too busy moving them out and worrying that he was never going to get through this day, to do more than notice, then forget, that for several heartbeats every one of his children had been paying attention to him. Passing Knight on the way into the school Neil couldn't resist silently questioning him with that universal gesture you make on the field when a teammate has blown a play, arms wide, shaking palms: where were you, buddy? Knight was busy looking the other way.

Chapter 2:

Doing All the Things You Must Never Do

In Neil's apartment: he lay in bed locked in a tight fetal ball, braced against the memories gnawing at him, vicious little monsters. He dozed and dreamed *that he stood facing a dirty white wall. Naked. Behind him were all the people he had ever known, friends, enemies, everyone. He became especially aware of the thirty-two sixth grade children he was supposed to be teaching. While they watched, pointing, giggling, his body began to sweat a corrosive substance like battery acid. He began to dissolve. His hands, now tear-shaped drops, were falling off his arms.*

To hide what was happening he turned to his right, feeling for a moment he had escaped. He had not. He was faced with the exact same dirty blank wall with everyone behind him watching as he dripped puddles of himself onto the concrete of the schoolyard. He tried to turn again, this time to his left, and when he realized he had turned back into the place he had been before he woke up, breathing hard, deeply disappointed that he was awake because, if it were possible, he would have stayed in that place forever, dissolving, his failures rumbling vaguely off in the distance. Instead, idly at first, then with greater and greater immersion, he watched an odd, distorted person, a hideous version of himself, twirl slowly around, screaming, *SHUT UP! SIT DOWN!* Struck again and again by the pain of what he was not doing.

Without warning he crossed a threshold and was *there*, in that classroom. His body flew open, hard as a plank, and he howled, aloud, very loud, "NO, GODDAMN YOU, NO!" He pressed a pillow against his face until he began to choke, raised his head to breathe and tried to settle back into that vague dread where memories wouldn't burrow through.

He had learned very early, probably before he turned seven, that when someone humiliated you you could not pretend it didn't happen. That was always the first thing you tried to do, but it was a waste of time. Nothing mattered, nothing, until you found a way to get even. But see, that was exactly what he was trying to do, here in this miserable bed: pretend it didn't happen.

He started this teaching caper believing it would be a snap. He would find the trick, pull it out of the hat, use it. *Easy as that, right, old boy? Two years go by, I age out of the draft, hand in that fucking IV-S. I'm so sorry, this was a big, big mistake. Though I certainly do thank you very much.* A snap.

What an unmitigated fool he was.

The very first thing he did when he got them to that room was to open the door and tell them to go in and find a seat, realizing only as he was swept aside by the wild stampede of children what a stupid thing he had just done. Now, in the replay, they went right through him, through his guts, a pack of children taking with them any remnant of control he had managed to hold onto. He never recovered from the trauma of that moment.

Wait. That was something he had to remember. He had lost control. He had from then on been unable to bring himself to a place where he could decide what he had to do next. What could he do to prevent that? Maybe he should write that down. He had to look at what happened and see what he could do about it. Maybe nothing. But, come on, man, he had been in worse spots than this. There was nothing life-threatening about herding around a mob of unruly children.

The situation did have certain unique difficulties, however, beginning with the fact that much of what happened in that classroom was caused by his total ignorance of what to do about it. That must be emphasized over and over again. He was *totally* unprepared for the situation.

For some unknown reason he had sat up. Why would he want to do that? He squinted at his bedroom window, which opened onto the fire escape. The window faced east and was the only opening through which by bending down and peering up he could see the sky. To see the concrete yard four floors below he had to go out on the fire escape, which he had often done on those hot August nights when he first moved in, leaning against the side of the building, sipping a beer and listening to the clatter, murmurs, the racket of pots and pans, a newborn crying, a raised voice, laughter, the music of the many people around him interrupted now and then by a siren singing of trouble and heartbreak. He had been so relaxed sitting there. Could that have been only a week ago? In another lifetime. He would never relax again.

From where he sat now on the edge of his bed he could see twilight spreading a faint blue on the air, deepening toward night. It was Friday evening, time to pick up your date, go dancing, then to your place or hers to undress in candlelight and fall naked into bed. He shook himself to throw off the fantasy. If he had any sense at all he would get his butt up and start figuring out what to do.

Now he sat in his living room at the desk next to the door. Staring at the wall. Wondering how he got there. He had to sort all this out. He winced: *SIT DOWN! SHUT UP! SIT DOWN! SHUT UP!* At a certain point they had become wary, even afraid, trapped in that room with that thing. It was wild, tormented, unpredictable, frantic. They actually began to scramble to their seats and if only for a split second became quiet. Until someone started the chaos again.

In the instance that came to him now, some boy behind his back made a belching sound, setting off a chain of belching laughter. Neil was somewhere in the middle of the room heading for some reason once again toward the back table. (Yes, of course, because there was almost always a group of boys back there playing some gambling game with their hands.) He whirled around and with the certainty of an angry boar charged at a small child with large brown eyes sitting staring up at him with a sweet appeasing smile. Neil grabbed the boy's desk back and front and heaved it and the boy aloft then slammed them down. With his face inches from the boy's he yelled, *DO THAT AGAIN! I DARE YOU!* The boy stared at him, grabbing for air, his lips moving in a peculiar reaching motion, like a fish out of water. From somewhere else a voice jeered: *It wasn't him. Stupid teacha.* Neil stood bolt upright, spun again toward the back of the room to catch the boy who made that comment and found himself staring at a mass of terrified faces. Except for the tall boy, Clyde, who met his glare with a small nod of his head, as if to say, *Yeah, me. What of it?*

Neil lowered his eyes without comment. He turned slowly and looked back at the small child he had terrorized, the child who now had his head down on the desk, hands on the back of his head, his small thin black neck straining, exposed.

It may have been then that Bernbach ushered that big girl, Arlene—he certainly wouldn't forget *her* name—through the door. Neil wasn't at all sure of the chronology of events. He had only a jumbled sense of failure after failure. He remembered that what Bernbach saw when he looked into the room was a mad flick of time. The horde had been driven into a momentary submission. Bernbach smiled at Neil and left. *Left.* Taking with him any hope of assistance, leaving Neil feeling abandoned and if possible even more helpless than before. Perhaps that's why he did what he did then? He refused to remember. Instead he drifted into a pleasant recollection of his fifth grade teacher, Mrs. Gunn.

The first time Mrs. Gunn approached him he realized she must be gigantic. He had always thought of his Aunt Connie as huge, but with Mrs. Gunn looming over him he understood that this woman was of another order of adult magnitude. Now with his older eye he could only confirm his ten-year-old perceptions. His aunt was a slender, petite woman. Mrs. Gunn was tall and heavy. She must have had a good seventy pounds on one-oh-five Aunt Connie. There was no physical resemblance between them at all. What linked them in Neil's mind was that they both totally approved of him.

When Neil made a picture of a red-breasted robin sitting on a tree limb you'd think he'd created a masterpiece. It was a direct copy of a picture he found in a book on birds. He hadn't traced it, but he hadn't worked from nature either. Mrs. Gunn thought this was the best picture of a red-breasted robin she had ever seen and up it went on the wall over the front blackboard and there it stayed for the rest of the year. Also, he wrote about bussing tables in his aunt's restaurant. He said you had to get the clattery stuff out of the way first. It went in a bucket under the cart. Of course, he meant the silverware, but that's not how he thought of it then. First the clattery stuff, then the spilly stuff, half-full water glasses and coffee cups, then the way you scraped the plates. Mrs. Gunn loved what he wrote even though he erased a lot and his letters weren't even. Up it went, right next to the red-breasted robin.

When Mrs. Gunn came into the restaurant, she and Aunt Connie would always talk about what a smart boy he was. And in the restaurant and in class too, Mrs. Gunn touched him on the back of the neck and across his shoulders in the same way his aunt did, molding him, laying ability and strength across his back. Mr. Gunn was a small man with a round shiny bald head ringed by hair like a laurel. Unlike most of the other regular couples they had no children. Also, they never seemed hurried or irritated with each other or the waitress or the world. Mr. Gunn was rumored to be some sort of expert in something about assembly line machinery and had tons of money, but here they were, regularly, in Connie's Corner, having the meat loaf special with mashed potatoes and gravy and Mrs. Gunn talking to Aunt Connie about what a smart boy he was, while he sat over in the corner hurrying up with his homework so his aunt would let him help bus the tables.

In the sixth grade everything changed. Neil's sixth grade teacher was Miss Slater, the daughter of a retired general, who lived with her father in a large house on the best street in town. That by no means placed her among the really rich. The really rich lived on large estates in the areas surrounding Lake Haven and usually sent their children away to the "finest" private schools. A few of the really rich, however, for various reasons chose to send their children to the Lake Haven Schools and these parents mounted a powerful presence in the PTA.

Miss Slater was one of the worshipful, perhaps the most worshipful, liaisons between those commanding few and the teachers and administrators of the school. Neil, sitting at his desk in his apartment, rummaging through these memories for the first time in years, heard his aunt say of Miss Slater, *She's not one of those old maids with some lost love. No man could ever have melted those frozen waters.*

But what stood out for Neil about these two teachers was that in Mrs. Gunn's class you pretty much sat like his class sat, in rows, without any differentiation, and you could sit near your friends. At various times desks got moved around. Why was that? For reading and math? He didn't remember. He did remember that a punishment for talking too much would be that you got moved to another desk.

In Miss Slater's class the desks were set up in three distinct groups based ostensibly on reading ability: Sparrows, who were the smartest, Bluebirds, the get-bys, and Bluejays, the dummies. The Bluejays sat with their backs to the blackboard, seated slightly forward so that they could move quickly to the side when it was being used. The door opened onto this group. The Bluebirds sat with their backs to the window facing Miss Slater, whose desk was just to the left of the door. The Sparrows sat to the left of Miss Slater's desk.

These birds were not really grouped by academic ability. Robert Zabliki was a Bluebird and everybody knew he was the smartest boy in the class. He did all these science projects at home just for the hell of it. Not only did he have a microscope and a telescope, he had his own Bunsen burner, for Christ's sake. In high school he won all the science prizes and was the class valedictorian. Even in sixth grade everybody knew how smart he was because in fifth grade Mrs. Gunn had him talk about stuff like what the moon's surface was like and the complicated mess he could see with his microscope in a single drop of water. He wasn't a Sparrow because his daddy managed, but did not own, the Texaco Station and did a lot of the mechanical work himself.

Bobby got into trouble with Miss Slater once because poor Jennifer did a problem wrong on the board and Bobby, after properly raising his hand and waiting to be called on, pointed out her mistake. The outraged Miss Slater lit into Bobby for publicly embarrassing a fellow student, though embarrassing students was one of her favorite teaching tools. It was not, however, one she used on Sparrows. Bobby never again said a word about anyone's blunders, though when a Sparrow faltered he would look at the board with raised eyebrows and shrug his shoulders. Miss Slater, the Hawk, usually caught these gestures, scanned the board until she located the Sparrow's error and suggested how to correct it.

Miss Slater's groups duplicated to a large degree the social and financial standing of the Lake Haven children's parents. Most of the Sparrows weren't from the really rich of Lake Haven. Matthew Reardon's father owned the drugstore and was the pharmacist. Cynthia Manning's father had the largest landscaping business in the area. Mr. Reardon and Mr. Manning were actually servants of the really rich, but most of their Sparrows flew off to prep schools.

So the moderately well off like Matty and Cynthia represented the elite in this class.

Of course, there was Lurlene. Her father, Mr. Stumph, was of another order entirely. He was the vice-president of a huge tobacco company down in North Carolina and was completely independent of everyone in town. Not only that, his ability to buy and sell land at favorable rates invested him with the power to lay fortunes on whomever his golden gaze might favor. He was rumored to be in line to become the next president of the Winston-Salem based tobacco company he represented. Lurlene, though new to the school, was certainly one of Miss Slater's darlings.

And then there was Jennifer, also a Sparrow. Her father was the president of Lake Haven Savings Bank. In spite of his grand title it wasn't likely he could afford to send his daughter to boarding school. And even if he had managed to scrape the tuition together Jennifer was not likely to have been admitted. Most of what Neil could remember of Jennifer, not only in Miss Slater's class, but in later classes as well, was how often she raised her eager hand to answer questions and how often her answers were not simply wrong, but spectacularly so. In twelfth grade—this had to be about Byron's famous swim—she suggested the Hellespont was the gateway to, you know, that place down under?

Now he was in the kitchen. Why? He stood for an endless moment in a grey space with the awful confusion of not knowing who he was or what he was doing. That sent him back to that room, 6-306, full of uncontrollable children, standing gaping at them without any idea what he was doing there. Standing there for an entire week not knowing what to do? In the kitchen? Heating water? Yes, for coffee. But...

After Bernbach ushered her in, that big girl, Arlene, marched over to a desk near the middle of the room where a slender girl had already begun to relinquish her place. *Thas my desk,* Arlene told her. The evicted girl walked quickly over to the windows, where with her arms folded over her belongings she turned back toward the class. She was a black girl with smooth light brown skin, her straightened hair cut short. Unlike the rest of the girls, who wore skirts or dresses, she wore jeans. Her blouse was a simple white short-sleeved top buttoned to a discrete V at her neck. She had a notebook and an actual book clutched in her arms. She glanced at Neil, then looked quickly away, more embarrassed for him, he was certain, than for herself. Had any of the others in that churning horde noticed her glance? It didn't matter. He couldn't let this go.

Neil rushed over to the desk where Arlene now sat looking up at him with a smirk. He clutched her by her arms, lifted her up out of the desk and pushed the desk away, yelling in her face, *I DON'T WANT YOU TO SIT IN THAT DESK! THAT'S MY DESK!*

DON'T YOU YELL AT ME YOU STUPID PIGHEAD! WHITEFACE! YOU AIN'T NO TEACHA!

I'LL YELL AT YOU ANY TIME I WANT! ANY TIME. (Never call a child a name. Never.) He leaned down to put his face inches from hers. *YOU STUPID BULLY.*

He relished the eeuws he heard all around him. He relished the concern he saw in her eyes. He wasn't normal. This man, this person, this thing, it wasn't normal. She was right. He didn't know what he was, but he sure as the Hellespont wasn't a teacher.

She moved away from him, over close to the door where she screamed, *YOU A PIGHEAD!*

To his immense relief she yanked the door open and ran out of the room. Of course, he would learn soon enough that this would only lead to further embarrassment. The next time she was ushered into the room he was running yet again at the gang of boys at the back table bellowing once again, *SHUT UP! SIT DOWN!*

Mr. Riley. **Mr. Riley**, a woman's voice, firm and demanding, called to him from the door. It was Mrs. Robin, the sixth grade teacher next door. Not only Neil, but the entire horde watched as she planted a hand firmly in Arlene's back. *Go sit down.*

I ain't got no desk, Arlene wailed, wronged, wounded. She looked pointedly at Neil.

Find one, Mrs. Robin said. To Neil she said, *Arlene was slamming her hand against my door. It would be best for everyone if you could keep your students out of the hall.*

Neil nodded at her obediently, as if he were a pupil, not a colleague. Now in his kitchen he raised his head to the ceiling and muttered a long, pained protest. *Agggggg.* After a moment he stopped and looked blindly ahead, then remembered the incident again in all its vivid intensity and raised his head and muttered a long, *Aggggggg.*

Had this happened on Monday? It seemed to Neil it had happened this morning. It must have been Monday, because he had spent most of the week standing with his back to that door preventing first Arlene, then the little one, Sheri? Yes, Sheri, from rushing out into the hall. And Mr. Bowtie, who suddenly claimed, *I got to go to the bathroom. I got to.* He had spent the entire week throwing one or the other of them back into that room. When in truth he would have loved to have ushered them all out with a sweep of his hand. *Oh, please, ladies, gentleman, be my guest. Go. Go!*

Most of the children had become intimidated by his size and lung power. At least until his back was turned. But not all of them. Arlene and that other one, that little ball of fire, Sheri, for example, seemed to need his rages.

No, that was only true of Arlene. It wasn't like that for the little one. She had to have his attention. It was not an exaggeration to say the need was obsessive. If he was focused on another student, especially if at some rare moment he was actually engaged in a positive exchange, answering a question about the math he had put on the board, for example, Sheri was sure to stand up and start stamping her feet, chanting, *Look at me, stupid teacha, look at me.* It was truly that obvious. *Look at me.*

Arlene, on the other hand, wanted to disrupt and destroy. That was her sole mission. And most of the time she pretty much succeeded. She was engaged in a particular kind of guerilla warfare, a constant rant, declaiming, *How come we got to have some white face pig? I ain't about to listen to no white face pig.* She never stopped. He was stupid, school was stupid, he was a white faced pig. *I ain't doin' nothin', I ain't stayin' here, I ain't gonna listen to you, how come you writing on the board? You ain't no teacha.* On and on.

He would tell her to shut up, would try to ignore her, would tell her again to shut up and finally unable to endure it any longer, would scream, *WOULD YOU PLEASE SHUT UP? I don't want to listen to you anymore. You've said you don't want to be here. Great. JUST SHUT UP. Put your head down on your desk. I'll leave you alone. You don't care about me? Well, guess what? I don't care about you either.* Oh, God, had he really said that? Yes he had, as he pushed his arms out like a madman, pushing her away. *Just sit there and be quiet and I'll leave you alone. I promise. I DON'T CARE WHAT YOU DO JUST SO LONG AS YOU SHUT UP!*

When was that? Late Tuesday afternoon? For the remaining hour or so left in the day she did exactly what he wanted her to do; she sat with her head down and at the bell when he lined them up to leave, once they were in the hall, she fled, down the back stairs. But she was back the next day, late, slamming into the room, her sidekick, Brenda, in tow, taking aim. *Stupid teacha. White face pig. I hate you. I ain't doin' nothin'. You ain't no teacha. I hate this stupid school.* On and on and on and on.

Every evening in his apartment he imagined bellowing, *IF YOU HATE ME SO MUCH, PROVE IT. GO TO BERNBACH AND TELL HIM YOU CAN'T STAND ME. REFUSE TO COME TO MY CLASS. DON'T LET HIM MAKE YOU COME HERE. PROVE YOU HATE*

ME. I DARE YOU. DON'T SHOW UP HERE TOMORROW. JUST DON'T. OKAY? DON'T SHOW UP HERE TOMORROW!

It was a fantasy with enormous power. And though he had not yet acted on it, he knew that any day now he might. No. He would go beyond making it a dare. He would make it a command. *TOMORROW YOU GO TO BERNBACH AND TELL HIM YOU WON'T COME BACK TO MY CLASS. I'M NOT ASKING YOU TO DO THIS. I'M TELLING YOU.*

He sensed in some remote area on the other side of insanity that there was something wrong with this fantasy. No matter. Get her to force Bernbach to transfer her to another class. Oh! Oh! If only he could!

What day was it that he'd told her he would leave her alone if she'd just sit there and be quiet? He thought Tuesday, but then it must have been again on Wednesday because he remembered turning to the rest of the class and telling them, *You see these problems I wrote on the board? I don't know how many of you copied them and frankly I don't care. But tomorrow you'd better hand them in or you get a failure for today.* It was Wednesday. Because Wednesday was the day when he actually tried to get them to do something other than, *SIT DOWN! SHUT UP!*

He was back now at his desk in the living room of his apartment, staring at the wall. Earlier—minutes ago? Hours? —he had as if in a dream remembered his own elementary teachers, Mrs. Gunn with her black shawl flying about her shoulders, a huge black angel; Miss Slater in her long beige skirts and white ruffled blouses. Neil wanted to remember Slater as a hook-nosed witch with an exaggerated chin, a finger-length mole sticking out of her cheek. In fact even as a child he knew she was a handsome woman with piercing blue eyes and long brown hair, her eyebrows straight composed marks that remained relentlessly set to severe no matter what the encounter. Something about this memory had a marijuana-laced intensity.

It was oracular. And it had the same grass-induced befuddlement. What was he supposed to remember? Mrs. Gunn, so wonderfully supportive, black cape flying around the room? Miss Slater pacing the aisles? So what?

One thing he had learned this week was that he could frighten them, most of them anyway. Make them tremble. Really. And he hadn't hit a single one of them. He had come perilously close, but he did solemnly swear, he had not hit a single one of them. He had restrained them, lifted them off each other, shaken them, but he had not done what he'd really wanted to do: whack the shit out of the little bastards. Especially that Arlene. Oh, how he longed to just let her have it, driving her into the back of the room, knocking her down, slapping her when she started to get up. It was a longing that extended from the top of his head down his arms to the tip of his fingers. Drive a left into her face, follow with a right using his entire body, twisting his fist on contact to do as much internal damage as possible.

Even in his crazed state he knew that would be too blatant. Better to set it up so it wasn't quite a hit. More like a slip of the elbow, you know? Hurt her and never have a problem. Your elbow jerks out. Pull the punch, but make it sting. He knew other teachers hit; they talked about it in the teachers' room.

The teachers who advocated hitting were, no surprise here, the same hardliners who insisted that memorization was the bedrock of learning and that strict discipline was the cornerstone of classroom management. Neil, who in his prep classes had been led to believe hitting was a thing of the past, learned that in this school at least it was openly practiced by several outspoken advocates, particularly his fellow sixth grade teacher, Mr. Knight, and the huge Mrs. Berry, a fifth grade teacher whose usual expression was a ferocious scowl and whose gait had the lumbering menace of a sumo wrestler. Her fervent cries for corporal punishment rang with conviction. She was the last noble warrior in a morally corrupt world.

Neil became aware of himself pacing the length of his apartment, from the tip of the kitchen to the bedroom window, back and forth, back and forth. He had no idea how long he had been doing this. He was shuddering, making spastic jabs at the air, ranting to himself in an emotional frenzy, *Bullies. That's what they are. Hitting children. Terrorizing them. Because they can get away with it. Come on, fuckers, try that with me.* He stopped and stood very still, remembering how he fought anyone anytime who tried to bully him. Would he fight this bully? This crazy teacha, this white face pig? He tightened his entire body as if it were a fist. He was crazy. Wanting to hit children. What was happening to him?

Which led Neil to think of that tall, handsome black boy, Clyde. His records said he was twelve, but he seemed older. Clyde was never openly defiant, not even when Neil confronted him face-to-face. In fact, it was only now in the quiet of his apartment that Neil realized he had always been aware of this boy's presence, all week long. While Neil paced the front of the classroom, Clyde paced the rear, shadowing him, forcing Neil to look at himself through the eyes of a heartless twin. Clyde, the boy squatting in Neil's conscience, saw right through him.

This man, he's bigger than me, so I guess I haf to take his shit. Thinks he's been around the block, bad motherfucker. Yeah, with a bunch of little kids. Except they running him ragged. And he cane do nothing about it and don't know nothing about nothing and ain't worth shit. How come we got this useless lowlife? Just cause he don't want to go die for his country he gets to be my teacha? Why? And while we at it, why do my older brothers haf to go over there and die while he stands around with his hands on his hips pissed off because he has to put off finishing law school for two years?

Neil yanked his head around. This wasn't Clyde. This was some evil tormentor with no sense of fairness. All he wanted was for this crazy voice to shut the fuck up. That was not going to happen.

Count it up. Two classes, at thirty-two children to a class, that's sixty-four children he plans to mess up over the next two years just so he won't have to die. He plays it smart and they stay dumb. Of course, not long after he does what he calls ages out I'll age in and it's not likely my black ass'll get that college deferment all those lily whites get. No, I get him, then I get the draft. And he wants me to SIT DOWN AND SHUT UP?

There was Clyde, sitting on the back table, swinging his legs, at ease, certainly looking at ease, entertained even? And there was Neil, cornered, baffled, unfettered, raging, cornered again. This man who was supposed to be their teacher stood turning in circles in front of the classroom, with no idea who these children were or what to do with them, with no books to guide him and no one to turn to. So what was the plan he came up with? Beat them up?

Wouldn't Clyde love that? The real Clyde, not some fabrication woven from his frustration and guilt, the boy who had spent the entire week cutting him to pieces. *How come we got to sit down? We don't do nothin'.* Absolutely true. *He yellin' cause he got nothin' to say.* No disputing that. And after another *SIT DOWN! SHUT UP! Why not BE QUIET for a change?* That was *really* annoying. Neil had considered making just that switch. Now it was out of the question. And when Neil yelled, *You! Yeah, you!* at a boy who had turned to talk to the boy behind him, Clyde had said, dryly, *His name is Javier.*

Can you imagine the fun Clyde would have if Neil started whacking the little brats around? *Ladies and gentlemen, behold! the world champion baby beater. What a specimen!*

Neil found himself now in the bathroom taking a leak. In his own defense he was telling that teacher, Mrs. Robin, the one who had brought Arlene back to the classroom, that he really did have a plan. When he learned there might not be any books he had intended to ask them questions about last year. For example, what readers had they used? What kind of math lessons were they doing at the end of the year? What was their fifth grade teacher like?

The idea of having a general discussion about their "academic progress in each subject matter," which was how he had phrased it in his plan book, proved to be so incredibly naïve he had to struggle against throwing the fucking thing out the window. He knew he had to keep that page. If he didn't he would try to deny he had ever been that ignorant. He shook a few final drips of urine from his penis, breathed deeply, bowed his head, shut his eyes and argued in his defense, *I didn't know children could be people.* He stood motionless, listening to himself. *No one must ever know, ever,* he thought, *what a thoroughly shamefully inexcusably stupid idiot I am.* He repeated to himself with the full-throated contempt the remark deserved, *I didn't know children could be people.*

Now he was back sitting at his desk, staring at his living room wall. He remembered again how each day he had counted on the arrival of the books, the books that had been promised for preparation week, then certainly by the first week of school, the week that had ended today.

The books that, incredibly, never arrived.

On day three? Wednesday? School was in full swing. He had been screaming and yelling for two days when he finally admitted to himself that, yes, the situation was actually as bad as he thought it was. He might never get books. With no idea what to do and with no one the least bit interested in his plight, that morning, on impulse, in the hour before he went down to get his children, he put twenty math problems on the board, making them up as he went along. Yes, $1+1=?$ Then, *if $X=1$ and $Y=2$ what does $X+Y=?$* Then: *14 divided by 2?* Then: *386 divided by 25.5?* Twenty problems scrawled across the board with no concern for difficulty, a random selection from his fevered brain.

Clyde: *Whas that? Chicken scratches. He cane even write.*

SIT DOWN! SHUT UP!

Quickly, too quickly, he learned the names of some of them. The tall well-developed black girl with the wide round underdeveloped chin that she regularly dropped in an astonished *gaw*, astounded that she could be upbraided for pushing or hitting, running around the room arbitrarily threatening some poor victim, when clearly, *gaw*, she had done nothing wrong, *nothing*, that innocent person was: *ARLENE!* Her sidekick, the girl with the haunted stare who when challenged froze into a protective shell, that was Brenda. Brenda was basically a quiet child, but with smiles and nods she gave Arlene just the moral support she needed to do her nefarious deeds with insouciance. Was the Lone Ranger really lone? Not on your life; Tonto, his faithful injin, was always there to back him up. *Yes, Keymosabe* (or whatever it was that ass-licker said to the masked man), that's effectively what Brenda said to Arlene all week: *Yes, Keymosabe,* which definitely put Brenda high on Neil's shit list.

Then there was Clyde. *Man, do you ever know his name.* Clyde, who moved back and forth in the rear of the room, a cool alter-ego to that heated fool who moved back and forth in the front. That boy calmly, without fuss, sat down on every, *SIT DOWN! SHUT UP!* and was up and at the back of the room the moment chaos was reinstated. That boy, Clyde, he was the one whose deadly comments seemed to come from the dark depths of Neil's other self.

Wednesday morning as soon as he got them into the room he told them, along with many *SIT DOWN! SHUT UP!*s, *Get out a piece of paper and a pencil and start copying down these problems, please.* A request that created an uproar. *What paper? What pencil? Copy what?! Those chicken scratches?!* Neil experienced an unexpected glee. He'd evoked expressions of anxiety in direct response to, for want of a better term, an academic request, one that a real teacher might make. Here was a legitimate opportunity to torment the little bastards.

Wide-eyed he said, *You were supposed to come to school with a three-clasp notebook, a hundred sheets of lined three-holed paper and two No. 2 pencils.* He knew this because it had been drubbed into him. This is what they were *required* to bring. He knew they hadn't because he had eyes in his head.

What notebook? What paper? What pencil? Required? Who said?

How many of you have notebooks? Bellowed several times to make sure everyone understood the question. He was actually having fun. As expected no one raised his hand. He knew at least one student who did have a notebook, the slender girl Arlene had displaced lo those many eons ago (yesterday?). Since the girl chose not to raise her hand, Neil had the good sense not to single her out. It may have been the only smart decision he made all week. She would surely have become a target for derision. Derision? How about an afterschool execution?

Meanwhile, no paper? No problem. *Oh, my little dears, do I have paper for you.* There were copybooks, an endless supply of them, at least fifty in his desk, another two hundred or more locked up in his back cabinet. Bernbach had assured him there were even more available on request. It was beyond comprehension. He had no real books, but he sure as hell had copybooks, hundreds of them. And he had hundreds of No. 2 pencils. Some suppliers must have a big friend in City Hall.

Still he sat imprisoned in this unwelcome reverie, watching now that feisty little black girl giving out the copybooks. That was a coup of sorts. Someone was actually doing something he had requested be done.

But his glimmer of pride and joy was fleeting indeed. He cringed, seeing the little boy with the bowtie grinding away at the pencil sharpener. What was that about? Ah, yes, the pencils. *How we gonna write when we ain't got no pencils?* Useless to ask, but Neil played the straight man: *Why haven't you got pencils?* To the obvious: *Cause we ain't.*

Who wants to give out the pencils? The little boy with the bowtie, who had been rolling his car back and forth on the floor, jumped up, shouting, *Me, me, me!* It was only now in his apartment that Neil actually took in the full import of this. An eleven-year-old boy playing with a tiny toy car? On the classroom floor in front of all his classmates? Was this normal behavior? No one teased him about it, which seemed remarkable to Neil. Others had set up a cry, too, to give out the pencils. There was an especially anguished cry from his little copybook helper, *I'll give them out. I'll give them out.* But Neil insisted, *No, he'll give out the pencils,* if only to keep him off the floor. He gave the boy a twelve-pack of No. 2s and the next thing he knew the kid had ground a pencil almost to a stub and was starting to do the same to another. With a lot of *SIT DOWN, SHUT UP*s along the way Neil made his way to the pencil sharpener next to the rear window. *What are you doing?* At least, he didn't say, *What the fuck are you doing?* The boy gave Neil his best why-are-you-so-stupid? look. *Sharpening the pencils,* he said. Implicit in his tone was a concluding: *moron.* Neil grabbed the rest of the pencils away from him. *Okay, great, you...* Do not ever under any circumstances belittle a child, call him a name, use sarcasm or otherwise attempt to humiliate him. *...little idiot.* Neil grabbed the boy's wrist and tore the stub of the pencil out of his hand. He bent and pressed the pencil at the boy's face. *If this pencil is sharpened the way it should be then you use it. From now on. Until the end of the year. Okay? This is your pencil. Okay? Here. Take it!* There were *ouuuu's* from all over the room. The boy, his eyes locked on the pencil, backed away from Neil, looked frantically past him, then took off around the back of the room, up the far side and out the door. Neil dropped the pencil on the floor. To the class, and he definitely had their attention, he said, *When he comes back, if he comes back, he'll pick this pencil up and* *use it or he'll bring in his own. Which he was supposed to do. Which you are all supposed to do! Which I expect you to do tomorrow!* Fat chance, but nevertheless put the demand out there; something else to hammer them with.

Bowtie didn't have the stamina of that big girl, Arlene. He was back in a matter of minutes pounding on the glass panels. Neil walked across the room, opened the door, reached out and yanked him in by his arm. Grabbing a handful of shirt he ran the boy over to the other side of the room. *Your pencil's on the floor. Pick it up.* And when he hesitated, Neil jerked him up and down like a yo-yo, his bowtie pulled up hard against his neck: *PICK IT UP!* When he picked it up Neil, still holding the back of his shirt, ran him back to his chosen desk, in the first row near the door. When Neil sat him down the toy car appeared from somewhere and ran up and over the pencil, up and over, repeatedly. The boy had his cheek down on his desktop watching this.

Now in his apartment Neil sat with his head down on his desk, in imitation of Bowtie. This was the position the children took when there was no other option, when escape was all that was left to them. Neil allowed himself a flicker of triumph. At one point or another he had driven each of his tormentors to this miserable place. He had managed to hurt them. *Little shits.* Then: *Well, they hurt me!* he snapped back at the voice that wondered how he could justify behaving like a vicious eleven-year-old bully. They thought they had this oaf cornered and they could play him to death. Instead, they found themselves locked up with a raving maniac. Locked up. Literally. Because Bowtie was the last one he allowed to leave the room. *From now on no one leaves this classroom. We'll all be miserable together, right here, from now on.* He turned the latch under the doorknob, which he was not supposed to do, thinking to himself, *Ever read* No Exit? The escapee could, of course, turn the latch, but that delay would give Neil time to stop the breakout. Bowtie was the first to try to take flight. He got nowhere. *But I have to go. I have to go!* To which with great pleasure Neil responded, *If you do, you'll have to sit in it for the rest of the day. I'm certainly not going to clean it up.*

Whoa, he mean. That was definitely Clyde. Reflecting back Neil realized that he hadn't managed to hurt all his tormentors. If Clyde had ever been hurt or terrified he kept it well hidden. Neil knew all about that, the necessity for keeping yourself together and the brooding pleasure of being able to do it. *You got something to say to me?* Neil asked him, walking back to stand in front of his desk. The boy brazenly rolled his eyes. *Yeah. Whas all that chicken scratchin' up there?* Neil, still locking eyes with his antagonist, said softly, *That's twenty problems. On the board. Copy them. Do them if you know how. Hand them in even if you can't do them. Or you get a fail for the day.*

Fail for the day? Fail for the day? Anxious cries, especially from the rows near the window. What bullshit! Where did he dig that up? Slater did that. *Hand it in or fail for the day.* It worked on some. He got: *How come?* And: *What chew mean?* And: *I ain't failing no day.* And the threat seemed to challenge something in cool Mr. Clyde, who said, *Even if we could read it, how we gonna copy it without no pencil and paper?*

The cry went up again. *How we gonna copy it without no pencils?*

His sometimes tormentor, the little black beauty, jumped up, volunteering, *I'll sharpen them.* To his dubious look, she said, *I gave out the copybooks didn't I?* And the girl with the frizzy hair sitting right in front of him, a strong looking, straight-backed white girl with a pug nose who put a Spanish spin on her words, informed Neil with certainty, *I'll give them out.* Little Black Beauty insisted she would give them out. *No, you'll be sharpening them,* Pug Nose said. Little Black Beauty smiled, a rare concession, and began to sharpen ten to twelve pencils at a time, which were then duly given out by

Pug Nose in a cool, organized manner that Neil envied then and now, as he visualized it in recollection, seeing her in her black skirt and white blouse marching up and down the rows as if to say to him this is how you do it.

Don't make idle threats. The chapters on "class management" in Neil's texts made euphemistic references to "realistic rules" and "consistency," but his professors at Hunter, experienced classroom teachers, were explicit, and adamant. If you make a threat, no matter what it is, don't back down or you're finished. They'll test every warning you make. At some point in the sharpening process Neil took a nice long pencil from Pug Nose, walked over to Bowtie's desk, and without any explanation put it down next to the stub.

His weakness may have gone unnoticed by most, but not by Pug Nose, who had stopped to watch him undo Bowtie's punishment.

Speaking of Pug Nose, wasn't that her following him yesterday and today? While he was standing at his bus stop waiting for the Crosstown. Wasn't that her? Yesterday at the corner of Amsterdam? In the exact same place today. Watching him. Why?

To ask him, probably, *What makes you think you could be a teacha?* What could he possibly say? He imagined himself spreading his arms out, crying, *I don't know what to do.*

They deserve better than that, she told him.

The truth was, he had been telling himself that from the very first day. *They deserve better. Not some bum who doesn't know anything wandering in off the street to beat the draft.* Rolling his head on the desk in his apartment, he longed to forget, to be free; if he could just quit; what a relief that would be; just quit and walk away. And leave them to what? Substitutes while Bernbach scrambled to find a replacement. How about a year of substitutes? Wouldn't that be better than a no-good draft dodger who didn't know his ass from his elbow? That guy who's gonna beat them kids up?

Think Miss Slater. Think how it felt to have that vicious bitch.

To have her seat you so you were called stupid every moment of every day. There were five other Bluejays. Two were from Spring Street like Neil, another one was the country club custodian's son and there were two girls who had parents working on fancy country spreads. The custodian's son was a smart capable kid whose family lived in a two room apartment underneath the country club pro shop.

Rick? Was that his name? Maybe. What Neil remembered was that they always played against each other at recess because they were the best athletes. Whether it was football, basketball or softball, they chose the teams, they got the games going, they negotiated the disputes, they respected each other, they were friends. But Rick was even more disconnected from the town than Neil. Immediately after school he took the bus back to the club, where he caddied and helped tend the grounds. Neil, wondering what happened to him, seemed to remember he had quit school to join the Army. If he did he was probably by now rotting belly-up in some Vietnam jungle.

It was Audrey, who lived two doors down from Neil's father, who suffered the most from Miss Slater's contempt. Once there was a hole in the elbow of her sweater and Miss Slater asked in front of the whole class if her mother couldn't find decent clothes for her. Miss Slater recommended the Presbyterian Seconds Shop or the Salvation Army. Ragtag Audrey the girls began to call her. By eighth grade boys were calling her Anything Audrey because, they said, that's what she would do for you. By junior year of high school she had disappeared. Had her family moved? Had she gotten knocked up? At the time he refused to think about her.

Thinking about her now sent shame roiling through his body. As preschoolers they played together. They made Kool-Aid in her mother's filthy kitchen, trekked up the huge hill to Aunt Connie's for cookies, poked each other's privates when his daddy wasn't home. When they started school he began to avoid her, which was easy enough because he now lived with Aunt Connie and spent most of his time at the restaurant.

He avoided her because from the moment Audrey entered school she was teased mercilessly, chased home almost every day, called *Spring Street Trash*. From the moment she entered school she was torn apart. They tried that with him, too. But when anyone called him a name, boy or girl, it didn't matter, he slugged them. When they tried to chase him, he didn't run. He turned and fought, bit, scratched; he was never satisfied until he got blood. Audrey ran and cried. She let them hit her and throw rocks at her. Neil couldn't be cruel to her, but he would no longer play with her. He had to protect himself. He couldn't protect her, too. He couldn't. By sixth grade they hardly spoke to each other. Thinking about her now, he cringed, shrank into himself, sat staring at her, a wide white face with large wet brown eyes, her lips pressed together, trembling, too afraid to show anger, too docile to show defiance.

What did all this have to do with those thirty-two brats waiting to pounce on him Monday morning? Well, clearly, he was willing to save himself at the expense of those kids. Then there were Gunn and Slater, take your pick: Gunn, the huge angel with black wings, flying around the room dispensing blessings or Slater, the icy white-bloused nightmare, stalking the aisles flinging out poison as she went. You could claim the comparison was oversimplified, but it wasn't. *Do you want to spend two years throwing poison at those children?*

But they all got copy books! And pencils! How about that?

It was a question that brought to mind the boy who smiled at him that very first morning in the schoolyard, a smile given freely, spontaneously, that boy who sat head on his desk as Neil was now sitting, miserable—what was his name? Morris. Yes. Morris. Morris sat with his forehead on his desk. That sweet kid. Neil had managed to hurt him once again. How? Neil caught Morris whispering to his friend, a small tight nut of a boy with wavy black hair. Neil yelled at Morris, *Do your own work. I won't have any cheating in my class.*

Morris, defending himself, said, *I wasn't cheating.*

Yes you were, Neil insisted. *I saw you. Do your own work.* To the class he said, *Put your name on the first page. Copy the problems on the board. Then do them.*

What you want us to do? That was Clyde.

Neil gave an exasperated sigh. *Put your name on the first page,* he repeated. *Copy the problems on the board. Then do them. How complicated is that?*

Morris, the boy he had accused of cheating, now lifted his head up and cried, *But we can't read them!* His voice gathered strength as he spoke. *I wasn't cheating! I was just trying to find out what they said!* Clyde, the tall boy facing Neil in the rear of the room, affirmed, *He's right. Cane you see? We cane read your writing.*

Neil rolled his head back and forth, trying to erase the memory. Standing there, so wrong, with no place to go—that was always the worst part. He had no place to go. They could run out the door and when he closed that avenue of escape they could still plop down in their seats and put their heads down.

Neil had walked slowly to the front of the room and stood facing the blackboard, his back to the class, the oaf cornered, exposed, without defenses. He turned and met them, so tired. *I'll read them off while you copy them,* he said, which gained for him from his very special student the inevitable, *I ain't copying no stupid problems. How come you want us to copy them? What chew mean copy them?*

While she ranted on he said, *I mean COPY THEM. YOU KNOW? COPY THEM.* He made scribbling motions with his right hand. *IS THAT SO (Neil, do not say fucking. And, by God, he didn't!) HARD TO UNDERSTAND?*

Gaw! He thinks he a teacha. And she was off on that track. On: *He ain't no teacha. Look at him. He don't know nothin'.* And on:

Look at him. He ain't no teacha. And on: *He don't know nothin'. He just think he does.* So she sang, endlessly, as he carefully read each problem, over and over, until it was time to take them to the library.

The library. How long ago was that? Two days. Forever? It was all a jumble. Wednesday. It had to be Wednesday because that's when his class went to library. So on Wednesday he managed to give out copybooks and pencils; he read the problems—oh, yes, over and over and over again. And either because they truly couldn't read his handwriting or, please please don't let this be the case, because they don't know, for openers, fractions, decimals, percent, long division or the simplest algebraic notation, he had to explain each problem, what it was asking, over and over and over again. Interesting, though, that the tall boy, Clyde, did seem to know his numbers and did, in spite of his pretended indifference, hand in a paper, not the next day, but that same afternoon. And, holy shit, he had gotten most of them right! (The ones he couldn't do he marked *=wha?*)

In the library, Mrs. Worash… What kind of name was that? Not Jewish that's for sure, given the cross dangling prominently down her bursting, though certainly respectably buttoned, bodice. Mrs. Worash, smelling of Johnson's Baby Powder, smiled pleasantly at him as he delivered his scraggly ill-tempered group to her room. Getting them there was both a relief and an embarrassment. He would be rid of them for nearly an hour and, hey, for that time they might actually learn something. But, of course, that nice lady could see how disorderly his class was; what a wreck he was. It was out there, waving like a battered flag. He couldn't do this. So there was no point in trying to hide it.

There were folding chairs lined up in the large space at the front of the library and when the children came in, immediately they straightened up and filed across first the front row, then the second, then the third. Worash snapped her fingers at the pretty little black girl—Sheri? Yes, Sheri—when she pushed Mr. Bowtie. Pauli.

That's right. Mr. Bowtie was Pauli. When Arlene started to take a seat near the rear Mrs. Worash said, *No, Arlene, I'd like to have you up here near me. You look so lovely today. You all do.* Then as if a witch had suddenly possessed her, she warned, *Any funny business from any of you and I'll have your mothers in here. You know I will!*

After a momentary glare she turned to him, sweetness and light again. He didn't know how they managed it. All the teachers around here were some mix of Gunn and Slater.

And how about you, Mr. Riley? Is everything all right with you today?

Neil was astonished to hear himself moan pitifully, *I don't have any books.*

Isn't that awful? It seems to happen almost every year.

But they told me I'd have the books before school started. I don't have anything for them to do.

Thinking about this now Neil cringed. He was so pitiful. Mocking himself, he thought, *Sniff, sniff, they told me I'd have books before school started. Sniff, sniff.* What he hadn't noticed that day that struck him now was that his class, sitting there lined up facing him in three rows, did not laugh. There wasn't a snicker. No angry needle from Arlene? No caustic thrust from Clyde? They didn't make fun of him. No one did. And it wasn't because Worash was protecting him. No one made any reference to that ridiculous display later in the day either. Maybe they didn't notice? Get out of here! The little devils noticed *everything.* Could it be they saw some genuine interest in their well-being? Not a chance.

The next day. Thursday. By the reckoning of his inner clock Thursday came an instant after he dismissed them Wednesday afternoon. W*hap* it was the next morning and he was picking them up in the yard again, failing again to keep them occupied for what was alleged to be six hours and twenty minutes when, plainly, it was forever.

Only Thursday was different.

What chew mean different? Don't fuck wid me, man.

No, really, Thursday was different,

  You shitting me? They were all the same. Dismal. Chaotic. Lost.

  Okay, I know memory does funny tricks, but I say different. And you want funny tricks? How about these?

On Thursday at least two rows, half the class, maybe even more, but at least those two rows next to the window right in front of his desk, were somehow—*God damnit, don't you dare say well-behaved*—but they were... okay, let's say... *careful now, somewhat, can I say somewhat? stable.* Quiet when he demanded it, paying attention when he tried to explain the lesson. And, come on, there were lessons.

  Oh, man, now that's pure bull.

  No, really, there were. Lessons. Sort of.

If there were anything like actual lessons on Thursday it was because on Wednesday in the library Worash said, *Come back at lunch, I may be able to help you.* And at lunch Mrs. Worash offered him a cabinet full of mimeographs, almost all of them neatly bound piles of paper left behind by one dear Sarah Weeks. Mrs. Worash, with a generous smile, said, *Take any of that material you want. I've got to clean that place out anyway.*

His hands were shaking and he kept his head toward the cabinet to hide his damp eyes. *Not till I've had a chance to go through it, okay?* Then carefully he said, sounding amazingly calm, *Actually, if you want, I'll clear it out for you. How would that be?*

  Would you do that? That would be such a help.

He was able to push only two of six piles into his briefcase that day. And that night he found treasures beyond belief. The fifth grade social studies curriculum focused on early man, the sixth, ancient civilizations, from Egypt to the Roman Empire. The theme for both was: All people are more alike than different. Hey, early man would be his warm-up for ancient civilizations. And thanks to the wonderful Miss Weeks he had master sheets for about ten lessons on archeology and early man in just this pile, and two full lessons, already run off, forty copies each. It was like stumbling on a paper bag stuffed with cash. Oh, no, it was much better than that. No amount of cash was going to buy you two full lessons, already run off, forty copies each, a whole curriculum mapped out and a treasure trove of other mimeographs still to be explored. Math lessons, readings in science, stories pilfered from *Seventeen* and *Scholastic* carefully edited for fifth and sixth graders with questions about vocabulary, the characters, the central dilemma. How could he be so lucky?

That was Wednesday night. And so on Thursday he was able to give two lessons. No. Better restate that. On Thursday he was able to attempt to give two lessons. First, of course, there was the matter of yesterday's math lesson.

What math lesson? You didn't give no math lesson.

Oh, yes I did.

You cane teach nothing. How you gonna give no math lesson.

Fortunately he had the paper Mr. Clyde Johnson had handed in the day before to prove that indeed there had been a math lesson. It was fortunate because he himself had certainly not had the foresight to copy down the problems. *Get out your copy books, please.* Was it a success or a failure that well over half of the students had managed to either store their copy books or take them home and bring them back? And that a small, but significant contingent, perhaps a dozen of them, had actually attempted to do the problems? And here's the amazing thing. Maybe even seven or eight of them brought in notebooks! And paper! And pencils!

Still he had to give out more copy books. Sheri insisted that it was her job to give them out and—what the hell?—she got it done.

Did someone mention pencils? Well, of course.

What pencil? I ain't got no pencil.

How many of you lost your pencils?
Stupid white face pig he think he doin sumthin.

Pug Nose, who sat directly in front of him and whose name by now he knew was Bianca, stood up and counted for him and just as she had done yesterday negotiated with an aggrieved Sheri that one of them would sharpen the pencils while the other gave them out. Then they spent all morning putting yesterday's problems on the board, copying the answers in their copybooks, putting their names on the paper and handing them in. Sheri took up the finished papers and placed them on his desk.

The reading lesson was a horror. Sheri volunteered to read and couldn't manage words as simple as *burial* and *journey*. Some children when he called on them refused to read, adopting some of Arlene's choice phrases to justify themselves. *You ain't no teacha. This is stupid. I doan have to pay attention to you.* But their outrage lacked conviction. The lesson, which was supposedly for grades five and six, was too difficult for them. In the meantime, Pug Nose (Bianca), and a small quiet brown child with wavy brown hair (was that Pedro?) and that quiet slender girl he could never quite identify, these three not only read well, but could answer the questions at the end of the essay, which was a brief description of the Pyramids, how they were built and why.

Today, Friday, he gave a math lesson, twenty addition and subtraction problems, which took them all morning to do, then spent most of the afternoon reviewing the Pyramid story. After that he hit them with a spelling test, ten words, which he put on the board in his best print, but called out in a different order.

We cane read no chicken scratches.

Of course not. That's why I call them hints.

Now in his apartment he reached under the desk and pulled a huge wad of papers from his briefcase. Papers to be graded, mimeographs to prepare lessons from. He intended to come up with at least four lessons a day for the entire week, with some homework every night. It would take the whole weekend, which infuriated him. It didn't matter. He felt some deep compulsion at work here. He didn't understand it, but he was actually going to have to try to be a teacher. Moreover, and somehow this involved a huge debt he owed Audrey, teaching did *not*, repeat *not*, include whacking kids around. Though, oh, God, wouldn't it be nice to at least once swat the living shit out of that bitch Arlene? No, it would not. And with a bitter, reluctant sigh he decided he couldn't fit child-beating into his educational methodology.

Chapter 3:

Roll Call

In Room 6-306: Neil had gotten his class up from the school-yard in ragtag fashion, but with no major incidents. No one was pushed, no one got hit and no one started screaming, not even Neil. After two weeks of chaos, any period of semi-calm felt like a major achievement.

In the classroom some kids made a beeline for their desks, put their jackets on the backs of their seats and began to visit with their neighbors. Others put their jackets on the hooks in the back before they sat down. Neil saw that Clyde, standing in the rear of the room, was watching Carmen, who put her shiny pale-pink jacket on a hook, walked away from it, then back to it, checked the pockets, then took it off the hook and carried it with her to her desk. After she sat down she lifted the jacket up around the back of her seat, tilting her head to make doubly sure it wasn't touching the floor. When at last she was settled down, in the territory Neil thought of as Las Senoritas', Clyde sat down too, in his area in the back where he seemed even now, with a crowd of boys milling around him, fiercely alone.

Neil announced that he was going to call the roll. No one, and as a kind of masochistic ritual he stressed this to himself: *not one of the thirty-two children in his class,* was paying attention to him. Sheri was passing bubble gum to the little girl who was known to Neil only as a familiar face. Mr. Bowtie—Pauli—and his sidekick, Sammy, with three other boys looking on, were in the back near Clyde playing the hand-game Neil had come to know was rock, pa-per, scissors. These were the wild boys.

Las Senoritas sat right in front of his desk. Pug Nose: Her

name was Bianca. Maldonado? He looked at his seating book. Yes. Maldonado. She was their leader. She had aptitudes that he had begun to rely on, organizing the flow of workbooks, pencils, paper; using calm and reason to moderate Sheri's aggressive need to distribute everything. Bianca would behave like a helpful adult, then without notice become a mouthy eleven-year-old. He didn't know what to make of her, but knew she had made a significant place for herself in his mental list of who's who.

Each morning her untamable wiry hair began the day corralled in a tight ponytail. Her searching brown eyes were always focused, never corralled. She looked bravely at anyone of interest, including Arlene. She sat first in row 4, right in front of Neil's desk. Sandra, the chubby one, was first in row 3. Carmen, the dark haired, dark-eyed beauty, sat right behind Bianca. During the first week they had each worn a white short-sleeved, or in Carmen's case, sleeveless, blouse and a blue or black skirt hemmed to just below their knees, except again that Carmen's was just above hers. This was a uniform of sorts that many of the Spanish girls had worn for the first week, but as the days went on their attire evolved into more colorful summer dresses, flowered skirts and ruffled blouses. At this moment these three, Bianca, Carmen and Sandra, were chatting quietly, about earrings, it seemed, because every once in a while one of them would touch one of her ear lobes and turn this way and that.

Pedro, a small, very dignified, very cooperative young Puerto Rican, and Morris, the quiet, stocky, friendly black boy, sat further back in rows 3 and 4. They had pulled their desks closer to play a paper game; hangman, most likely. The cluster of boys sitting near them watched, making an occasional comment. These boys, who formed a loose group around Pedro and Morris, were more or less the well-behaved gang.

Row 4 ran parallel to the windows and Norbert, near the back of that row, sat craning his Norberthead on his long neck, checking his perimeter. A number of the girls, Marta especially, were busy decorating the covers of their notebooks. He knew Marta's name because she wrote it over and over on her cover, with spacious flourishes that she then inked in. Both Norbert and Marta stood out for Neil because of the intensity of the fear that seemed to rule their lives. Norbert lived in terror that the moment he let down his guard he would be attacked. Marta lived in terror that she would be noticed… and that she would be ignored.

"Class," Neil said in a normal voice. Not one person in the room paid the slightest attention to him. He was so tired of shouting. "Class," he said louder.

Sheri, with impeccable timing, smiled her beautiful smile and pointed her outstretched right hand at the curious specimen standing in front of the room. "Look at the teacha. He talkin to hisself."

Neil didn't just want to shut her up. He wanted to make her as outraged and miserable as he was. He lunged toward her across the front of the room, screaming, "SHUT UP!" He stuffed his hands in his pockets with his last shred of control. "ALL OF YOU IN YOUR SEATS!" he shouted. "SIT DOWN! SHUT UP!"

He whirled around, hands on hips, chose his next target, moved quickly toward the boys in the back, rolling up his sleeves as he went. They scattered. Clyde, already seated, watched him warily. Then a moment came when everyone was seated, everyone was quiet. Everyone was watching him.

"All right, let's just sit for a minute," Neil said, extemporizing. He had forgotten what he was supposed to be doing. The roll, of course. The roll. He glanced at his watch, appalled that it was only 9:15. Hours ago, exactly thirty minutes by this lying timepiece, he'd led them up from the yard. Still, they were quiet.

"Okay, then. Marta Albanez."

The door flew open, banging against the wall, and Arlene shuffled in, whooping gaily, "Here I am, yawl!"

"Sit down, Arlene."

"What yawl doin'?" she asked in Brenda's direction, oblivious to Neil.

"Sit down, Arlene!"

He moved toward her. Arlene ran to her desk, but did not sit down. She stood facing him, inviting him, of course, to chase her. Because he now stood near the door the temptation to walk out and not come back, which began every time he came into this room, nearly overpowered him. It was like a magnet, that door, so powerful that for a fleeting moment he forgot Arlene, the class, all consequences. There was only the longing: walk out.

The chorus brought him back quickly enough. A litany of his missteps, inadequacies and out and out failures were sung to him in thirty-two merciless voices.

"He cane do nothin'," Arlene told Brenda.

"You ought to *hit* her." Sheri said the word *hit* with a vicious twist of her shoulders.

"You shut up!" Arlene told Sheri.

"He ain't strict like Mrs. Robin," Paulie chimed in.

"She ain't like you," Sammy told him.

"He doan do nothin'," Arlene said.

"Thas cause he cane," Clyde added.

The object of these observations, all six foot one, one hundred and eighty pounds of him, stood staring, speechless, helpless.

"I'm tired of this ole seat. I ain't gonna sit here no more. I'm gonna sit..." Arlene looked around, then suddenly took off at a run around the back of the room and toward the front.

No, Neil decided. *She's not going to do this again. Ever.*

Arlene was making a beeline for Carmen's desk. When Neil saw where she was headed, he moved quickly to head her off. Before she reached Carmen Neil was able to grab her arms and flip her around to face the windows.

"You aren't going to do this," he said.

When he let her go, she turned on him, furious, fists flying. He made his blocks as hard and painful as possible, but that wasn't really satisfying. What he really wanted, craved, was to unleash a flurry of jabs, full force, messing up her face, breaking her ribs, giving her as many long lasting reminders of his attack as he could before she fell. What stopped him was the look on her face as she saw the brute he had become.

He pushed her away, using minimum force, compelling himself to be careful. Arlene, however, managed with great flair to stumble backwards, making a spectacular drama of staying upright. Then unintentionally she lost her balance and fell. Her head just missed the edge of a desk. Neil rushed back to make sure she was all right, but when he held out his hand to help her up she raised her right palm to ward it off. Her face was turned away from him, her eyes squeezed shut. She was, rightfully, expecting a fist.

Neil stepped back and shook his head. A flush spread through his entire body, a burning thing he wanted to hide. He turned and fled to the front of the room, found himself facing the blackboard, shuddering, the weight of all those eyes stripping his defenses down to the truth. They knew. Naked beast. He had been ready to beat her up. Do serious damage. Yes. Kill her. Who was the bully?

He turned to face the class. It wasn't a silence he could appreciate, but they were silent. He raised his hands, both palms open. "Arlene, I promise. I won't hit you. Ever. But I'm not going to let you hit other people either. I'll stop you any way I can. If I have to I'll carry you down to the office and tell them to call your mother and then you and I will stand there till she comes. I WON'T LET YOU BULLY THIS CLASS. I'LL BULLY YOU INSTEAD." He looked at Brenda, Clyde, Morris, Norbert. "I won't hit anybody, but I won't let any of you hit anybody either. I'll stop you any way I can."

Arlene had gone quietly to her desk, where she now sat with her head down.

Carmen was standing next to his desk. "Sit down," he told her. "That's your desk."

"You didn't hurt Arlene," Bianca reassured him.

She spoke quietly, the way a grownup might comfort a hurt child, the way Aunt Connie would say to him when he was in third grade and came into the restaurant all torn up after a fight at school, *Come on, sweetheart, it ain't that bad.*

"How you gonna stop us if you don't hit us?" Pauli asked.

"SHUT UP! JUST SHUT UP!" He walked back to his desk, where he thumbed absently through his pad to today's lesson plans. They were, to his astonishment, still silent, still. He quietly checked off their names. They were all there, of course, all thirty-two of them. None of them were ever absent.

After *Call Roll* in his plan book he had written *Spelling*.

Into that blessed quiet he requested in a firm, teacherly voice, that they, "Please get out a pencil and paper. I'm going to give you your preliminary spelling test."

"I ain't got no pencil," Sammy said.

"I'll give out the pencils," Sheri said.

"I want to give them out," Pauli said.

"I won't let you," Sheri said.

"I ain't gonna do nothin'," Pauli said and flopped his head down dramatically, his arms spread wide across his desk as if in torment.

So now both Pauli and Arlene were sitting with their heads down. What a blessing. Then Arlene sat up.

"Pauli is sooo hurt," Arlene crooned. "He like in a movie." She waved her hands in the air like wilting petals. "Poor hurt Pauli."

Pauli raised his head. "See?" he spat at Neil, noting the general injustice that prevailed in this classroom because of this teacha who, obviously, cane do nothin', so why should he?

"SHUT UP! BOTH OF YOU. NOW!"

"Gaw. He all a time yellin'," Arlene said. "Cane nobody even think."

Neil started bellowing, enraged. "I CAN YELL ALL DAY IF I HAVE TO. I WANT YOU TO SHUT UP! BOTH OF YOU!"

"You should calm down, Mr. Riley," Bianca advised him.

Neil stared at her. She met his gaze briefly, then looked down, her cheeks flushed. *My God, she's embarrassed for me,* he thought. *She's right to be, of course. Calm down. But how?* It wasn't even ten o'clock. There were still more than two whole hours until lunch time. And an eleven-year-old child was mothering him.

He took a deep breath. "Who hasn't got pencils? Raise your hands, please," he said with the best teacherly voice he could come by, which as a matter of fact sounded pretty damn teacherly.

"Gaw, there he go, thinkin' he's a teacha."

Chapter 4:

Murderers

In Roger's living room: Dylan was insisting she made love just like a woman. The party was in full swing, the smell of grass and cigarettes choking the air.

"You're late," Roger said, greeting him at the door.

"How can I be late?" Neil asked. "We didn't set a time."

But his interest had already moved past Roger to the woman standing next to him. The moment he stepped into the apartment she had trained very blue eyes on him while insisting on wearing a lavender dress that flowed down her body like water and exhibited her spectacularly naked white shoulders and sturdy arms. The two thin straps holding her dress aloft were obviously there to make him wonder what would happen if they weren't. Unfortunately, his appraisal included the fact that the man standing next to her was too comfortably close for her to be alone. The sense of disappointment he experienced surprised him, particularly since even if she had been available, he wasn't.

Roger gripped his arm, flashing a grin at Neil's wavering attention. But there was something tight, insistent about the way he said, "I told you around nine."

"And I said when I get here. I walked across the park. And, man, I've got to take a leak like you wouldn't believe."

"'Hi, Roger,'" Roger said. "'I'm so glad to see you. It was so nice of you to call and invite me to your party.' It's been over a month, buddy."

"Come on, Roger. I've just been through the worst three weeks..."

"Wait, listen to this." Roger held up his hand for silence.

And Dylan whanged, louder than all the noise, that she broke just like a little girl, which the guitar underscored; then Dylan brought it home on his harmonica.

"Isn't that great?" Roger pressed. "Like the band was playing right here." He pointed at the floor between them.

"You didn't finish," the woman standing next to Roger said. "'I've just been through the worst three weeks...' You can't leave us hanging like that. What have you just been through?"

Her dress didn't make it to her knees and she clearly wasn't wearing a bra, but Neil managed to pull his eyes up to her very complicated regard of his regard of her. His hands ached to go to the indent at her waist, to be right *there*.

"Neil, this is SeeSee. SeeSee, this is Neil, my best friend," Roger said.

"That's the letter C twice," she said. "For Cecilia. This gorgeous hunk of man is my twin brother, Charles." She took the arm of that man, her brother, who nodded at Neil while taking a hit on the roach Roger had just handed him.

Neil saw the resemblance. They had the same slightly flat face and angular cheeks, the same straight nose and firm U-shaped chin. Their faces were vaguely reminiscent of those old photos of American Indians. To Neil the brother was the pretty one, younger looking, with pouty lips. They had the same slender body, but she was broad-shouldered, with well-defined arms, while in his grey pants and white silky shirt with, of course, three buttons open at the neck, he looked thin and soft. The salient point was that he was her brother.

"Take a hit," Charles said, offering Neil the roach. As he did this he checked Neil out the way Neil wanted to check out his sister.

"Uh, no thanks. I can't. I..." As soon as Neil said, "have to work tomorrow..."

Roger groaned, "He has to work tomorrow!" Then, arms spread, eyes widened to emphasize his can-you-believe-it, "Never mind that tomorrow's Sunday."

"What do you do?" CC asked, blue eyes unwavering, eyebrows raised.

She might actually be interested. And even though he was about to pee in his pants he rushed to answer her. "I'm a teacher. Well, I mean, this is my first year. Actually, I'm starting my fourth week." And he would have kept going had he not had to cross one leg over the other and bear down hard and explain, "If I don't go piss right now I'm going to hose down the whole place."

CC put a hand on his shoulder and a palm on his chest inside his jacket. Her touch, even through his shirt, came with a rush. She stood on tip-toes and leaning on him said into his ear, "Go to the bathroom."

And surely her touch would have given him permission to touch her in return and against his better judgment he would have, but just then the group of six or seven people standing in the middle of the smoke-filled living room shifted. Bobby, Neil's former roommate/landlord, bent forward to offer someone Neil didn't know a light for his cigarette. The bodies of both young men curved over the flame in Bobby's cupped hands. Then when they stood and stepped back Neil saw Amy sitting stiffly in the overstuffed chair in the corner. At that exact instant she saw him, shot up out of the chair and headed straight for him.

"God damn you, Roger! You said she wouldn't be here."

"That's why I was waiting for you at the door."

The second Neil knocked Roger had opened. Neil thought it was unlike Roger to be hovering like that. He loved to mingle. Did he think waiting there would soothe Neil's anger?

"You should have told me. Damn!"

"You didn't give me a chance. The minute you come in you have to piss. Betty invited her. They're good friends, Neil. I didn't know until this afternoon. I swear."

"No. I mean you should have called me. I wouldn't have come."

"I tried to call you. You didn't answer your phone. You should get one of those answering services, for Christ's sake."

Neil stared at him. It was true. The phone had rung several times that afternoon and he hadn't picked up. So what? Roger shouldn't have let this happen. Neil wanted to just turn and walk out the door but couldn't because he would end up urinating all over himself. He looked toward the bathroom down the hall to his left and back and suddenly she was standing right in front of him.

Amy was a stunning presence. She had black hair and skin that seemed so thin and white you expected to see through it the way you could see through to the veins and organs of a poster on a doctor's wall. She must have been doing dope; the pupils of her eyes were like black holes in the surrounding white, with her irises nearly invisible. When he first saw Carmen, the gorgeous child in his class, he had thought that at last he had seen a girl more beautiful than Amy, with clearer skin, more appealing features, but that was simply not the case. The haunting siren's call of her face had once seemed marvelous to him. Now he felt it as an affront, cowardly, the way he had felt as a kid when in a fight some guy began to bite.

"Why haven't you called?" Amy asked.

"Because I told you I wasn't going to call, remember?"

"No, you said you'd be busy, but you'd call the first chance you got."

"Amy, that's an out and out lie. I never said that. I said, it's over, I said, goodbye. And right now I'm telling you I'm going to the bathroom, after which I'm clearing out of here."

There was an old-fashioned bolt on the door that Neil, knowing Amy, slammed into place. And just to prove he hadn't been paranoid she jiggled the doorknob. When he could finally let go he felt such joy that for a moment it seemed he didn't have a care in the world.

As he washed his hands he was vaguely aware of how clean the bathroom was. Usually the tiled floor was sprinkled with dusty wet spots and drifts of hair. Tonight the floor was scrubbed and dry. There were no dirty panties hanging on the doorknob and none drying on hangers on the shower rod. The porcelain of the old-fashioned legged tub and the sink both showed wear, but were also clean. The fixtures had been polished to a shine. This neatness was Roger's doing. Roger's East 9th Street room had been spotless, everything precisely organized. Living with sloppy Betty must, in this way at least, be an agony for him.

Roger and Betty's housekeeping habits had at first drifted without purpose at the edges of his mind, but as he reached for the doorknob and the certainty of Amy they tightened into the proud reminder that however nasty things got, he didn't have to answer to anyone but himself. Then, as he yanked open the door, ready for whatever might come, he glimpsed CC turning to watch the fiasco he must now stumble through. He took a deep breath and accepted the fact that things would only get worse.

Amy had been leaning against the wall opposite the bathroom door. She leapt forward wildly when he stepped out and grabbed his jacket, holding on as if he were a life preserver. "Take me home with you. Just tonight. *Please.* I'll never bother you again."

"That's such bullshit. You've got to leave me alone. You've got to."

"You don't know what it's like. I walk on the street and I'm looking for you. I have panties with drippings of you. I sleep with them under my cheek."

"Oh, Jesus, Amy." He felt so exposed. "I don't want this."

"Songs. That stupid Billie Holiday song you love so much. Everything reminds me of you. I go over in my head everything we ever did. I don't understand what I did wrong. I'm yours completely. I always have been. Is that it? That I'm so easy? But I couldn't play hard to get. It would be such a laugh."

"Do you hear what you're saying? You never played hard to get?"

"I could change. Anyway, that's not what I meant."

"Hi," CC said, suddenly leaning against him, putting a hand on his back. She looked very elegant in a long camel's-hair coat with a black velvet collar. "I thought we were leaving?"

Neil untangled this strange threesome, Amy clutching his front, CC leaning against his back, by forcing himself sideways and putting his arm inside CC's coat, right at that place on her waist he had longed to embrace. He caught his breath at the pleasure of doing exactly the thing he wanted to do. Amy lurched back as if she had been slapped.

"I'm ready. Let's get on outa hea," he said, imitating Paulie, his bowtied child.

"You don't know what you're getting into," Amy said to CC. And then to their backs as they walked toward the door, she screamed, "Murderers!"

Chapter 5:

No One Can Do Me Better

On Broadway and 92nd: under the neon glow of the pharmacy they turned and faced each other. CC put her hands on her hips, opening her coat to her dress, to her neck, to long strong legs. She cocked her head and stared up at him. Neil stood with his hands in his jacket pockets, not quite meeting her eye. This was too sudden, too strange; she was too mesmerizing. He didn't know what to say.

CC shook her head with an exaggerated frown.

Neil took a deep breath.

CC stretched her arms out, wing-like. With her eyes on his she pressed her palms left then right, back and forth, her body snaking from the hips. She said nothing, watching him, forcing eye contact, then turned her back on him, black hair swinging from a wooden barrette. As her head rocked back and forth, hair shimmering in the red and blue neon, she slowly lifted her arms and let them fall, opening and closing her coat like wings. She was a bird unable to fly away, a bird in a torment of indecision. Neil was baffled, wondering if he had jumped from the frying pan into the fire, thinking, *Then let me burn.*

She suddenly turned and came down to earth, which was when he realized she had done this dance on tiptoes, in plain brown flats. With a start, as if stepping from a bleak passageway, he felt himself emerge into the evening.

She held her hand out to him. "Hey," she said, "we just met at Roger Casper's party. Remember? I'm CC Harp. I named myself CC when I was too young to say Cecilia."

Neil took her hand. "CC, listen..." But he couldn't think of any-thing to say.

"All right," she said. "I'm listening."

"Okay." He let go of her hand, shook his head, fell silent again.

"Okaaay," she urged. "That's a beginning."

"Thanks for helping me out," he said. "I really didn't need her tonight."

"She seemed a little insistent."

Neil laughed.

"Look at that," she said. "A smile. Even more than a smile."

"I..." He didn't go on.

"You?..." she urged.

"I don't know what to say." He was thinking of how his hand had felt on her waist. He was thinking of all the work he had to do before Monday. He imagined his own dance, an agonized palm to his forehead, a leap off toward the crosstown bus stop, frozen in midair by passion, regret, lust. Of course, he would never have the nerve to act out this fantasy.

"That's good, that's good," she was saying. "We can work with that. What is it you don't know what to say?" she asked, pulling with her hands as if to draw a long string of words out of his mouth.

She was clearly enjoying herself and Neil was enjoying her, too, feeling her gentle teasing as an invitation, which was exactly what he wanted. And he knew he wouldn't respond. Couldn't. It was impossible.

"I guess what I'm thinking is that I'm really lousy company," he said. "You might be better off if you went back to the party."

"I can't go back to the party. The smoke was awful and I was getting a headache. I was about to leave when you came in. And besides, if I went back to the party I'd bet my entire bundle your little sweetheart would come flying after you like a bat out of hell."

"God. That's exactly what she would do. Please don't go back to the party."

"Can we walk? South?"

She grabbed his arm and pulled him back from the direction he would have taken, toward the crosstown, toward home.

"Let's head down to 79th," she said. "By this time you can almost always get a booth someplace."

"I can't do that," he said. "I don't have the time."

"You were about to go to a party." She was indignant, like Sheri. (*How come you say that?*) "That's three hours. C'mon. I get three hours for saving your life."

"Dutch," he said. "I can't afford a big tab."

"I pay," she said. "You pay next time."

They stopped for the light at 92nd.

"You know what they say about poor boys, don't you?" she asked.

"Not really."

When there was no traffic they ran across the street against the light. On the south corner in front of the toy store she said, "Poor boys want to get even."

After another block he said, "You know what they say about rich girls, don't cha?"

"Not really."

"They can't ever get enough."

"Touché, smart ass," she said.

"Now we know all about each other," he said.

She took his arm. "An old married couple." She ran her hand over his bicep. "Whoa. Muscles. You are tense though. You've got to let go."

That, of course, was what Bianca was constantly telling him. He shook his head, trying to throw the class out of his thoughts. *If only for a moment,* he pleaded with himself. He said, "I can't.

It's how I feel. Like I'm about to explode. All the time. Like I'm sick." He stopped and held up three fingers. "Three weeks," he said. "Three weeks and no books. I can't believe it. You wouldn't believe it. We're supposed to have two readers, a social studies book, a math book, books... I don't have any books. This is New York City, the largest school system in the country. After three days I got stuff from the librarian. Mimeographs, lessons. It's not like books, but it's something. I prepare and prepare. For what it's worth. The kids run around and try to beat each other up." He choked, staring at some distant disaster. "I don't believe this. I'm not crying," he insisted, taking a swipe at his face with the back of his hand.

CC reached up and with the sleeve of her coat wiped off the tears that had trickled down his cheek. "Of course not," she said.

"All this whining, I'm so embarrassed." When he had something like control he shouted angrily at the sky. "Where did this come from? I don't know what I'm doing. I never know what I'm doing."

CC had put her arm around his back, pressing her body in close to him, holding them together. She turned to face him and placed her palm on his jaw, her fingers cool against his cheek.

"It's okay, it's okay. Keep talking. Tell me about it. What is it?"

"Everything," he cried. "No, not everything," he snapped at himself. "My class. My kids. I don't know what to do. I'm awful," he howled. "I'm failing. I've never failed at anything before, *ever*. Yeah, well, you're failing at something now," he came back at himself.

"What's the matter, honey? She givin' you a hard time?"

This from a black person who in very very high heels was nearly as tall as Neil. This person, High Heels, had long powerful naked legs, and very clearly in her daylight life was some version of a he. Tonight, though, she was definitely of the female persuasion. She was barely wearing a miniskirt, one that flared inches above her red panties. A skimpy jacket opened to a bright red lacy bra. The bra made a substantial statement, though somehow Neil doubted its veracity. She wore thick rouge circles on her cheeks, glossy lipstick and inch-long eyelashes. It was this mask Neil saw, not her face. She was peering into their embrace as if through a window.

"I can do you better," she insisted.

Neil straightened up and put his arm around CC's waist, gasping with pleasure. "That's just the problem. Nobody can do me better. She does it all." He squeezed her more tightly. She nuzzled against his shoulder. Out of nowhere he had an erection.

"We could do a three-way," High Heels suggested.

"No. I'm only good with her," Neil said. The way that sounded surprised him. It didn't sound like he was joking.

"Well, anyway, maybe you could do me a dollar?"

"That I could do," and he reluctantly untangled himself from CC, pulled out his wallet and passed over a one. He checked his wallet again before putting it back in his jacket.

Walking now, quickly, to put distance between themselves and any further to-do with High Heels, CC said, "That was fun."

Neil's head snapped around to look at her. "Fun? Never show you're vulnerable on the street." He knew he sounded pompous, but couldn't help adding, "It's the first rule of the city."

She was shaking her head, smiling, but with a kind of frown, as if to ask him what on earth he was talking about. "The first rule of the city?"

"I'm trying to apologize." He put his arms across his chest. "I put you in a bad spot." He was walking with his head bowed.

She reached out to stop him. "That's not what happened. Really. You handled her perfectly."

He faced her, straightening his shoulders. Suddenly he let go and chuckled, blinking his eyes in disbelief. "I don't know if perfect's the word. Aghast would be better. But you're right, it was fun. I don't think that person was a she though."

"Oh, yes she was. I think she considered herself the complete female. And I think she enjoyed us. Or anyway saw something she wanted."

"My money," he said.

"Oh, no, she didn't need your money. She saw me holding you and wanted someone to hold her too. It was fun for us; sad for her."

They walked along in silence. He didn't know what to say. He was too confused. Some part of him wanted to reject the whole scene. *She saw me holding you.* Was that true? Absolutely. He had been held; he had allowed it. *Allowed it? You longed for it and when she held you, you felt completely at peace. At peace? Your prick went rock hard and has stayed that way, poking out there like a fence post right this minute,* which made him realize that until she materialized he hadn't had a sexual thought for weeks. *All right then, fun.*

As they walked occasionally CC would tug his arm. "This is so pleasant," she told him. And later, "It's such a beautiful night." To Neil the sidewalk was jammed with your typical outlandish Broadway mix. To CC? "It's wonderful how everyone is out tonight." Each time she delivered one of these small bursts Neil would sense her body stir, like a bird's did as it lifted its head to sing. *Pleasant, beautiful, wonderful. Fun.*

Chapter 6:

Groovy

In *Silhouettes*: a bar and grill on 79th west of Broadway they were led to a booth near the kitchen by a pretty dark-haired woman. Looking around, he worried that conversation would be difficult because of the noise. In fact, the music from overhead speakers, the voices at the bar and the intermittent clatter through the swinging doors offered a kind of privacy. They could hear each other and yet were enclosed in layers of sound, especially the cool mix of a jazz ensemble, a gorgeous trumpet, not playing a standard. *Miles*, he thought. *It had to be*.

Sniffing the air, Neil said, "Ahhh, cigarettes, beer and hamburgers." He pointed a thumb back at the kitchen. "I've spent my entire working life in places like this. There isn't a job here I couldn't pick up and do this minute."

"How about prep?" the waitress asked. She had come from the kitchen and Neil hadn't noticed her standing there. "We haven't had a prep man for over a month."

"I'll keep that in mind," he told her. "The cook must be going crazy."

"You got that right," she said. "He'd probably quit if he didn't own the place. And I'd probably quit, too, if I wasn't his daughter." She wiggled a thumb at her chest. "Guess who does the dishes." She put a menu in front of each of them.

"You grew up here?"

"Ten years. Since I was nine. I couldn't serve, but I could always bus." She looked at CC as she said this, including her in the conversation.

She was thin, of medium height and wore a black dress that buttoned right up to her neck. The buttons were white fuzzy balls. It was a kind of prim maid's outfit except that the hem of the skirt was only a few inches longer than High Heels' had been. The disappointment for Neil was that her legs were covered with black tights. A black band held curly red hair off her face and caused her ears to stick out. She had light freckles across her nose and a quick, easy smile.

"Ha, I started even younger," Neil told her. "I was bussing in my aunt's place when I was seven. It's called *Connie's Corner.*"

"Is it a bar?" the waitress asked. She held her pad to her mouth and looked back at the kitchen. "I'm not supposed to have conversations with the public." As explanation she said, "We're really short-handed. It's all family."

"Is the hostess mom?" CC asked, pointing toward the front.

"Step-mom. Mom couldn't take it anymore. I shouldn't tell you that. My daddy says…" She deepened her voice. "'Be friendly, but don't fraternize.' I'd better get your order before I get killed." She straightened up and got back to her script. "Would you like something to drink?"

"Do you have a wine list?" CC asked.

"Red or white, that's all I know," the waitress said, pressing her lips together and looking at the ceiling. "I'm sorry." Then she leaned toward CC, whispering. "They have all kinds of bottles up there, but I don't know what they are." She giggled. "Don't tell Daddy. I'm supposed to know." Now she was holding her pad against her chest with both fists.

"It's okay," CC said, smiling. "I'll have a scotch on the rocks and some water on the side. I prefer Dewar's if you have it." She waved dismissively. "But that's not important."

Neil was studying the waitress. "Are you in school?"

She brightened, then sighed, "Part-time. Hunter." Then she gave a back-to-business frown. "We have a special on pitchers tonight.

Draft Bud. Fifty cents, if you get a burger."

"Sounds good to me," Neil said. "What's your major?"

"Dramatic Arts." She seemed about to elaborate on that, but with a sudden change in tone asked, "Would you like time to look at the menu?"

"Dramatic Arts? You mean acting don't you?" CC asked.

And to her affirmative nod, Neil said, "Sounds like waitressing's gonna be a lifetime career."

"Thanks a lot," the waitress said, swatting at him with her pad.

"Okay, but listen," Neil said, "maybe I won't have to look at the menu. Let me tell you what I want and you tell me what you call it."

"Shoot," she said.

"A cheeseburger with bacon, lettuce and tomato, and a large serving of fries."

"It's called a cheeseburger with bacon, lettuce and tomato, and a large serving of fries," she said, smiling. "Steak fries or strings?"

"Oh, yeah. Steak fries."

"How'd you like your burger?" She was back to business.

"Medium."

"How bout you?" she asked CC after writing his order.

When CC looked up at the waitress Neil realized how closely she had been watching him. He felt a particular sadness pass through his mind when she looked away and was momentarily confused, as if seeing a familiar face that he couldn't put a name to.

"No, nothing thanks," CC said. "And skip the scotch. I'll share the pitcher with him."

"Okay, then," the waitress said, with a slight curtsy.

The silence when she left felt awkward to him. He sensed CC's legs moving under the table, crossing, uncrossing, restless, as if she were suddenly uncomfortable.

"Well, that was interesting," she said finally, studying him. "Three minutes flirting with a half-naked co-ed and I learn all about you."

"Flirting? More like commiserating." He leaned forward to say in a quiet voice, "These are hard times for Mr. Silhouettes and our young waitress is catching some of the pressure."

"How do you know that?"

"When you're raised in a restaurant, there are things you know. By osmosis? Like this is Saturday night, probably the biggest night of the week and he's only got one waitress? And she's his daughter? And he's alone in the kitchen? And his wife is playing hostess, cashier and busboy. And one bartender, which is his only labor expense, unless he's a buddy moonlighting for tips. So I don't have to be a genius to tell you money's a problem." He rubbed his fingers with his thumb. "Things are tight. Very tight."

"You think this affects our waitress?"

"Huh? There she is, barely old enough to serve liquor, working her butt off to do her part, when she'd rather be taking in the off-Broadway scene or partying with some young stud."

"Is that what it was like for you? Stuck working Saturday nights when you'd rather be out raising hell?"

He laughed. "I loved working Saturday nights. I loved the whole scene. And believe me *Connie's Corner* wasn't struggling financially."

"Does it...? Say it again, what's it called?"

"*Connie's Corner.*"

"Does it still exist?"

"Oh, yeah. Bigger than ever. And on Saturday night everyone in Lake Haven has to put in at least one appearance or they haven't been out."

"Lake Haven. And you were the Saturday night waiter?"

"One of them."

"And all the Lake Haven girls got a chance to come in and order you around?"

"You could say that."

Unexpectedly, what he wanted to tell her was how he loved being the charming helper, handling difficult customers with grace and respect, seeing the surprise on the faces of classmates and their parents when he was polite and helpful. Most of all he loved the proud lilt in Aunt Connie's voice when she'd bark out something like, *Neilly, water for number three!* and he'd call back, fully cooperative, *I've got it.* He couldn't tell CC any of this because the memory of those performances embarrassed him enough to cause him to immediately shift his mind to something else. In this instance it was the uneasy awareness of how eager he was to talk to this woman.

"Tell me about your aunt."

"Oh, no, I've answered enough questions. Now it's my turn. And by the way, I'll pay for this," he said. "You don't have to buy me dinner."

"Not a chance. This is on me. Then you owe me. And one more question, just for the record. How old are you?"

Head held high, he looked down his nose at her and told her through tight lips, "I'm twenty-four. Twenty-four and a half, to be exact." With a sweeping gesture across the table, "And Madam?"

She imitated his haughty look, her chin aimed at him. "I'm twenty-seven. Twenty-seven and ten months to be exact."

He did a quick calculation with his fingers while she held his eyes with her stare. "You'll be twenty-eight in December?"

"December 10th. Shall we continue these introductory matters? Your name is Neil Riley, yes?"

"Yes. Neil Riley. And you are CC, two capital c's, for Cecilia. Might I ask, are there periods after each C?"

"No periods. And my last name?"

"I don't think I've been given that information."

"Harp. I am CC Harp."

The waitress brought their pitcher and two glasses on a round tray. "Your burger will be a few minutes," she said, carefully setting the pitcher down. After placing a glass in front of each of them, with great concentration she lifted the pitcher and filled CC's first, then Neil's, each slowly so as not to create too much head. Neil and CC allowed their eyes to meet briefly, nodding.

"Thank you. That was perfect," CC said, lifting her glass.

The waitress beamed. "You guys." She clasped the tray with both hands and shivered. "You guys are so groovy," she said and went running off toward the front.

"Groovy?" CC frowned. "She obviously means you. How do you feel about that?"

"Me? You're the one who sent her into ecstasy."

When he reached for his beer she asked, "Are you looking at your watch?"

"Huh? No." Then, "Shit, it's after eleven! For how long? At least an hour. For an hour I've hardly thought about school. My God." He crumpled forward. "I'm sure as hell thinking about it now."

She kept looking at him and in the dim light her eyes—he would have said they were black except that her pupils were so plainly black, showing then that the irises surrounding them were more the deep blue of a moonlit sky—seemed to reach in and monitor his every thought.

"What?" he asked.

She smiled. "I'm just curious. I might not have realized how tense you are if this scene…" She made a circle with her hand, her head then nodding at the bar. "…hadn't been like a magic pill. From the time we walked in here you've been another person entirely. No, that's not accurate. The pill analogy is though. You're the same person but it's as though something really mellowed you out." Her voice trailed down on those last two words and her head rolled, indicating how loose he had become.

It's not the place. It's you, he thought.

They both leaned back now, gripping their glasses, maintaining eye contact. As unnerved as he was by her stare, he was also pleased. And he enjoyed the freedom it gave him to stare back. Slowly, without apology, he went from her dark startling eyes to her long black hair. In the dimness her white skin had a golden luster, her wide strong cheeks were even more prominent, her jaw more firm. But his attention focused especially on her nipples making small points on her dress. He wondered what her breasts would feel like in the palms of his hands, a speculation that drew his attention to his recurrent hard-on.

Meanwhile, across the table, CC's glance down indicated she wasn't blind to his interest. She made eye contact again and brought her glass to her lips, effectively covering her chest with her arm. It occurred to Neil that nipples, like erections, made their own reckless declarations.

"I know what you're thinking," she said.

"What?" Would she dare say it? *You're dying to fuck me.*

"You're thinking, this is all very nice, but it's getting late and I have to go."

That was so woefully right. He had to do those stupid lesson plans. Everything else, including this beautiful woman, was just a distraction. How pathetic was that? He blew out a huge breath. "You don't know the half of it."

"Maybe not, but I do know some of it. You said you'd never failed before…"

He shook his head, waving his hand in the air. "No, no, it's a stupid thing to say. Of course I've failed, but…" He hesitated.

"But not like this," she offered.

"No way. This is…"

"Awful."

"It is," he agreed. "Awful. Oh, God, yes, awful."

"Why?"

He stared at her. Why? The answer came immediately to mind.

Before he could suppress it, he blurted recklessly, "What I'm doing. It's not right." He enclosed his right fist with his left and pressed, hard. Blue veins swelled up his wrists.

CC very carefully moved her glass, then his toward the wall of the booth. She circled his hands with hers, gently caressing the tight knot of knuckles, pulling softly, easing his grip open. Then she pressed their palms together and locked their thumbs. "Take some time now to let go. Seriously. Just relax, do nothing, just for a few minutes. Tell yourself you don't have to go anywhere or do anything. Just for a few minutes."

"But I can't shut my stupid mouth…"

"Please don't shut your stupid mouth," she said.

"I start to have fun and believe me I haven't had fun in eons and then I look at my watch and see what time it is and I start to think of all the stuff I have to do before Monday and I feel everything come crashing down on me."

"I think I know how that feels."

"Do you really?"

"I'm guessing, but it feels like you think that if you aren't super prepared then you won't be able to exert any control over all the things you have to do."

"Exactly. I keep thinking of all the stuff I have to do."

"All the stuff…?" She left the question open, watching him.

"Yes, everything," he said in a rush. "All the planning. All the thinking." He held a hand up, a claw, and shook it. "I keep thinking how stupid I am. Believe it or not, it never occurred to me that sixth graders are people." Oh, God, had he actually told her that? He glanced at her for a moment; then his entire body tensed as he gazed into his unfathomable ignorance. "It never occurred to me that eleven-year-olds have feelings, needs. I'll tell you this, though, they don't need me." He suddenly fell back and looked around self-consciously. "I'm sorry. God, I'm so sorry. I don't know where all that came from. You're probably wondering what you've gotten yourself into. Would you like to leave? This must be embarrassing for you. I know I'm embarrassing myself." If he didn't shut up he was going to start banging his head on the table.

"You're not embarrassing me." Truly she was just watching him. And she actually looked interested. "And I don't want to leave. Talk some more about what you have to do."

"Oh, man, that would take forever. What I'm thinking right now is I don't have time to talk about anything."

"Yeah, well, we have three hours." She laughed, pointing at his alarmed expression. "I know, I know. Okay, we have until you finish dinner."

"All right, then," their waitress said. "Be careful. Everything's really hot." As she said this she put a huge platter in front of Neil. "Can I get you anything else?"

CC pulled back to make room for the platter. "Josie?" she said, reading the girl's nametag. "You're Josie?"

"That's me. Josephine." She giggled.

Meanwhile Neil reached behind the napkin holder, picked up the catsup bottle and began to unscrew the top. The two women watched as he snaked a small roll of catsup around the top of the fries. He picked one up, dipped and turned it until it was drenched with catsup, then put it in his mouth. He savored it with closed lips, chewed it slowly, then sighed.

"I'm going to just eat," he said. "This is too delicious."

"I think we've lost him," CC told Josie.

"He looks hungry," Josie said. She beamed. "Let me know if you want anything else." She touched the handle of the pitcher, still three-quarters full. "More beer?"

"God, no," Neil said.

"We'll think about it," CC said. After Josie left CC said to Neil, who was pouring catsup on his open burger, "You're going to have trouble closing that thing."

"Just watch," he said, putting the two piles together.

As he jammed the closed bun into his mouth she widened her eyes in mock horror. "Just don't choke to death."

He stared at her, chewing.

"You *are* starved. When was the last time you ate?" she asked.

He chewed, holding up a finger, signaling wait. After a sip of beer he said, "I had a bologna and cheese sandwich just before I left for Roger's. That was lunch."

"Don't you even take time to eat?"

"When I can. I open a lot of cans. I heat stuff up and pour it over bread. Sometimes I skip the heated part." He took another bite of his burger.

"That's it? Canned foods?"

"Yeah, well, and Cheerios. And milk. And bananas. And peanut butter and jelly. I'd really be up the creek without peanut butter and jelly. And I almost forgot. The poor man's speed. Coffee and chocolate bars." He took another bite. "Wost wa wite wazy," he said with his mouth full.

"The subtitles on that read?..." She spread out the thumb and forefinger of each hand. "'I lost weight like crazy?'"

He nodded. As they looked at each other, Neil felt a shiver of satisfaction, as if he had just lowered himself into a magic pool. His hard-on was only part of it. He remembered the healing feel of her fingers on his hands, how she actually listened to him when he talked. And with all this he suddenly had a voracious appetite. He could taste the food, hear the music, see the marvelous person sitting across from him. The protective layer he had been wrapped in for the last few weeks had evaporated.

And his reaction to this revelation? He wanted to know what time it was. He looked down at his plate and sneaked a glance at his watch as he picked up another fry. It was almost midnight. He was still hungry, but it had become just food, not manna. This woman was a stranger, not a magician. And the music had stopped. He would end the evening in the same morose hole he had been buried in all along.

As if she had sensed his mood change, CC pulled herself forward and offered up this non sequitur. "Roger says you're the genuine article." There was a provocative cadence to her voice, and a hint of haste.

Neil took a sip of beer, looking at her over the rim of his glass, then asked, "What does he mean by that? 'Genuine article.' Sounds like I'm a Persian rug."

She laughed. "What he said was you don't try to be anything you're not. I think he has a crush on you."

"I'd give a hundred to one he didn't say that."

"No, I said it. Men get crushes, though they would never call it that. Roger calls it best friends. Speaking of which, when he introduced you as his best friend, talk about double-takes. You jerked like he'd given you a whack." She threw her head back to demonstrate.

"I didn't know I was so easy to read."

"Oh, no, not so easy. Some people would take it as a compliment to be called a best friend. You didn't seem to like it at all. I wonder about that, but I certainly don't understand it." Racing on she asked, "How do you know Roger?"

"We met when we rented rooms in Bobby's East 9th Street digs. Bobby has this big sprawling apartment. The whole fourth floor of a building. Ninety bucks a month. Heat and hot water. Anyway, most of the time. Renting out rooms to suckers like me, he makes his rent and a little on the side. But it was a good deal for me, too. For forty a month I had a place to flop and keep my stuff. If you're going to NYU Law it's practically like living on campus. I was in the library most of the time anyway. Or at that great Horn and Hardart's on Third Avenue where you can sit all night with your overcooked dinner and cold coffee. So Roger and I have known each other for what? Two years maybe? We moved in at about the same time, June before the fall semester. Then he and Betty got engaged and he moved out. Bobby was his best man when he got married. I was surprised to be called his best friend, that's all."

"Roger, Bobby, all those guys, why are they in their third year and you're teaching school?"

"For one thing, I ran out of money. I had a scholarship, but it wasn't enough. I'll finish, believe me."

"But why teach if it's so hard? Why not do prep, for example? The money's probably better."

"You got that right. The real reason is with the new law if you take a student deferment you get one year of post-graduate school. Then they can draft you till you're thirty-four. So I finish law school, report my change in status and I'm drafted tomorrow. That is not going to happen. I am not going to fight that fucking war."

"I totally agree," she said. "It's an outrage."

"I could care less about that." He leaned forward. "Why on earth would I want to fight for this country? In the town I grew up in there were two slummy streets. My dad and I lived on one of them." He snickered. "Spring Street. From the first grade on I had to fight my way to and from school. And everybody always assumed I started it. I was that Riley kid. Nobody gave a shit about me except my aunt. Nobody. I have more in common with the Vietcong than I do with those creeps in Washington. So do the guys on our side. Kids, a few years older than my kids…"

He rolled his eyes at the ceiling. "My kids? Where did that come from? I certainly didn't spawn that assorted bunch of maniacs. My kids. Jesus, I better watch my mouth. I mean the boys in my class. If they don't stop this war, the boys in my class will be there, too, in a couple of years. And this lottery they're talking about? What a joke. I'm telling you they ain't gonna draft no rich white boys. And they ain't gonna draft me." He leaned back, made a face and brushed at the air as if to clear away a bad smell. "Wow. I'm sorry. I'm really weird tonight. I don't know what's gotten into me. I haven't talked to anyone, you know, just talked, like I was a person just talking to a person since..." He thought about it. "I don't really know when." He squirmed at that and tensed to stop himself from squirming.

"So if you teach, you avoid the draft?" she asked.

He stared at her for a moment, then rushed on. "Yeah. Believe it or not, local boards can declare certain occupations essential. In Alabama it might be pipefitters, in New York it's teachers. So the City says I'm IV-S and in two years I'm twenty-six and free to go. Okay, I've talked enough. Too much. It's my turn to ask the questions."

"No, wait, I'm not finished with you."

He laughed. "Oh, yes you are."

"No, I'm not," she said.

Neil laughed. He was thinking of Arlene's stubborn intonation and sassy twist. "Yes, you are," he said.

"Am not," she said, grabbing one of his hands.

"Am, too," he said, grabbing her other hand.

"Am, too," she said.

"Am... Oh, no, you won't trick me. Creep."

"No. Just intrigued," she said.

Their eyes met. She seemed as pleased as he was that their hands were gripped tightly over the clutter on the table.

He couldn't help himself. He said, "You are lovely."

"Not nearly as lovely as your little dark-eyed beauty. Amy? What about her?"

"I'm starved," Neil said. "Here are these fantastic steak fries and you keep asking questions."

"So eat, piggy." She threw his hands back at him. "You already had bologna and cheese today. Isn't that enough?"

"So how did you meet Roger? Are you one of Betty's friends?" he asked.

"No. Wait. You get to ask me about Roger, but you won't tell me about your girlfriend? You're avoiding something here."

He finished chewing then said, "I'm not avoiding anything. I'm just saying you don't get to ask all the questions. Okay, here's a deal. You tell me about Roger, I tell you about Amy."

"Hah, that's a deal. Cause there's nothing to tell. Roger's more a friend of my brother's. We all went to the same school for kids who couldn't or wouldn't go to public school. You saw my brother. Could you see him at Seward? He'd've been killed the first day. So anyway Roger and Charles, my brother, they're the friends. And Roger and I were the literary lights. He edited the newspaper and I published the *Walden Reader*, a sort of catchall journal of poetry and prose. The poetry was mostly mine."

Josie appeared at their table. "Is everything all right?"

"Yes, but you have to tell us why we're groovy," CC said.

"I know you've got problems, but everybody does," she said to Neil, who laughed and nodded in agreement, "but that's groovy too. I mean... " She looked up as if the words she wanted were on the ceiling. "You're both so here." She dipped her knees and did a quick wave of her hands. "Not just here, but *here*." Another quick wave. "Know what I mean?"

"Yeah, I do," Neil said.

"Of course you do," CC said, "seeing she's the cutest thing that ever lived."

"Are you mad at me?" Josie asked her.

"Not for a minute. Not for a second," CC said, touching her wrist. "He's going away tonight and I'm probably never going to see him again. It's not easy."

"Oh, God, that's terrible," Josie said. "Why?" she asked Neil. Then before he could answer, she gasped and said, "You're going to Nam."

"No, no, it's not that." He looked at CC. "I've got a job. I've got to go and she's got to stay. It's just one of those things."

"I'm so sorry. Really." Her eyebrows plunged into a tragic V. "Oh, God."

Neil, looking at them both with wary eyes like a dog protecting his bone, picked up his burger and took a huge bite. "Am solly ealy ungar," he said.

"I think what he means is that he's sorry about all this heartbreak, but he's really hungry," CC said.

Neil drank more beer. "I'm really hungry," he agreed and took another bite of hamburger. The music was back. A sax singing, long slow urgent.

The two women watched him.

"What?" he asked.

CC put her hand out as if presenting him to Josie. "Groovy?" she asked.

Josie smiled. "Well, yeah, sort of. You know what I mean?"

CC sighed. "Yeah, I sort of do."

"More beer?" Josie asked

Neil shook his head.

"Anything?" she was looking at CC.

"No, I'm fine."

"Wait," Neil said as Josie turned away. The moment he eased up the jailor stalking him grabbed him, insisting it was time to go.

CC held a hand out, palm up, to stop him from saying any more. "Let me say it, okay? We'd like the check."

How had she known exactly what he was going to say? She was worse than Bianca. He felt her watching him as he wiped at the catsup on his plate with his last fry.

She chuckled.

"What's so funny?" he asked.

"Nothing really," she said. She waved a hand back and forth across the table. "This evening, I guess. The way you're under so much pressure. It's not funny haha. I laughed because it's not funny haha."

"Oh."

"We might never see each other again. I guess that deserves some kind of laugh."

The only thing he could think to say was exactly what he felt. "I wish I didn't feel the way I feel. I can't tell you how much I wish I didn't feel the way I feel."

"That's okay. But before we call it an evening, could you tell me about Amy? You promised, you know."

"I promised? When?"

"Oh, yes. If I told you about Roger? Remember? You promised."

"Okay, yeah, but…"

She looked down at her glass, which was almost empty. She slid the glass carefully to the center of the table, hefted the pitcher and filled it. "Want some?" she asked him.

He shook his head, *no*.

She took a drink and ran a satisfied tongue over her lips. She had a way of grabbing him with her eyes, which was what she did now. "You promised."

"It's hard to talk about someone…" He grimaced. "Someone who drives you *nuts!*" He leaned back. "Okay, but first I need to catch up." He filled his glass and downed half of it.

"Tell me about Amy," she insisted.

"The reason I'm having a hard time with this is… Do you think it's fair to talk about a woman you… you know, a woman you know is in trouble?"

"Ah, how nineteenth century: the gentleman is compelled to

protect the lady's good name. Dare I mention that the lady in question announced to all and sundry that she sleeps with undergarments anointed with the gentleman's emissions. Putting aside with great reluctance any diagnosis, such as extreme fetishism stemming from childhood sexual abuse, I can still confidently conclude that the gentleman and the lady have been, um, intimate. She also made it clear that he had failed to follow through on his promise to call her, though as I remember it, he alleged he had unequivocally ended the relationship. Given the public nature of this dispute and that she indicated that we, that is, he and I, were murdering her, I have a claim to, no a need to, no, a right to know the nature of this relationship, if only to defend myself from possible retribution. I only mention that I rescued you from her to let you know that though this places you deeply in my debt I haven't demanded any sort of repayment. Yet."

Neil laughed. "Holy shit! You're a lawyer!"

"Oh, no, much worse: a businesswoman. And I know when a deal is about to go bad. You entered into an agreement with me. I expect payment. Tell me about Amy."

"Yikes. Yeah. Well, you did help me out of a painful confrontation."

"At great peril to my wellbeing, sir."

"Oh, absolutely. No doubt about *that*. And I am deeply grateful."

"All right, seriously, you don't have to reveal anything about her you think is wrong. But I am curious. And since we're all connected, I should at least know how dangerous she might be if I meet her again."

"I… my guess is she's more of a danger to herself than to anyone else." He thought for a moment. "The most important thing about her to me? She never ever saw me. I don't quite know how to describe this. I dated her…" He counted on his fingers. "…four times, five if you count the night I took her home after we had dinner at Roger and Betty's. That's how we met, at Roger and Betty's. Then we had a typical first date. I say typical, but looking back the problem was there from the beginning. We went to a movie at the Eighth Street, had espresso, that kind of stuff, but already... Okay, already she'd ask me a question then answer it. Did I know why I was so attractive to women? Before I could finish saying, no, I didn't... she jumped in, telling me, I'm the Robert Ryan type, sexy but sinister."

"Yeah, I can see the Robert Ryan overtones, with maybe a touch less menace. Did you make good grades in school?"

"Actually..."

"I bet you did. You're very well spoken to be so sinister."

"All right. Okay. Please don't."

She smiled, nodding. "I'm sorry. I just wanted you to know I understood. So if this went on all evening, well, why did you see her again?"

"Okay, look, I mean, all right, time for shameful admissions. This woman could have stepped out of a movie, she's so gorgeous."

CC's right hand flew to her cheek as if she had been struck. Hard.

"Ouch. What happened?" he asked.

"It's a nerve thing. I'm okay. Go on. She is gorgeous, no doubt about it."

"So here's this knockout telling me I'm this sexy sinister guy and I'm saying to myself, whatever turns her on, and on the swing of that dirty little turn things became very strange." He paused, looked at his beer, took a sip.

CC pointed an accusing finger at him, giving it a quick jerk. "Right *there*. You're censoring something. Not fair. If you leave certain details out..." She suddenly relaxed and dropped her hand to the table. "You have every right to protect yourself. So she's irresistible. Go on."

"I'm trying to think how to say this. On our second date, at her house, she's cooking. And from her point of view, this is something like an engagement party. I don't think I'm exaggerating. I had become whatever it is you are when someone can't live without you. She called me her soul-mate. Are you with me?"

"Oh, yes," she said. "Soul-mate."

"Yeah, right, and furthermore… now, let me see if I can convey at least some of the nuances of this… it was apparent to her, if not to me, that she was also my soul-mate. She told me that. Oh, man, this was so weird. To me. Let's be fair. Maybe it's not weird. But to me it was weird. I started wondering how I could get out the door. Only, wait, I won't censor this. I was wondering how I could get laid without too many incriminating lies before I got out the door. Pretty sick, huh? Still proud that you rescued me?"

CC shook her head. "Are you kidding? Typical male behavior." She held an arm out at him as if making a presentation. "You're so normal, it's amazing. Though I have to say that touch of guilt, while charming, *is* abnormal. Okay, go on. Did you get laid?"

He shook a fist. "Nailed her."

"Well, all right!" She leaned into the blow she threw at him. "But did you get out the door?"

He laughed. "Well, as you may have noticed, not really." He took a deep breath. "I'm uncomfortable with…" He pursed his lips.

"You don't want to make fun of her."

"No, I don't."

"It's my fault. No more joking around. Okay, so I take it getting out the door, as you put it, proved a lot more difficult than you had anticipated."

"A lot more. Listen, in some way I don't completely understand…" He waved a finger back and forth between them. "…talking about this seems wrong. You're… good at asking questions. That's certainly not a fault. I just… I don't want to put Amy down. I don't understand her and I don't want to make it seem like I do. The crux of it for me, and this is what's so wonderful about talking about it, I don't think I ever fully understood before, the crux of it for me is…" He grabbed at the air. "…there was never any reality to hold onto. For me. I'm speaking strictly for me. She wasn't/isn't/ never could be my soul-mate. We weren't soul-mates. She said we were; I said we weren't. No matter what we talked about that's what we were really talking about. Do you understand?"

"Yes, I think I do. Shall I demonstrate?"

"Oh, God, I can't wait. Okay, demonstrate. But only once."

"I don't care what we're talking about, what we're really talking about is how we're going to end this evening."

He stared at her and when he understood, looked quickly at his watch. "Holy shit, it's 12:15!"

"I think I've made my point. I do understand the problem of underlying issues. You've been a pumpkin for fifteen minutes. Where is our Josie? We need to get the check and go. But before I go looking for her just tell me, did you try to explain to Amy this difficulty in communication you perceived in your relationship?"

He shook his head to show how confused he was. "I'm trying to perceive the difficulty I have keeping up with you. Why do you know exactly what's going on while I'm totally at sea."

"Because all you can think about is how your world will fall apart if you don't go to work while I…" She paused then said, "While I want to know how things are between you and Amy. From your point of view. I know you can't speak for her."

"Things are over. Over, with a capital O. I told her in no uncertain terms that I wanted to end the relationship. On our third date. I was very very clear about it. She begged me to see her one more time and like an idiot I agreed and it was the same old shit. "

"What did she do?"

"She told me that I knew she was my soul-mate. That I didn't really want to break it off. Actually, she insisted that I couldn't break it off."

At that moment Josie put the check in front of Neil.

"Oh no, this is mine," CC said, reaching over and picking it up. "Wait," she said to Josie. She looked at the bill, studied it for a moment, twisted around to get her wallet out of her coat and took out a ten and a twenty. "Keep the change."

"Oh, wow, thanks. You guys come back, okay?" Then quickly, "Not because of this," she said, holding up the twenty.

"I know," CC said. To Neil she said in a level voice, "It's time to go."

He helped her with her coat and then as he put on his jacket she helped him. There was an awkward shuffling before he suggested he needed the bathroom and she admitted that she did too.

When they stepped outside she asked, "Where do you live?"

"97th and Lexington."

"Wow. El Barrio south. Pretty exclusive."

"Only the best," he said.

"I want to get a taxi. I'll drop you off."

He stepped to the curb.

"No, wait," she said. "I'll just be a minute."

She went back inside; he had no idea why. He paced restlessly from the curb to the door of the bar. How had he let this evening go on so long? How could he let it end here?

After a few moments she re-emerged. "Sorry to keep you waiting. I wanted to write something down." And to his slightly quizzical look, she said, "I don't have my purse. Pencil and paper? Write?" She made squiggling motions with her right hand.

Luckily, perhaps because it was late, they were able to get a taxi almost immediately. CC gave the driver directions, first to Neil's, then back to hers, at 82nd and Riverside. Before he could comment on how out of the way it was for her to take him home she reached over and took his hand.

"Here. A souvenir." She put a matchbook into his palm.

Holding it up and squinting he saw a slick black design with a white circle in the middle. Inside the white circle were two black profiles facing each other, or looking again, it was a white vase outlined in black. On the other side was the name, white on black: *Silhouettes*.

"What? Oh, from the bar."

She tapped the matchbook. "You didn't ask for this, but inside is my name, address and telephone number. Numbers. I included my work number. I certainly won't call you and I may not be available if you call me, but... anyway, I won't hold my breath."

"Thank you," Neil said. His response felt entirely inadequate.

After that they sat apart, in silence. Neil wondered what they would do if they were sitting in a plane bracing for a rough landing. Then he knew. They would have held hands. The walls flying by the cab as they passed through Central Park made it seem as if they were burrowing through a tunnel. More than ever he felt compelled to take her hand, but couldn't. Then they were out of the park, passing Fifth. When they reached Madison Neil leaned forward and told the driver to let him out at the corner of 96th and Lex. Almost immediately the cab stopped, throwing Neil back to a place where they would go their separate ways. He felt CC move toward him, her hand finding his cheek, her mouth wet and open on his. "So long, old friend," she said, letting him go. "You are definitely the genuine article, groovy, here here, know what I mean?"

Neil turned back and spoke to the dark outline of a woman with legs gleaming in the light of the street lamp. "Goodbye, CC. It was fun. I really mean it." The cabbie peeled off the moment he shut the door.

Chapter 7:

Wanting the Genuine Article

In Neil's apartment: he paced back and forth from the kitchen to the bathroom. He could hardly lift his feet he was so tired, but he couldn't unwind. He felt like he'd been slipped a benny. His mind hurtled through recollections of the evening, his focus ricocheting like a pinball from trigger to trigger. CC sat up on the scoreboard, her eyes always on him, watching.

He remembered her tits (*Riley, do you have to always be so crude? Can't you at least say breasts? What about nipples? Even doctors say nipples.*) nipples hard against her dress. Being a connoisseur how could he not have pursued the possibility of examining that lovely pair? He cringed, worrying that he'd actually told her he didn't have time to check out her tits, breasts, nipples. No. He hadn't. He had been maybe not a perfect gentleman but pretty okay given the slimy sex maniac he was in real life. Anyway, the conversation hadn't gone in that direction, on the surface at least. No, everything had been about his misgivings, his anxieties, his failures. *Oh, God, what a jerk she must think I am.*

Consider this. She ran the whole evening. I was the resisting flower. Oh, no, you Jezebel, you can't buy me with a cheeseburger with bacon, lettuce and tomato and steak fries on the side. No, not even if you throw in a pitcher of beer, which don't forget you shared.

That feeling, that she was available, was definitely in the air. The feeling that he wasn't was definitely in the air, too, stinking to high heaven. And here he was staying up all night anyway. Realizing that what enticed him wasn't her nipples, but those gorgeous eyes watching, that smart face listening to him, immersed. She *listened.*

Who had ever listened? Not Connie whose questions were aimed at edging him back to Lake Haven. Amy? *Come on, Amy?* But not just Amy, not just Connie, most people, himself included, asked questions to corral their quarry into a particular stall.

Are you saying CC didn't do that? I'm saying CC asked then listened, trying to understand. Come on now, do you really believe that? What about all that stuff about age? She was probably trying to tell you you're too young for her. Yeah, but what about her questions about teaching? What about her curiosity about me? And he had fallen all over himself to tell her anything that came to mind. He couldn't shut up. Why had she shown up now? He didn't need this. Oh, yes, he did. He needed this. That was the problem.

At least he didn't tell her his best friend was a freeloading wildcat who'd drop him the minute those bowls in the kitchen went empty. Speaking of whom, where was he? It was after 2 a.m. and he hadn't shown his smelly self. Out tomcatting, the slinky bastard.

As Neil stumbled back and forth he picked up his jacket and hung it in the closet, remembered as he walked away that she'd given him that matchbook and rushed back to the bedroom. He fumbled it out of his jacket pocket, then hesitated, as if expecting to find it unreadable. How amazing, what she had written was perfectly comprehensible. Though he had no plans to contact her, how could he? there was something reassuring about this offering, as if he had received it this minute. Without any further thought, he undressed and crawled into bed.

Where he found that in spite of or because of everything he stared with vivid wonder at her legs shining out of the darkness in the back seat of the cab, at her nipples hard against her dress and simultaneously with these experienced again the shock of pleasure he'd felt when he held her waist at Roger's. As he masturbated, he couldn't, or wouldn't, imagine her naked. He wanted the genuine article. To climax he went to that first time Cynthia, his high school girlfriend, closed her mouth around his penis. Back in the here and now, exhausted, drifting toward sleep, full of regrets, upset and dissatisfied with every aspect of his life, most of all that lame, 'It was fun. I really mean it,' he heard the cat drop from the window sill. It was called a purr, but what that guy did sounded more like the growl of a small motor boat. Anticipating dinner.

Even if he hadn't heard the quiet landing on the floor from the window he always left open he would have heard that growl and smelled the stink of tar and sour garbage and, tonight, the pissy smell of cat sex. He turned to watch a mass blacker than the darkness, one white paw flashing, flow over and put a nose to his palm, a greeting of sorts, before he went on into the kitchen for the now expected bowl of dry cat food topped with scraps—*bologna tonight, old buddy*—a bowl of water and a small dish of milk. After he ate the cat would curl up on the towel, *his* towel, in the middle of the living room couch to sleep for a while. He was usually gone by morning.

At least one of us got laid, Neil thought.

Chapter 8:

Define "I"

In his apartment: the next morning with bright sunlight streaming through the window Neil woke up with the thought: he had no time. He immediately reached for his pad. *Spelling*, he wrote. Twenty words and their meanings. Too many? Hell, no, lazy little fuckers. Easy. Give em easy or so it would seem. But provocative. He wrote, "I." *Define "I", smart ass*, he challenged himself. *Me? Myself? Ain't so easy, huh? Look it up.* Webster says: "Someone aware of possessing a personal individuality." No way. But also, and he wrote, *Myself. How about that? And how about aware? That's a good one. Oh, yeah? What the fuck does aware mean? Come on, come on. Knowing something. Oh, man, lame dick. Well, then?* Webster: "Having or showing realization or knowledge." *Not so bad. Aware: Having knowledge.* He would put the definitions on the board all mixed up and have them choose five. No, ten. *Damn, if you gonna give them the answers at least make it ten.*

For some reason he was standing in the kitchen. *To make coffee? Fix a bowl of Cheerios? Never mind. Get your ass out for a run. How about words that sound alike but have different meanings? I and eye. Oh, yeah, give it to me, baby! And eye, that's easy. The organ you see with. Be a little more elegant please.* Webster? Oh, Jesus! "A specialized light-sensitive sensory structure of animals in nearly all vertebrates, most arthropods and..." *on and on and what the hell's an arthropod? Okay, but here:* "The image-forming organ of sight." The organ animals see with. *Eye: The organ with which animals see. Can you live with that? Arthropods?* He looked it up.

93

Insects and other creepy crawly things. *So, arthropods? Uh, not this week, kiddies.*

See and sea, there and their, so and sew. Take that, you little fuckers. Words that have several meanings? Like? Can you think of another? Yeah, foot. Linguistics 101, how words come to be, how their meanings shift over time, why language is important.

Can't you just see it? Professor Riley sitting comfortably on the edge of his desk discussing Chomsky's innate language thesis. Back in the here and now, face it. You do have a choice: teach sixth grade or go to Canada. Or even, hey, how about getting killed killing gooks? My goodness. I've got choices up the wazoo.

And so we find our numb-nut draft dodger trying to prepare for his Monday morning chaos—sorry—class. Remember that Monday is tomorrow and that following Monday are four more very long days, 8:30 to 3, with an assessment of each day's failures on the bus ride home, and more prep in the evening, and then it will be Friday afternoon, that blessed time that is the longest time between Friday at school and Monday at school.

He was standing in his underpants in the middle of the living room holding his funky jeans. Why? *To get out, west on 96th to the park, wind down to 59th and head back up and out.*

He turned to a fresh page in his pad and wrote *Social studies,* then erased the "s" in studies and wrote "S." *Moving right along.* He still didn't have any books. He had been promised they would come last week. According to Mrs. Bane that delivery had been dropped off at another school by mistake. The administration there, being moral educators, had for the good of their children commandeered the shipment. The principal had even filed a formal complaint regarding the fact that her school had been scheduled to receive their books after Bane's.

What did all this mean? He had no books and yet every minute had to be accounted for.

Chapter 9:

The Third Word Is Care

In Room 6-306: in the first week of October some work actually got done. And one day without warning a huge tractor-trailer drove up bringing books. Neil's class got: a math book, two readers, a dictionary and a social studies text, forty copies of each. Neil was ecstatic. It was as close to a good day as he could imagine having, which didn't mean there weren't rough patches. Sheri: "How come Morris always carrying stuff?" Arlene: "I don't want that scraggly ole book. I wants a new one." Brenda: "Miss Weeks had this book last year in the fifth grade." Clyde: "Why we need to know about *Our Ancient Heritage*? Them ole peoples was stupid."

In any case Neil was not about to overestimate his progress. Some work was getting done, yes, but that didn't mean the class was meeting the requirements of the sixth grade curriculum. Nor did it mean that Mr. Riley was meeting the requirements of a sixth grade teacher. What amazed Neil was that neither Bernbach nor Bane had sat in on his class once since the beginning of school, not *once*. But Neil evaluated Mr. Riley every single day, every single moment, and his report card had barely changed. But it had changed. It had risen from straight F's in subject expertise, classroom management and knowledge of learning differences to D- in all three areas. However, since he now devoted his entire waking life and, he suspected, much of his sleeping life to this job he had to give himself an A for effort, a peculiar circumstance for which he had no explanation whatsoever. He had planned to coast through this caper. Having learned that coasting wasn't going to happen, he could still have veered into just get by. Instead he was wrestling mightily to actually do the job.

On Monday afternoon in the second week of October, Neil asked, "Marta, would you give out last Friday's spelling tests?" and told the class, "Let me have all the hundreds back and she'll put them on the bulletin board."

Sheri, as always, was right there. "I want to give them out. Shoot!"

"Marta, please give them out."

"She'll take them from me," Marta said. She gave her fatalist's futile shrug.

"No she won't," Neil said emphatically.

"Yes I will," Sheri said.

"No you won't," Neil said to her. "You gave out the math homework, remember?"

"I didn't give out no math homework."

"Yes you did," Arlene said.

"No I didn't. Shoot!" Sheri said. "Keep yo ugly self out of it!" she shouted. Then she and Arlene spontaneously smiled, wide deep smiles, sharing that telepathic joke, the punch line being, Neil understood, *Look what we doing to that poor stupid teacha.*

Neil handed the papers to Marta, who began to sort them.

"Everyone else get out your spelling notebooks and I'll give this week's pre-test." As he thumbed through his notebook for the words he saw a streak from the corner of his eye... his mind flashed on those cartoon blurs Bugs Bunny made as Elmer Fudd stood helplessly by... and looked up to see Sheri snatch the papers from Marta's hand and fling them into the air.

Marta went to her seat, shaking her head, her shoulders rounded in defeat. "I ain't gonna pick them up," she said. "She'll just knock them down again."

"Would some concerned individual please pick up the spelling tests for Marta so she can hand them out?"

Half a dozen kids, Morris and Pedro, Arlene and Brenda, Sammy and Pauli, rushed to pick up the papers. It became a contest to see who could pick up the most. Desks scraped and teetered, elbows flew, threats were made; it was every man for himself.

"Okay!" Neil said. "OKAY!" he yelled. "STOP! SIT DOWN!"

He went around and took up the spelling test papers from the various students who held them out to him, then quietly, without comment, picked up the rest from the floor himself.

"I don't care," Sheri said. "I ain't doin nothin."

"You better care," Neil said. "Most of the people out there," he flung his hand toward the windows, "they don't care about you. And if you don't do nothing and you don't know nothing they won't care about that either. They'll just let you be poor and messed up and all the time angry. What you've got to do..."

"I ain't listening to you," Sheri said.

"What you've got to do," Neil said louder, "is learn to take care of yourself. Sooner or later you've got to learn to do that. And reading and writing and arithmetic are tools you'll need to..."

"I ain't listening to you, dumb stupid ole teacha," Sheri said, sticking her fingers in her ears.

"...SURVIVE!" Neil shouted. "DON'T YOU GET IT! YOU DON'T KNOW HOW TO SURVIVE OUT THERE!"

Sheri jumped out of her seat and ran to the door.

"Sheri, don't you leave this classroom," Neil ordered.

SLAM.

"Gaw," Arlene said.

Without sorting them Neil walked around from person to person to hand out the spelling tests. Were they watching so intently because they knew how painful this was to him? Were they enjoying his suffering?

"You ought to hit us," Morris announced.

"No I shouldn't. I promise you, I never will."

"Mr. Knight does," Morris persisted.

"That fag. He better not ever put his pukey white hands on me," Arlene called out.

"No more calling out. Get ready for your pre-test. Arlene, it isn't polite to call people names."

"Well, it's true. He all a time tappin' some boy on his butt. I ain't lyin'."

"Okay, *okay*, now get ready for your pre-test," Neil repeated and looked at the door, where Sheri peeked in, beaming. "Oh, man!" Neil exclaimed, shaking his head, allowing himself to let out the edgy laughter he had been trying to repress.

Relieved giggles popped out all over the room. Neil walked quickly to the door, but by the time he opened it Sheri had already disappeared around the corner, where Neil knew from past experience she stood on the top step of the stairway pressed against the wall.

She was back at the door before the third word.

"Pedro, would you be so kind as to go out and invite Miss Wallace to rejoin us?' When Pedro and Sheri were back in their seats he said, "The third word is 'care.' Would someone spell care for us?"

Bianca, of course, and Pedro and Pauli and Morris, who probably didn't know, all raised their hands. But so did a girl in the middle of row three. Neil walked over and peeked at his roster. It wasn't that he had forgotten her name. He didn't know it.

"Harriet, can you spell care?"

"Care," she said. "C-a-r-e. Care."

On the board under the first two words Neil wrote '3. Care:'

"Could you define it?"

"To like somebody?"

"That's exactly right," he said. "Wow, Harriet, good job."

On the board he wrote, 'to like.'

"The dictionary says, 'Suffering of mind,'" Bianca called out.

"Bianca, please don't call out. Raise your hand if you want to say something."

"She jealous. Teacher's pet. Somebody else got it right."

Arlene stuck out her tongue when Bianca turned around to look at her. Bianca, of course, stuck her tongue out back.

Neil drooped his shoulders in exaggerated frustration. "Arlene would you please stop calling out? Bianca, would you please stop calling out. Harriet, thank you so much for raising your hand."

Sheri raised her hand and called out, "What's the first two words? Shoot!"

"If you'd been here you would've heard," Neil said. He pointed to the board. "There they are, 'across' and 'place'. You'll have to catch up as we move along."

"I ain't been nowhere," she said, indignant at the suggestion. "What you talkin' about?"

"Uh, Sheri, weren't you just out in the hall?"

"Me? I wasn't in no hall."

Neil narrowed his eyes. "You weren't just peeking in that door?"

"Heck no."

"Oh, my dear injured lady. I am so sorry. It must have been a case of mistaken identity."

"That's what it was," Sheri said.

She frowned and then as he continued to stare, her smile bloomed irresistibly.

"Okay," Neil said, trying to remember what he had been doing. "Right. Bianca is right, though she shouldn't have called out. Like so many of the other words we've studied, care has a number of meanings and one of them is a feeling of suffering or worry. But the one used in our reader and that we'll work with is your third word. So please write 'care: to like'. I care for this class."

Clyde snickered.

"What's the definition of 'across'?" Sheri called out. "I cane read that scratchin'."

"'On the other side,'" Neil read from the board with exaggerated weariness.

"Well, if you'd get somebody else to write for you we could read it," Bianca said.

"I can't even get somebody not to call out, how am I going to get them to write?"

Chapter 10:

Another Disaster

In Mr. Bernbach's office: Neil jumped up and howled, "You've got to be kidding. You want to dump another disaster on me?"

He had been sitting in a chair facing Bernbach, who remained complacently behind his desk. Now on his feet Neil turned, glanced at the door and knew down to his bones that he couldn't leave this office until he was dismissed. He sat back down.

"Disaster is an exaggeration, don't you think?" Bernbach said. "You've got to understand my problem."

"I think disaster catches it just about right. Charles doesn't belong in my class. He belongs in special ed." After a moment's reflection he asked, "Why are you doing this to me? I'm a brand new teacher and I'm getting all your worst problems. It's like you want me to walk out. That's it, isn't it? I'm so bad you want me to quit."

"Bad? You're not bad."

"I'm terrible. You should fire me. You'd just rather I walked out."

Bernbach smiled. It was a smile that purported to be completely unpremeditated, amused, friendly, forgiving; a smile so calculated that it caused Neil to shiver.

"You're doing much better than anyone could have expected. In less than six weeks you've learned to keep your kids out of the halls. It's very impressive."

Neil studied him for a moment. Then he said, "You're betting I won't walk out, aren't you? You're thinking you can throw anything you want to at me. Because I have to take it. Of course. Because I'll be up shit's creek without a paddle if I walk. Up Hanoi's ass."

"You won't walk and it doesn't have anything to do with Hanoi's ass. I've been in this business nearly twenty years and I know when someone's going to walk and it won't be you. You can stomp around all you want, but you won't walk. You can't." Bernbach jabbed a finger at him as he said this. "You couldn't live with yourself." He pressed at his temples, pulling his eyes into slits. "Okay, here we go. I'm going to be honest with you."

As if to emphasize the significance of this moment he paused and put his hands on his desk one on top of the other, still looking Neil in the eye. Neil with effort managed not to say he'd bet his last dollar Bernbach had never been honest about anything with anyone.

"Travers was one of the best teachers ever. You can still see it. Her class loves her. Poor slow misbegotten souls, she treats them like they're as precious as her own. But she's barely here. Half the time she doesn't know what day it is. She got bumped up to district because she wanted to get her thirty years in and she deserved that. But the district, the city, can't afford to have her, at her salary, sitting around sorting paper clips. So I got her. Am I making myself clear? Sort of like the way you're getting Charles."

"I'm not getting Charles. It's not going to happen."

Bernbach sighed. "You're not listening to me. You don't have a choice."

"Oh, yeah? How come? Why not Knight? I've got thirty-two kids; he's got thirty."

"Oh, Mr. Riley. Can I tell you something in confidence?"

"I can't keep secrets."

Bernbach kept looking at him, nodding. Neil fancied for a moment he had finally penetrated the man's slick exterior, that he was going to lash out with honest-to-God-damn anger. Bernbach closed his eyes, opened them and continued to stare.

"If you ever repeat what I'm about to say I'll wring you out like an old rag. I'll claim you're trying to libel me. I'll put a mark on your record that'll make it impossible for you to get a job doing anything anywhere."

"Gaw, he mean."

Bernbach smiled. "I can be your daddy or I can be hell."

"Maybe you should just tell me what's on your mind."

Bernbach made a fist. "Knight's got me over a barrel, okay? Unlike you, he didn't have to quit law school to teach; he sits there and studies."

"I wouldn't have believed it was possible if I hadn't seen it myself."

"Do you know how he does it?"

"He has the world's best collection of mimeographs."

"Would that keep your crew quiet?"

"For two or three seconds. Maybe."

"Right. So how does he do it?"

"I have no idea. It's kind of amazing."

"He has a goon squad. Richard and Loretta. Anybody who gets out of line, Richie and Loretta can kick, pinch, punch, as long as they do it quickly and keep it out of sight. Anybody complains, his enforcers say the squealer's lying and Knight backs them up and the squealer gets a double dose of kicks, pinches and punches."

"You know this and don't stop it?"

Bernbach shrugged. "His class is quiet. He's got it under control. They're not in the halls."

"I don't believe you're telling me this."

"Frankly, I don't either. And for the record? I'm not telling you this. You're the kind who might try to do something about it. It's just that right now you don't have any credibility," he added. "Okay, but Richie? I hate to say this, but some kids are just mean. Psychologists have a label for them. Psychopaths. You ask me, they're just mean. John's like that, too. You wish Robin had taken Arlene, but I'm telling you, she did you a big favor. Now, can you see why I can't give

Charles to Knight? Richie wouldn't leave Charles alone no matter what. He couldn't. Then Charles would erupt and kill Richie and you'd have a homicide on your conscience. How'd you feel about that?"

"Two for one. Good day's work."

"Now that's exactly the kind of thinking I'm looking for in my teachers."

"Speaking of Arlene..."

"Which we weren't."

"I'll trade you. Give Knight Arlene. Richie may be psychopathic, but he ain't stupid. Arlene would chew him up and spit him out before he could kick, let alone pinch and punch."

"You're not listening to me," Bernbach said.

Neil had come to realize this was one of his rhetorical feints. You disagree he ducks with a 'you're not listening to me' and dances away.

"You're not listening to me," Neil said, smiling a broad false smile. "I'm offering you a deal."

"I told you, Mr. Riley. Neil. Can I call you Neil? You can call me Ron, in private of course. In front of the kids I'm Mr. Bernbach and you're Mr. Riley. So, Neil, if you want to have Arlene removed from your class all you have to do is compile an anecdotal record. I'll bet we could have her off to a special class within a month."

"Right. Arlene's pushing Carmen out of her seat and I'm going to go my desk and write, 'ten thirty, Arlene is grabbing Carmen and tossing her across the room.'"

"Did this actually happen?"

"Did Arlene toss Carmen across the room? No, but she would have if I'd let her."

"You stopped her?"

"Of course. You're not listening to me."

Bernbach smiled his scariest smile. "Be careful, Neil. I am your boss, a fact that seems to sometimes escape your attention."

"And as my boss you're giving me all the assistance and support a new and inexperienced teacher needs. I'm attending to that."

"You... This..." Bernbach stood up and went to his window, which was closed with the blinds drawn. "This is Knight's last year," he said, fiddling with the strings that pulled the blinds. "He has enough sick leave to walk out of here and not come back until May and in the spring, when he has his finals that's probably what he'll do and I have to prepare for that." He looked at Neil. "Do you think Bane spends even a minute worrying her bleached-blonde head about any of this? But that's not your problem, is it?" He pressed a palm to his forehead. "How many of your kids were absent today?"

"What?" Neil squinted to emphasize his wonder at this non sequitur.

"How many of your kids were absent today?"

Neil formed a zero with the thumb and second finger of his right hand. "None. Not one. Not Arlene, not Sheri, not Paulie, not one."

"Right. And it was the same yesterday and the day before. And I'd give you three to one there were at least five kids absent from Knight's, and about the same from Travers'. So you and Robin, probably, had a perfect attendance today. So why?"

"I can't imagine."

"Your kids feel safe, Neil."

"Huh?"

"Your kids know they can spend six and a half hours a day five days a week not worrying about being beaten up, knifed or shot. You'll be there. And it's not because you're six-ten two hundred and fifty pounds either."

Neil knew this exaggeration was meant to be an insult; it also revealed a short man's envy. And it informed Neil he should not belittle Bernbach's size until he was ready to quit the job.

"It's because you won't let them get hurt. Some other guy big as you might actually want to see the blood fly, but the kids, they call you 'the teacha who don't like fights.' You think you're having a hard time and you are and maybe the kids feel nervous about that cause they don't know if you'll last. But they want you to last, Neil, that I know. They really really want you to last. And so do I. Why do you think I put up with your insolence? You're worse than Clyde."

"I'll take that as a compliment."

"I'll tell you something. You remind me of myself twenty years ago. I was going to be a dentist, would you believe it? But dental school costs money and teaching paid pretty good for a Jew boy from the Bronx and then there's this certain young lady and then you're married and she's in the family way and how did that happen? And all at once twenty years have gone by and you're sitting in your office with this young goon *who won't listen to you!*" he snapped. "So here's my sixth grade. I got one good experienced teacher, a black militant who wants my job. I got another so so experienced teacher, a putz who's gonna walk out on me any day now. Then I got this teacher who's losing her marbles. She's terrific one minute and off in dreamland the next. And, last but not least, I got this kid who don't know his ass from his elbow, who's got a real problem with authority and, guess what? is smart, gutsy and strong. He keeps his kids out of the halls and actually has lesson plans. My God, lesson plans! In a notebook! For a week!"

"That guy, is that the one you dumped all your worst problems on? It's not lost on me, you know, that John was mine, too, before he made a suicidal remark to Arlene about some aspect of her anatomy."

"That's right. That guy. And he's the guy who's taking that nutcase Charles because he understands that I have no choice and he has no choice and that's what this job is all about."

Chapter 11:

I Made Something

In Room 6-306: it was always so quiet in the early morning before he brought his class up. Neil put his brief case on the chair behind his desk and rummaged past the math, spelling and social studies homework, his planner and four texts, to the art supplies he had gotten on sale at a street fair in Roger's neighborhood on Saturday, five sets of what seemed to be brand new colored markers, six colors to a set, for (he couldn't believe it!) twenty cents a pack.

He had gotten them in the vague hope that in some distant future when things were more settled he would try teaching an art class at least once a week. There was no arts teacher in this school. And yet on his bulletin board were four beautiful pictures done on vanilla construction paper by one of his quiet ones.

Last Wednesday Sandra had raised her hand and asked if she could come up to his desk. *I made something*, she said and handed him the pictures. One was a series of jack-o'-lanterns, seven in all, evil, funny, sad, snaggletoothed, vivid. Another was a headless horseman holding a pumpkin type head under his arm riding hell-bent for leather along a winding brown road. The background was green except for a leafless tree with a skeleton dangling from it. A third was a series of costumes and masks, a witch, a hobo, the tin man from *The Wizard of Oz*, a goblin. The last picture was her masterpiece. A young prince knelt before a lovely princess. He held a white high-heeled shoe to her naked foot. He was in black formal attire. She was in a white gown with a veil. She looked more like she was dressed to walk down the aisle at her wedding than to waltz until midnight at the ball. Around them in haphazard fashion were other clothes suitable for travel. A sports jacket and slacks for him, and for her: a sundress, a sweater, a neat blue vest over an off-white blouse, a formal dress, two skirts. And in the bottom right-hand corner an open suitcase waited to be packed and carted off to what had to be their honeymoon.

Sandra, these are beautiful, he told her. And they were: imaginative, pleasing in arrangement, tasteful in color and very well drawn. *For Halloween,* she said, waving a hand at the stark room that for her must be a torment. *Thank you,* he said. And then from Sheri, *I wants to see. Shoot.* He showed the pictures to the class and with Sandra's permission allowed Sheri to stand on a chair and put them on the bulletin boards along the wall next to the hall.

The administration had discouraged any activities centering on Halloween and for once Neil had been in total agreement. These children were already primed to feel terror, be furious and go wild. Why encourage them? But the pictures were too good to be ignored and could he really reject the offering of this reticent girl who had suddenly stepped forward and revealed herself? Even if he had thought the pictures were terrible, he would have put them up. But he thought they were wonderful: funny, scary, romantic, so silly, so incredible.

Today, Thursday, the day before Halloween, he stopped at the bulletin board on his way to the back and examined Sandra's work once again, so pleased once again. When and if the pictures were supplanted by others he would frame them, especially the pumpkins and Cinderella and her prince.

At the supply cabinet in the back corner across from the window he put the colored markers away. Someday his class would use them. He promised himself. But not today.

It was so quiet that for a moment he felt lost. He turned and faced the empty classroom. From the rear. Not his usual perspective. So incredibly quiet. He stared at his desk, sitting catty-corner to him in the front next to the window. Every day thirty-three pairs of eyes turned to that desk or, since he was hardly ever still, to his figure roving in the front, up and down the aisles, pacing, chasing Arlene. Four rows. Nine desks to a row.

Last night, thinking about his class—did he ever not think about them? —he had done one of his periodic head counts. He had twenty-four students who were under most circumstances fully cooperative. Or, well, reasonably cooperative. Don't get carried away. But, yeah, they did their assignments, turned in their homework, sat at their desks, were quiet when he asked for silence. Well, anyway, sometimes. Another five were for one reason or another troublesome not because they were behavior problems, but because he didn't know what to do with them: Bianca because she was so unrelentingly perceptive, Norbert because he was so disturbingly fearful, Clyde because of his cutting resistance. The other two, Samuel and Brenda, troubled him because they followed slavishly after the wild ones, Arlene and Paulie. And Sheri. What was he to do with Sheri? And now Charles. *After all, Mrs. Robin took John,* Bernbach had said.

But Neil suspected that an experienced teacher would love this class. There were so many opportunities to learn, to sharpen your skills. If you knew how. If you weren't an abysmal failure.

And yet even Neil had to admit some things had changed.

Chapter 12:

Lining Up Nicely

In the schoolyard: his twenty-four or so solid citizens were, loosely speaking, on line. Arlene, Brenda and Sheri were, naturally, at the far corner of the fence, probably harassing passersby. Clyde stood back from the lines, with Pauli and Sammy horsing around him like little brothers he was babysitting. Charles stood in his own space with the hood of his sweat shirt pulled down level with his eyes. Norbert stood near him, looking around incessantly for danger. Neil felt Norbert was protecting not only himself, but Charles as well, and that it was an act of great bravery. If anyone tried to make fun of Charles, Norbert would have to do something. What would he do? Neil had never once seen them speak to each other, but by some means they had become fellow travelers. Dare one suggest friends?

Somehow this tableau, the schoolyard, his line of students standing patiently, the troubled ones out there dripping on a broken Dali dreamscape, was etched like a watermark on everything he thought and felt, a constant that lay waiting to ambush him the moment he thought he could relax.

Clyde saw him come through the school doors and approach the lines and began a slow, cool stroll timed, Neil knew, to bring him to the back of the lines just as Neil reached the front. Then Clyde stopped and turned back and said something to Norbert, who looked toward Neil and lurched forward after Clyde, followed immediately by Charles. It crossed Neil's mind that while Norbert was out there to protect Charles, Clyde was there to protect them both, the two most vulnerable creatures in the class. No one would mess with them because Clyde wouldn't let them. What was it with that kid? There wasn't time to examine that question now. Nor could he let himself fret about the fact that he didn't know half these children or that instead of spending time getting to know them he'd once again spend most of the day reacting to Arlene, Pauli and Sheri. *Stop it, man. Your job's to make it to three o'clock. Yeah, Mr. Riley, not a problem.*

Bianca, like Clyde, had seen him the moment he walked out into the open and had nudged her two compatriots. Just behind Bianca, in her shadow, was a pale girl, hunched around the notebook that she clutched desperately to her chest, which was, much to her consternation, Neil surmised, swelling into adolescence. Her name? Yes, yes. She was first on the roll, Albanez, Marta, reading level 4, could never ever line her numbers in straight columns and usually out of ten problems got at least two wrong answers just because of that.

"Good morning, Mr. Riley."

"Good morning, Bianca."

"Did you get to have your coffee?" Apparently Bianca's mother was a coffee drinker, too, but she liked hers with sugar. Neil's had to be black, no sugar, as strong as you could make it. She had noticed his thermos the very first day and she delighted in this similarity between her mother and Neil. It seemed to tell her something about him, reassure her. What Neil had learned about Bianca from their talks about coffee was that she was an only child living with her mother and an aunt, that her mother was a nurse and that Bianca was responsible for much of the shopping, cooking and housekeeping.

"Not yet. When I get my free period," he said, looking out toward Arlene and her crew. True to form Sheri was on her way, rushing to get on line, not because she didn't want to cause him trouble, but because she was afraid she'd miss something. Neil motioned the other two to come on in, knowing they would not. He had on occasion, stupidly, much to everyone's delight, chased them around the schoolyard. Now he just let them be, secretly, shamefully, welcoming the few moments he would have in the classroom without them before they came bursting through the door to disrupt whatever was going on.

"Come on, line up, please. As soon as you're straight, we'll go." Then to his own surprise as much as to hers, he asked Marta, "Did you do your math homework?"

She smiled nervously, looking at some spot near his knees. "Me and my mommy did it. She just checked them," she added quickly.

"Did she help you with the columns?"

"Yes."

"What'd he say?" Sheri asked the world at large as she arrived on the scene. But she must have heard, because she then said, "So? I did my homework, too."

"Well, I'm glad to hear it," Neil said. "Now if you'll just line up nicely..."

"I am lined up nicely. Shoot."

"...we'll be on our way."

Chapter 13:

I Must See You

In Room 6-306: the children went through their usual morning rituals, putting their coats up, or arranging them on the backs of their chairs, settling in their seats, checking the books they had left on the racks under their desks, each one of them looking up at him at some point with, he felt, an anxiety he shared. What happens next?

Mrs. Robin's class, the gold standard, waited at the door until she ordered them into the room, girls first one day, boys the next. This he had witnessed. Then, he was told, by rows she ordered them to put their coats on the rack on their assigned hooks. Meanwhile, her children sat quietly, hands folded on their desks, until she finished the roll and told them what their first assignment was. This miracle of classroom management had been described to him on a number of occasions, prefaced with, *You should do like Mrs. Robin. You should...* then he would be informed of what amazing feat Mrs. Robin accomplished that if imitated would correct the particular deficiency he was at that moment guilty of. He knew no class of his would ever behave the way hers did, first of all because he would never be able to exercise such control over thirty-three feral creatures, but also because he didn't want to. The idea of such a regimen filled him with envy, pointed up his inadequacies and repelled him to the depths of his being. He wanted something else for his class. He didn't know what it was. He did know it wasn't the anger and anxiety he always had these days.

"So, what we gonna do now?" from Sheri as he silently checked off the roll. They were, as usual, all there, everyone but Arlene and Brenda.

"Fractions," Neil said. "We're going to continue our review of fractions. You boys in the back, sit down please. Get out last night's homework, please." He looked at his roster and picked a name at random. "Javier, would you collect them for me?"

"How come you ask him?" Sheri complained. "You never ask me."

At this there were loud groans of protest, not just from Neil but from Bianca, Clyde, Pauli and Sammy. Javier stood up, but he stood by his desk and eyed Sheri.

You little bitch, he thought. *Why do you think you're the only person in the world?* Aloud, he said, "Are you kidding? I never ask you to take up the homework?"

"So? You didn't ask me today." She shook a silent fist at Javier.

"I ain't gonna fight no girl," Javier said, probably as worried that she would kick his butt as that he would have to hit her.

Neil sighed. "Pull out your homework and hand it to me as I come around to pick it up."

Neil had them hand him the papers rather than just put them out to be picked up because if he didn't Sheri would race around ahead of him, snatch up as many papers as she could and rush them up to his desk.

"What we gonna do after arithmetic?" Morris asked as Neil headed down Row 1.

"Social Studies. I have a lesson on early man."

"Mr. Riley, you should put the lessons on the board," Bianca said.

"What? I'm sorry. Could you all stop calling out."

"That's right," Clyde said, "so we know what's happening."

Neil, who had started down Row 3, suddenly turned and looked around vaguely, having completely forgotten what he was doing. He came to his senses fast enough realizing Sheri must be about to swoop down on those papers. But, no, her expression had changed, too, and like him she had turned to look at Bianca, who was watching him with her usual canny scrutiny.

"He's thinking it over," Bianca told them.

"It's not a bad idea, actually," he said, stepping to the board. He copied from his planbook: *Schedule, Thursday, October 30, 1969.* He looked up to see Clyde standing, pointing, with his hand on his mouth as if to hide his laughter.

"What?" Neil asked.

"You write worse than me," Clyde said.

"We always have trouble when you put stuff on the board," Pedro said, apologetically.

"Except when you real careful," Morris added.

"And print," Bianca said.

"And it still ain't so good as all that," Sheri informed him.

"Well, we can't all be artists like you," Neil said.

Which brought a broad smile of pleasure to Sheri's beautiful black face. "I guess not," she said.

"Let somebody else write it," Bianca said.

"Do you want to do it?" he asked, holding the book toward her.

"Me? I'm worse than you."

"Who wants to write the schedule on the board for me?"

Eight hands shot up: Marta, Carmen, Sheri, Sandra, Sammy, Gloria, Susan, Karen. Sammy? He couldn't print a single letter without erasing it six times. The others were all credible possibilities.

"If I choose someone... maybe I'll do it alphabetically..."

He was stalling. The logical choice was Sandra, because she had by far the best script of any of them, and as he had learned over the course of the semester she read quite well, much better than her Iowa Skills scores had indicated. Furthermore, she was completely reliable. But for purely irrational reasons he wanted Marta. Because? Because once he had noticed her a hoard of pictures of her had come tumbling out of his memory bank. She had sat unnoticed for weeks, drab and lost, longing for Bianca's friendship. She had a fairly decent script, though it was embellished with curlicues. In fact she spent the time in class when he was distracted developing new and different superfluities, which then appeared in her name on her homework pages. He'd have to convince her all those flourishes were not the mark of good penmanship. Also, her lack of confidence would require patience, reassurance, work. To put it delicately, Marta would take time. Sandra would just do it. In spite of all that, or maybe because of it, it was Marta that he really wanted. It would be like touching her with fairy dust. Now that he had noticed her, which had given him a rare sense of accomplishment, she represented for him all the ignored and unnoticed in the class. If he started alphabetically, he could choose her without seeming to give special preference. It wasn't a sly and devious scheme. It was simply logical.

"I'll start with the a's," he said, as if this were the only way of doing things. The gooey falseness of his voice reminded him of Mrs. Bane at her lovey best. Whether it was this or the flagrant unfairness of his plan, Bianca and Clyde would have none of it.

"Naw," they both groaned, and repeated, emphatically, "Naw." They looked at each other and smiled and sang it again, a call to arms, "Naaaaw."

"You can't do it alphabetically," Bianca said.

"Why not?" Neil asked.

"You've got to choose the best," Bianca said.

"It has to be fair," Clyde said.

Neil, who was leaning against his desk, suddenly clawed at the edges of the desktop, wondering if he were having some kind of seizure. A flood of energy had suddenly rushed through his body. It took him more than a few bewildered heartbeats to realize that what was bothering him was joy. He was practically giddy with the stuff. Because? Could it be because two of his biggest pests were in point of fact, albeit in their typically annoying fashion, making a constructive suggestion? They weren't just trying to waste time or avoid work. Of course, they were doing that and were, as usual, questioning his authority and demonstrating, as usual, their superiority to him—Clyde his moral superiority, Bianca her superior competency—but they were doing this to shape the organization of the class. They were showing that it mattered. This was not especially new for Bianca. But Clyde?

Neil took a deep breath. He could step down hard on them and pick Marta or he could let loose a genie he didn't understand, probably couldn't control and longed for with every ounce of his being.

"How?" he asked.

SLAM. The door burst open, and banged against the rubber cushion on the wall designed for exactly an event like this. Arlene stepped into the room.

"Hey, yawl! Here I am!"

"Oh, God, why can't she just die," Bianca muttered, audible only to the other two Las Senoritas, Sandra and Carmen, and to Neil.

She got giggles from her friends. For Neil it was a wish too close to his own to be considered funny.

"Why doan you just go away," Sheri said right out loud.

Her anger was real, palpable. A chorus of "Yeahs," from around the room supported her. Neil was struck once again by the physical courage of that small being. She was intrepid. She would speak up when no one else would dare. Her insistence on asserting herself was a revelation. And for this moment at least he loved her for exactly who she was.

"What'd you say?" Arlene asked. She was outraged, but not wholly comfortable with it. Something was different. The chaos and distraction she brought wasn't welcome. Neil was flabbergasted.

"You heard me," Sheri said, standing.

Sheri was preparing, he knew, to run behind him if need be. He might be that stupid teacha, but he was nevertheless her refuge of last resort. Her strategies were shameless.

"No, wait!" Clyde was on his feet, pointing at Neil. "This is good. It's about him."

"What'd he do?" Arlene asked.

"Admitted his handwriting was worse than chicken scratching," Neil said. He had never quite appreciated musical comedy. The idea of someone bursting into song in the middle of a conversation had always seemed to him kind of dumb. And yet, that's how he felt, like bursting into song. *This is so unbelievable,* he would sing. *So wonderfully inconceivable. I'm happy with my class and it's incredible.*

"You said it," Bianca said.

"Somebody said something about what we gonna do today," Clyde explained.

"Me!" Sheri sang.

"An he goes on about fractions an stuff an she..." Clyde pointed at Bianca. "...says, 'You should write it on the board,'" shaking his hips in accompaniment to his high voice, and in fact catching something of Bianca's always outspoken self-confidence.

"You said it too," Bianca shot back, smiling, pleased it seemed, by his portrayal of her.

"I said it too. Shoot," Sheri said.

Clyde looked at her for a hard moment then continued. "So she says," and here came Clyde's Bianca again, "'You should let somebody else do it.'"

"She auways got somethin' to say," Arlene opined.

"Oh, an' you don't?" Pauli asked.

Arlene smiled.

"So we decided you got to pick the best," Clyde said.

"And we got to figure out how to do it," Bianca said.

"It's gotta be fair," Morris said.

"Do you want to be considered?" Neil asked Arlene.

"Me. I cane write as good as you."

"Me neither," Brenda said, which was a lie. Next to Sandra Brenda probably had the best script in the class. But she didn't want the job and Neil wouldn't want her if she did.

"Can I make a suggestion?" Neil asked.

"Maybe," Bianca said.

"Let's have a contest."

"Oh, bull," Arlene said.

"No, maybe he's right," Bianca said.

"Yeah, that's the only way," Clyde said.

Arlene, who was inching toward her desk, wasn't sure how to take this contradiction. They were agreeing with the teacher over her? And her usual angry response to this would be inappropriate. They were in the middle of something no one, not even Arlene herself, wanted to interrupt. What's an angry rebellious bully to do?

Ask exactly the question the teacher secretly wanted to hear.

"What kinda contest?" Arlene asked, not quite addressing Neil, but more an area just to one side of him.

"The people who raised their hands should copy what I wrote on the board on a piece of paper. Don't put your name on the paper. We put your papers on the bulletin board and go on about our regular class work and one by one everybody goes up and votes on the one they like the best. You can vote by signing your name."

"So how will we know who they are?" Pedro asked. "Somebody could say I wrote that one, even if they didn't."

"I'll go around and assign numbers to the contestants. I'll write down the names and numbers on a piece of paper and we can look at it after everybody has voted. But first I have to finish picking up the math homework."

"I'll pick it up," Sheri said.

"You can't it pick up. You're one of the contestants."

"That's right," Sheri said.

"I'll pick it up," Javier said, graciously.

"Would you?" Neil agreed. "I'd appreciate it."

And, though it was difficult to believe, someone other than Sheri actually picked up the papers.

"Okay, you eight who wanted to compete, please raise your hands again." He wrote down the names and assigned numbers starting in the middle of his list. The entire class watched him intently as he engaged in this highly sensitive process. "Okay, when you're finished, raise your hand and I'll pick up your work and put your number on the page, then one by one we'll vote. Okay?"

"Okay, Mr. Riley," Clyde said, waving his hands like a conductor.

"Okay, Mr. Riley," the class said in unison, as if Mrs. Robin had suddenly taken over the proceedings.

Neil faced the blackboard, then turned around and looked at them in astonishment. "Who are you?" he asked the class at large.

"6-306!" Pedro announced with pride.

At that moment the door opened and there was Bernbach peeking in, smiling broadly, very likely about to comment on what a well-behaved class Mr. Riley had when Neil saw movement in the glass panes of the door and Bernbach stumbled in as if he had been shoved. Amy—oh, for God's sake, *Amy*—rushed past Bernbach and across the front of the room in a beeline for Neil. It could only have taken a few seconds, one for each step, say, for her to reach him, and yet it seemed to Neil, or would seem in memory, to have taken a very long time indeed, as if slow motion wasn't a movie device, but something that actually happened. The number of impressions he registered in those few seconds amazed him.

First there was the silence. No one spoke. Or moved. Or perhaps even breathed. Surely there were sounds off in the distance, some class in the yard, traffic out the window, a distant siren. They didn't penetrate here. There was no sound in Room 6-306.

Then there were those thirty-three pairs of eyes glued to every move he and Amy made.

And then there was poor Bernbach's stricken face. He was a man who had been seduced and abandoned, wooed then tossed aside. Neil could see it. Amy was a dream, a drug. Bernbach had drunk deeply of her dark brown eyes, the soft promise of her crimson lips, the sweetness of her smile. Only to be rudely dropped for that gangly young no-good first year teacher standing there like the stupid inept fool he was. How could she?

And the room, which moments before had been a vibrant, lively place where willy-nilly children grew and where, if nothing else, the teacher was learning how ignorant he was, that room had suddenly become a shabby, scruffy hovel, smelling of baby powder, cheap perfume and Charles, and underlying it all, the ever present tedious drift of chalk.

Because Amy, in her beige pants suit and low-heeled silver-buckled brown suede shoes, white silk blouse with the ruffled collar, bright red lips and pure white oval face, had walked into the room, making everything around her seem drab and dingy. This was, Neil knew, her field outfit. Amy, after only three years on the job, was a supervisor with the New York City Child Welfare Protective Services. When she went out it was usually a desperate case that required immediate intervention. She was almost always accompanied by armed plainclothesmen. Neil imagined the cops escorting that gorgeous welfare girl to take a baby away from some druggy felt it was good duty. Today Amy must have done what she had to do with the baby, released her partners and, finding herself near Neil's school (Betty would have told her where it was), decided to drop in on him.

Of course, Amy would have known you don't just drop in on a classroom teacher and this was confirmed by Bernbach's, "She *said* it was an emergency," offered apologetically to Neil over her shoulder, the emphasis on *said* revealing that he now knew he had been duped.

Neil planted his hands on her shoulders to prevent her from wrapping herself around him right there in front of *all of them*. She reached out and grabbed his shirt. Neil thought that to anyone astute in human relations this grappling should speak volumes. It did not to Amy.

Bianca blurted, "That's not his wife."

"I must see you," Amy said, loud enough to project to the rear of a massive auditorium. So certainly they all got it loud and clear in the back row. God forbid Arlene and Clyde shouldn't be in on the action.

"Mr. Bernbach, if you could just watch?..."

"I'll give you two minutes," Bernbach snapped.

The fact that Bernbach wasn't happy with this scene, which after all he had created, was the only aspect of the situation that Neil enjoyed.

"Come on," Neil said, already heading for the door.

In the hall Amy threw herself against him, wrapped her arms around his back and clutched his shirt at the shoulder blades.

"For God's sake, Amy. Let me go."

She pressed her head against his chest. "Oh, God. I can hear your heart. Oh, God."

"Shit," Neil said. "Don't you know where we are?"

"We're here. I've got this moment. They can't take this away from me."

Neil grabbed her arms at the elbows and whipped them out and around behind her back. Now they were standing with their bodies locked tightly together; his hands holding her arms by the wrists at the small of her back. She was breathing heavily, deeply aroused. He knew in some dark primordial place that if he wanted he could have ripped her pants down, thrown her against the wall and fucked her right there, regardless of the consequences to either of them.

Neil said, "This is so sick," not at all sure to whom he was speaking.

"It's not. It's everything. Nothing else matters. Don't you understand?"

"NO! No, I don't understand. Don't touch me!" He pushed her away and held her upper arms, squeezing hard. She closed her eyes and gasped, with pleasure he realized. "Do you have any idea what you've done to my class? What do I have to do to get rid of you?"

"See me. Just one more time."

He heard a sound and looked behind him. Pauli's nose was mashed against the middle glass panel in the door, Sheri's right next to his. So where was Bernbach? He felt Amy wiggling free of his hands and tightened his grip.

"Just one more time," he said with a sigh of surrender, of desperation, of defeat.

"When?" she asked.

"Tomorrow night. It's Friday." The longest time between school on Friday and school on Monday, the one night in the week he allowed himself to let go, that night.

"You'll answer the door?"

All those gratuitous buzzes from downstairs, was that her? Even the one last week after midnight?

"I'll answer the door."

"If I call tonight, will you pick up?" She had him pinned to the mat. It was no time to ease up.

"If I'm home, I'll pick up," he extemporized. "Seven. Tomorrow night. The last time. Do you promise?"

"I swear it."

"Say it. I promise this will be the last time I'll see you."

"I promise. This will be the last time I'll see you."

"Now you've got to let me get back to my class. You've got to."

"I'll see you then," she said.

And when he let her go to his immense relief she actually turned and walked away.

Going back into the classroom felt like stepping back into the ring against a gigantic opponent who would show no mercy. And even so his sense of relief lasted.

"Thanks," Neil said to Bernbach.

Bernbach, who was obviously having his own difficulties with this encounter, walked past him brusquely. He said not a word.

The moment the door closed the class erupted.

"Oh, Neil, I gots to see you," Arlene said, rising and sashaying toward Brenda. Some other time Neil would have been forced to laugh out loud. He was in no mood for laughter now.

"Mr. Riley, whoa, she baaaaad," Clyde said.

"She's like a movie star," Carmen said. She faced the ceiling with her eyes closed, pinching the lobes of her ears with her fingertips. "Didcha see her earrings? They matched her lipstick perfectly. *Perfectly.*"

"They were probably real rubies," Sandra said.

"Is that yo wife?" Sammy asked.

"Man, she was sumpin," Hector opined.

"You got that right," Morris agreed.

And Pedro? His head, too, was tilted toward the ceiling, his eyes closed, enraptured. He was very likely committing to memory every aspect of Amy that he could call to mind.

Bianca was staring furiously at the top of her desk. "She's not his wife."

Chapter 14:

Fundamental Truths

In Room 6-308: Mrs. Robin was sitting reading at her back table, back straight, both feet planted on the floor. She always ate lunch in her room because she was no longer welcome in the teachers' lounge. Last year there had been a series of strikes, and Mrs. Robin had crossed the picket line each time. She had come in even when after the first two strikes the parents stopped sending their children to school. Nothing had ever been said directly to her when she came into the lounge. Any teachers who were there simply stood up and walked out. All this had been explained to Neil by the gym teacher, Miss Tobin, who was also the shop steward. It was apparently acceptable for Neil to both visit with Mrs. Robin and eat in the teachers' lounge because he was new and "had to learn." And, too, he'd made it clear to Tobin that he was a staunch member of the UFT and wouldn't have crossed the picket lines. Mrs. Robin had never discussed any of this with him.

"Your door was open so I thought maybe..." Neil hesitated just inside the room. He held up his thermos with one hand and his lunch bag with the other.

Mrs. Robin got to her feet, none too quickly, Neil noticed, and said with a sweeping gesture of her hand, "Me casa es su casa."

"You didn't have to get up," he said.

"Yes. I need to get my lunch bag. I was hoping you'd drop by. I made this gigantic egg salad sandwich this morning with just a few bacon bits crumpled in. My eyes are always bigger than my stomach. I barely ate half of it. I was going to send the other half to you for your free period if I didn't see you at lunch time."

"Ah. It's the bacon bits that make my mouth water," he said.

It would have been futile to reject her offer. She would have, as she did the one time he dared to say no, slammed it down in front of him with a, "Now you eat this. You can't get by on that pitiful lunch you bring in. Big as you are and still growing. You can have your peanut butter and jelly for dessert." So it had become routine for her to give him these mouthwatering half-sandwiches that were near mini-meals.

Now as he slumped into the chair she had slid out for him, she asked, "Have a problem, Mr. Riley?"

"I don't know where to begin. Actually, yeah, I can begin with Arlene's going to beat up Bianca after school."

"Oh? Why?"

"It's a long story."

"Tell me."

"Yesterday a friend of mine dropped by."

"Would that be your Movie Star Wife?"

"News sure travels fast around here."

"Brenda and Sharon are friends and Sharon tells me everything. 'Course we don't know it's his wife, but they say she was more beautiful than just about anybody. She has to be somebody.' And since "somebody"..." Mrs. Robin made the quotes with her fingers. "...can only be a movie star, it follows she is?..."

"A supervisor with the Bureau of Child Welfare. She'll probably end up the director in a couple of years and they'll plaster her picture all over the city and the evening news will feature her every time there's some sort of mess up with a kid. That's nasty. I've made it sound like she's riding on her looks. In fact, she seems to have an uncanny sense of what to do in the most horrendous situations. It's not easy to decide when to wrest a baby out of its mother's arms. I know I couldn't do it."

"I don't think I could either."

Neil thought that she probably could if she had to.

"But how does this relate to our girls, Arlene and Bianca?" Mrs. Robin asked.

"Arlene came in late this morning as usual and announced, 'Mr. Riley, it's your wife!' At which point she sashayed... Ever seen Arlene sashay?"

"Unfortunately, I have."

"Over to me. 'Oh, Neil, I gots to see you.' And Bianca said, and I don't know how she's so certain of this. I don't particularly feel the need to explain the intricacies of my private life to my class and I've sure as hell never discussed Amy with them. Bianca said, 'She's not his wife.' Then Sheri said..."

"Do we need that language to pursue this matter, Mr. Riley?"

"What?"

"I'm referring to your unnecessary mention of the nether world."

"My huh? Oh, yeah. Okay. Sorry."

"What did Sheri say?"

"'How you know so much, Miss Smarty Pants?'"

"Our Sheri certainly takes up a lot of space to be so small, doesn't she?"

"And Arlene picks it up. 'Miss Knowitall. You watch out or I'll kick your ass.'"

"Mr. Riley, please. Not in this room."

"Sorry. Sorry. Dang!"

Mrs. Robin smiled. "So Arlene threatened Bianca. Is there anyone Arlene hasn't threatened?"

"Yeah, but Bianca..."

"Never a shrinking violet."

"Who doesn't always know where her best interests lie, says something like, 'Will that make you any smarter?' You know, something that implies Arlene's not the brightest student in the room, probably the most cutting remark you could make to Arlene, and there you go. Arlene's not bluffing any more. Now she's really... uh, the word that comes to mind wouldn't go over well here."

"Furious," Mrs. Robin said. "Livid. Incensed. The English language has a plethora of vivid expressions to describe our emotional states."

"Livid's good. I'll take livid. So there you have it. Arlene's livid and she's going to kill Bianca this afternoon after school. I'm going to walk Bianca home since her building's near my bus stop and I'm going to call Arlene's mother tonight."

"Did you tell Arlene that?"

"I most certainly did."

"Where are they now?"

"In the lunch room, I guess. I figure Bernbach and his crew will keep them off each other until I pick them up."

"My guess is this will get patched up. If you call Arlene's mother, she'll lock her in her room until Monday. Arlene may decide this isn't worth it."

"Lock her in her room. Really?"

"Mrs. Whitman is one of those all or nothing parents. Consistency isn't her forte. Let them run wild or put them in a corral. She'd just as soon do nothing. But if the teacher calls, she'll feel she has to do something just to show you."

"God, I hope they patch it up. Is mention of the Deity?..."

"I could never understand the need to take the Lord's name in vain, but perhaps in His infinite wisdom He'll choose this once to take it as a prayer and give you some assistance. I'll be interested in knowing how this turns out. Walking Bianca home is fine in this situation because of where she lives."

"It happens most days anyway since she's generally there, hanging out with me until my bus comes."

"You didn't let me finish. You must never walk with someone to or go inside one of the projects."

"Why's that?"

"Listen to me, Mr. Tough Guy, and listen carefully. Every inch of those hallways, every stairwell, every elevator, is somebody's territory. Do you understand? You will be trespassing with every step you take. Maybe you could display some manly something or other with one or two of those people, but not with six or seven and not when at least one of them will be carrying a gun. I would hate for us to lose a sixth grade teacher in the middle of the year. No substitute could take your class. It would ruin things for all of us."

"But kids live there. Arlene and Brenda live there."

"And they have brothers and uncles and cousins. They know which way to go and they go quickly. There are alliances and people watching out for them. You would have none of that. And just so you know, the kids don't always make it home safely. Last year one of my girls was being gang raped every afternoon. *Every afternoon.* It was the toll she had to pay to get to the door of her apartment. We only found this out because one day she refused to go home. Refused isn't the word. Couldn't. She simply couldn't bring herself to enter her own building to go to her own home. She wouldn't identify her attackers. She alleged she didn't know them." Mrs. Robin said all of this through gritted teeth. "She was so hurt."

"What happened to her?"

"I don't know. She went to live with a relative somewhere. She will be scarred for life. I do know that."

"I'm not going to go wandering into no projects."

"You got my meaning?"

"I got it loud and clear."

"Another thing. No matter what you think of Arlene, it's not likely she would be accosted, but if she were, could you imagine her keeping it to herself or being shy about identifying her attackers? And if you've ever wondered why Brenda trails after her like a shadow think of the protection Arlene affords her. I'm not saying that's the only explanation for their friendship, but it helps to feel safe in a not too friendly world."

"Safe with Arlene. Now there's a thought."

"Just think about it. Now eat your sandwich. We have to go soon."

Neil ate the half sandwich, slices of whole wheat bread cut diagonally loaded with egg salad spiced with pieces of bacon on a huge slice of tomato laid on a large dark green leaf of lettuce. It was delicious. Mrs. Robin watched him eat with the fixed attention she probably used to monitor a student working through a problem at the board. And from the broad smile that was his reward when he finished he knew he had gotten it right.

"There is something you should know about Bianca."

"Uh-oh."

"It's nothing bad. In fact, it's quite good. Last year Bianca tormented her fifth grade teacher half to death. Sarah Weeks. Miss Weeks had my class last year. She was in her third year, so she wasn't totally inexperienced."

"Just moderately so," Neil said.

"It takes five years to become a journeyman, Mr. Riley. Five years. Then you're ready to learn how to really teach. Anyway, Miss Weeks was conscientious, but she was too sensitive. If you're going to fall apart every time some child smart-mouths you you'd better find another profession. And Bianca, as you've pointed out, will express her opinions."

"So Bianca was in the top class? That's where she should be."

"Until she was moved to Mrs. Duane's. Mrs. Duane had Knight's class."

Mrs. Duane was a very fat—corpulent would probably be Mrs. Robin's expression—black woman, a disciplinarian who made Mrs. Robin look like a pussycat. Duane and Robin had been friends before the '68 strikes. They were natural allies in a way, black middle-aged women with children at home and teachers of the old school with enormous dedication to their profession. But Duane was an ardent Union member and the moment Robin crossed the picket line their friendship was over. *Over.*

"Miss Weeks and Bianca actually came to blows. What happened was that Bianca said something..."

"She probably advised Miss Weeks not to be such a Nervous Nelly or some other inappropriate and perceptive proposal," Neil interjected.

"That would be our Bianca. Weeks slapped Bianca. That was not a matter of debate. Everyone, including Weeks, who apparently felt completely justified, agreed that Weeks drew first blood. Bianca slapped her back."

"That would be our Bianca," Neil said.

"So Miss Weeks strongly recommended Bianca be sent to a class for uncontrollable children. She was actually thinking of pressing charges. Does the word overreaction come to mind? Not to mention Bianca would have had a better case. Bernbach, of course, sorted it all out in his own inimitable way."

"So let me get this straight. Bernbach actually gave me Bianca thinking she would be a problem too? I mean, he really stuck it to me, didn't he?"

"You underestimate Bernbach."

"I would never underestimate Bernbach."

"He gave you Bianca because he thought you'd be the best teacher for her."

"Oh, stop it."

"We all have our drawbacks, Mr. Riley. Let he who is without sin cast the first stone. He's the stabilizing force in this school."

"He's a slick manipulator," Neil said.

"Intelligent..."

"Self-interested..."

"Energetic..."

"Deceitful..."

"And experienced. And in this case he was exactly right. You were the best teacher for Bianca. She and I would have been oil and water." Mrs. Robin put her hand to her mouth, as if to tell him a secret behind her palm. "And I would have drowned her." She stood up and stretched her back. "But that probably wouldn't have been the best thing for her."

"No. Drowning's not always best."

"So here she is. Last year she was a major problem, this year she's thriving. Can't all be just chance."

"But where's the problem? She's an excellent reader, a natural leader and perceptive, maybe too perceptive for her own good. I'm lucky to have her. Of course, like Sheri, she isn't too shy about expressing her opinions."

"Fortunately for all concerned Miss Weeks didn't have Sheri."

"What happened to Miss Weeks?"

"She was able to find a job near her home. She lives in one of those Westchester places. Tarrytown, maybe? Let me state the obvious. For a child to learn he must first be taught how to succeed. Miss Weeks as of last year still could not grasp that fundamental truth about teaching. She might even be temperamentally incapable of learning it. I'll tell you this: she still believed it was the child who failed when he didn't do well."

"Can I ask you something about Clyde?" Neil asked.

"Ah, Clyde." She looked at her watch. "Not today. We have to go." She was collecting her glasses, a notebook and her pen and putting them in her purse.

Neil groaned as he got to his feet. "Oh, drat and phooey," he said.

"It's not nice to make fun of an old lady."

"I don't see any old ladies around here. Just this teacha always gonna wash my mouth out with soap."

"My daughter, who is almost exactly your age, has a much better grasp of the English language than you do because her mother has not allowed her to opt for ugly, clichéd expressions that don't fully communicate the matter at hand."

"But girls always do better at language stuff than boys. Everybody knows that. And anyway I'm learning," Neil said. "Livid. That's my word for the day."

"You are learning, by leaps and bounds," Mrs. Robin said. "And miracle of miracles you are definitely not temperamentally impaired."

"Under the tutelage of an excellent teacher."

"Okay," she said. "Here's a test of that excellent teacher's abilities. What is the fundamental truth about teaching?"

"Uhhh. Duh."

"I thought so. You didn't hear a word I said. You were too busy, I suspect, thinking up some way to josh an old lady. But the failure is really mine because I didn't think about the level of the child I was trying to reach."

"I think I have just been sliced and diced and didn't even see it coming. I do need to know. What is the fundamental truth about teaching?"

"Oh, no," she said, looking at her watch again. "Fundamental truths will have to wait. Besides, they have a way of operating even when you don't quite know they're there."

Chapter 15:

An Answered Prayer

In the schoolyard: Arlene and Bianca were playing a hand game on the order of patty cake patty cake. "Boogey man boogey man you don't scare me, I got a daddy mean as can be."

As she passed Neil Mrs. Robin looked back at him and crossed her eyes. Neil sputtered and hid his mouth with his fist as if he had a cough and walked over to the fence to hide the kind of welling jubilation that surely came with an answered prayer.

Chapter 16:

What Kind of Job Is This?

On West 96th Street: Neil lugged his bulging briefcase with first his right arm and then his left as he walked to the bus stop. Bianca skipped along beside him, then skipped ahead and stopped and stood waiting for him. She had done this several times. Each time she would eye him appraisingly, head cocked to one side, as if trying to make up her mind about something.

This last time when he caught up with her he shook his head, laughing. "What?"

"Do you always wear suits? Some teachers wear jeans to school."

"Well, first of all this is not a suit. It's khakis and a jacket. That's not as formal as a suit."

"But you sometimes wear a suit,"

"That's true."

"What would you wear if you were going to the park?"

"Jeans probably. Khakis. I wouldn't be carrying a briefcase, that's for sure."

They had finally reached the bus stop and Neil thought he could see his bus just coming off Broadway onto 96th. To ease the burden on his arms he lowered his briefcase so that most of the weight rested on his shoes. This was only a temporary solution since bending forward to hold the handles placed the stress on his back.

"Is that heavy?" she asked, indicating the briefcase.

"Yes, it is," he said.

"I could carry it for you."

"Not today."

"Okay," she said. "It's probably too heavy for me anyway."

She was carrying her notebook and her dictionary and a Nancy Drew mystery. Harriet had hooked her on Nancy Drew during their Wednesday library periods. Improbably, Harriet, his bright quiet one, and Bianca, his bright anything but quiet one, were becoming friends. When had that started? How had it started? What did they talk about? It seemed to Neil he was completely in the dark when it came to the emotional lives of his children. Of course, it was only in the last couple of weeks that it dawned on him they had emotional lives. Now here he was with this eleven-year-old child and he had no idea how to talk to her. He looked up to check where the bus was. Still three blocks away.

"That lady yesterday, she ain't your wife, right, Mr. Riley?"

"You should say, 'Isn't your wife.' You know that."

"All right. She isn't your wife. She isn't is she?"

"Bianca, I'm not going to discuss my personal life with you."

"I'm not going to discuss my personal life with you," she repeated with a prune face and mocking diction.

That face, all her features scrunched toward her pressed out lips, was her "don't bullshit me" response to any rebuff and its rhetorical majesty never failed to charm him. Did she know that? Of course she did.

And her rebuttal went straight to the heart of the matter. "She shouldn't be coming running in like that then. We have a right to know who she is. And you didn't want her to touch you. I saw you."

You always see everything, he thought. "You're right," he said aloud. "She shouldn't have come running in like that. Okay, for the record. Tell everybody. She's not my wife, she's just a friend." He craned his neck. "My bus is coming," he said, relieved. Wearily he lifted his briefcase, remembering that Amy would be visiting him tonight. Halloween. How appropriate. To hide his inner exhaustion he asked Bianca, "Are you going trick-or-treating tonight?"

"In my building. I'm not pretty like she is, am I?" Bianca asked.

"Who?"

"That lady. She's so pretty. I'm not, am I?"

Neil looked down at her, suddenly alert to the pain wrapped around the words. He dropped his briefcase to the sidewalk and knelt down so that their faces were almost level. "Bianca, you are pretty. *Very* pretty. And you're smart and observant and strong. You play fair and you don't let anyone bully your friends. Everything about you is exactly right. You should be proud of who you are. You should be glad to be so strong."

"Carmen's prettier than me."

The sting of it shot right through him. "Carmen is pretty," he said.

He looked up for the bus, then ordered himself to forget the damn thing. He looked her directly in the eye. She still had to stare up at him, her face anguished and wonderful.

"I don't want to take anything away from Carmen," he said. "But you, Bianca, you are special. And you're very attractive. Let Carmen be the way she is and you be the way you are."

"Do you like me?"

"You know very well I like you."

"You think I'm bossy. Everybody does."

"I think you're outspoken." He stood up. "It's different. Look it up. I'm serious. Study it. Memorize it. It's good to be outspoken."

"You're the best teacher I ever had," she said.

"I doubt that." He was not by any measure anyone's best teacher, but her saying he was touched a deep unwanted need.

He heard the wheezing of the bus's brakes and turned toward the street. The doors sissed open and he grabbed the bar and swung his briefcase up the step and lifted himself up after it.

"I like you a lot, Mr. Riley," she said.

"Thank you. I'm glad. Have a good weekend. Outspoken," he

said. "Look it up. Extra credit!" he managed just before the doors shut.

The bus was half-empty. He sat on one of the long side seats near the rear. He stared at a chewing gum wrapper on the floor, elated; a mess that wasn't his problem.

What kind of job is this? he wondered. One minute he had to make sure a girl didn't get mauled by a girl twice her size. When, *whew,* that was settled and he thought he could let himself go, that same child hovered around, lit on the palm of his hand and begged him to nourish her. The thought of how easily he could have crushed her terrified him.

He leaned back and closed his eyes. If it weren't for this goddamn war he'd be playing half-court pickup in the park near Minetta after spending the morning in the library. Tonight being Friday the plan would be to get stoned out of his gourd with some coed and fuck through the grass clogged air to Joplin's soaring *Summertime*. This year he would have graduated. Next year he'd be earning twelve K minimum. He'd get to his desk by nine to review contracts to make sure they said what all the parties agreed they would say. His major decision for the morning would be what kind of pastry to have when the coffee truck came. Then, of course, he'd have to decide where to eat lunch. He could go to the bathroom any time he wanted. On the way home his carefully chosen *slender leather* briefcase would contain a couple of work items he probably wouldn't get to and the latest *Stones* album he would surely get to first thing.

Well, goodbye to all that. The Tet offensive made it official. He wouldn't see law school again until he turned twenty-six.

He lurched forward, gripping his briefcase with both hands. *As a starting teacher I make $6,800 a year.* He flung this silently at the boob he imagined sitting on the seat across from him.

He made him resemble that balding fortyish jerk who owned the shoe store back home in Lake Haven. He wore a mismatched suit, a shiny blue jacket lighter than his pants. He was one of those, *They spend too much on education, the schools are terrible*, guys. He'd tell you, *Teachers' salaries should be cut in half, they get too many holidays and then they get summers off too?! My taxes pay for that?* One of those guys who spends his days seething behind a false smile.

Neil wanted such a guy, ached for such a guy. He'd break his jaw, kick his teeth in, then bending over him: *You prick. After deductions I take home under $100 a week. I spend at least $10 of that on books and supplies for my class. In this huge bulging snap-open canvas briefcase, in addition to a reader, the social studies book, the dictionary and the sixth grade arithmetic book are the homework assignments I gave Thursday, the math and spelling tests I gave today and the social studies mimeograph that was the follow-up to their reading lesson on the development of agriculture along the Tigris and Euphrates. All of this has to be graded this weekend so I can hand it back on Monday. I have all these books so I can prepare next week's lessons. Do you understand? You shit! You asshole!*

He sat there with the briefcase on his lap, the pressure on his quads nothing like the pressure on his brain. He rolled the whole vile load onto the seat next to him and laid his arm across it wearily, so tired and so tired of being tired. Oh, and don't forget Amy, at seven sharp.

So why was he grinning? Because he knew she'd look it up. He fumbled around in his briefcase and got out the same faded red cloth-covered dictionary she would use. *Outspoken: unrestrained in speech; direct; open; frank; opinionated; forthright.* Bianca.

Chapter 17:

Friday Night

In Neil's apartment: the bell on his wall jangled at 6:50 p.m. There were three flights of stairs, quite a climb, but the knock at the door seemed to come only seconds after he buzzed her in. Neil allowed himself a moment to wish this wasn't happening, took a deep breath and let in Amy.

Who swirled through the door in a dark blue woolen coat, the hood cradling her head, framing her white skin and wind touched cheeks. The coat was fitted from her neck to her waist and smooth and flowing from her waist to her ankles. It was held closed by three sets of wooden clasps anchored in grey suede patches embroidered with small red flowers on curled green stems.

How Carmen would have loved that coat. And the wispy turns of the stems would have thrilled Marta. Neil decided it would take close to a thousand dollars, a month's expenses for Carmen's entire family, two adults and two children, to pay for it.

Without a word Amy threw herself at him, locked her arms around his back and squeezed. The door was still open and he wanted to maneuver to close it without seeming uninvolved in her embrace. Then in a fit of exasperation, at her, at himself, he just lifted her up, worked the two of them to the door and shut it. She did not let go. He resolved then that he would outlast her, that she would let go before he did. He wanted one instance where he could not be construed as the guilty party. It became imperative.

It became impossible. He gripped her arms at the elbows and yanked them down tightly at her sides.

"I'm getting stiff," he said, letting her go.

140

Her head moved around in strange jerks. She peeked to her left at the kitchen, then to her right at the vestibule leading to the bedroom. "It goes straight through."

"It's a railroad."

"There aren't any doors."

"The bathroom has one."

"It's awfully small."

"Thirteen paces, twenty-six steps, from the kitchen cabinets to the toilet bowl. Not all of us can afford a fancy village setup."

"I want to take the tour." She was already on her way to the bedroom. The light flicked on. "I don't believe it. You make your bed," she yelled.

The made bed was a statement: *No sex happens here.*

He heard metal scraping; that would be the hangers being pushed back and forth on his clothing rack. The opening and closing of drawers; those would be from his bureau. Apparently she did this with no hesitancy, not a shred of self-consciousness. Though surely she knew her behavior was outrageous. Betty once told him Amy had been beaten up by one of her dates. Black eyes, a busted lip, the guy had really whacked her around. Betty told the story as an example of the hazards of being a single woman in New York. At the time Neil, who hadn't yet met Amy, wondered why she hadn't called the cops. But by their second date he knew why. Getting knocked around was what she wanted.

"The bathroom is teeny," she called out.

He could hear her open the cabinet over the sink. He clenched his fists, but stayed where he was. After all, aside from her terrible compulsion, what was being exposed by this search other than his razor, toothpaste and sloppy housekeeping?

She whisked past him into the kitchen, where she looked first in his frig and then in the cabinets above the sink. There was a sense of release in her body, a feeling of a job well done, that she brought with her back into the living room.

"What's for dinner?" she asked.

"You're not staying for dinner," he said.

"Oh." She began to unclasp her coat. "Not a lot to eat anyway that I could see."

"Just enough for me. Two beers and a deli sandwich."

"You have a pet?" she asked.

"Me? God, no."

"I see a bowl of food on the floor and some water."

"My roommate. He spends most of the night getting laid, comes in about midnight to freeload off this sucker, sleeps a while, then takes off again."

"You're talking about an animal, right? Not a person."

"A cat."

She removed her coat. It would be more accurate to say she disrobed. She was wearing a shimmering white gown, the kind favored by movies before the code, designed to make women as close to naked as possible. In the movies the dresses were ankle length. Amy's was hemmed two inches above the knee. It tied halter-style at the neck, leaving her back bare. Neil knew without asking that it was made of silk and bought perhaps just for this occasion.

"Ewww." She had started to toss her coat on the sofa when she noticed the cat's towel with the greasy black splotch in the middle that was his mark. "What is that?"

"That's where he sleeps. Right in the middle of the couch. Don't mess with it, please. I can't imagine what he'd do to me if you moved it."

"Where can I put this?" She held the coat aloft.

"How about across the desk?"

His desk, against the wall next to the door, with the hard-backed chair in which he spent most of his waking hours when he was home, the desk from which he had swooped all the papers and stuffed them into his briefcase. If she went for the briefcase, he would have to stop her. But she couldn't possibly know how important that scruffy looking thing was to him.

She laid her coat across the desk. Her dress was loose at the sides so that her left breast was now on display and remained so as she examined the row of books he had lined up across the back of the desk. "*Science for Children,*" she read. "*All About Weather.* Okay, but Dostoevsky's *Idiot*? You? Dostoevsky?"

"I put it there to impress you," he said, thinking she knew exactly how to work him. *It's not going to happen,* he promised himself.

She held the book up, examining it. "No, I think you're actually reading it."

"All right, I confess. I'm reading Dostoevsky's *Idiot*."

"There are two toothbrushes in the holder," she said.

"What?"

"Who uses the other toothbrush?"

Neil pointed to the cat's towel. "His morning mouth is beyond belief."

"I'm serious."

"Really? You're serious. About what? What the fuck business is it of yours that there's two toothbrushes in the bathroom. Why are you here? What do you want? You blackmailed me into this, so now you tell me what this is all about."

"You know," she said, putting her hands on her hips.

"That sick shit? I'm not doing that anymore."

"You're still seeing that flat-faced cow you left Roger's party with. That's her toothbrush, isn't it?"

"Not all of us can be frail little flowers like you."

"You were seeing her even before we broke up, weren't you?"

"Broke up? How could we break up? We never had anything to break up from, don't you know that? God, you have no idea how I see this. And you could care less."

She stared at him with long-suffering dignity, patient, tolerant. "She can't be staying here. There aren't any extra towels. And no woman would put up with that!" she said, pointing at the cat's lair.

"That's true. I spend all my time at her place," he said. "She has this incredible apartment overlooking the East River."

He was being facetious, but quickly realized that possibility wouldn't occur to her. It would be impossible for her to imagine he spent all his waking hours either preparing for his class or in the classroom. And yet how could she not see that? In her mind his life seemed to be a labyrinth of lust and desire. The only reason there were no panties in his drawers, lipstick and eyeliner in his medicine cabinet, a full refrigerator was, as he had just admitted, because he was always lounging around in that woman's apartment.

"Amy, you said you wanted to see me. Okay. You see me. Now what?"

"You know very well."

She reached behind her neck, untied the straps and let the dress fall to the floor. Now she stood there, a small, white, perfectly formed woman wearing only a pair of sheer panties. Not much taller, really, than Carmen, smaller than Arlene. Neil stood ensnared in the net-like bristle at her groin. His mouth was thick, his pulse racing; his brain had almost ceased to function. But not quite. He imagined at least one stratagem: run into the bathroom, lock the door and scream for her to leave. *Why not? A prudent man must always have his wits about him.*

He dropped back on the couch. She fell to her knees between his legs.

"Make me blow you," she said. She was breathing hard, an addict on the verge of a fix.

He thought of putting the cat's towel over his fly. *Like garlic. Like a cross.*

"Right. Make you," he said, and just the thought of that, pressing her head down, having her resist, taking her by the neck and forcing her, became the talisman he needed. She would fight. He would really have to make her. "I can't," he said. "I don't want to."

As he said that, to his immense relief it actually became true. He had worried that he couldn't resist her. But he didn't have to resist. He had lost the desire. "Amy, please, put your clothes back on. It's over."

And it was quite clear he meant it. *Oh, my God,* he thought, *I'm not a total sadist.*

"I knew it," she said.

It was like watching a movie roll backwards; she stood up, stepped into the dress, pulled it up, tied the straps behind her neck. The monster that had overwhelmed her retracted back into a beautiful young woman. He couldn't believe this was happening. It was too easy.

"You should go," he said.

"You can't wait to get rid of me."

"I have a lot to do."

She put on her coat. "Will you walk me to the train?"

"Yeah, sure."

She waited for him while he got his windbreaker from the bedroom. When he came back, without comment, she headed out the door and down the stairs.

Chapter 18:

The Coat

On East 96th Street: she removed her hands from the waist pockets of the coat and with elbows tight against her body and her forearms out she twirled once and curtsied before him. "What do you think of my coat?"

"I think it's beautiful," he said. "You look like a Cossack's wife."

"I got it at one of those resale places on Canal. For twenty dollars! Can you believe it?"

Her smile was exquisite. She was so incredibly beautiful. He remembered the dress she wore beneath the coat, how it had fallen away from her body. But he was able to keep on walking, keep on talking. "No. Twenty bucks? I thought it must have cost hundreds."

They were standing under the streetlight on the north corner of 96th and Lexington. The subway station was across the street. He felt anxious to get her over there, to say goodbye.

She said, "I know. It looks very expensive. And it fits me perfectly."

"Yes. It does," he said, though he didn't look at her to confirm it. The light changed. "We can go," he said, stepping off the curb.

When they reached the south side of 96th she grabbed his elbow. "When I bought it, I pretended you were there. I tried it on for you. You loved it."

"Oh, right, I've really got an eye for women's clothes."

She shook his arm. "Look at me." And when he did, she continued. "I supervise seven caseworkers, one a man in his fifties, another a woman in her thirties with two children. I review their cases, evaluate their narratives, go out with them to make sure they know

146

what they're doing. I have to make life-changing decisions every day."

"I know that," he said. She had described one of her cases to him. Her responsibilities were enormous. In fact, that was her job, to make harrowing decisions.

"My caseworkers all think I'm very together. They think I've got everything. I pretend we're seeing each other. I talk about you all the time."

"You shouldn't do that."

"I won't anymore." And because he had quietly removed his arm from her grip and looked back across the street, she startled him by saying, "Why can't you pay attention to me for even a minute?"

He felt he could have asked her that exact same question. "I'm sorry. I keep thinking of all the work I have to do," he said, which was only half true. He was also thinking that if she would hurry up he could still have his evening off, savor those beers and relish that sandwich.

She gripped his arm again. "Please look at me," she said.

His eyes had wandered again to the other side of the street.

"I know you could never love me the way I want you to," she told him.

He thought, but did not say, *I never loved you.*

"I also know you never wanted to hurt me."

That wasn't quite true, but he felt no need to argue the point.

"That's why I'm so crazy about you."

And certainly no need to comment on the aptness of that choice of words.

She tightened her grip on his arm. *Here it comes,* he thought. *The begging, the screams, the fit.* He braced himself.

"You could save me," she said.

"Amy, I'm just a guy. Really, just a guy. And right now I'm in it up to here." He put his hand about six inches above his head.

She shook her head, smiling. "No, no, you're not just a guy. Not to me. You're the lover who couldn't hurt me. That's so funny. I mean, it completely contradicts that angry young man image you project." After some thought she said, as if offering the solution to their differences, "We could help each other."

Get better at rough sex, he thought. Aloud he said, "I've got this friend."

"Girlfriend," she said.

"The woman I'm talking about is around fifty-five years old," he said.

"As if that mattered."

"Amy, listen to me, please. Her name is Mrs. Robin. A really good sixth grade teacher. She has deigned to help me. I don't know why."

"I do. She wants to seduce you."

"No. She doesn't. Wait a minute. You know what?"

"What?"

"You're right. She does want to seduce me. But not the way you think. She's helping me because she wants me to survive. She wants me to learn to teach. She's doing it for the kids."

"What's this got to do with me?" Amy asked.

"Nothing. Absolutely nothing. Don't you see? The only woman in my life is a married fifty-five-year-old black woman with a daughter my age. This woman is mentoring me because she wants me to help a bunch of poor scrappy kids living on the edge of disaster. I don't want to suck her, I don't want to fuck her, all I want to do is pick her brains. That's where I'm at. See? It has nothing to do with you. I'm flailing around, lost, baffled."

And, he thought, *I desperately need someone to know that, can't you see? Can't you see how your absolute refusal to listen to me is such a hassle? I can't stand to be around you.*

"I could say the same exact thing," she said.

She seemed completely unaware of the laughter that bubbled out of him, a lapse that only reinforced his notion that they were saying exactly the same things to each other while ignoring every single word the other said.

"One final request," she said, "then I promise, I'll be gone."

"What?" he asked.

"Oh, God, the way you said that. It'll only take a minute. I promise. I hope this never happens to you. That you'll want someone who doesn't want you. I mean, I'd wish this misery on you, but I'd be too jealous if you loved somebody the way I love you."

"Amy, what?"

"Pick me up and kiss me. You did that when we first got together. You'd lift me off the ground and hold me like you were never going to let me go and you'd kiss me."

He lifted her off the ground and kissed her, deeply, sadly, truly wishing she could get the care she needed and knowing he couldn't have given it to her even in the best of times.

She put her face in his neck. "I want to smell you. I want to remember this. Please don't say goodbye when I leave. Okay?"

"Okay."

As soon as he put her on her feet she turned and fled down the subway steps. He stood for a few moments staring at the entrance. He crossed the street, but couldn't help looking back, expecting her to suddenly come running screaming after him. She didn't. It was hard to believe but she was gone.

At home finally he flopped exhausted on the couch and meticulously planned how he would over the course of the evening slowly eat, drink, undress and go to bed. He ordered each task in his mind. Anytime he began to brood about Amy or worry about his class he would get up and do the next thing on his list, beginning with taking off and hanging up his windbreaker. Back on the couch he discovered himself looking at the paperback lying where Amy had left it on the desk. He immediately got up and went into the kitchen, got the bottle opener from the utensil drawer and popped open a beer. There was no chance in hell he was going to read, especially not that book, not tonight. He savored the beer, sip by sip, and planned how he would unbutton his shirt. Several times he delighted himself by deciding not to take a shower. He did not hurry. He did not do or think anything that could be considered productive. He occupied himself with the exquisite luxury of wasting time.

Part Two:

The Hard Surface Beneath 1969

Chapter 1:

A Math Lesson

In Neil's apartment: light was streaming through the bedroom window when he woke up. He pulled himself out of bed, emptied his bladder and made the coffee. Almost ten o'clock. He had slept for over nine hours. It was his longest sleep in months. He had his regular Cheerios with banana and, still hungry, a peanut butter and jelly sandwich. The cat had eaten, had his water, taken his nap and split. Whadja expect? Neil's evening with Amy was a bruise that would have to heal itself. It was Saturday, the first day of November, and he had a math test to grade.

He had been told by all and sundry, the teachers of his education classes at Hunter, Mrs. Robin, Bernbach, all the great authorities, that the sixth grade arithmetic curriculum was essentially a review of the concepts that had been taught from first to fifth. This was a fucking lie. Sixth graders would sharpen their skills with more complex problems, they said, but nothing new was introduced. Bull shit. Of course, at the end of the year if it seemed appropriate the teacher had the option of doing some basic algebra or of introducing different number systems. Fat chance. Anyone up for a little set theory? Give me a fucking break.

His class, with the exception of Charles (always with the exception of Charles, who was illiterate and could barely count from one to ten), did understand the four basic operands, could for the most part add and subtract numbers in two or three columns (most using, but not understanding, the "carry" notation), could multiply with one multiplier and could do division with a double-digit divisor as long as there was no remainder. Six of his students knew all this and were ready for much more; another twenty-two knew it well enough to continue with what was essentially fourth grade math, and five needed remedial work in the basic concepts.

Now this. Last week he had reviewed basic fractions: notation and finding the common denominator. Really basic. They could all recognize and write what part of the pie chart or bar graph was colored in black as long as only one of the parts was black. It was therefore true to say that thirty-two of his students could recognize 1/2, 1/3rd, 1/4th and 1/5th. On the test everyone (except Charles) got those four problems right. Only twenty-eight or so could see that 4 black parts of 5 were 4/5ths and only about twenty-three of his scholars knew that 1 inch on a twelve inch ruler was 1/12th and if 3 of the 4 fruits in the bowl were apples and 1 was an orange, 3/4ths of the fruits were apples. Only Clyde, Pedro, Bianca, Brenda, yes, Brenda, Harriet Wilson (his elusive girl wonder) and David Wade (whoever he was) knew that 1 and 1/2 inches of a 12 inch ruler was 1/8th of the ruler.

Asked to "Reduce to the lowest denominator:" the entire class knew that 2/4=1/2. Sheri, Sammy, Raul, Constance and Alicia did not know that 4/8ths was also 1/2. Once you left the comfort of the divisor by 2, Sheri ("I ain't gonna do no arithmetic" and, indeed, she did not) and many others lost their way. 3/15ths became, variously, 1/2, 1/10th, 2/7ths or nothing. Arlene actually got that one right. But only that fantastic six, that is, Clyde, Pedro, Bianca, Brenda, Harriet and David knew that 3/16=3/16. Others tried =1/2, 1/4th and 3/4ths. Some (wisely) put nothing.

Out of twenty problems Cole, Javier, Marta, Steven, Gloria and many others, that middle of the class, middle of the room, quiet, unknown bunch that went largely ignored because he didn't have to chase them around the room, constantly ask them to sit down, continually tell them to stop calling out, that group got between eleven and fifteen of twenty problems right.

For extra credit, and for his information, Neil threw in five more problems: a simple addition of 1 and 1/2 plus 2 and 3/4ths, a simple subtraction of 5 minus 4 and 1/3rd, an addition of 5/16ths plus 3/4ths, a multiplication of 1 and 1/2 by 1/2 and a division of 4/5ths by 1/5th.

The final results of the test were that—drum rolls please—most, twenty-three in all, scored in the 55% to 75% range. Sheri and Alicia scored 35% and Sammy, Raul and Constance got 40%. Pauli, Morris and Norbert (Norbert?) got 70%. Marta, God bless her, got a whopping 75%.

Okay. But Brenda got 100% on the regular test and quit. Did she refuse to do the extra five out of defiance or ignorance? It was hers to know, his to find out. Sloppy Bianca got 105% because on the regular test she reduced 4/8ths to 2/4ths instead of 1/2 but was able to do two of the extra five. David Wade got 110%. Harriet got 115%. Multiplication and division of fractions were as yet beyond Harriet and David. Still, they were ready to learn them, the elusive Harriet, the unknown David.

With regard to Clyde and Pedro it got tricky. Clyde got all twenty-five: 125%. Pedro? Well, now, Pedro. Neil hesitated, realizing he was on the brink of a decision that might upend his entire existence. God damn this job. Back in Lake Haven, when he was considered vicious and uncooperative and would get every single answer right on a test, including some little trick the teacher threw in to assess the students' alertness, Neil experienced the injustice of having some goody goody the teacher liked get the same grade as he did in spite of the fact that the goody goody didn't see the little trick and got it wrong. Well, in this instance Pedro did not finish the problem, 5/16+3/4=. He left it 17/16ths. Not Clyde, who finished the problem with the correct answer, 1 and 1/16th (as did that Harriet). And here was Neil, thirteen years later wanting to let bright, energetic, sensitive, cooperative, compassionate Pedro slide. Well, goddamnit.

Pedro: 120%. And Clyde: 125%. *And you?* He groaned. *You'll let Clyde know he was the only one to get a perfect grade. Yes, and you'll do it publicly. Yes you will, if you want your 100%.*

There were so many problems suggested by this test that a veil of hopeless weariness rose up when he tried to think of how to confront them. His class by and large was ready to do fifth grade math. Could Neil really take the rap for this? His class was supposed to be the second brightest. This year it was Mrs. Robin's turn to have the most academically advanced class, the nice, middle-class achievers. She even had five white kids (a problem Neil would definitely not have been able to handle). But Neil's class was supposed to be bright, too. The street-smart hard cases. Well, they were bright. Whether they were street-smart or not depended on which street. Neil didn't think they would do too well on Grand Street in Lake Haven, the Connecticut town where he grew up. But no matter who or what they were, most of them didn't know fractions.

He sat for a long time staring at the wall. Where had he been? For four days he had "reviewed" this stuff and most of his kids, three out of four, barely understood what he was talking about. Why hadn't he known that? Okay, but this test gave him the situation. They needed remedial work in fractions. No shit, Dick Tracy. But that was only one of his problems.

Another was that he had at least four levels of arithmetic here when he didn't feel competent to teach one. And don't forget, at least six of those children, if you threw Brenda in with his five other geniuses, probably loved numbers. Rolled them around in their heads like sour balls. Fractions, division, decimals, oh, God, give 'em to me, give 'em to me. Oh, God, oh, God. Disgusting little perverts. And David Wade? Comes roaring in out of the blue.

Still, it wasn't all bad. Aside from the fact that math was a huge slice of the basic curriculum, it could also be a way to help Clyde with his language arts program. He loved math and hated reading.

Okay, put the problem another way. Forget for the moment that he and Clyde had serious emotional conflicts. Just focus on the fact that here was an obviously smart kid who was good at math and read poorly. How could he, Mr. Brilliant Teacher, use that?

More. How could he teach what he didn't care about himself? To children who deserved as good as they could get. Put bluntly, Clyde and Pedro were better at math than he was. The whole business of multiplying and dividing fractions was as fuzzy a practice to him as it was to Harriet. How the hell do you cut 1/3 into 4ths? Why bother? You know? Why not call it one and cut it into quarters? And how come when you divided a fraction by a fraction you got a larger number? If he sat and thought about this he could come up with the proper explanations, but who the hell *wanted to*? Just because it took innumerable geniuses thousands of years to develop this stuff, why was it supposed to matter to him? He was with Sheri. "How come I gotta know about arithmetic? Shoot!"

And back to that other nagging question, the one he kept avoiding, the one about class management. What was he supposed to do with Harriet? And Brenda? And now David? He got out his roster. Harriet Wilson. Row 3, Desk 6. Behind Cole. Between Karen Mathews and Constance Andrews. Who the hell was Karen Mathews? Who the hell was Constance Andrews? Where was David Wade?

Where was Neil Riley? What the fuck was he doing? Dumb stupid pathetic helpless scared selfish shitfaced draft dodger. How dare he call himself a teacher? He didn't know half of the children in his class. They were probably lucky. That way he couldn't fuck 'em up.

He told himself he shouldn't let this failure get to him. Too late for that. So the next step was to call on his expertise in failure and misery and do what he had to do, live with it one minute at a time. He went for a long run, then treated himself to Chinese and three Buds and spent the evening continuing his reading of *The Idiot*, a novel unlike any he had read before, though not an unalloyed pleasure. It sure as hell wasn't escape.

First of all the central character, this Prince Myshkin, the 'idiot,' had no defenses, never blamed others for his failings and never judged or condemned anyone. That didn't mean he ignored their failings, though. He wanted people to care about each other, to put aside selfishness and ambition and act compassionately, which seemed pretty stupid to Neil. It seemed pretty stupid to Myshkin, too, who kept apologizing profusely for being so kind.

Neil's reaction to Myshkin was exactly like that of the characters in the novel. He had to be a phony, a nut, an idiot. By demanding nothing, he demanded everything. He was infuriating and superb. He was unbelievable and stupid and magically beautiful. And Dostoevsky wouldn't let you deny him. He was there, alive, on the page.

Okay, this 'prince' told a story about a troubled girl he gave comfort to in the Swiss village where he was convalescing from epileptic fits. The young woman had been seduced and abandoned by a traveling salesman, ostracized by the people of the village, including her mother, and tormented by the children. The prince treated the girl kindly and convinced the children to treat her kindly, too. After that "I was always with the children," he said, insisting that children were by nature loving and kind, good and gentle and in possession of a natural understanding that was invariably underestimated by adults. It was the same or similar crap he was encountering in his reading of Jonathan Kozol.

"I was always with the children, only with the children..." Myshkin says. "It was not that I taught them... they can teach us."

Neil held the book out and shook it. He wanted to shake Myshkin out and slam him to the floor. "Bullshit! What bullshit! Oh, God, oh, God." He threw the book at the wall. He was sweating. What was going on here? Why should he care what a character said in a novel written one hundred years ago? Oddly enough he and Myshkin were the same age, twenty-four, but that's where any similarity between them ended. *What you need to know about me, you... you idiot, is that in less than two years, on March 25, 1971 to be exact, I'll be twenty-six, too old to draft and ready to get on with my life. And I know from pretty good sources, like for instance the book jacket, that you're going to be insane.*

Neil stared at the floor for a long while, then got up and got the book and sat down and continued reading.

The next day, Sunday, he allowed himself another twenty pages of *The Idiot,* then graded the spelling test. He was fairly pleased with the results. At least they were passable. He had hated spelling when he was in school, but now it was an essential part of his language arts program, such as it was. It increased the students' word recognition and, more importantly, having to look up, read, memorize and write the definitions was a task they all understood and took satisfaction from, Sheri perhaps more than anyone else.

On his Sunday run he kept thinking of Clyde. According to Clyde's scores on the Iowa Basic Skills he read on a fourth grade level. Neil wondered if he was even that good. He had been tested for poor eyesight, dyslexia and stupidity, but he had 20-20 vision, no dyslexia and an IQ on a verbally administered test of 110. Neil suspected that was a low score reflecting Clyde's problems with testing, but even so, 110 was above average. Whether he was 110 or 140, Clyde had begun to do the spelling homework, so that in a given week he was able to spell 16 to 18 words right and knew from at least three to all five of the definitions Neil asked for, with the understanding that sentence structure and subject verb agreement weren't Clyde's forte. Moreover, *Clyde was actually studying,* which according to his records was not typical.

Clyde's reading problem had been diagnosed, finally, as "poor attitude," a copout if ever there was one. Neil's diagnosis was "fear of failure" and when he was really pissed at Clyde he was tempted to tell him that and explain the derivation. "It's your limp dick, shit-face. You're impotent." That would probably not be beneficial and certainly wouldn't go over well at home, but metaphorically speaking it was closer to the truth than "poor attitude."

Watching Clyde read was painful. His eyes would bulge, his throat constrict, his face break into a sweat as he read, laborious-ly, "The—bbboy's—na—naame was Myyy—" Neil would ask, "What's the ch sound?" "My-chall." "No, the other ch, like a k, ka." "Michael." "Right."

Neil had stopped calling on him to read. Instead he asked him to summarize what someone else had just read and then would sometimes ask him to justify his summary. "You said they were going to visit the Statue of Liberty. Where does it say that? You don't have to read it, just tell me where it says that on that page. Which sentence in which paragraph?" He did this with Norbert and with Cole, too. They, too, seemed verbally adept, but afraid of reading. This way these three had to follow along, deal intuitively with the concepts of paragraphs and sentences, and at least rec-ognize selected words. A gleeful moment for Neil would be when one of them, most likely Norbert, would say, "See, right there, it says..." and then read the sentence. Was this instructive? It cer-tainly wasn't a technique he learned in any of his classes. But the boys went along with what he was doing. They may even have appreciated it.

Most of the children wanted to read and couldn't wait to be called on. It was, among other things, an opportunity to be recog-nized by their teacher, to have him actually look at them and admit that they were in this classroom. That did not mean, however, that they understood what they read. The eager readers, too, were asked for summaries and often came up blank. A source of deep satisfac-tion for Neil would be when one of his limp dicks would jump in and add to the reader's summary.

It was, of course, a measure of his limitations that all the children used the same reader. He taught to the middle range of his class. Both Bianca and, yes, according to her Iowa score, our Miss Harriet, were reading far above grade level. Pedro and Brenda scored at just about grade level, but Neil was convinced Pedro could read and understand material that would baffle many high school students, particularly scientific concepts. With regard to Brenda, Neil didn't know where she stood, academically or emotionally. She never raised her hand to volunteer to read, but always knew the place and always read perfectly when called on. At the other extreme Sammy and Alicia could only grasp the most basic ideas. "The cat was black." They got it. The cat was of the color that is universally referred to as black and they could point to the blackboard to support their contention. "Why do you think the cat jumped on the counter?" Silence. "Well, then, start with what the cat did. What did the cat do?" Silence. Okay, that was Sammy and Alicia. Charles couldn't read. Period. Basically he hid out under his jacket. Once in a while he would peek out furtively, but he'd dive back under the moment Neil or anyone else might happen to notice he was sneaking a look.

So. On his Sunday run Neil pushed hard for an hour even though this should have been a light day. He would be sore tomorrow. Good. It would give him something to think about other than his inadequacies. Which were? Too many to enumerate but surely included...

He was walking, warming down, ruminating, and he ruminated right past the Jewish deli. The Italian deli, across the street, was open on Saturday; the Jewish deli was open on Sunday; God bless New York City. At his front door it dawned on him he had to get something for dinner if he didn't want to open cans and he turned around and headed back up 96th.

His biggest shortcoming? He hardly ever knew if what he was doing was effective.

Okay, forget that. What did he know was wrong? What was his

biggest failure? Something he could put his finger on and say this is wrong.

You really want to know?

Maybe not.

I'm going to tell you anyway.

Whisper it to me.

Arlene.

The albatross Bernbach had slung around his neck. The affliction Neil used to excuse all his defects. He didn't want Arlene in his class. Well, she didn't want to be there. But there she was: the difficult child, the class bully, a little treat for first year teacher Neil Riley. She was without a doubt headache number one. Because? He couldn't control her. She controlled him. Somehow he had to turn that around. He had to figure out a way to give her migraines.

He looked up to find he had walked past the deli again and was almost back at Fifth Avenue. He had to focus. He had nothing decent to eat in his frig. *Come on! If you don't want Dinty Moore Stew again tonight you've got to focus.*

He ordered a pastrami on rye and as he watched it being made ordered another one. The counter man threw in a side of cole slaw and Neil had him add a garden salad and two cups of potato salad. The cat was going to love that kosher pastrami, if there was any left. And hard to believe, he was actually looking forward to Monday. School or corrections, school or Canada. Watch out, Arlene. Hell take the hindmost.

Chapter 2:

Let's Do It

In the schoolyard: Bianca saw him come through the gate and waved as if they were old friends. He smiled and waved back, then quickly questioned whether he should have. *Don't smile until December,* the old timers said. The other students on the line had turned to watch his approach. Eager to have him take them up to class? *Don't get carried away, Riley.* The schoolyard, the dreamscape of lined concrete stretching up and out forever, preyed on him even as the children organized themselves. It was the hard surface beneath everything else.

Pauli and Sammy ran to join the line. Norbert and Clyde, like two guards standing watch out on the corners of the perimeter, slowly herded in Charles. Arlene and Brenda were nowhere to be seen.

"Good morning, Mr. Riley," Morris said.

"Good morning, Morris. Hey, Pedro. You and Clyde on the math test. Too good, man." He pointed at Clyde. "You were the best. You'll see."

Clyde pursed his lips and turned his hands palms up, as if accepting applause. Robin moved her class out, then Neil nodded, "Let's do it," and, could this be happening? they followed him quietly, quickly, up to 6-306.

Chapter 3:

Fed Up and Enjoying Every Minute of It

In Room 6-306: Sheri stood at her desk and read the schedule that Neil had already put on the board. "*Mathematics*," Sheri read, touching her heart with her right hand. "I cane wait. And look, yawl, *Reading. Science*? We got to go to that ole Mizz Perry?"

"Every Monday," Neil said.

"Nawww," Charles groaned.

Neil moved to the back and put a hand on Charles' shoulder. "It'll be okay. I'll take care of it."

Last week Perry had spent the first fifteen minutes of her class trying to get Charles to sit up straight and take his jacket off. Charles finally rushed her, pushed her against the blackboard and ran back to 306 and Neil, who was sitting having his coffee and laying out the social studies homework for grading. That was the end of that free period. He pulled the story out of Charles, sort of, then went to tell Perry he had Charles, not to worry.

"What are you going to do to him?" she asked.

"Keep him for the rest of the period," Neil said.

"I mean, how are you going to punish him?"

"He's going to miss science."

"He pushed me, Mr. Riley." She was really saying, *You're pushing me, Mr. Riley.*

"What are you going to do?" he asked her. "You're the one he pushed."

"You're his teacher." She squinted to show how unbelievably dense he was.

"So are you," he said, mirroring her squint. Later when he was

164

turning this over in his head he kept wishing he'd said, *What am I going to do with you? You pushed him first.* Instead he said, "I'll talk to Charles. It won't happen again."

"It had better not," she said.

And that was how they left it.

Now Sheri stood reading the schedule, rather well, actually.

"Miss Wallace, could you read the schedule without editorial comment? Your feelings about Mrs. Perry might get us confused. What's next?"

"I doan know," Sheri said. "I cane read all that scratchin'."

"You cane write worth a dang, Mr. Riley," Pauli said, doing a pretty good imitation of Clyde.

"How come we never had that contest?" Bianca asked.

"What contest?"

"To get somebody else to write on the board," Clyde said.

"Not today," Neil said.

"How come?" Bianca asked.

"Not today, Bianca, okay? Stop calling out."

"Everybody else does."

"Yes, I know. Sandra, would you hand out the math tests, please."

Sandra looked over at Sheri.

Neil looked over at Sheri, too, as he said, "Don't worry about Miss Wallace. I'm riding shotgun. You have nothing to worry about."

Neil stood right next to Sandra, giving her the papers for the first row and walking her down the aisle as she handed them out.

"I don't never get to do nothin'," Sheri protested. Tears were rolling down her cheeks. "It's not fair."

Neil steeled himself with a *fuck her.* When they were at the end of row one Neil said, "Sammy, would you come help me, please?"

Brenda, Clyde, Arlene, Charles and Norbert were the only ones in the class who didn't want to give out papers, yet Sheri threw a fit if she wasn't allowed to do it every time. Even if she had just given out a set of papers, *even if she was already in the process of giving out a set of papers,* she would attack anyone Neil gave another set to. She simply couldn't allow anyone else to do this chore except Neil himself and that was only because she couldn't stop him. Neil couldn't find anything in her anecdotals that indicated she had been like this in earlier classes. Calling out, insulting the teacher, creating disturbances in the library, assembly, special classes, they were all there, but nothing like this.

Neil had come to resent this behavior almost as much as Arlene's antics. It was unfair, it was a nuisance and it had to stop. Someday maybe a hundred years from now he'd tell the funny story about the tiny gorgeous little black girl who couldn't let anyone else hand out the homework papers. But right now, as petty, stupid and incomprehensible as the situation was, it was another landmine constantly about to go off. He had decided that he had to dig it out once and for all and defuse it.

At the end of row two Neil turned and said, "Marta, would you come help me give out the papers for row 3?"

"I ain't never goan do nothin' in this class again," Sheri cried.

Neil turned toward her, shouting, "WHAT HAVE YOU DONE SO FAR? NOTHING! YOU HAVEN'T DONE ANYTHING! YOU SIT THERE AND TALK OUT AND DO NOTHING!"

"I give out the papers," she said and turned her head away to hide her tears.

Neil?

He turned quickly toward the front of the room. As if in a dream, he had heard a voice calling his name coming from the direction of his desk. It certainly wasn't Bianca. She was looking down, staring at the top of her desk. Anyway, the voice had been male, calling as if from a long distance away; asking him to consider what he was doing?

So now he was becoming a delusional freak who heard voices.

So be it. Until the men from the funny farm came and tied him up in one of their white canvas suits he would see to it that whoever wanted to give out papers in his class would give out the papers—as long as it wasn't Sheri. Sheri was never going to give out another piece of paper as long as she was in this class. Making certain of that. That's what he was doing.

"Pauli, would you please come help me give out the papers for..."

SLAM! The door flew open and in walked Arlene, followed tentatively by Brenda.

"Hi, yawl, I'm here!" she announced and then stared at the faces looking at her in silence, at Sheri two seats down row one with her head in her hands and now at Neil who was walking quickly toward her. "What jawl doin'?" she asked him.

"Do you have a note explaining why you're late?" Neil asked.

Hands on hips she said, "I don't need no note."

He grabbed her by the shoulders and flipped her around and out the door. To Brenda, who had edged inside and was standing a few feet into the classroom against the wall he said, "You, too. Out."

She strained her head forward, as if trying to understand him.

"Brenda, I said OUT!"

She jumped at the command, terrified, and keeping her eyes on him moved quickly past him and through the door. Neil stepped into the hall. Arlene was pressed up against the wall, looking trapped.

"Neither of you will come back into my class until you have a note from home explaining why you were late this morning. Is that clear?"

"No," Arlene said.

Neil ignored this. "You can get your notes today or bring them in tomorrow. But if you're not on the line at 8:30 a.m. tomorrow morning, notes or no notes, don't bother to show up. Am I being clear? No note, no class, come late, no class."

"How are we going to get the notes now?" Brenda asked.

Neil put his palms out. "It's obvious. Go home and get them. That's where you were for the last hour, right? At home? Weren't you at home?" he asked in Arlene's face.

"I can't go home," Brenda said.

"We ain't goin' home. We goin' in there."

"No, you're not. I'm not going to let you."

"Where we gonna go?" Arlene asked.

"I do not care. If you don't have notes explaining why you were late you are not my responsibility. You can go where you want to, do what you want to, but my advice to you is you go home and get the notes. Today or tomorrow, it doesn't matter to me."

"I can't," Brenda said, pleading.

"Then go spend the day with Mr. Bernbach. But don't come tomorrow without those notes and don't come late or I simply won't let you in my classroom."

"I ain't gonna spend no day..."

"I don't care what you're gonna do, Arlene. I'm finished talking to you."

He went into the classroom and closed and locked the door. He walked quickly over to his desk, got out his notebook and a pen.

"That's why we're not having your contest," Neil said to Bianca. *God damn fucking little bitches,* he added to himself.

He walked quickly back to the door, where he wrote:

Mr. Bernbach,

Arlene and Brenda came late to class, arrived at 9:47 a, without a note. I sent them home in accordance with memo of underst between union and admin. No child is to be admitted to class late or after absence

Neil Riley 11/3/69. 6-306

Neil tore the note out of his notebook and jotted out a copy for himself. It was a mess, but it pretty much did what he meant it to do. Meanwhile, his students, the entire crew, watched him in total silence. It was probably the longest period of silence that had prevailed in this classroom since they had entered it two months ago. There was a slam of hands against the door. That would be Arlene. Neil didn't turn to look. He hoped she didn't break one of the glass panels, but then again, if she did and really cut herself badly maybe that would wake everybody up. Why, with a cut violent child even Mrs. Bane might get involved. If Mrs. Robin got involved Neil was prepared to tell her to butt out.

"You can all get out your math books. Pauli, would you get the math test papers that are on my desk and give them out to row 4. And Sheri, if you move, I'll throw you out of here in a heartbeat and I won't let you back in unless you show up with your mother."

"Damn, Mr. Riley, you be bad," Clyde said.

"Please don't call out. Look at your grades. As you can see we need to do a little work on fractions." There was more slamming on the door. "Some of you actually did fairly well. You'll see. I'm going to put the passing papers on the bulletin board. Actually Marta will do that for me."

The slamming had stopped. Neil turned, unlocked the door and stepped into the hall. The two girls were nowhere to be seen. Down the hall past Robin's door and around the corner at the top of the stairwell, that was where you hid while you licked your wounds and planned your next move.

He closed and locked the door and still standing there said, "Morris, take this note to Mr. Bernbach, please. I want you to use the middle stairway and I expect you to go straight to Bernbach. Put the note in your pocket and take the bathroom pass. I expect you back here in fifteen minutes max. Okay?"

"Yes, Mr. Riley. I'll be right back."

"Good." Then he did what he had promised himself he would do. "There was only one person who got a perfect grade on this test, and that was Clyde Johnson. Congratulations, Mr. Johnson. Not only did you get a hundred percent on the regular test but you got all the problems from material we haven't covered yet. You are our most brilliant mathematician."

"Yeah, right," Clyde said, smiling.

Pedro was staring down at his paper.

"Second only to Clyde was Pedro Rodriguez, who messed up on one problem. Right, Pedro?"

"Yeah, I see." He snapped his fingers. "I knew that didn't look right."

"Can I see what he did?" Clyde asked.

"I didn't change 17/16ths to the whole number."

"Is that all? Ah, come on, Mr. Riley," Clyde said.

"Does anybody know what they talkin' about?" Sheri asked.

"Me," Bianca said. "I got that wrong, too. What's wrong with 17/16ths? Why not just leave it?" Bianca asked.

Neil was stunned. They were actually discussing the test.

"It's in the directions," Pedro said.

Would anyone else want to be clued in?

Pauli asked, "What problem number yawl talkin' about?"

Why did this have to happen now? Here he was standing with his back to a locked door, two of his biggest headaches wandering the halls, Sheri ready to go through the ceiling, and his students decide to have a discussion about the math test? There was no justice.

"Number 23. You got to go to the whole number," Pedro said.

Just then there was a knock on the door. It was Morris, who came in breathing hard.

"Mr. Bernbach got Arlene and Brenda and he said tell you he comin' up to see you."

"You gave him my note?"

"Of course." Morris looked up at him as he sat down, wounded that Neil doubted him. "I told you I would."

"I know. I know. It's really important, that's all. I appreciate what you did. Thank you," Neil said, realizing now that Morris had gone on a dangerous mission for him and was still at risk. Arlene might see Morris as a traitor and want to retaliate. It was something Neil had to keep in mind as this situation played itself out.

There was another knock on the door. Mr. Bernbach. And when Neil opened the door he saw that Arlene and Brenda were standing right behind him.

"Want to tell me what's going on here?" Bernbach said.

"Wait. First." Neil held up his palm in the stop position. "Want to ask that question again? One professional to another."

Bernbach looked at him for a moment, then said, "I received a note from you and a minute later two of your students showed up at my door."

"I guess you were the lesser of two evils," Neil said. "I actually told them to go home."

"You told them to go home. On what authority?..."

"According to the memorandum of understanding between the Administration and the Union, no teacher should admit a student into his or her classroom after an absence without a note signed by a parent explaining the absence." Tobin had discussed this memorandum at the last union meeting. She wasn't actually certain it had been implemented. It may have been something merely proposed. Neil didn't care. He was ready to bet it all, draw for the inside straight and walk away naked if he lost. It felt good to be in this place. He was fed up and enjoying every minute of it. "I can give you exact details of the date, paragraph and wording of the memorandum if it becomes necessary," he lied, "but I'm quite certain I've correctly stated the memorandum's intent. Arlene and Brenda attempted to enter my classroom at approximately 9:50 this morning, one hour and twenty minutes after they were supposed to be here. I noted the exact time in my memo to you. Neither of these students had a note explaining her absence. I informed them I would not admit them to my classroom without the required note and advised them to take steps to obtain said note."

"Said note? Why are you talking like that? Jesus, I'm never going to hire another lawyer as long as I live."

"I'm not responsible for Arlene and Brenda. I will not be responsible for either of them until I receive a note signed by a parent explaining their absence. These two girls can't come into my classroom. Is that clear?"

"That memorandum was because of the situation at Garibaldi."

Neil knew this was true. On any given day at Garibaldi Junior High School there was a fifty percent absenteeism rate. He had heard that twenty-five percent of the students stayed home out of fear for their physical well-being. The other twenty-five percent wandered the halls robbing, molesting and mugging anyone (including teachers considered vulnerable) they caught in the halls during classes. If someone was injured severely enough to cause the district problems an attempt was made to hold the classroom teacher of the perpetrator responsible rather than the administration. The UFT wanted the memo to address this problem. Bernbach seemed to assume it had been implemented. Or in his own inimitable way he too was bluffing. So you had two scam artists trying to out con each other. Educators extraordinaire.

"The memorandum fits this situation exactly," Neil said. "These students were absent from my class and they have not given me the required excuse slip. Therefore, they should not be in my class."

"Why are you doing this? And what's with all the 'students were absent' and 'required excuse slip?' These kids were probably hanging out in the bathroom and came to class a little late."

"I have no idea where these girls were and apparently neither do you."

"You know what, Mr. Riley, this discussion is over. These kids belong in your class. That's it."

Neil stood with his back to the door of 306. "These students are not coming into my room without an excuse signed by their parents. I expect you to back me up on this since I am following the edicts of the administration. However, if you want to make an issue of it, I'll go to the union and to the PA. In the meantime, I'm telling you, they are not coming into my classroom."

The two men stood glaring at each other.

Bernbach sighed. "Okay. I'll take them downstairs. But I won't forget this."

"YOU WON'T FORGET IT BECAUSE I WON'T LET YOU!" Neil shouted.

Bernbach studied Neil's face. "You've got to ease up, Neil."

"I've got to finish a math lesson and take my kids to science," Neil said.

As Bernbach led the girls away Neil heard Brenda cry, "I can't go home, Mr. Bernbach. I just can't."

"Neil, when you deliver your class to Mrs. Perry come and see me, okay?"

"I'll be there."

Chapter 4:

Dirty Little Secrets

In the hall: on the way to the science classroom Charles stumbled along like a drunk, veering from one side of the hall to the other. Both Clyde and Norbert hung back to stay behind him.

"Keep them moving," Neil told Pedro. He stood and waited for the back of the line to pass and then walked along beside Charles. "It's going to be all right. I promise. Anything happens I'll be down at Bernbach's. You come down and sit outside his office. Okay?"

Charles kept on stumbling along.

Neil looked over at Clyde. "Okay?"

Clyde pressed his lips together. It was a gesture like gritting his teeth. "Okay," he said, annoyed.

Clyde understood what he was really asking. *Do you care what happens to Charles? Do you? If you do, help me out.* And Clyde was forced to admit he did and would. That was Clyde's dirty little secret. He cared what happened to people, especially the vulnerable. He didn't like to see them get hurt. If he could, he would try to protect them.

Knowing this, using it, Neil felt as Bernbach must feel: manipulative, guilty, gleeful, justified.

His class, led by Pedro, stopped at the door of 302. There was some funny business between Sammy and Pauli, but Morris stopped it. Neil walked quickly to the front of the line.

Mrs. Perry was standing astride the open door. She favored black short-sleeved pullover blouses and colorful ankle-length skirts. She was tall for a woman and at first glance slender. But Neil's eye went quickly to her ample love handles and large stomach, the latter spilling over the top of her skirt as if she had just swallowed some animal and was slowly digesting it. She had a strong nose, sharp brown eyes that were magnified by the lenses of her eyeglasses and a protruding lower lip she kept moist with a flicking tongue. Her hair, dyed a very black black, puffed out in two buns at the sides of her head. She wore large dangling earrings, bright red plastic circles, the reflected red moving up and down the silver temples of her eyeglasses. She moved slightly from side to side as she faced Neil in the doorway, as if to keep him and his unappetizing bunch from entering her classroom.

Why was this happening? What should the classroom teacher do? Neil would have loved to present these questions to that lovely silver-haired woman who had taught the basic prep class in his training program. The professor was a principal in a school similar to this one, but otherwise in no way resembled Bane. The class was called, *The Elementary Classroom: What to Expect* and he could hear her asking, in her decidedly New Yawk accent, "Formulate da problem."

Neil would say, *Okay, a special subjects science teacher has determinedly embarrassed a boy in front of his whole class. She has told him out loud that his behavior is unacceptable. To the boy (it took me a while to understand this, but eventually I got it) his behavior is an essential survival mechanism. He lives in a cave, which he does because he has to. From his point of view suddenly for no reason this woman wants to drag him out and flay him alive.*

I should add that, much as he might want to, the classroom teacher, for purposes of the story let's call him Neil Riley, can't portray himself as the righteous hero in this scenario. His own initial feelings about the boy, we can name him Charles, resembled those of the special subjects teacher, who we'll call Mrs. Perry. To Perry, as he had been to Neil, Charles is a needless burden on an already intolerable assignment; he is a filthy, unwanted disruption. Only slowly, far too slowly, does our Neil learn the boy desperately wants help, is cooperative enough if allowed to keep his cover and responds with giddy shivers to any sort of friendly acknowledgement and with giggling joy to praise.

All right, but now that the classroom teacher, Neil, has become an enlightened authority on this damaged child, the professor/principal would surely ask, *with it seems a reasoned, if rudimentary plan of action, shouldn't he share his insights with Perry in a friendly meeting?*

Fuck that, Neil thought. *She should have known better.*

Standing face-to-face with Perry, Neil's own dirty little secret shook him with its clarity. He didn't want a solution. He wanted revenge.

Perry undulated in the doorway of her classroom, ready to strike. "Is he here?" she asked.

Neil was ready. He looked to the rear of his line. "Hey, Charles, come mere, buddy."

"Wait. What are you doing?" Perry asked.

Charles shuffled up to Neil, who put his arm around him. Neil was always struck by the similarly between the way Charles and the cat reacted when he touched them. First they froze, then relaxed and, shivering, offered themselves up to the contact. They smelled the same, too, that sour sweet festering smell of unrinsed garbage cans in the back of *Connie's Corner* where Neil had thrown the day's scraps, a smell seasoned with just a touch of urine.

"Charles has agreed to sit in the back with his jacket over his head. He understands that if he doesn't call out or make a disturbance, you won't mess with him."

"I won't tolerate such behavior," she said. "Who do you think you're talking to?"

"Mrs. Perry, you don't get my point. I want my class, my *entire* class, to have science. If you don't want them, we'll get Bernbach to switch us to Johnson," which was unlikely because too many teachers had already requested this and Johnson's schedule was full. Even so Perry wouldn't want to have yet another teacher trying to dump her.

"You know very well that's not necessary."

"That's good. That's good. Excuse me." Neil, his arm still around Charles, edged past Perry and into the room. "Go find a seat."

Charles moved quickly to the back of the room, sat down at a desk near the rear window and covered his head with his jacket.

"Now just a minute, Mr. Riley."

"It's gonna be okay. I promise you. Just leave him alone. It's gonna be all right."

"I'm not going to tolerate any misbehavior from that boy."

In a nod to his former lovely silver-haired professor he said, "He'll be quiet as a mouse. Seriously. You just leave him alone. He needs to have a cover. I'm working on it. He'll be fine. I have to go. When you take them down to lunch let Clyde and Norbert handle Charles. Okay?" Then: "Hey, buddy," he called out and Charles actually peeked at him. "You take care now."

With the same cool step he used to saunter past a gang on the street, he strolled off to his next confrontation, with Bernbach.

"How come you don't have to do no science? Shoot," Sheri called after him.

Neil turned back and shrugged, flattered, as if in spite of everything Sheri considered him one of the class and felt he should be tortured by Perry right along with the rest of them. Well, Sheri might forgive him his trespasses but it was unlikely Perry would. And now Bernbach.

What a wonderful day.

Chapter 5:

Problems

In Mr. Bernbach's office: the door was open when Neil got there. Bernbach remained seated as Neil entered. He pointed to one of the two chairs facing his desk.

"Sit down, Neil."

They were folding chairs with black padded bottoms placed about a foot apart. Four more chairs like these were closed and stacked against the rear wall. The room was small, hardly big enough for the desk and these two chairs. A conference that included parents, the student and a teacher would be a tightly packed affair indeed.

There was a window behind Bernbach, with blinds that, it seemed to Neil, were always closed. On the wall to the visitor's left were Bernbach's diplomas, certificates and awards. On the right and back walls were pictures of turkeys and reindeer, a snowman and stick figures of girls jumping rope, a boy standing with his arms spread.

"I prefer to remain standing," Neil said.

"Oh, cut it out." He waved away Neil's resistance. "There are some things I need to tell you."

"Okay," Neil said. "Tell me. I'd still prefer to remain standing."

Bernbach took a deep breath and blew it out in a long patient discharge. "Suit yourself." He clasped his hands together. "So, how's Charles?"

"Charles?" Neil asked in turn. The tone and squinty face he used to let Bernbach know how exasperating and irrelevant the question was seemed very like one of Bianca's favorite tools. "He's Charles," Neil added. "He sits all day with his jacket pulled over his head. I don't know what to do with him," a statement that didn't feel truthful but was, very much so.

"He's staying in one place," Bernbach said, "taking in the situation. That's pretty good."

Actually Neil agreed. At least Charles had a desk, a place to be and even, improbably, a friend. Neil ached to tell Bernbach about Charles and Norbert, he wanted desperately to discuss the run-in with Perry, but any of that would suggest he wanted advice. Worse, it would look like he respected Bernbach's opinion. The thought darted across Neil's mind that he couldn't blame the man for not giving him support when he insisted on behaving like a stubborn brat. By the time Neil had recovered his equilibrium, reminding himself that no matter what, Bernbach shouldn't have dumped his worst problems on a first year teacher, he had sat down. He thought of jumping up again, but realized that would only call attention to his childishness.

A faint smile skipped across Bernbach's face, but he quickly changed his expression to a look of concern. He said in a soft, sympathetic voice, "Neil, I get the feeling this job may be too much for you. Is that so?"

Neil sat up straight, surprised by how hurt he felt, how insulted. He felt himself spiraling out of control. He wanted to challenge Bernbach to a fight, slap his face and walk out, lean across the desk and tell Bernbach to keep his condescending feelings to himself. He looked straight at Bernbach as he considered these options. Bernbach blinked then returned the stare.

After a noticeable pause Neil said, "Arlene and Brenda were over an hour late for class today. I won't, I can't admit them back into my classroom without a note from their parents explaining why they were late. I don't know where they were, I don't know what they were doing, I can't be responsible for their behavior or their well-being. If I admit them without a note I'm making myself responsible. I can't do that."

Bernbach drummed the fingers of his right hand on his desk. "If you keep this up Brenda's going to get kicked out of her house. She'll end up in foster care. Do you care about that?"

"Brenda knows more about that than I do. Does she care? How about you? You seem to know something. Do you care?"

"I care a great deal," Bernbach said. "I also care how you address me."

"Me, too," Neil said. "I care how you address me, too."

"Now you listen to me!"

"I will when you speak to me with respect!"

Once again they were staring at each other.

Bernbach sighed. "I could fire you this very minute."

"Why don't you? You really should, you know. I'm terrible at this. You just said so." He tilted his head, a coy Sheri. "Of course, I'm also brand new. And I've been given especially difficult children who shouldn't even be in that class. But, yeah, hey, I'm bad at this. For example, it baffles me that when I want to stop two of my students from coming in late every day, *every day,* I get no support whatsoever from my administrator. None. Nada."

Bernbach tilted his head slightly. "Okay," he said, "now hear me out. If anything I say sounds disrespectful, please, I want it understood, I'm not trying to insult you."

"Anymore," Neil said.

"Please, Neil." More softly, he repeated, "Please." He clasped his hands together and pressed them tightly. "First of all given that you're totally unprepared..."

Neil sprang forward.

"Wait, wait. It's the truth and you know it. You're totally unprepared. Now given that *fact* your class should be all over the halls, running out into the street, going nuts not just on you, but on all of us. One of these days we're going to get a substitute in one of the upper classes who's absolutely incompetent and you'll see what I mean. But you..." He held both hands together and aimed at Neil with his two pointer fingers. "Well, I don't quite know how you do it. I mean none of your students look particularly battered and yet there they are, in the classroom. That's enough right there for the rest of us. You keep your children in the classroom." As he relaxed his hands he said, "Okay, now listen. Brenda's father caught her mother in bed with another man. A mutual friend? I dunno. In the improbable way these things happen Brenda's father let the man go, then shot his wife, Brenda's mother, through the head. Brenda was a third grader. She was eight, nine. This was three years ago. She was a very bright, happy little person. Scrappy when she had to be, but basically cooperative, eager, easy to love. Her father is serving twenty to life for aggravated manslaughter. Why wasn't it murder? You're the lawyer. You tell me. But anyway, her aunt, her father's sister, took her in. Okay? With me so far? Her father's sister's husband wanted no part of this at the time and wants no part of it now. He didn't have kids and didn't want any. He agreed to this guardianship under duress. It happened all at once. Brenda was already there. But for him she's nothing but an emotional and financial burden. You send her home like this I guarantee he'll pull the plug. It's the kind of thing he's looking for."

"Brenda shoulda thought of this before she started coming in late every morning. She's just one of my problems. I've got a few others. Thirty-three to be exact. And as I said some of them are extra special. Rumor has it 6-306 is the place for extra special problems."

"Every class has its share of problems, Mr. Riley."

"Okay, so why is Brenda, who was in the top class last year, in the second class this year? Mrs. Robin couldn't handle her?"

"Brenda's aunt wanted to get her away from Sharon."

"So now she's in the clutches of Arlene? That's an improvement?"

"That's one of the ironies of the business. You think you've solved a problem and you've only created a new one."

"That's exactly what's happened here. You thought you had this patsy who didn't know his ass from his elbow and it turns out he's so crazy it don't matter. Neither of those girls is coming back into my classroom without a note from their parents, or guardians, as the case may be. I'm doing this in accordance with district policy. If they go someplace else, that's none of my business. They are not my responsibility."

"Brenda goes home at night and sits in her room. You've probably noticed she does her homework. She doesn't have anything else to do. She can't watch TV or listen to the radio, she can't talk to anyone on the phone. She most certainly can't go out."

"Sounds like foster care would be a blessing."

"You're not listening to me. She wouldn't go into a family. She'd go to a group home. The first night they'd strip her bare. They'd leave her nothing but her naked self. Then they'd take that away. She couldn't just hide. She'd either learn to fight, to the death, or she'd give in, be somebody's slave. Either way, she would not ever again be Brenda."

"Think they'll teach her to get to school on time?"

Bernbach breathed deeply. "What's the matter with you, Neil? I thought you were a mensch."

"What's the matter with me?" He asked the question to the empty chair next to him. "What's the matter with me?" he asked, turning back to Bernbach. "Maybe I'd like to feel that the solution to every problem isn't handle it yourself and, oh, by the way, here's another little problem I'd like you to handle. Okay, here's what I'd like. I'd like for Arlene to go to Knight, where she belongs, and for Brenda to go to Robin, where *she* belongs. Failing that, as long as they're in my classroom I expect them to abide by the district's rules, the school's rules, and when I insist on that, I'd like the administration, specifically the principal and the assistant principal, to back me up."

"What do you want?"

"*I just told you,*" Neil said, frustrated. "How could I be more explicit?"

"I meant specifically. Make an offer."

"I just did! Send Arlene to Knight. Send Brenda to Robin."

"Here's what I'll do. I'll take responsibility for Arlene and Brenda being late just to stop you from whining about it."

"Whining? You're the one who's not listening. I'm not whining. I'm telling you what I want."

"And I'm telling you what I'll do. I'll take responsibility for Arlene and Brenda being late."

"Explain to me what taking responsibility means."

"What do you think it means? It means I'll take responsibility."

"So Arlene and Brenda are going to spend their days in your office?"

"You're not listening to me. I'm really getting tired of this."

"I'm glad. So now maybe we'll get back to the subject. Are you going to see that Arlene and Brenda get notes from home?"

"I'm... You know what?"

"What?"

Bernbach stared at him.

"What?" Neil repeated.

"I'll give you a note for each girl, dated today, stating that I have been informed that she was late without an excuse, that this is a re-curring problem and that if it continues I will require her to come in with her parents for a conference with me before she is allowed back in the classroom. In return you will admit both these girls back into your classroom after lunch. If you do not, I will file charges against you with the district office and begin proceedings to have you fired. You can make whatever counter charges you want, but regardless of what the policy is on unexcused lateness, you exceeded your author-ity when you ordered those girls to leave the school grounds and I'm going to give you another note, also dated today, telling you that. The next time one of your children comes in late without an excuse, you send the child to me. You do not have the authority to send anyone home. Do you understand?"

"Yes."

"Another thing. You and I are not friends. You are Mr. Riley, I am Mr. Bernbach. Your employer is the City of New York, and as your supervisor I am the City's representative. Is that clear?"

"Yes."

"Arlene and Brenda are coming back into your class after lunch. Do you understand?"

"Yes, sir, Mr. Bernbach, *sir*."

"God. You know, Neil? Under no circumstances do you ever want to go into the army."

Chapter 6:

I'm Waiting

In Room 6-306: Javier was reading aloud from the social studies book when the three o'clock bell rang. Arlene, Clyde and Pauli all jumped up and ran to the back of the room to get their coats.

"Javier, stop reading please. We will wait until everyone is in his seat." Neil was standing with his back to the door.

"That's the bell, Mr. Riley," Morris said.

"Please don't call out, Morris. Look at the schedule. We did the math, although it took us most of the morning and we finally got through the reading."

"And went to lunch late," Sheri said.

"And went to gym late," Sammy said.

"We aren't leaving until we finish the schedule. We still have to do our social studies lesson."

"I'm leaving," Arlene said.

"We're waiting for you to sit down, Arlene."

Pauli, seeing that Clyde had sat back down, carrying his coat with him, did the same.

Neil decided to ignore the coats. "We're waiting for Arlene to sit down so we can continue the lesson."

"That man is crazeeee," Sheri said.

Arlene had marched up to Neil. "Get outta my way. I got to go home."

"You're much more likely to get there if you sit down and keep your mouth shut." Neil looked down at her, smiling. "I'm not going to let you leave."

"Sit down!" Sheri ordered.

Arlene turned on Sheri, who sat just behind Pauli in the front of the first row. "You shut your mouth."

Sheri smiled her wide sweet red and white smile, ready to run. Arlene used this encounter as an opportunity to move farther away from the front door and closer to her desk.

"He ain't gonna let us go till you sit down," Morris said.

"Who you talkin' to?" Arlene said, turning toward Morris.

Morris stood up. This was a first. "I'm just tryin' to explain. Don't get loud."

"Sit down, Morris. And stop calling out. Arlene, you should sit down, too. But we can wait. The building closes at 4:30. That's when we have to leave. If we don't finish the social studies by then, we'll pick it up tomorrow and start off even more behind."

"Sit down!" Clyde shouted. "Can't you see he means it?"

"Don't you be telling me what to do! Gaw. All right then." She sat down and gathered her coat around her angrily.

Neil waited a beat, then said, "Javier, please continue reading."

"'What is a dig?'" Javier read.

"You read that," Arlene snarled.

"Javier, please wait." Neil tilted his head with a hand cupped to his ear. "Any more smart remarks?"

"Yeah, less go home," Pauli said.

"Keep it up," Neil said. "I've got..." He looked at his watch. "... one hour and twenty minutes."

"Yawl shut up," Brenda cried. "I got to go home. I got to, Mr. Riley."

"Then don't call out. Ready?" He listened. Quiet. "Okay, Javier."

"'What is a dig?'"

At 3:35 Neil said, "Listen to me. I'm going to let you get your coats one row at a time. Quietly. Any pushing or shoving or calling out and we stop and everybody sits back down and we wait. If you don't believe me, try me."

He waited. Everyone in the room watched him. No one called out.

"Row three, since no one in your row got up to get their coats out of order, please get up now and get your coats and sit back down." He progressed through row four, then two, then one. They lined up quietly in the hall outside the room. Brenda had started to cry. Arlene looked at her and then glared at Neil, but didn't say anything. He moved them quickly down the stairs and when he shoved open the outside doors they bolted and ran, amid shouts of, "That man crazeee." "He meeeean." "I hate that man."

Back in 6-306 Neil sat down at his desk, exhausted. But almost immediately, restless, unable to relax, he got up and walked to the back of the room, then to the middle, between rows two and three, placing his hands on the backs of desks number five in each row. Who sat here? He had no idea. He went back to his desk and got his roster out. Cole Nelson and Javier Alvarez. In front of them were Morris Carter and Hector Viera. Harriet Wilson sat behind Cole, Constance Andrews behind Javier. He sat down at Constance's desk. Connie! His aunt's name. How could he not remember her when she had his aunt's name? What did she look like? It was November 3rd. He had been with this class since the 8th of September and he could not recall who Constance Andrews was. And Harriet Wilson, one of the smartest kids in the class, was just a presence, not someone he knew.

The boys he knew a bit better because he sometimes did the slow pitch for them when they played three-up. Cole was a pretty good hitter; Javier was fast and could catch a ball. Javier usually played first base. What could he remember about their schoolwork without looking at his records? Nothing.

Yet they all did their homework, kept their mouths shut and sat in the middle of the room. The average middle. They were there every day and he never saw them. He stood up and walked slowly back to his desk to collect his things. Surely there had been many days when he felt more miserable, but this one had to rank near the top.

"You look like I feel," Mrs. Robin said.

Neil started, then smiled. "You startled me."

She was standing in his doorway, weighed down by two full shopping bags, one in each hand.

"I'll carry those to your car if you want," he offered. "Just let me put on my coat and get my briefcase."

She set her bags down, but frowned dubiously when he picked up his own jammed briefcase. "Who's going to carry that?" She pointed at his bag.

"Me," he said. "I can manage two bags in one hand."

"Five years ago I would have been outraged by your offer, sir. But that was five years ago. I usually get one of my boys to help me, but I had some decorations I wanted to put up and completely forgot about this stuff when I took my class down." Then she pointed at his windows. "You'd better close those or Mac will have a fit."

"You're absolutely right." He quickly closed the three windows that were open at the bottom and used the pole to close the three that were open at the top.

As they were walking to the stairs she said, "I know that stuff is heavy, but my back goes out at the drop of a hat these days and I'd rather see you struggle a little than end up in spasms for a week."

"It's not a problem," Neil said between breaths.

"I hear through the grapevine you've been out there bothering Mrs. Perry."

"Uh-oh. Better tell me what you heard."

"She complained to Judy that you were insolent with her and that it was a union matter because it was a question of you abusing other teachers."

"Judy?"

"Tobin. Gym teacher? Shop Steward?"

"Oh, okay. Remember I ain't been here since the olden days."

"I keep forgetting that you're just out of sixth grade yourself. Okay. I know how Judy operates. She probed a bit and found out that you insisted Mrs. Perry take Charles with the rest of your class. Judy then told her, and I can tell you from personal experience she didn't stand on ceremony, that it sounded to her like you were just asking Perry to do her job. I know about this because Judy broke her sworn oath never to speak to me again to tell me. I don't know if Perry was stupid enough to complain to Bernbach, but since she took it up with her shop steward I suspect she knew Bernbach would have thrown her out of his office. Judy didn't tell you all this herself because that would have been a violation of Perry's privacy. Why telling it to me, a sworn enemy, isn't a violation of Perry's privacy will remain one of life's mysteries. I do suspect she wanted to let me know she knew about our..." Mrs. Robin pointed a finger back and forth between them. "...conversations and approved of them. She is a teacher first, and like every real teacher in this school wants you to get as much help as we can give you."

"What should I do about Perry?"

"Nothing. I'm assuming you were exceedingly diplomatic. You were weren't you?"

"Well, maybe. Maybe not."

"In the future I suggest you do what you think is right, but lead with that truly winning, if rare, smile of yours."

They had made it downstairs. She held the door open for him. He heaved himself through.

"This is embarrassing, Mr. Riley. I shouldn't let you do this, but I have to."

His left arm, with which he was carrying both her bag and his briefcase, had begun to tremble with weariness, but he felt that if he stopped to take a break she wouldn't let him continue. "It's all right," he insisted.

Finally they made it to her car and he heaved her bags onto the back seat as she directed.

"John, Mr. Robin, wants me to retire," she said. She put her hands on her hips. "I said, 'Then what would I do?' I'll tell you what he *wants* me to do. Stay home and clean house and fix his dinner, which by the way I already do. But he can't complain how hard his day is. How bad the weather was. He just has to bury his face in the sports section and keep his big mouth shut." She shut the car door. "Let me ask you something."

"Shoot," Neil said. He braced himself for some prying question about his personal life that he really didn't want to talk about. But he couldn't possibly say no to her.

"Are you ready for Parents' Night?"

"I'm sorry?"

"Has someone talked to you about Parents' Night? Have you thought about your presentation?"

"My presentation?"

"Mr. Riley! Good heavens!" She put her head in her hands and shook it, growling.

"Are you okay?"

"Just a little frustrated. It's on the calendar and I guess they figured if you had any questions you'd ask them."

"They in this case being?"

"Never mind. You'll probably get a reminder like the rest of us in Monday's handouts. Next Wednesday is Parents' Night. From 7 to 8:30. Parents are invited to come in and visit their children's classrooms. The teachers—that's you, in case you didn't know—are expected to be there in their Sunday best with a little presentation about their curriculum and their goals and then to meet individually with the parents who want that. Wear that nice blue suit of yours and keep your jacket and tie on."

"You're shitting me!" He reached out helplessly. "I'm sorry. I didn't mean to say that."

"You don't know a thing about this do you?"

It wasn't lost on Neil that the importance of this information outweighed his egregious use of profanity. This was fucking serious. "You're right. I don't know a thing about this. Nothing."

"Okay, here's what you need to do. Prepare a little speech, short, ten minutes at the most. You say what you've covered in math so far and what you intend to cover. Then you explain your language arts program. Then have the folders ready for all your kids so you can talk to their parents. You know. Who's your child? They'll probably tell you right off anyway. Then you tell them little Pedro's strengths. What you really want to do is to get them to talk about little Pedro. What you want to do is to listen carefully. You'll learn volumes. *Volumes.* We'll talk about this some more tomorrow."

"You better believe we will."

"I do have to go. Mr. Robin really does expect to have his dinner ready when he gets home, even though his commute is one mile and mine is four through downtown traffic." She looked at his face. "Seriously, now, you'll do fine. I know you will."

On the bus he sat biting his lip, pulling at his chin, rubbing his forehead, scratching his head, massaging his temples. He looked like a man having a nervous breakdown. People getting on the bus and moving to the rear where he sat took one look at him and turned and moved back up toward the front. *A presentation?* he thought. *My language arts program? My curriculum? Who is your child?*

Part Three:

Parents' Night 1969

Chapter 1:

Let He Who Is Without Sin

In Room 6-308: Neil was struck as always by the contrast between his plain old classroom and her vivid space. Over the blackboard at the front of her room were ever changing pictures related to the social studies program. This month, pictures of the pyramids and of digs at various sites in Egypt. Other pictures, mostly by students, lined the long wall next to the hall. These were seasonal, related this month to harvest and Thanksgiving. In the back at each corner were study desks with reference materials on the shelves. Next to one was a bookcase with an extensive library of novels, stories, science books and subject related comics. Next to the other was her famous tomato plant. The room drew you in, seductively asking you to come here, look at that. What's over there? Come see.

Mrs. Robin was sitting, flawlessly straight, at her back table. She looked up at him over her reading glasses when he came in. There was an inward focus, a care, in the way she laid her book on the table.

"I hoped you would drop by. This will be our last chance for a long lunch this week."

"They would have to be shooting in the halls to keep me away. Parents' Night? Next Wednesday? One week from today. I'm thinking I'll probably get the flu. It's the day after Veterans Day. Two days off."

"First things first, Mr. Riley. In that brown bag over there?... Right! That one."

"What's on the menu?"

"Honey-cured ham on Bavarian black bread with some home-made cole slaw. There's a container of my string beans, too, lightly steamed. And a fork." She made as if looking into a bag and twirled her finger to indicate he should look for it.

"You know I can't eat until we talk."

"Are you expressing feelings of anxiety?"

"Whatever gave you that idea?"

"In that other bag, the shopping bag with the handles? Get me the loose-leaf notebook."

He handed her the notebook and she flipped it open, pulled out several pages and handed them to him. Under the heading *Meeting Your Parents* was a printed outline of the presentation he needed. It was in three parts, Math, Language Arts and Questions for Your Parents. He studied it avidly, the points to be covered popping off in his mind like pills of relief. He hadn't allowed himself to realize how helpless he felt until he had some means with which to confront the problem; the problem being his complete and utter ignorance. He was sitting opposite her at the table when he looked up. He hadn't known until then that he had sat down.

"Oh, my God. That's thanks to my existential deity, not a vain curse," he said quickly. He shook the paper. "I can borrow this?"

"It's yours. I teach a couple of courses at Hunter and that's one of my handouts. *After* I've had my students prepare their own, of course. I'm making a special exception in your case."

"I'll feel like such a fraud. This comes from years of experience."

"At least you won't have to get the flu."

"Okay," he said, picking up his sandwich. "But..."

"Why don't you concentrate on your lunch, Mr. Riley?"

When his mouth wasn't completely stuffed, still chewing, he asked, "Could I be Neil? I mean, could you call me Neil? At least in private?"

"I could except that I have one of you at home even more adamantly male than you and he would not take kindly to me being on a
first name basis with another man—regardless of the circumstances.
You are a student whom I mentor. Can you accept that?"

"Yeah, well, I guess, since it's the truth. Still, that's pretty old-
fashioned, don't you think?"

She stared at him.

"I don't mean any disrespect," he said hastily.

"He's a good man, a very good man, a good husband, a father to
his children and a deacon in the church. And *that*," she said emphatically, "is all we are going to say about *that*."

"Yes, Mrs. Robin."

She smiled. "Good." She moved to push her book to one side but
suddenly winced, sucking air. She closed her eyes and sat very still,
drawn into a rigid pause.

Instinctively Neil's hand had gone out to her and he sat like that,
motionless, his hand outstretched, while he studied her shamelessly,
beginning with her closed eyelids, patient if not calm, and her long
black lashes. It was one of those intervals that in retrospect would
seem to have lasted much longer. Her mouth was clamped tight,
her forehead creased with three long lines, her attention apparently
focused on simply staying still. There was nothing white, European,
about her features or her color. She had a broad nose and thick lips, a
strong chin line and prominent cheekbones. Her skin was very dark,
a rich warm darkness, and Neil, hardly admitting it, wanted to place
his palm on her face, on her neck. She was a proud strong beautiful
woman, a Negro woman, she would tell you, with enormous presence, he would say. Regal. He knew he was not supposed to see
her in such pain, and even though he did see it he was supposed to
pretend he hadn't, but he cared. How much he cared only added to
his distress.

"Mrs. Robin?"

"I'll be all right," she said. "My back is in spasm and when I move a certain way it feels like someone jabbed me with an ice pick."

"Jesus!"

"No," she said, with a slight smile, "He wouldn't do such a thing."

"Well, but maybe he could cut you some slack."

"Young man!" She looked at him sternly, then let go. "I know how you feel about my religion. But if I'm expected to tolerate your godless existentialism I expect you to tolerate my devotion to Jesus Christ and the Holy Spirit."

"Yes, ma'am. I will. I do. I'm sorry. I'm just worried about you. Truly, I'm sorry."

"Good. A little contrition is a healthy emotion in one such as you. Anyway," she sighed, "you're not to worry. Back spasms aren't fatal, just intolerable."

"I played football in high school. I know about back spasms."

"Would you please eat? And then I suggest we run over my little handout to see how you should adapt it."

"Okay, but you know what? It's still not going to hide the fact that I don't know diddly. The parents come in, I stand up and *boom* I go running out the door."

"I seriously doubt that will happen. You'll be prepared."

"Yeah, prepared. Prepared to pretend I'm a real teacher. It's embarrassing. Clyde and Pedro are better at math than I am. Harriet keeps asking me about the books she reads and I haven't read a single one of them. I think maybe I read *Peter Pan*, or saw the play. I'm not sure. *The Secret Garden*? What's that?"

"You have a treat in store."

"Every day I learn how little I know, how little I teach, how inadequate I am to this incredible task. I can't stand up there and tell them I'm actually teaching. I can't."

"I can tell you you're fine till the cows come home. That's not the point, really. The point is you've got to stop thinking about yourself and start thinking about your job."

"Okay. Tell me."

"What do you want for your children?"

"What?"

"What do you want for your children? Who do you want them to be when they grow up?"

"Oh, wow, I don't know. I want... What kind of question is that? But, okay, yeah, I want them to be able to take care of themselves. I want them to know they can handle the crap that's bound to come their way. I want them to hold their heads high, get decent jobs, pay the rent, have loving relationships, have a lot of interesting activities going on around them. A warm safe place to live, food on the table, people they love, the ability to think about what's happening to them, to get what they want; that's what I want for them."

"Why, yes, I think you've gotten most of it," she said, quietly clapping. "Though I didn't hear anything about service to the community."

"Service to the community?" He smirked. "That's what you do instead of hard time, right?"

She stared at him for a very long time, making him very very uncomfortable.

"I don't put up with smart remarks from my students."

"All right, no smart remarks, just straight talk. We all believe in freedom of speech here, don't we?"

"The abuse of freedom is usually a harbinger of its collapse."

"This is just a frank inquiry. Why on earth should my kids care about their community?"

Mrs. Robin took a deep breath and closed her eyes. Neil, who with each one of his ill-advised remarks shouted at himself, 'shut up!' still could not stop the acidic contempt he felt for feel-good pabulum. He knew that on her side she was in some manner counting to ten.

"The children in this community are more fortunate than most."

"What?" Neil said, screwing up his face in mock amazement.

"Many of the children in this school have lived in this neighborhood all their lives. Most of them come from stable environments where at least one person has a job. Some of them come from homes where there is a Mommy and a Daddy. This provides opportunities for our school. And the school is stable, functional. You have no idea about the poverty that exists in New York City or how it can overwhelm a school."

"I know from poverty."

Again she looked at him, studied him, unabashed, as if in some way he belonged to her and she was trying to think how to arrange him. A tuck here, a pat there, but surely a firm slap right here! She made a long loud raspberry with her lips. A mouth fart. From Mrs. Robin? "You don't know from poverty."

"I know from poverty," he said again.

After a pause she nodded. "Maybe you do. That would explain some things. But somebody took you in. A big tall handsome specimen with brains, a B.A. and two years of law school. Somebody helped."

"Yes, they did... She did," he corrected. "In defiance of a whole community."

"She?"

"My uncle's wife. Yes, she took me in. Anything I got, I got from her. Get. Still. She's still there."

"God bless her. She thinks about what's best for you?"

"Always. Whatever I need, she gives it to me." *Anything,* he thought. *Food, clothing, money, whatever I want, she gives it to me. Almost. She wouldn't give me sex.*

"Then if only for her on Parents' Night you need to think about what's best for your children. You can give your little performance." She pointed to the handout. "But that's not your real job. Your real job is to look and listen, to learn as much as you can. Forget about what you are and aren't doing. Put it in a basket and toss it out the window. Think about this. In a few months you'll be out of those children's lives forever. Their parents, on the other hand, will still be there; which for the most part is a good thing. For the most part. Unfortunately not all parents were made in Heaven. To the extent that you can you need to be aware of what your children are coping with at home, you need to think how you can assist them with those relationships."

"Oh, come on. That's too much to ask."

"It most certainly is, but even so the children will demand it. The question is whether you're going to deny that and push through with your eyes shut tight or whether you're going to try to be as sensitive as you possibly can to the fact that for this brief period you are father mother brother sister friend to every child in your classroom. For this brief time you are one of the most important people in their lives, perhaps the most important."

"You've really got me scared now."

"Well, you shouldn't be. Deeply humbled and respectful and as conscious as you can possibly be of your children's needs. That's what you need to be."

"Okay, so I pretend I know what I'm doing. I say I'm moving them through their numbers, I say I'm getting them to read. I pay close attention and try to find out who I'm talking to. But what if Clyde's parents come in? Arlene's? I mean, I need to know why Arlene, John and Clyde were held back. What was that all about? So they weren't reading on grade level; neither is three-fourths of the sixth grade, right? I mean, they must have been about average given the population. Bernbach says they were told if they went to summer school and got their reading up to grade level they could go on to Garibaldi. Which, of course they didn't do. Grade level? I coulda told them it was a hoax. They might improve, but they aren't going to get to grade level. Arlene says they were promised they would be promoted if they went to summer school. Period. No strings attached. I understand she's not the most reliable reporter, but she must have been given some enticement. Arlene? Summer school? There's no way. She had to have been promised something. I don't think I've been given the full story. You're always defending Bernbach, but he conned them and he's conning me."

As he took another bite of his (*her*) sandwich he looked up to see that tears were streaming down Mrs. Robin's face. He chewed quickly, then washed down what remained with coffee.

"Mrs. Robin?"

"That's not fair. Ron, Mr. Bernbach was adamantly opposed to holding them back and yet he's the one who has to take the blame. It was Bane's decision. Yes, but let he who is without sin cast the first stone. I went along with it. Last year Travers had the top class. She had Clyde because she was the one who could handle him. She probably just didn't have it in her to go one more round for Clyde. I had the three class, the equivalent of Knight's group. Arlene and John were in my group. Think how much fun that was for me. Knight had your group, the two class. They'd never give him the top class and he wouldn't accept it if they did. Too much work. Colby, who's at Seward now, had the four class."

She stared at him. She seemed to think she'd explained the situation.

He shook his head. "Did I miss something?"

"Bernbach did not want them held back."

"Well, yeah. I mean, what I asked was why were they held back?"

"And the answer is: they shouldn't have been! *Okay*?"

Neil raised his hands palms up in surrender. "Okay, okay."

Quickly, exasperated, as if to a badgering cross-examination, she blurted, "Bane wanted to please District. I wanted to... to make it hard for Bernbach to make life hard for me."

203

"I am totally confused."

"You know there were strikes through the fall of 1968."

"I have been told that in many ways by many different people."

"The first strike was at the beginning of school, for two weeks. Three teachers crossed the picket lines. I'm sure you know all about that."

"Yep. Know all about it. Sort of."

"And of course the kids showed up. Why wouldn't they? School's supposed to start. So there's Bane, Bernbach, Shirley Mayer, Janice Smith and me. No one from the office would cross the lines. Mac's union got the UFT's permission to cross because of safety issues, but he's not about to work with kids. Five adults, six hundred children. Can you imagine? We herded them into the auditorium. Bernbach didn't want us there. He's pro-union, adamantly so. He thought we should have stayed out. I know that because unlike me he's not one to beat around the bush. He said, and I quote: 'Don't you know you're cutting your own throat every time you cross those lines?'"

"He had a point."

"It was bedlam. After the first day we did the purportedly responsible thing—no, it was unequivocally responsible; it just felt like a failure—we sent the children home with a note explaining that for safety reasons it was better if they did not attend during the strike. Then a deal was struck. As long as the City and the UFT continued to negotiate in good faith teachers would stay on the job. This lasted about two weeks and the UFT went out again claiming the City was negotiating in bad faith. The children who showed up this time were the ones whose parents were militantly opposed to the strike or who had no place else to go or whose parents simply didn't know that anything was going on. Charles, for example, showed up every single day, if only because the breakfast and lunch he gets at school may be the only meals he gets and the picket lines and signs and whatnot were just more weird paraphernalia these crazy people put up to make his hard life harder." Her voice was strangely flat, without affect, but tears were running down her cheeks. She took a tissue out of the box of tissues she kept on the table.

Neil thought that if he had a box of tissues on his back table within an hour half of them would be all over the room and the rest would have disappeared.

"Mrs. Robin, you don't have to..."

"Yes, I do. I have to tell you this. You're right. It's something you should know. Nothing got done that first semester. About this time last year we were finally giving out books. But even that was chaotic. Mac had thrown all the deliveries into the supply closet. What does he know about readers? The strain on teachers was unbearable. Very good teachers believed fervently the union was justified in its demands. For very good reasons. We are grossly underpaid. Classroom size was forty. The UFT wanted thirty. They finally settled on thirty-six. Anyone knowledgeable who could look you in the eye and tell you thirty-six children to a class is an acceptable agreement is either cynically indifferent to the truth or in deep denial. And yet with each passing day teachers went marching militantly up and down in front of our school the chances for our having a decent year came closer and closer to zero. Things didn't begin to settle down until after the Christmas break."

"Okay."

"Okay, what? Okay, old lady, it's obvious you aren't going to answer my question? Okay, just stop beating around the bush and tell me what happened? Okay, I'll tell you. If things were bad at our school can you imagine what they were like at Garibaldi? What they should have done was close that school down. Rethink the whole junior high school program. No school would have been better than what they had after the strike. Once again they denied the problem. There was no school at Garibaldi last year, only a terrifying chaos.

"At the end of the year the call came down from district. It was very hush-hush. Don't let it leak to the papers. Hold back your worst behavior problems. So..." She enumerated them with her fingers as she said, "Arlene, John and Clyde were held back. They were told it was because of their reading scores." She made a face. "As you've pointed out they're about average for the population we're talking about. If the decision was based on reading scores at least sixty children should have been held back before them. They knew something was suspicious, but they never got a straight story. As I said, Bernbach fought it."

"That's no surprise. He didn't want to deal with them another year."

"What is your problem with that man? Is this some father figure thing? He fought it because he knew it would damage the children." She wiped her cheeks. She had recovered some of her verve. "And now he's the one who has to pick up the pieces. And he's too honorable to do the 'I told you so' number. And too busy dealing with them another year."

"I can see singling Arlene and John out for their behavior. But Clyde? Because he's proud? Because he's stubborn? He's a pain in the ass... I'm sorry. How can I put this? Clyde can wear on one's nerves, shall we say, but that's not like Arlene's constant annoying frustrating demanding irritating obnoxious persistently out of control, did I mention annoying? behavior."

Mrs. Robin said, "Almost every day that he came to school last year Clyde got into a fight. He cut school at least once a week, probably a lot more. I didn't have him and I didn't want him. He was put in Travers' class, the top class, where the children's academic abilities could only exacerbate his feelings of inadequacy. He was put there because Travers loved him and could deal with him. She still loves him. And he loves her. He was very protective of her. On the days he was there I'm sure some of the fights were because someone made fun of her. Bernbach couldn't put him in with Travers this year. It would have been unfair to Clyde. And you want to know something funny?"

"Oh, yeah, absolutely. Ha ha. Tell me something funny."

"I think you were hired because Bernbach saw who you are and sensed you could work with these children. Clyde hasn't had a single fight this year. It's a minor miracle. Maybe because he knows he'd have to deal with you first? But if he's afraid of you, why is he here every day? And he's working. You've said so."

"Why would that be?" Neil asked. Then, ashamed of the anguish in his voice, he sat upright, squared his shoulders and said, "Assuming this model citizen you've described has any resemblance to the real Clyde."

"Has he had any fights?"

"No."

"His attendance is good?"

"He's here every day," Neil said. Then he repeated, with a frustrated shake of his head, "Every single day."

"And he does his homework?"

"He's stronger on the math side than he is on the language arts side, but, yeah, he does his homework."

Mrs. Robin smiled. "I'm not prepared to say we've got ourselves a model citizen, but I will say we've got a boy who wants to impress his teacher."

"Mrs. Robin, that is such bull..." Neil swallowed, made a circular motion with his chin and came out with, "fooey. That is bull fooey in the nth degree."

Mrs. Robin was peering at him, waiting, he was sure, for his capitulation. Did she really expect him to agree that Clyde, who had it in for him from the moment they laid eyes on each other, wanted his approval?

"I... Whoa. You're really serious about this?"

"Oh, yes, I'm very serious. You and Clyde, two of a kind. My guess is Mr. Bernbach recognized this immediately. You both care deeply about people's feelings and for cultural and personal reasons are deeply ashamed of it. You must give Clyde time. More to the point, you must give yourself time. You'll see. All you need to do is to continue this intense..." Laughing, she suddenly threw her hands in the air as if scattering fate to the wind. "...truly odd journey you've begun."

"You think this is funny?" Neil cried, anguished.

"Oh, Neil, I'm not laughing at you. I'm enjoying the marvelous turns situations can take."

"The marvelous turns situations can take?" Neil repeated. "Marvelous? I don't have the slightest idea what I'm doing. Turns? My class is a shambles. Situations? Here's one. I'm ashamed to face their parents. Hi, I'm Mr. Riley, the fumbling bumbling idiot who keeps your kids from running wild in the streets. We don't do much in 6-306 but, man, we make a lot of noise not doing it."

"You have a full program in progress. Your class is academically challenged every day. Now here's the real wonder. You're a strong, attractive white man who can relate to these children. Black children. Brown children. Your children. You stand there every day pushing them, to think, to care, to cooperate, to learn, to be alive. You provide them with the safety to do that. And you certainly don't look down on them."

Neil shook his head. "You make it sound so tidy. And *successful*. But, you know, I can't help going back to that friggin', no, sorry, truly, sorry. That awful person Bernbach. He wanted to stick it to me, didn't he? Arlene, Clyde, John, Bianca, Sheri, Pauli."

"You are so anxious to do him in. But have you tried to see the world through his eyes? He has over six hundred children to worry about; twenty-four classroom teachers, twelve floaters, a less than active principal, a three story plant. It's happening every minute, while you sit there sipping your coffee. Think about what goes through his mind as he's driving to work. You took this job. He saw an opportunity. That's *his* job."

"It's about that time. We should be going," Neil said. He tightened his thermos and put it in his briefcase.

"You don't ever want to hear anything good about him, do you? You just can't accept the fact that if he's using you, it's because he should." Then in another tone of voice she said, "Neil."

He smiled at her use of his first name.

She corrected herself. "Mr. Riley."

"Mrs. Robin," he said, looking at her, still smiling.

"It's always going to be hard. And no doubt you have a lot to learn. And, yes, regardless of how distracted he is, Bernbach could give you more support. But you're doing it. You are. It's rather special, frankly."

"Thank you," he said, standing.

She stood, too, carefully, awkwardly. They remained opposite each other for a moment, paused, as if there were more to be said.

"We should go," Mrs. Robin said.

Chapter 2:

What You're Not Doing Is Just Fine

In *The Silver Moon Cuban-Chinese Restaurant*: a shadow fell across the table where Neil was sitting with the spelling assignment spread out in front of him. He looked up to discover a woman—in her mid-thirties, was his guess. She wore a navy beret over short brown hair and a dark brown trench coat with the belt cinched. Her only make-up was pale lipstick on full lips. She had hard lines across her forehead, a prominent nose and a steady gaze through brown eyes. At ease, with her chin less unyielding she would be sexy, but Neil's thought was, *Uh-oh, cop.*

"Mr. Riley?"

"Yes?"

"I'm Eva Maldonado. Bianca's mother?"

"Ah. Mrs. Maldonado. This is great." Not to mention a relief. What misdeed weighed on his conscience enough to make him think the police were after him? How about impersonating a teacher? "Sit down, please." He pushed the papers back into a file holder, trying to keep them in alphabetical order. "The spelling assignment. We did it in class today."

"I'm sorry to bother you."

She sat on the edge of the seat opposite him, her legs in the aisle, not fully committed to this meeting. Her coat opened to reveal the skirt of a white dress. Her shoes and stockings were also white. Of course, a nurse. Now he remembered.

"I have the evening shift and I couldn't make it tonight, but I wanted to see you. Bianca said you would be here." She smiled. "She knows all about you. Or thinks she does."

Neil returned her smile. "She knows a lot."

"Is this all right? My coming here?"

"Absolutely! I would have regretted not seeing you."

She swung her legs under the table. Neil sat with his hands folded, not quite sure how to begin. Should he practice his little mini-lecture?

"You gave her a very good report card."

"She's one of my best students."

Suddenly Mrs. Maldonado reached across the table with both hands and enclosed his in a tight grip. Tears came to her eyes. "She's so happy! She loves school." She waited a moment, containing her tears. "She goes on and on. At breakfast. She tells me. She gets everything right. All her papers are on the bulletin board. You don't let nobody beat anybody up. You give too much homework, but she does it anyway. Everybody says she's the teacher's pet." She stopped again. Steadied herself. "The teacher's pet? Last year they wanted to throw her out of school." She looked down at her hands gripping his. With an apologetic wave, she withdrew her arms and crossed them tightly in her lap. "I'm so grateful."

"I am too. Bianca... She's very special... Mrs. Maldonado, are you okay?"

"I had to hear this. I thought maybe she was making it up. I knew she wasn't lying. I know when she's lying." She said this with a mother's firmness. "But delusional? Would that be the word? Wanting something so much, you begin to believe it's real."

"She's not delusional. I have four students who are at or above grade level in all their subject areas and she's one of them."

"She's very smart."

"She's very smart," Neil agreed.

"Too smart for her own good."

"No," he said. "That's what I need to say to you. She's very perceptive and very competent and sometimes she sees how things should be and she gets impatient, like with me, and she's not too polite when she says what's what."

"She's like that with me! You see that!"

"Sometimes she's dead wrong and then it's okay. I mean, it's annoying, but she's just a kid and she doesn't know better. It's when she's right, and she mostly is, that's when it's really annoying."

"That's exactly what happens. You know?"

"Okay, so our job is not to get annoyed. It's to accept the fact that this eleven-year-old child is smarter than we are, anyway sometimes, and to try to convey to her that diplomacy and patience with others a bit slower than she is will get her more than her usual..." Neil made a claw of his right hand and snarled. "...my way or the highway approach."

Mrs. Maldonado laughed out loud. She shook her finger at Neil. "You know her."

"Not like you, but, yeah, I know her. But this is what I have to tell you. Next year."

"Oh, my God. Garibaldi. I don't know what to do."

"Do you always work the evening shift? The reason I ask is that you should join the PA, the Parents' Association."

"It's the best shift for me and Bianca. My sister lives with me, but... Well, anyway, she's there. I work three days, then I'm off four, because I work twelve hours, six to six."

"God."

"Yes, but then see I'm home all day four days. I could get more involved."

"You have to. And just as important, you have to make sure Bianca gets into the Academic Program. Don't forget that. They may try to type her out of it."

"Because she's Spanish?"

"Not really. At least a third of the kids in the program are Spanish. It's because of her spotty record. That's why you've got to be firm with the school and know your daughter is as smart as or smarter than anybody they've got. But you've got to be firm with Bianca that sometimes she has to *cooperate*, that it's not cowardice to *cooperate*. If there is a problem with the school you've got to go in and sort it out and get specific things they want her to do and make her do them. I mean as long as they're reasonable. That's one of my biggest jobs right now with her, by the way. Not just to yell at her when she's impatient or gets smart. But to try to explain, she's not the only person who knows the answer or has an idea or thinks she's right."

Mrs. Maldonado was nodding, but her attention seemed to have drifted.

"I'm sorry," Neil said. "You know all this better than I do. I'm..." Just a kid, he started to say, because he wanted to be open with her and because... yes, because he wanted her sympathy. But he was a teacher, her daughter's teacher, and this was advice he was compelled to give her.

"No, I don't know all this. I need to know what to do. Maybe I just need a kick in the pants. She..." She shook her head.

Neil suddenly felt self-conscious. "If I sound like a know-it-all it's because I worry about the next three years. She's got to make it to tenth grade."

"I let her take care of me too much. I come home tired, she makes the breakfast. She calls me mommy, but who's the mommy?"

The question made Neil realize that the conversation had forked and they weren't listening to each other. He wanted to talk about how to approach Garibaldi; she needed to talk about her relationship with Bianca. He straightened up, made eye contact.

"It's hard to be a working parent," he said.

"With no help! My sister. Okay, she's there nights." She looked over his shoulder, pulling at her right hand with her left. "Half the time with some guy. Okay, not half the time. Sometimes. And she pays her part. But basically it's just me and Bianca and a lot of the time I don't know what to do. And she's so smart and like you say, lots of times she knows what to do. I mean, she *thinks* she knows all the time. But too much I let her take over. Like what we need to get at the store, getting to the doctor. And I'm a nurse!"

"You're worried you give her too much responsibility?"

"She's just a baby." She suddenly looked directly at him. "You, too. You're so young. I'm sorry, I shouldn't say that should I? Anyway, you don't act so young. I haven't..." She pressed a finger against her lips, then clapped her hands together lightly. "I haven't talked to anyone like this since forever. God. But you know her. That's so incredible. That you know her. I should shut up."

"Bianca's a very healthy, intelligent child. It's sometimes hard to deal with her because she's so smart. Your relationship with her may have problems, but you've let her be the person she is. Now for the next few years she's going to need a lot of support to hold onto that person. I need to insist on that. That you've got to look out for her best interests when the system isn't interested in her at all."

"How do I do that?"

"Don't let them tell you she's bad or stupid or give you some other general kind of put-down. Don't let them tell her that. Get specifics. What did she do? What can she do to correct it? Talk particular behaviors. What's wrong? How can she change it? Be there for her, in the school, when you can. Let them know that they'll have to deal with you, but also let them know they *can* deal with you. And Bianca, too. She's got to be able to say: what do you want me to do? and, assuming it's not destructive, do it. She's learning some of that from me, but you know...?"

"What? What do I know?"

"I'm not good at this," he said.

"What?"

"I don't really know what I'm doing."

"Well, thank God for that, mister, cause what you're not doing is just fine." She leaned toward him across the table. "Bianca loves school. You know what? She loves you. Your movie star girlfriend?" Mrs. Maldonado clapped her hands and laughed. "I've never seen anybody so jealous as Bianca. She stomps around." She pulled back her head and tightened her lips. "'She's not his wife. He don't even like her.' Silvia and I say, 'How do you know that?'" Through tightened lips again, "'I just know.'"

"Well, I'm flattered."

"You should be. I think you're the first man she's ever liked. She hates most of Silvia's boyfriends." Then in a conspiratorial tone, "Actually, so do I."

"Mr. Maldonado?"

"Her father? He vacated the premises seven years ago, never to be heard from since."

"I'm sorry."

"I'm not." Her eyes widened at this and she suddenly pressed her hands to her cheeks and ran them down her face until they came together in a prayer at her lips. She closed her eyes and made a slight shaking motion with her head. Then she sat up straight and with her hands in her lap took a deep breath and said, "Mr. Riley, I'm not the complete babbling idiot I appear to be at this moment, I assure you. There are times when I am a fully sane adult who can actually carry on an intelligent conversation without spilling her guts all over the table. It's just that... Bianca is my life. My *life*. And to talk to someone who knows her. Who cares about her. It's such a pleasure." She clasped her hands together under her chin. "Oh, my God. Such a pleasure." Her eyes squeezed shut then opened. "Okay, but now, please, you don't think too badly of me?"

"Badly of you. Oh, wow. No."

There was a long silence. Neil looked at his watch.

"Am I keeping you?" she asked.

"No. I've still got more than an hour. I was just checking."

"I'll probably be a little late. I should go." She made no move to leave. "If there's a problem you'll call me?"

"Absolutely," he said.

She looked around. "Do you come here often?"

"I like the rice and black beans. And they have this dish, I call it pulled pollo con leftovers. It's a half chicken they pull apart and throw over a bed of rice. They use a red sauce with ingredients from whatever vegetables were served the day before. It's always delicious. I learned about this place from friends who live in the neighborhood. I get lots of takeout on my way home." He smiled. "I was never much of a wine man, but you order wine, they give you a water glass full." He held up his hand, his thumb and pointer finger stretched wide. "For two bucks." He shook his stretched fingers. "Two bucks!"

"Not tonight," she warned.

"No way."

"Maybe after," she said.

"I'll just be glad to go home."

"I should go," she said again, looking down at her seat. "What did I do with my beret?"

"You're wearing it."

She reached up and touched it. "Oh, my God, I'm losing my mind." She stood up, but something was holding her. "She's going to be all right, isn't she?"

"She's going to be fine," Neil said, thinking that was as true as not.

Chapter 3:

Welcome to Room 6-306

In the school: as Neil walked up the stairs to the third floor he became sharply aware of the echo of his steps in the empty building. It was 6:30. He wanted to be early. Probably no one would show, but he needed to set up and review his presentation one more time. Halfway up the staircase he stopped, remembering the totally unrehearsed, unplanned presentation he had given Mrs. Maldonado. *My God, what did I do?* He had given unequivocal advice to the mother of one of his children. Furthermore, he didn't regret one word of it. Bianca needed more care, more support. Mrs. Maldonado gave her too much responsibility, which might not be any of his business; however, letting her know how to help Bianca survive Garibaldi was.

But why? This was what stunned him. How much he cared what happened to Bianca. He flat-out cared. He wanted her to survive, to thrive. Smart, capable, involved, attractive, lively, courageous, outspoken, able to reach out, able to take responsibility, able. He wanted Bianca to flourish and grow. He wanted that for all of them. *Even for? Don't you lie now. Yes, I even want Arlene... No! Yes! ... to flourish and grow. That riff I gave Robin? Came straight from my heart. I long for them to live, be whole, have a life. It's like a constant prayer. Oh, shit, what's happening to me? Oh, phooey and darn. Don't tell me I love my children.*

Well, right now, as a matter of fact, I might remind you that you don't have time for a lot of mushy wallowing. You happen to be in the middle of one of the biggest challenges of your two century-long months at this incredibly torturous ordeal. Parents' Night?

Remember? You've got act like you're a teacher? Remember?

When he got to his room there was a couple standing waiting at the door; Sandra's parents, it turned out, Mr. and Mrs. Ortiz. After he ushered them into the room he hung a sign on his door that had been made for him by one Miss Sandra Ortiz.

Welcome to Room 6-306
Mr. Riley, Teacher
Please Come In

Neil asked them to sign his attendance sheet and told them he would ask for conferences in the order in which their names appeared on the sheet.

"We could do that conference now if you wanted to get it over with," Mr. Ortiz said.

"Sure," Neil said, though he had planned to take out his notes and review them. As he had with Mrs. Maldonado, he stressed that Sandra should sign up for the Academic Program.

"No, Sandra will go to Saint Mary's," Mr. Ortiz said.

Neil said he thought that was a good choice for her. "Does she ever draw stuff at home, pictures, that kind of stuff?"

"All the time. I can't get her to do nothin' else."

"She's very good," Neil said. "Check out the bulletin board. Those are her pictures up there."

"What's wrong with her work?" Mr. Ortiz asked.

At that moment the door opened and a man in a tuxedo rushed in. "I'm sorry to interrupt," he said breathlessly. "Pedro's father." He touched his chest. "I have to go to work," he said to explain his abruptness. He greeted Mr. and Mrs. Ortiz. "Eduardo, Maria." To Neil he bowed slightly. "Please, thank you. I hear all about you. I must go. That's all I wanted to say. Thank you." And he was gone.

Neil quickly wrote his name down on the list. And the note: *couldn't stay.*

"I'm sorry. You were saying?"

"Sandra, she got all B's. Last year she got A's. Is she bad? Every night we hear, no TV, pappy, I got to do my homework. But B's? We don't understand."

Report Cards! How he had hated them. It wasn't until his junior year of high school that he felt he had begun to be judged fairly and then, still, he felt his grades suffered because he was *that Riley kid.* Apparently last year Duane, who had had most of his kids, graded them largely on how well-behaved—in Duane's class, that would mean how submissive—they were. Sandra had gotten all A's in Duane's class. Neil had decided to base his report cards on academic performance, not his personal preferences. He now realized it was a decision that was going to cause him trouble. Sandra's performance in almost every area of study had been in the low to mid 80s.

Neil took a deep breath, reminding himself to continue flailing, even if he felt himself sinking with the weights of ignorance and inexperience tied firmly around his neck. "Sandra is a good student. She works hard. But did you know she's not reading on grade level? She's reading on a fifth grade level. The work she does in my class is extremely neat. She writes like a professional calligrapher." And, indeed, he had given her an A in penmanship. "But she doesn't always think things through. She seems to be in a hurry to get the right answer, but doesn't focus on the meaning of the subject. The same with her math. She wants the right answer, but doesn't always think about what she's doing."

They were nodding. Did they understand?

Neil took another deep breath. If he was going to learn how to do this fucking job he was going to have to do what he thought was right. They could run him out of town on a rail, but he would go out shouting the truth as he saw it. "I think in the past Sandra has gotten grades based on her good behavior. But that won't matter when she gets to junior high. Her grades will be based on her test scores. And if she's going to college..."

"College? She ain't going to college! She's going to finish high school and get a job." Neil felt the heat of Mr. Ortiz's stare. Sandra was definitely not going to college.

Others were coming in the door and Neil had to excuse himself to give them the sign-in sheet. He explained to the group, now about eight people, four of whom seemed to be alone, that he would like to give a brief presentation and then have individual conferences. When Neil got back to them the Ortiz's were whispering to each other, having what seemed to be a heated exchange.

"I have to end this now."

"That's all right," Mrs. Ortiz said. "Sandra's having a very good year," she said firmly.

"We can't stay. I got to get back," Mr. Ortiz said. He hesitated slightly before accepting Neil's hand, but then shook it firmly and left with Mrs. Ortiz hurrying after him.

As Neil began his presentation the door opened again and Mrs. Ortiz edged in, waving apologetically for him to pay her no mind. He was saying that competence in math is basic to almost any job short of digging a ditch. He stopped, thought about it, then said, "Wait? How deep is this hole supposed to be?" And he got some laughs!

He outlined the sixth grade math program, at the end of which his students should be able to do long division with a remainder and with decimals, do fractions in all the operands and convert fractions to decimals and vice versa. In line with this they should be able to work with currency. And they should be competent in most forms of measurement, ounces, pounds, inches, feet, yards and miles, have some knowledge of conversions to grams and meters and also be able to work with time.

At first the room was a blur, but slowly he began to distinguish individuals in his audience, notice things. Right in front of him, the woman in Bianca's seat, the man in Sandra's, was a well-dressed middle-aged black couple; the man, who wore a three-piece suit, had a substantial waistline, the woman, even heavier, wore a flowing ankle-length navy dress decorated with small orange dots.

Another black woman sat alone, in Pedro's seat in Row 4. Her long coat was draped across the top of the desk. She wore a denim wraparound skirt and a light blue man-tailored shirt. Her unstraightened hair was worn close, not as a wide 'Afro.' She wore silver hoop earrings. Her only other jewelry was a large watch, which he noticed because she had just then turned her left wrist to surreptitiously peer down at it. Neil felt he had seen her before. Absolutely! At the PA meeting he had attended. She was President of the PA! Oh my God! President of the PA!

A couple, Spanish he guessed, sat in the front seats of rows 3 and 4, the man in neat jeans and a bomber jacket open to a spotless white shirt, tired, nearly nodding off to sleep, the woman in a yellow flower-patterned dress. Her short skirt revealed good legs (don't look again). She wore several bracelets, blue, yellow, red, on each wrist and long dangling blue glass earrings. Even at a glance he could see that her cheeks were heavily rouged.

A thick-set, bordering on obese, grandmotherly black woman in a black dress sat with difficulty at Sheri's desk. Behind her sat a thin dark younger woman who talked to her constantly. About what? Why couldn't she shut up? Mrs. Ortiz had been sitting right behind this woman, but soon got up and moved over to the middle of row three, where her attentive gaze reminded him of Sandra's.

A man, "high-yellow," with a cane, dressed in dark pants, a striped shirt and a windbreaker, sat in the seat right behind Carmen's, his brown overcoat folded neatly on top of the desk and his brown fedora resting securely on top of it. He sat straight with his cane straight up at his side. He appeared in spite of the simplicity of his dress elegant, sophisticated.

Neil realized he didn't know the name of the child who sat in that desk. Now as he continued his little talk he was bothered by that fact. Who sat there? He guessed it was a girl. It was appalling that he didn't know.

He took a deep breath and looked down at his roster. Maria Rivera. He couldn't remember what Maria looked like. He shook his head. *Keep going.* He stepped out from behind his desk and with feet shoulder width apart, his right hand firmly on his hip, his left extended, he said, "To continue," and realized he had forgotten what he was supposed to say. He turned back toward the desk, where mercifully he had left his outline, and blurted out, "Language Arts."

He cleared his throat and told them that many educators believed that if one could read at a sixth grade level, one could with determination become educated in most areas of human knowledge. So what did that mean, to read on a sixth grade level? (He was in all of this shamelessly plagiarizing Robin's handout. If what he said wasn't true, at least it wasn't without some reference.) It meant that one had an instinctive sense of the structure of the language, which in English was subject verb object. He briefly explained that. Then he said that one needed a sight vocabulary of most of the basic functional words, the fundamental verbs and the fundamental nouns that were necessary to walk the streets, shop the shops and use the transportation systems of the places where one lived and worked. Opinions about just how many words were needed in this basic set varied from expert to expert, but were generally placed at between fifteen hundred and five thousand, although some recent studies indicated that one could function fairly well in a language not one's own with as few as five hundred words. The sixth grade reader also needed to be able to use phonics to unlock unfamiliar words. He went into a brief explanation of what phonics was and was not. He said that in his opinion it was not, as some claimed, the only reading skill one needed.

It was here that he saw he was beginning to lose his audience. He had never had Miss Talker and Mr. Nodding Out, but now Nodding Out's wife, Mrs. Legs, to his dismay crossed them more and more often, and the well-dressed couple had begun to fidget. The heavy elderly woman who was the target of Miss Talker remained inscrutable. The PA President, Mrs. Ortiz and the elegant gentleman were the only ones still listening. Neil knew he had to finish up quickly.

Context was another word skill that could be learned, he told them. If you saw a long word with several syllables beginning with r in a sentence that read, 'put the milk in the *refrigerator,*' you might be able to make an intelligent guess that the word was refrigerator.

But the most important thing, he wanted to emphasize, was comprehension. He repeated the word with emphasis, trying to wake up Mr. Nodding Out, alert Mrs. Legs, let them all know what he considered to be the most important point (and it was his point, only briefly mentioned in the handout, but crucial to Neil): You've got to learn to actively read the page, to ask yourself questions. For example, why was this article or story or advertisement or brochure written? What is its purpose? Entertainment? To impart information? To sell me something? Comprehension, he stressed, was essential and was obtained by active reading, which he repeated was that constant questioning of the material. He ended his little speech there and as he did five more people walked into the room.

Two of these newcomers were a tall thin plainly dressed black couple. The man wore an open black overcoat over an open jacket showing a flannel shirt and grey work pants. The woman carried a light blue overcoat with probably a faux fur collar. Her long dark navy dress was sprinkled with small red dots, roses perhaps. Their faces were like the dual masks, tragedy and comedy, that often adorn Playbills. The man's mouth was turned down in what appeared to be a permanent scowl. The woman had a quiet, sweet reassuring smile.

The next person to walk into the room was one of those spectacular women you might see cast in a movie as a very expensive, very beautiful hooker. She was tall and slender and wore a long fur coat opened to a silky white blouse with the three top buttons undone and a very fashionable black miniskirt. Her legs, naked, long, smooth, deep chocolate, now joined those of the yellow dress woman, making two areas of the room that were off-limits to Neil's eyes. The man following her with his hand planted firmly on her back was nearly as tall as Neil and much broader. He was not fat. He moved with the confidence and grace of a very fit heavyweight. His face wore a watchful you-do-not-want-to-insult-me expression. He was dressed in a long leather jacket, a purple shirt and a pair of faded jeans. A leather strap crossed his chest, a fact that registered with Neil after some confusion: *Holy shit. He's wearing a gun.*

The fifth person to come in was a small very bent old woman. Neil gave the big man the sign-in sheet, explained it and asked him to pass it on when he was done. The bent old woman had begun registering her disapproval of the proceedings from the moment she walked in the door. It might have been here that Mrs. Ortiz left the room. Neil wasn't sure. It was only later that he remembered that she had stayed and then without any further interaction with him was gone.

"I ain't gonna sign no paper," the bent old woman declared. "I'm here to find out why my grandson got C pluses. He never got no C pluses before."

"I'll be happy to discuss that with you. That's why I'm having these conferences. Who is your grandson?"

"I don't want no conference."

"But how else could I explain..."

"Just tell me. Is he bad?"

"Who?" Neil asked. "Who are we talking about?"

"Simon Wolf," she said.

Who the hell is Simon Wolf? Neil wondered. *Could he be that kid who sits near Arlene? Sweet easy smile. Never causes any trouble.* He said, "If you'll wait your turn, I'll be able to show you his folder."

"I don't need his *folder*. I need an explanation. He always made A's, always."

"If he made a C plus in a subject it means his test grades averaged about seventy-five percent," Neil said, and C pluses were probably too kind since the tests were based on fourth and fifth, not sixth, grade material. A seventy-five actually suggested a student was working at a level significantly below his grade. "But I'm not going to discuss any student's work publicly." He turned to address the others. "On the report cards next to the grades of two of the items, Language Arts and Mathematics, are numbers, like five or five point five or six. Those numbers tell you how your child scored on the Iowa Basic Skills Tests compared to other students around the country. No matter what grade I give my students, that's the number the school uses to determine how he or she is ranked in ability."

"What's Simon's score?" his grandmother asked.

"Look on his report card," Neil said.

"I'm askin' you," she said.

"And I've already told you. Wait your turn, talk to me privately."

"I told you..."

"Yes, ma'am, you did. You told me. And I told you. Now, I've got other parents here I need to talk to. What I can do is call you on the telephone..."

"No, you ain't gonna call me on no telephone."

"Then if you don't mind, I want to talk to these other parents." He picked up the sign-in sheet. "Mrs. Wilson?"

"What time you gonna call me?" the bent woman asked.

"Tomorrow night around seven?" Just what he wanted to do, call an angry grandmother. "Could you sign the sheet and put your telephone number next to your name?"

She pointed a finger at him. "You have my number in Simon's *folder*," she said, managing to convey just how filthy that thing must be. Then she left. And what was peculiar about her leaving was that she shut the door carefully behind her, quietly, as if to avoid disturbing him any further.

On the sheet he wrote, *Wolf??? Telephone number??? Call grandm 7 pm. Her name!* and called out again, "Mrs. Wilson?"

Chapter 4:

Complicated

"I'm Harriet's mother," she said.

"Right. Yes. Of course," Neil said. "Have a seat."

And the President of the Parents' Association sat down.

He reached into his file drawer and extracted Harriet's folder and scanned his Summary Page. He had looked at Harriet's record before with wonder, gratitude and a sneaky denial. One he didn't have to worry about, he would tell himself, seeing that her homework and test scores were, in a word, perfect, her attendance record excellent, her behavior excellent, her class participation excellent and her Basic Skills scores as high apparently as the K through 6 tests would go, 9.0. Now suddenly he was confronted with his deceitfulness. What could he possibly claim he was doing for Harriet? Why hadn't he pushed to have this child transferred to Robin?

"Looks like you've got a full house. I won't be too long," she said. "Mainly, well... I wish I could protect you." She threw a hand back toward the door. "That woman loves her grandson, you know?"

"I know."

"This must be quite an adventure for you," she said.

Something like a giggle bubbled out of Neil's mouth. It wasn't exactly the professional response he would have preferred. He hadn't expected empathy, least of all from her.

"Mainly, I wanted to make contact," she continued. "And to apologize for what happened at the PA meeting."

Two weeks ago on a Monday all the teachers got a handout in their boxes inviting them to a PA meeting scheduled for that coming Wednesday. Neil had decided what the hell? And that Wednesday he had hung out at the *Silver Moon* until he could show up promptly at 7 p.m. at the room that doubled as the AV (Audio-Visual) and conference rooms. At a table long enough to accommodate about a dozen people eight women, all black, sat talking and laughing; that is, until Neil walked in, when abruptly there was complete and utter silence.

This woman, Mrs. Wilson, President of the PA, sat at the head of the table at the far end.

"Good evening," she said to Neil. "Welcome."

A woman sitting a few seats down from her leaned forward, with the back of her head to Neil, and asked, "Is he a parent?"

To Neil Mrs. Wilson said, "Would you mind introducing yourself?"

"I'm Neil Riley. I teach sixth grade?" He said loudly, "I'm a teacher."

The woman leaned forward, again showing Neil the back of her head. "A teacha? How come he here? I got some serious business tonight."

"Did you have some particular matter you wanted us to address tonight, Mr. Riley?" Mrs. Wilson asked.

Neil stood up. He was tired. It had been long day. When wasn't it a long day? "Yeah," he said. "I do have something to say. I guess it's a question." He was fumbling around in his briefcase. He knew he was about to do something he would regret. And yet at that moment it had felt so good to pull out that flyer and hold it toward the group, all of whom were looking at him except the woman who had so openly objected to his being there. "Madam? Lady? You! The one who won't look at me!" And when she still refused to look at him, "THE ONE WHO HAS SUCH SERIOUS BUSINESS TO DISCUSS! Why on earth did you put this in my in-box?" He threw the flyer on the table and walked out of the room. It was a great exit. He felt commanding, powerful and right, and almost immediately petty, dismal and wrong. He thought of running back in and begging their forgiveness. He thought of filing a furious complaint with the UFT. He thought of... trying to sweep the whole incident under the rug. He went home and got his lesson plans ready for the next day and slept badly, worrying that he would be punished, that he had appeared weak, that he had been rude, that he had been too accommodating, that he wanted to forget the whole thing, that he wouldn't be allowed to forget the whole thing, that he was weak to want to forget the whole thing, that he would never ever know what to do with this incredible fucking impossible goddamn motherfucking, *Mrs. Robin get out of my head,* golly gee job!

Now Mrs. Wilson put a neatly folded white bag on his desk. "Brownies," she said. "An apology and a peace offering. Harriet said you were a coffee drinker. Most coffee drinkers I know love chocolate. I felt so awful about the way you were treated."

"I love brownies," he said.

"I was the one who put those flyers in the teachers' mailboxes. The executive committee, that's me and two of the other women who were there, agreed to do it without a vote. I pushed for it. I was to blame. I was wrong. I'm so sorry. But Mrs. Shapely, the one who was your welcoming committee? Her behavior was inexcusable and I told her so. I keep wanting to apologize, to explain."

"Please don't," Neil said.

"All right, I won't. But about the flyer." She made a face. "I won't do that again. I've been president of the PA for three years." She made another face. "I won't do that again either."

"Mrs. Wilson, we need to talk about Harriet. About next year. About Garibaldi."

"I know all about Garibaldi. My son was there briefly year before last and we pulled him out. He's exactly the kind of boy to get himself killed in those halls: smart, athletic, capable. We've got him in John Dewey up near Columbia. It's a little artsy fartsy for my taste, but Matthew loves it. Especially since he's a shoo-in for varsity basketball. He claims only eight boys in the whole school can hit the backboard. That's where Harriet is going, too. Good old John Dewey Prep. It's a copout, but I'm not sacrificing my children to a hopeless cause."

"Yeah," Neil said. "I know."

She studied his face for a moment, then laughed. "What a year this must be for you. But for Harriet? She's made a real friend. That's a first. I mean, she has friends, but no one she has enjoyed quite like this. She has always been so reserved. And here she is every night on the phone with Bianca." She made a jabbering motion with her hand. "Talk, talk, talk. Homework, what this one did, what you said. The Wilson household knows a lot about you, Mr. Riley."

"Bianca and Harriet are friends?"

Mrs. Wilson smiled. She seemed to enjoy his surprise. "I think Bianca is drawn to Harriet's intellectual abilities. And Harriet is dumbfounded by Bianca's fire. Where do they sit?"

He pointed out their desks and in doing so remembered the other parents scattered around the room waiting for him.

"Is there anything else we need to talk about?" Neil asked.

"No. I think things are going just fine," she said.

"Just fine. Right. So what I need to know is: why is she in my class? She could have been in Robin's class. Seriously. It's much more..."

"Schooly..."

"Challenging."

"She chose your class. We had a furious fight about it. I wanted Robin. Think about it," Mrs. Wilson said. "This was in August. She didn't know who you were or what she was getting into. You came sight unseen. You could have been anybody. Another Knight, if you pardon my saying so. But she wanted your class. It's as if she knew something. About what, I dunno. About herself. She was determined. To do something on her own terms? That's certainly part of it. And she's fascinated by you. She knows you're struggling. She says you're complicated."

"Complicated?"

"Remember, this is a very bright, sensitive child. Not to mention a pampered daddy's girl. With her, complicated is about as good as you're going to get. Just remember this, Mr. Riley, when you're plodding your way to school tomorrow morning, wishing to God you were back in bed with your gorgeous Movie Star."

Neil grabbed his temples.

"I'm sorry," she said smiling. "I had to get that in. Anyway, at least one little girl is up and at 'em so she won't be late for your class." She glanced at her watch. "I should let you go. Enjoy your brownies."

"Thank you. I will."

"Godspeed, Mr. Riley." And she was gone.

Chapter 5:

Are You Jewish?

"Mr. and Mrs. Carter?" Neil called out. The next names on the list. Carter. Morris' parents.

"Reverend Carter," the man in the three-piece suit corrected him.

The well-dressed couple, both looking to Neil to be at least in their late forties, got up and stepped forward. Neil quickly got another chair from the rear of the room. He bit his lip. He should have thought of this.

"I don't want to wait around all night," the tall man with the permanent scowl called out, standing. "We got no complaints. If Brenda's bad you just let us know. We'll tend to it."

"You're Brenda's parents?"

"Guardians," the man corrected, already at the door. The woman, his wife, rushed up to the desk. She had a pen in her hand. "Mrs. Green, on your list," she said. "Please let me write my number," she said, writing it down, then looking apologetically at the Carters. "I'd love to hear how she's doing. Call after..."

"Let's go, Mabel. I ain't waitin' all night."

"...eight. He has his shows."

Next to Green and her number he wrote: *after 8 pm Brenda's aunt.*

Mrs. Carter began, "I don't want to sound like that woman who just walked out, but I was disappointed in Morris' report card. He always got A's before you."

It seemed to Neil that the Reverend was scrutinizing him; not just his responses, but his suit, his shirt, his tie. Neil was grateful to Robin for insisting on the suit. "Show them the respect they deserve," she said. The union rep, Tobin, said this was an event agreed upon in the contract as an informal meeting requiring casual dress. He could have worn his usual khakis with his tie folded away in his briefcase. And he would consequently have been sweating bullets now while the impeccably dressed Rev. Morris Carter Sr. examined him from head to toe or at least as close to toe as their seating arrangements would allow.

Neil said, "Morris is averaging just about 80 in his test scores in math. He's got about a 90 in spelling, so I gave him an A. His reading comprehension average is a 78 so, yeah, B, though it's a low B. According to his scores at the end of the year last year he wasn't on grade level in math or reading. Duane chose to give him A's. I would have given him B's, but only if his grades were like they are this year."

"Do you believe in the Lord Jesus Christ our Lord and Savior?" Mrs. Carter asked.

"Now, Jennifer," the Reverend said.

"No, ma'am," Neil said, looking her straight in the eye.

"Then what right have you got to give my son B's?"

Neil shut his eyes and shook his head, showing how irrelevant he thought the question was. "Your son's grades are based on his skills, not his religion."

"How can you judge my son and not believe in Jesus? Are you Jewish?"

"No, ma'am, just plain ole unaffiliated American."

"What's your education?" the Reverend asked.

"I have a B.A. from the University of Connecticut, where I majored in history," he told them. To himself he said, *I'm on leave of absence after two years of NYU Law, where I have a 4 point. I also earned nine credits in education this summer and need six more to obtain a permanent New York State Teacher's Certificate. Or maybe it's seven? I'm not sure.*

"How long have you been teaching?" the Reverend asked.

Neil looked *him* straight in the eye. "Two and one-half months," he said, "give or take." Thinking: *Yes, you're right. I'm woefully under-qualified to teach your son and probably would have melted into a humiliated, apologetic, remorseful pile of guilt if you had questioned anything but my belief in that rabble-rousing son of probably not Joseph who should have about as much to do with this discussion as whether I like my bread plain or toasted. Plain, by the way, because I don't have time to toast it.*

"And Duane. She taught Morris last year. How long has she been teaching?"

"I have no idea. A long time, is my guess. Let's say twenty plus years." *Compared to this crypto-draft dodger's couple of weeks, is that your point?*

The Reverend smiled. "Fools rush in where angels fear to tread. I always noticed those numbers next to the grade but I honestly never thought about them. Isn't that a shameful admission?"

"The question for me is why?" Neil said. "He's a smart kid, and so personable. But he doesn't always think about what he's reading. There's some disconnect. He can say the words, they're familiar to him, they even seem to make sense to him, but he doesn't always make sense of them. You know what I mean?"

"He doesn't take in the import of what's being written."

"That's exactly right. Sometimes he does and sometimes he doesn't."

"And you think you know how to change that?"

Neil wiggled his hand. "Sort of. *He's* got to change it. I think that when he reads he's got to ask what he's reading for. Even if it's a story. You know? Why do I like this boy or girl? Why don't I like that one? Where is this taking place? And on and on like that. Actively engage with what's happening."

"Why did the Lord order Abraham to sacrifice Isaac? Is that a good example?"

Right out of Kierkegaard, Neil thought. "Ask him," he suggested. "If he doesn't know don't tell him. Ask him to think about it. Why would God do such a thing? See what he comes up with."

"This has definitely been instructive," the Reverend said, rising.

Mrs. Carter looked up at her husband. "We're leaving?"

"For the time being. We'll be interested to see how this matter develops," he said to Neil.

Mrs. Carter reached out and placed a small black book in his hands. *The New Testament.* "I want you to have this. I always carry an extra copy with me."

For us infidels, Neil thought. "Thank you," he said.

"I think you ought to read some of it every night before you go to bed," she told him.

"We will be going now, Mrs. Carter," the Reverend told her.

Chapter 6:

Those Numbers and Things

"Mr. and Mrs. Torres?" Neil called out.

Mrs. Legs nudged Mr. Nodding Out and they stood up and became—Carmen's parents. As they approached the distant floral odor that had been wafting faintly about the room now became a thick haze that enveloped the area around Neil's desk.

"Sorry to be so tired," Mr. Torres said. "I drive a delivery truck. Up at four, out there six latest. Restaurant provisions. Diners mostly."

He was a dark well-built man in his late thirties with a receding hairline. Mrs. Torres carried a black coat over one arm. Her short sleeveless yellow dress exposed those nicely formed bare legs. Legs Neil could not avoid seeing from the corner of his eye. He wondered—he could not help it—if he looked would he see her panties? *Oh, my God, Yahweh, Jesus, Somebody, here I am trying to do my job and I am coveting my neighbor's wife. Thou must appreciate the beauties of nature. That may not be in Mrs. Carter's New Testament, but Jesus would have known it. He wasn't an idiot.*

Mrs. Torres' face seemed to be rather pretty in a pert girlish way, with a small curved nose and regular features, though it was hard to know exactly what she looked like because of the mask she wore: long black false eyelashes, a thick loop of eyeliner around each eye and two large circles of red on her cheeks. The finishing touch was her very red, very glossy lipstick.

"Thank you so much for coming," Neil said to Mr. Torres.

"Oh, you don't need to do that," Mrs. Torres said as he flipped open Carmen's folder. "We came to see you. I mean, you know," she continued quickly, "to ask if you wanted to know anything about Carmen. Is she behaving?"

"She's very well behaved," Neil said. *Driving poor Clyde half-crazy, but that couldn't be held against her.*

"Well, then," she said, standing up. "We have to go. Johnny, he has to get up so early," she cooed, as if talking about a baby.

"Okay, but..."

"No, no," she said, reaching out and putting her hand on Neil's, "as long as she's being good things are fine, ain't that right, Johnny?"

"That's about it," Mr. Torres said, looking at the hand with which she had pinned Neil's to the desk.

"How old are you?" Mrs. Torres asked, leaning in toward him.

Neil turned his head to Mr. Torres. "Carmen needs to pay more attention to her homework." *Though I can see now why she thinks earrings and lipstick are far more important. And who knows? She may be right.*

Mr. Torres locked eyes with him and smiled a broad warm smile. "Carmen, she likes this class. That's good."

Mrs. Torres finally removed her hand from Neil's, but continued to stare at him.

To her he said, "I'm twenty-four."

"Oh, my God," she said. "And you look even younger. Well, as long as Carmen is having a good time. I mean, you know, with those numbers and things that you talked about."

And they were gone.

Chapter 7:

Absolutely, Totally, Understandably Insane

"Mr. De Angeleno?"

"D'Angeleno," the elderly man with the cane said, standing, briskly, without any need of the cane, or so it seemed to Neil. "It's D apostrophe A, dan not de."

"Sorry," Neil said. "And who's your child, Mr. D'Angeleno."

"Norberto."

"Norberto?"

"Norbert, Norbert," he said impatiently, sitting down. "It should be Norberto. Like me. But his father hardly spoke English and certainly couldn't read it, so it became Norbert on his birth certificate. Norbert. It should be Norberto. I'm his grandfather."

Neil put a note next to Norberto D'Angeleno's name on the sign-in sheet: *Grandf Norbert Rosado. Norberto. which prefer?* He opened Norbert's folder.

"Does he live with you?"

"Yes. And my daughter, his mother. His father has another wife, another family. I don't think he's married to her either."

"What did you think of Norbert... to's report card? That seems to be the theme this evening."

"His report card is the best ever. Nobody ever liked him."

"I didn't grade him on how I felt about him," which wasn't quite true. Neil had a grave, worried sympathy for Norbert that encouraged him to grade him a bit more generously than his test scores would allow. Also, he was deeply in Norbert's debt because of his friendship with Charles. But Norbert could understand what he read, could do most of the math problems and did need a boost. Fuckit, man. Norbert gets A's. Was it fair? As fair as Simon Wolf's C pluses.

"He comes to school every day," Mr. D'Angeleno said, as if it were information that had somehow escaped Neil's attention.

"Yes, he does. Is that unusual?"

"It is a miracle, Mr., what did you say your name was?"

You know my name, fucker, Neil thought. "Riley," he said.

"His attendance in the past was maybe every other day. And on the days he came I had to drag him, threaten, bribe, scream." He smiled. "This has been an easy time for me. I have developed some bad habits, like strolling along Broadway and enjoying a donut and a cup of coffee at *Donut World* and reading *The News* every morning."

"Sounds like heaven to me," Neil said.

"Close. We would agree, I think, that a beautiful woman like the one who just left would add to that significantly."

"That is true. A beautiful woman would add to *The News*." He thought of *that* woman, at *Silhouettes*.

"But I am old and don't have much time and must take what I can get. And that brings us to why I am here. Garibaldi."

"Yes. Garibaldi."

"It is a very bad place."

"Yes, I know," Neil said.

"Do you know? Do you really know?"

"No, not really. I was there once. For a job interview."

"You should go back there then. Take that job."

"Yes, well, but I've got my hands full here."

"No, no, I mean next year. You should go there to teach. You could watch out for Norberto. If he knew you were there. If he could see you. Do you understand? If he could be in your homeroom, they call it, and come back to you if there were problems."

"Mr. D'Angeleno, I teach here. They expect me to come back next year. What you're asking isn't practical."

"I don't have long to live. Is that practical?"

"Are you sick?"

"I'm seventy-six years old. Do I have to be sick, too? He's very sensitive. Norberto." His eyes had begun to water. "Things are not so easy for him as for some other children. I bring him to school and take him home." He rapped his cane twice on the floor. "This is why they do not pick on an old man and a frightened boy. This stick. I am not afraid. But I did not live with a monster when I was child. I am not one to judge. Nor you either."

"No, sir, I know that."

"I know you do." He stared at Neil, furious. "This is why I want you to go to Garibaldi."

This is absolutely, totally, understandably insane, Neil thought. He met Mr. D'Angeleno's furious gaze with calm: paper covers rock. He hoped. "I am not going to Garibaldi," Neil said.

"Then Norberto will wither and die. You think I exaggerate? I do not exaggerate. Over time, he will crawl more, get smaller inside, retreat more, get smaller, be killed or kill himself."

Neil looked at his watch, partly because he was truly worried it was getting late, but more because he wanted to end this interview and meant to tell D'Angeleno that. He felt helpless and it was a feeling that was hard to endure. He said, forcefully, "Norbert will have to learn how to cope. It is our job to think of ways to help him." *Oh, God,* he thought, *that's exactly the kind of thing Bernbach would say.*

"That's ridiculous. The child is terrified beyond belief. Someone like you would not understand."

"I understand this. If you decide nothing can be done, it's likely nothing will be done. And this. He is very *very* brave. He has befriended a boy who has grave problems. Norbert… Norberto could be ridiculed for this friendship, but he is willing to take the chance. He is not terrified beyond belief."

"You know, I don't appreciate being lectured to by a child. Well, at least I have this. For now Norberto comes to school; he *wants* to come to school. I guess I had hoped for more from you."

"Mr. D'Angeleno, I will do the best I can," Neil said.

With a sniff and a hard silent look D'Angeleno stood up and walked out the door.

Chapter 8:

What's a Good Teacher?

To his four remaining conferees he said, "I'm sorry to keep you all so late. If any of you prefer, I can call and have our conference on the phone."

The incessant talker raised her hand as she said, "I'm just here with my mother."

And in fact there were only two more names on the list.

"Mr. and Mrs. Carver?" Carver? Neil couldn't think of any student named Carver. But what did he know? He was only their teacher.

"We'll just wait," the big man in the leather jacket said and as he spoke Mrs. Carver put both high-heeled shoes on the floor and opened her legs slightly.

Oh, God, why do I have to be such a sex maniac? Neil complained to the indifferent Existential Silence to which Mrs. Robin was so incredibly deaf.

"Mrs. Cross?"

"Pauli's grandma," the heavyset woman said. She had been sitting sideways in the desk and now with one hand on the back of the seat and the other planted on the desktop she pushed herself up and waddled toward the front of the room.

The incessant talker, talking, saying she would just come with her, it wasn't no bother, she had best be there, wonder what Pauli up to anyhow... was suddenly shut down by Mrs. Cross, who turned on her and said, "Sit down and be quiet. I need to talk to this teacha." To Neil as she approached the desk she said, "I didn't have no problem with Pauli's report card. Except for behavior."

She better not have a problem. Pauli's grades were based on his test scores and homework and not his behavior (which Neil graded a D plus). His grades in Language Arts (B+), Spelling (A), Math (B) and Social Studies (B) were the best he had received since second grade.

She lowered herself into the chair next to the desk, breathing a sigh of relief, and said, "That ain't why I came here."

As Neil said, "Okay."

She was saying, "I came here cause I heard you don't believe in hitting. Well, that ain't gonna cut it with Pauli. He runs and squirms and puts hisself in every place but the right one. Thas why you having so much problems wid him. The only way to get that child to listen is swat him upside the head. Now I heard you a good teacha. But let me give you some advice. Not if you don't hit. They ain't gonna listen, believe me. I been around the block a couple of times and I know. Don't need no fancy degree to understand *that*."

Neil knew he was very tired because he was staring at his thumb and suddenly he had poked it in her eye and her eyeball had come squirting out of its socket. It was, thank God, a sudden brief nightmare. He breathed a sigh of relief. She was still sitting there glaring at him and he was still mildly shaking his head. But it had been a deliberate stab and that fleeting belief that he had yanked her eye out had given him deep gratification.

"Mrs. Cross, I can't hit the children."

"Why not? You some kind of Rastafarian?"

Neil's eyes widened at his own audacity. "I'm a boxer. I'm trained as a boxer. I hit Pauli and hurt him? Legally? I'd be up for assault with a deadly weapon. It's like I used a gun." As he spoke he made his hands into fists.

"I didn't know that," she said, looking at his fists. She adjusted herself better to the chair, pulled her head back and studied him more closely. For the moment she seemed to be out of advice.

The boxer story was, of course, a thumb in her eye. When he was in sixth grade as punishment for attacking some boys who had tried to bully him he had been sentenced to train at a PAL gym every Wednesday evening for two years. It had been a thoroughly enjoyable penance. So in college after he failed to make the football team as a walk-on defensive back (in all of one day of tryouts) it made perfect sense for him to take boxing classes to fulfill his PE requirement. If he were ever called for his blatant fabrication he could insist it was perfectly valid. Come on. It had some faint validity.

What wasn't valid was his anger at Pauli's grandmother. Yes, he had decided once and for all he would never ever hit a child, but there were times... He could hear Mrs. Robin clucking her tongue and telling him, *Let he who is without sin cast the first stone.* The silver lining in this exchange was that he was now wide awake.

"So what you gonna do bout his behavya?"

"Teach him how to duck. Then you can't hit him upside the head as much."

She actually smiled. "I'll give 'im a feint, then swat 'im when he comes up." After a moment she said, "You look really tired, hon. You better get yourself home and get you some sleep." Then her smile widened.

And Neil thought, *Okay, here comes something.* And he was dead-on right.

"Course what I heard, you busy nights even when you at home."

"Grading papers," Neil said. "Reading textbooks. But that other thing you heard? You said you heard I was a good teacher? Could you tell me what that means? What's a good teacher?"

"One that don't think Negro chillren are stupid," she said. She gripped the bottom of the chair. "Where's that damned girl. Annie! Get over here!" As Annie rushed up Mrs. Cross said to Neil, by way of introduction, "One of Pauli's aunts." (pronounced ont, not ant) "I had three girls. Pauli's the blessing at the end of a long road."

"Pleased to meet cha, Mr. Riley. I heard from Mrs. Wright, that's Sharon's mother. Sharon is in Mrs. Robin's class. She said you was tall. You pretty tall."

"Let's go, Annie."

"We got to go now," Annie said, "but it was a pleasure to come in here and look around and see how tall you..."

"*Let's go, Annie!*"

"Yessum. Goodbye, Mr. Riley. Like I said, it was a pleasure to meet you."

Chapter 9:

Junebug

Neil looked at the large man in the leather jacket with the gun holster slung across his chest and his beautiful slender companion in her short black miniskirt. "Mr. and Mrs. Carver?"

The purple shirt suited the man like pink booties would a tiger. But it did go with that miniskirt.

"Why don't you come over here?" Mr. Carver said, turning Marta's desk around so that it faced his.

Mr. and Mrs. Carver were sitting in the third seats of Rows 2 and 3. That lethal boxer with fists of fury did as he was told. He walked over and sat in Marta's desk. Meanwhile, Mrs. Carver was wiggling her desk around a bit. They were suddenly in a tight threesome. Neil took a deep breath. She gave off a light floral scent. Roses. The man, like Neil, favored Brut.

Assuming it was the Mrs. who had parented the unknown child, Neil looked her in the eyes, a dark worried brown, then focused on Mr. Carver. Before anything else, Neil decided he had to deal with that weapon. It might be legal, but it wasn't appropriate to wear it in an elementary school and certainly not in his classroom. He braced himself for a messy confrontation, but Mr. Carver headed him off at the pass.

"The reason I'm packin'," Mr. Carver said, "is cause somethin' came up and I have to be there."

Mrs. Carver leaned forward to catch Neil's eye. "He's a police officer. I'm Clyde's mother."

"I'm his step-father," Mr. Carver said.

Clyde's mother! Neil would have said mid-twenties, but subtract twelve from twenty-five you come up with thirteen. Still, she couldn't be thirty; not even close. Neil sat up straight as a pole, wide awake, braced for anything. *Your job is to find out all you can,* Mrs. Robin had said. *Well, how about this.* She had obviously had Clyde at a very young age, hadn't given him up to anyone, and the way she said that, *I'm Clyde's mother,* she hadn't even considered it. Better note, too, that being a step-father wasn't anything to apologize for.

"I'm a detective," Mr. Carver said. "Not a whole lot of us colored boys walk around in regular clothes. On the street they call me *The Carver.*"

Neil nodded respectfully. *I'll call you whatever you tell me to call you,* he thought.

With a wave toward the other side of the room where Simon's grandmother had voiced her objections, Mrs. Carver said, "I understand how that woman was so upset. With her grandson's report card? I've had problems like that with Clyde. But not this last report card. I couldn't believe it! He got A in math! and B's in spelling and social studies."

"And a C plus in reading. Which we need to talk about," Neil said.

"But he is reading. He brings books home. C plus is pretty good for Clyde."

"And he's taken to grabbin' my paper, at least the sports page," The Carver said.

At that moment the door opened and Mrs. Robin stuck her head in. "I'm sorry to interrupt, Mr. Riley. I just didn't want to miss you. I have a favor to ask of you when you're done. I'll be in my..."

Mrs. Carver had turned around to look at the door the moment Mrs. Robin spoke. Mrs. Robin looked at her then pushed the door all the way open and put her hands to her cheeks and screamed. She went: euweeuweeuwee. Neil jerked around, checking the floor, thinking she saw a rat. Then he realized she was giving voice to that particular female ululation (at least he had never heard it uttered by a man) that was a long loud outburst of joy and sorrow, the sound a woman makes seeing her daughter in her wedding dress.

Meanwhile, Mrs. Carver, with astonishing athleticism, leapt out of her seat making the same sound: euweeuweeuwee. And rushed in her high heels toward small tired vulnerable-looking Mrs. Robin who was now uttering, "Oh, my goodness, oh, my goodness."

"Mrs. Robin, Mrs. Robin." Mrs. Carter was crying.

"Junebug, Junebug." Mrs. Robin was crying.

The two men inadvertently made eye contact and Neil noted how they were both scrupulously careful not to display any eye movement, twitch of the lip, headshake, anything that could possibly be construed as a comment on these proceedings. After that unfortunate encounter Neil knew they could not look at each other again; they had to keep quiet; anything like a smile from either of them would be a serious impertinence. And he knew if they could both keep their cool they would each be profoundly indebted to the other. Most of all, they could strut they butt cause they knew what's what.

"I know you've been around the school sometimes," Mrs. Robin said. She was not one to keep feelings of reproach hidden. "You could've come see me."

"It was always a bad time," Mrs. Carver, Junebug now, said, and somehow not quite unexpectedly burst into tears again.

Mrs. Robin, who would have stood a good half a head shorter than Junebug without those high heels, had to reach to pat her on the back. "I know, I know. It's all right. I just would have loved to see you."

"Me, too," sobbed Junebug.

"Well, he's growing and he's a mighty fine lookin' boy and he's got hisself a good strong teacher," Mrs. Robin said.

"Can I introduce you to my husband?"

"Chile, you better."

Neil and The Carver, hearing this, were on their feet. And, Neil knew, they both had the same sappy just-tell-me-what-to-do grin on their faces.

"This is my husband, Police Detective John Carver."

"Good evening, Mr. Carver."

"Evenin', ma'am. Pleased to make your acquaintance."

"Mrs.?" Mrs. Robin hesitated, then to Junebug, "Carver?"

Junebug nodded proudly.

"Congratulations. Mrs. Carver was one of my best students ever."

"That's not what you told me," Junebug said.

"That's what your report card said, honey."

"Yes, ma'am."

"And look at you all grown up and beautiful." She looked her up and down the way a man would. "Umm, delicious," she said. Mrs. Robin jerked a thumb at Neil and told Junebug from the side of her mouth, "He's one of my best students, too, an' I don't tell him either." Then to Police Detective Carver she said, "It was a pleasure meeting you. I realize you probably had to wear that thing you're wearing but it would have been better to keep it out of sight."

"Yes, ma'am," he said. "I realized that already."

Mrs. Robin told Neil, with a nod that seemed to say he was doing just fine, "I should let you get on with your meeting."

When she was gone Junebug, Mrs. Carver now, announced, hands on hips, "And that's Mrs. Robin."

"Yes, ma'am," Neil said.

Mr. Carver was laughing, then serious. "Mr. Riley, we got to ax you. It's important."

They were standing now in a tight circle facing each other. Neil stepped back a little. Mrs. Carver leaned in against her husband, but somehow it was to appease him, not to seek support. Something about whatever this was separated them. "When Clyde got held back I didn't know what to do. It didn't seem right," she said.

"It hurt him," Neil said. "It was like a slap. He didn't deserve it."

"He didn't. He didn't deserve it." She said this emphatically. "An' it did hurt. Really bad." She seemed to lose her train of thought.

Mr. Carver tightened the grip of the hand he had on her upper arm. "Go ahead, baby. Say it any way it comes."

"They was having trouble, John and Clyde. They... They're both my men, you know. *I'd kill for them.* I mean, it was okay before we was married. It was good. They got on just fine. Then we got married and he started fightin' and he'd come home and wouldn't say nothin' and John was good. I mean it. He was. He is. He's good. He let him be. And then they did that to him, held him back? An' I thought," and here she talked as if she were a total idiot, "well, all right, they say it's a good thing and I guess I'll just go along and," here she suddenly changed her tone to reflect the fury she felt, "it was like they beat him up. You give me trouble, you little black puke face, well, we'll get you good. And that's the way he felt. That they'd gotten him back.

"And he got you an' I thought, Oh, Lord, this is gonna be a mess. An' it wasn't. It wasn't. My God. A big ole nasty-tempered white man? I'm sorry."

"No, it's okay. I get it."

"A first year teacha? Oh, Jesus, Lord, an' a class full of them kids." She pointed at Neil. "I thought what's he gonna do? But most of all," and she made a gesture to indicate the outside world where Clyde resided, "I thought, what's gonna happen to my child?

"Well, first of all, I know this sounds awful, but I think he, well, I think he thought you were funny. 'Like a rookie they shouldn't put in yet,' is what he said. Then he said, about you, 'He's getting better,' and so was he. Bringing home his books? Doing homework? Huh? Then here comes his report card and I'll tell you," she said, pulling back and putting her hands on her hips again. "He by God got the best report card ever and he talks to John at dinner, asks him about his job, and he plays ball down at the rec center and don't fight. Well, less he has to. And you said, on his report card, now tell me if it ain't true, you said that he's the most gifted math student in your class. You said that?"

"Yes, ma'am, I said that. And as you may have heard tonight my report cards are an honest reflection of how my students perform."

"But maybe I could add somethin' here, hon?" Mr. Carver asked. He put an affectionate hand on her hip.

Neil knew from his own vivid memory of doing just that with his not quite one-night stand. Who was? CC. Yes, her name was CC. Neil knew how much pleasure could be involved in taking a woman's hip.

"All right," Mrs. Carver said.

"What we need to know. We thinkin' of moving. Some of my people got a place in Queens, in a nice neighborhood. And we could probably get a place there, too. Rent to buy would be the way we'd go. If we did that Clyde would go to a different school."

"He wouldn't change in the middle of the year," Mrs. Carver put in quickly.

"Next year," Mr. Carver said, closing his eyes and shaking his head.

Neil got it. Whether they should move, and when, was under serious discussion, but her preference for staying at least through the school year had been decided. So what was the question now?

"The school would be better, harder," Mr. Carver said. "And there's some racial stuff, white and black."

Neil was shaking his head. What had been a stressful evening had suddenly become an impossible one. His entire body was now on red alert. *I can't tell them what to do.*

As if he were reading Neil's mind, Mr. Carver said, "We ain't axing you to tell us what to do. We just want to know what you think. Like, you know, if it's a really bad idea or what. Just what you think, is all, as his teacher. We won't hold nothin' against you."

As his teacher. They were asking him to behave responsibly, like a teacher.

It was happening too quickly. When he had pushed his opinions on Bianca's mother he hadn't quite realized the declaration he was making: *I am Bianca's teacher, I care about her and what I think matters.* This time around he couldn't plead ignorance. Next year he could become a law student or a short-order cook in a Calgary luncheonette. It didn't matter. At this moment, right now, he could take an active role in influencing a child's life or he could shrug it off with a credible: *Still, I can't tell you what to do.*

"I can't tell you what to do," he said. "But..." and felt himself stumbling over an emotional line he had never meant to cross; leaping. "...I care what happens to Clyde." He rubbed his forehead with his right thumb and forefinger and went with the fall. "I can only tell you this. I went to Garibaldi for a job interview. There were papers strewn all over the hall, potato chip wrappers, you know, trash. And there were lockers, all up and down the hall, you know, those school lockers, a lot of them with the doors dangling open. It looked like the aftermath of a war."

"I've been there," Mr. Carver said. "That's exactly right. It is a war. Different gangs have they own places in the halls, they own bathrooms. Fights go unchecked, kids get mugged every day. Every day, okay? Every day some kid gets beat up, sometimes enough to go to the hospital. They can't keep teachas, parents keep they kids at home."

"And nobody does anything?" Neil asked, relieved to let The Carver take the lead.

"It was always bad, but it sort of drifted along. After the riots everybody expected it would get better. And it wasn't so bad they couldn't pretend. But after the strikes it just got worse. And this year

I think it got even worse than that. So now it's impossible. Maybe somethin' will happen. Maybe not. For a long time the schools chancellor, especially, and the district administrator and Lindsay hisself didn't want cops in there. We'd be disruptive, they said. It wasn't necessary, they said. Bad publicity is more like it. Man, you don't know the lies people will tell to save they jobs. Now they gonna lose they jobs anyway and they screamin' where's the po'leeeese, when of course we're gettin' cut back and don't have the bodies to send in there to really make the place safe. They got two uniformed guards there now. And Lindsay? This time he fought the Council to keep them there." He snickered. "They get beat up, too."

He pulled at Mrs. Carver. "What I think is if we stay up here I oughta drive Clyde down to my sister's neighborhood anyway. She'd vouch for him and he'd at least go to a school where you can walk the halls."

"He wouldn't know anybody," Mrs. Carver said.

"So? The people he'll know at Garibaldi? He'll be better off not knowing them."

"It's just so hard. What about his reading?" she asked Neil.

"It's getting better." Neil suddenly buried his head in his hands.

"Mr. Riley? You okay?" The Carver asked.

"I don't know. I don't know." He shook his head. "All of my kids." He stood up straight. "This is the kind of decision... It's impossible." He was thinking of the cocky, *'I'll do my best,'* he had given Norbert's grandfather. Aloud he said, "What do they do? They stay home, terrified, or they join a gang and become outlaws? Is that the way it is? Look," he said to Mrs. Carver, "it's your decision to make. But if it were up to me I'd put Clyde in a more stable environment. If I could I'd put all my kids in a more stable environment. This situation is insane. And no one's doing anything about it."

"That's exactly what I think," The Carver said, satisfied. "Hon, I got to go. I got to take you home first. "

"Mr. Riley, it was so nice to meet you," she said pleasantly, as if they had been having coffee and cake at a luncheon.

And they were gone. *But what about Clyde's reading?* Somehow it didn't seem as important as it had before. *It's your decision to make,* he had told her, but then: *If it were up to me I'd put Clyde in a more stable environment. If I could I'd put all my kids in a more stable environment.* He cringed at his audacity. *Well, wasn't that the truth? But Mr. Riley, are you prepared to work to establish that stable environment?*

Chapter 10:

One of My Favorites

In Room 6-308: when he came in she asked, "Are they gone?"

"Yes. They were the last."

"All dressed up like a hussy," Mrs. Robin hissed. "It's disgraceful. And she was so sweet. And smart? My goodness, she was smart as a whip. And so pretty. It made your heart ache to look at her."

It still does, Neil thought. *And other parts of your anatomy, too.*

"And now? And that big Poe-lice Officer wearing that thing in here. How could he? Sometimes I can't stand it. She dresses like that for *him*. That's not *her*. You know that, don't you?"

She does wear it well though, he thought, but he had the good sense not to say so.

"For him and for Clyde, so he'll have the protection of a father." She was throwing books in a bag, furious. Suddenly she stopped and looked at him. "And look at you. Stumbling-down tired. I wanted to ask you to carry some stuff for me. But maybe I should be carrying you."

"No, no, I'm good. I just didn't sleep much last night."

"Worrying about Parents' Night, huh? Well, it wasn't so bad, was it?"

"What do you need?" he asked her, not sure that it wasn't even worse than he had expected. Because it wasn't over. Because he had never felt so alone. He wanted to ask her why she had never told him about 'Junebug.' Why hadn't she said Clyde's mother had been one of her pupils? Had she disapproved of Junebug's pregnancy? Or had she somehow thought she had failed one of her children in need? Perhaps she felt Neil would be better off not knowing... Not knowing what? What he knew was that he didn't dare approach the subject with her. And he couldn't tell her how bothered he was by the Garibaldi conversation either. She might realize that what really upset him was that he didn't want to do this, be a teacher; it was too much; it was changing him; he didn't know what was happening.

But most of all? He was very very tired, that must be it, though it didn't feel that way. What he felt was that most of all he needed to talk to someone about what was happening to him. What he felt was a need, a longing, something he didn't understand and that he knew very well was not ever going to be fulfilled.

"You look terrible," Mrs. Robin said. "I have a bargain for you. I can't let you take that bus home tonight. If you help me carry my displays down—most of which, by the way, I didn't use—I'll drive you home."

"Don't you take the West Side?"

She lived in the twenties, in the Chelsea district.

"Not tonight. You help me, I'll double right back."

"That would be fantastic."

As he waited on the sidewalk with their stuff he thought how wrenching the evening had been. And how satisfying. *Yeah, and where were all the other parents?* he thought in a huff, sounding just like Mrs. Robin. Then he thought how much he had resisted doing this evening; how he had actually contemplated pretending he was sick. What if you were Arlene's mother? Or Sheri's? Would you want to come in and listen to some young smart aleck tell you how much trouble your child was? He should call all the parents, not to complain, but to chat. *Oh, God, let me be,* he moaned. *Next year,* he thought.

Before he could realize the full import of what was going through his head he noticed two dark figures loitering against a fence about half a block away, in front of the apartment complex next to the school. He immediately stiffened for trouble, then just as quickly relaxed. That jacket hooked over the head of one of the figures? That had to be Charles. And could that be?... His mother! Come for Parents' Night?! That was her. Neil felt certain of it. He had to acknowledge her. He wanted to hear what she had to say about Charles.

But he didn't feel he could leave the bags sitting unguarded at the curb. He knew how valuable his briefcase was to him, as useless as it would be to anyone else. Surely Mrs. Robin would feel the same way about her bags of displays. Even if he had felt confident no one would bother with their things (which he did not) he would have worried that Mrs. Robin would think he was irresponsible to leave them to... do what? Chase down two specters that could or could not be Charles and his mother? The minutes went by and Mrs. Robin didn't appear. It was maddening. He couldn't let Robin down. He couldn't let Charles down. He didn't know what to do. Why didn't she come? Why was this evening so relentlessly difficult?

It probably took her less than fifteen minutes to get the car and drive around from wherever she had found a space to pick him up, but it seemed like hours. When she finally arrived and he had thrown her stuff in the back seat, he told her what the situation was and asked her to leave him.

"You put your briefcase in the car and go see who that is. I'll sit right here. I mean it. And don't you hurry up either. I'm not going to leave you."

He tapped the frame of the door. He wouldn't have dared grab her shoulder, though that's what he wanted to do. He walked briskly over to Charles and the other person, cloaked, black, facing the fence, gripping the fence, tight, hanging on.

"Hey, buddy. I thought that was you."

Charles was holding his notebook against his stomach. It was tied with some sort of cord. Maybe the kind of elastic you'd put in the waist of sweats? This was to hold his library books?

"Ma mummm," he mumbled.

Which Neil translated as, 'My mother.'

"Mrs. Franklin," Neil said.

She gripped the fence even tighter.

"Thank you so much for coming tonight. It gives me the opportunity to tell you how well Charles is doing. Has he shown you some of the homework he's been doing?"

She nodded her head vigorously.

"He's been writing his numbers and he does letters and he can sign his name. He plays in the yard with the other kids."

She nodded.

"He probably didn't say it, but you must have guessed; he's one of my favorites."

She pulled herself against the fence and nodded her head wildly and without warning went running off toward Amsterdam. Charles looked at him.

"Go, go," Neil insisted and watched Charles rush off after his mother.

In her car, Mrs. Robin said, "There's a seat belt. You clip it across your lap."

But he didn't understand what she was saying. Down that corridor? There were more corridors and classrooms with teachers who would not let him in. The last corridor narrowed and narrowed. He was crawling up a narrow hollow that he knew would soon close in on him. His mother, though he knew very well she was dead and gone to heaven, was saying...

"Mr. Riley? Neil? I'm sorry, you have to wake up."

He raised his head. He was looking at a woman—an amazing angel with eyes like black coals in a glowing velvet face—at her hand shimmering on his arm like a fiery handcuff. Bianca said, "That's not his mother." For a wrenching moment he felt an enormous sadness and then he was back, sitting with Mrs. Robin in her car at the corner of 96th and Lexington. The street light caught her face in profile, her hand was in a pool of light at his shoulder. He had had a dream that he could not remember, but that had left him with a deep sense of longing. Was this grief? He knew he had felt like this many times before, though he couldn't remember a single instance.

"It's almost ten," Mrs. Robin said. "I drove around the block a couple of times." She chuckled. "I almost took you home with me. Mr. Robin would have loved that."

"I went to sleep?"

"The minute you got in the car. You did manage to shut your door. I did your seat belt. You are one very tired young man."

"I'm so sorry. God. Gosh. Sorry. I really am a lot of trouble."

"You are a handful. I'm not sure of what, but it's a lot more than trouble."

"Whatever it is, I bet you know more about it than I do."

"Out of the mouths of babes," she said. "Just get some sleep, Mr. Riley."

Chapter 11:

Tell Me Everything

In his apartment: on Thursday evening at exactly seven he began trying to call a Mrs. Marvin Wolf, the person listed as Simon's "Primary Contact." Her "Relationship to Student" was listed as "Grandmother." This had to be our lady of the "I don't want no conference" encounter. Neil had Simon's folder on his lap. He could clearly remember two exchanges with him. Once at random he picked his name from the roster to go to the board to do a long division problem. As Neil did so he realized he had no sense of who Simon Wolf was. There was a boy sitting in that seat; he rose when Neil called out "Simon Wolf;" it was likely that was Simon Wolf. What was memorable about the incident was that in his nervous haste to get to his feet Simon had dropped his notebook on the floor.

The other time that Neil could remember speaking directly to Simon had been when he caught him looking at Arlene's paper during a spelling test. Neil had to go to his roster to look up his name before he could say, "Mr. Wolf, if you can't keep your eyes to yourself you're going to earn yourself a zero."

Simon buried his head in his hands and shook it hard. He said nothing to defend himself. Neil remembered thinking at the time that it was more likely Simon was checking to see if Arlene had the right answer than that he was trying to copy it. Neither of them would win any spelling bees, but Simon certainly had the edge when it came to language arts. A curious aside about Simon for Neil was that he seemed to be a friend of Arlene's—an actual friend, not some minion she kept under her thumb.

And then he remembered another encounter with Simon. Wasn't

he the boy who during that terrible first week of school Neil had accused of making a belching sound? Neil had lifted the petrified boy and his desk and slammed them to the floor. Now, based on what little he knew of Simon, a quiet, shy child with a sweet smile, it was highly unlikely he had done anything so disruptive. Neil had lashed out blindly, which of course he shouldn't have done, and hurt an innocent child. Yeah, well, one thing was certain, that wasn't one of the things he meant to discuss with Simon's grandmother.

As it turned out he wouldn't be discussing anything with her.

The telephone was busy and remained busy for an entire hour. Neil tried the number at ten minute intervals from seven to eight then gave up. At five after eight, with Brenda's folder in front of him, he dialed Brenda's aunt, Mrs. Green. He was so used to getting a busy signal that he wasn't at all prepared for the immediate "hello" that came after one ring.

"I was waiting for your call," she said.

Should he have dialed at exactly eight? "I appreciate that," Neil said, fumbling around, looking for the paper with the notes he'd made to help him conduct the conference. Where was it? It had been right in front of him. He found it on his knee, under Brenda's folder. "I'll give you a report on Brenda's progress, but first, do you have any special concerns?" he asked, reading from his notes.

"Tell me everything," Mrs. Green said. "Everything. Good and bad. I just want to hear about her."

"You have her report card?"

"Right in front of me." She began to cry. "It's the best she's gotten in a long time."

"She's a good student."

"Oh, my Lord."

"Mrs. Green, are you okay?"

"I'm fine. Tell me what happened today."

"Today? Nothing special."

"Tell me anything," she insisted.

"I had difficulties with Brenda at the beginning of the year. Her best friend..."

"Arlene," Mrs. Green said, dragging the name out of her mouth.

"...has difficulties."

"To put it mildly," Mrs. Green said.

"Okay, but it took me a while to see they're very different. And I've come to understand, I think, that Brenda needs Arlene."

"Oh, and just how is that, pray tell?"

Neil chuckled. "I can see you don't exactly approve of this friendship."

"To put it mildly."

"Who you talkin' to?" Neil heard a man's voice say. That would be Mr. Green.

"Excuse me," she said. Her voice suddenly became muffled, but he could still hear her, saying, "It's Mr. Riley, Brenda's teacha at school. I ax him to call me." And to some muffled response from him, she said, "Ain't no problem. I ax him. He say she doin' juss fine. Juss a few more minutes."

Neil realized she had been speaking to him one way, with school talk, the kids called it, and to her husband regular, as they would say.

"Mr. Riley, are you there?"

I'm hangin', he thought. "Yes, I'm here," he said.

"I don't appreciate her friendship with Arlene one bit," she said, not missing a beat in their conversation.

"Okay, but," and here he shamelessly filched from the wisdom of Mrs. Robin, "there's a positive aspect to their relationship."

"Oh, please."

"No, really. It took me a while to realize it, but Brenda tends to be fearful."

"You're being careful. She's scared out of her wits."

"And Arlene is about as close to fearless as you can get without getting knocked down by a mail truck because you think it won't hurt you."

"She's not fearless. She's crazy."

"No, she's not fearless and she's not crazy. She's troubled. But she's tough and she's gutsy and Brenda uses that. Arlene is teaching Brenda that the world isn't as scary as it sometimes seems."

"That's something I never thought about."

Me either, Neil thought. *Robin revealed it to me. But I don't need to tell her that.*

"And Brenda is teaching Arlene. For one thing, Brenda can speak proper English."

"School talk," Mrs. Green said.

White talk, like you, he thought. "Yes. But it's more than that. Brenda knows the value of being able to operate in different worlds."

"If only she could cash in on that knowledge," Mrs. Green exclaimed.

"Well, she's getting there. Her behavior in my class is much better, which separates her from Arlene. But this has caused some changes in Arlene, too."

"I'll tell you later," Mrs. Green said in a sweet affectionate voice.

"Ma'am?"

"I'm sorry. Not you. It's Brenda. She just poked her nose out the door." In that other voice, she said again, "I'll tell you later. I promise." Then, "Mr. Riley?"

"I'm here," *juss hangin'.*

"Brenda is changing," Mrs. Green said. "She's starting to come out of herself. She dared to fight to get the phone for fifteen minutes every night. To discuss her homework with Bianca." She laughed. "Like with all that whispering they really discuss their homework. And now I have something *she* wants to know. She knew you'd be calling and she's in her room going crazy waiting to hear what you said."

"I hope you tell her everything."

"Everything?"

"Everything. It might just set off some sparks in that excellent brain of hers. But I want to tell you what I've told her. And I want you to tell her what I said. You asked what she did today. Well, the answer is nothing she didn't have to do. She only participates when she's called on. I want to see more effort. If I give a hard problem for extra credit on a math test I want her to do that problem. If I ask a question about what we're reading, I want her to raise her hand if she knows the answer. I call on her and bam she's knows exactly what it's about. So why didn't she raise her hand? I want her to show more initiative."

Mrs. Green laughed. "Chile, you are something else."

"Why you say that?" he bounced back.

"I expected you to be all huffy and give me nothing. At least, I half expected it. Listen." She was suddenly whispering. "I have to tell you this. Because you're a man. And you laugh and shout and look at people. It's good for her. Even if you're... I dunno. So big and tall. I have to get off now. Someone's coming."

"Even if I'm white?" he said.

"It's a fact of life, isn't it? The way things are?"

"Yes, ma'am."

"Thank you for calling, Mr. Riley," she said, suddenly quite formal and proper. Mr. Green's ugly head must have appeared on the horizon. "I appreciate the good report..."

"Excellent report," Neil said.

"Excellent report," she repeated. "And we will expect Brenda to continue to improve, especially in her participation, over the coming months. Goodbye, Mr. Riley." And she hung up.

Neil stared at the phone wishing for more and thinking about Brenda and about living in dual worlds. That led him to think about his incredible young colleague, Bianca Maldonado, who lived in multiple worlds in two languages and stayed exactly who she was in all of them.

Part Four:

The Days Grow Shorter 1969

Chapter 1:

Opening Windows

In the schoolyard: Brenda was already on line, talking to Bianca. *Talking to Bianca?! Of course, talking to Bianca the way she did almost every night on the phone. Why hadn't I known that?* Harriet and Sandra stood with them, a small tight circle. Arlene, back by herself, without Brenda now, shuffled forward with dramatic weary droops of her shoulders to the back of the girls' line just behind Brenda, who had nervously stepped back there the moment she saw Neil.

Norbert and Clyde left their outposts, herding in Charles. Pauli and Sammy, who had been circling Clyde, followed after him. They all looked so different to him now after nearly three months as their teacha, even more so after the whipsaw encounters on Parents' Night. Had that really only been a week ago?

Now the boys were known figures, yeah, with problems, but not ciphers without substance. There was Norbert (*Norberto?*), thin, scared and long-legged, perched precariously between the figures of his grandfather, the chevalier, and his father, the brutal thug, his jeans hitched high, his jacket zipped tight, braced for the attack that would inevitably come. On the other side of the perimeter was Clyde, the tall cool athlete, dressed in the same style as Norbert, but worn so much more easily; Clyde, chosen son of the fabled beauty, Junebug, stepson of the monstrous intruder, The Carver; Clyde, wanting nothing more than the opportunity to fight for justice and truth and, of course, revenge. Norbert and Clyde, Fear and Anger, were more driven than most of the others to find answers, were more tuned to the precariousness of 6-306.

Between them staggered the hooded drifter, Charles, son of the tortured woman of the shadows. Surely he was the ground from which they all had come, wordless needs peering out of the darkness at a panorama arcane, threatening, beckoning.

Pauli, spiffy as always, costumed today in a half-length black overcoat opening to a tight brown Beatles suit, all three buttons of the jacket done up to the stiff white shirt collar and bright blue snap-on bowtie. As improbable as it seemed, his outfits were so much a part of him no one teased him about them. After meeting Pauli's grandmother, the huge woman with the iron fist, Neil grasped a vision, however askew, of a world of manners and decorum. And Pauli, even when he was Clyde's humble squire, managed to transform his grandmother's outfits into wild, dramatic statements. Sammy, small, with large ears flying out from each side of his head, his dusty matted hair somehow defining his unformed, unkempt nature, Sammy followed Pauli because he had to follow somebody; and Pauli, whatever misgivings Neil might have about him, had inner drives and needs that made him twist and fly down problematic aisles regardless of the consequences.

These five boys, Neil's outlanders, managed to reach the rear of the line just as Neil arrived at the front on a grey bleak day with large black storm clouds climbing into the western sky.

"Good morning, 6-306," Neil said cheerfully.

And he got, "Good morning, Mr. Riley," from his regulars, Pedro and Morris and Las Senoritas and the vast unknown middle. It wasn't an overwhelming response, but it was friendly, with no sense of irony or rancor.

Then, because he had sworn to himself that he would try each day to pay attention to at least one child he rarely singled out for anything, a child who was a complete mystery to him, he caught Simon's eye. Simon, when he saw Neil look at him, looked quickly away in mortal terror. Neil was absolutely not under any circumstances ready to deal with Simon today. So he chose from the unknown middle: "Connie?" Of course, Constance Andrews, a little chunky, average height, very black, broad nose and at this moment with those lovely brown eyes looking up at him in an apprehensive *what did I do?* stare. Neil wanted to hug her, tell her it was okay, tell her she shared a name with his aunt, the only person in the entire world he trusted. He said, "Pretty good on the math quiz yesterday." She actually got six out of ten, her best ever.

Then he turned his attention to the girl whose mother had piqued his interest like no other. "Harriet?" Harriet Wilson, quiet, light brown, attractive without being assertive about it, with thin, expressive lips and a high forehead. Unlike her mother, she straightened her hair, but she wore it short and brushed back, which was rebellious enough for a sixth grader.

"Yes, Mr. Riley?"

She was about average height for her age and stood just in front of Bianca and just behind Constance. The girls were the ones who made the determination about their place on line. They measured themselves constantly and changed places based on their findings. To Neil these three looked to be exactly the same height and for the moment straight as boys. *Girls on the cusp of menses. Oh God.* Another challenge he was totally unprepared to deal with.

As this went whizzing through Neil's mind he was preparing to move his class out the moment Mrs. Robin's went strutting by, stuck-up little reading-on-grade-level bourgeois snots that they were, and trying to focus on Harriet, who should have been with that elite bunch, would have been an elite among that elite, and had chosen to be in this class, insisted on this class, where she remained carefully anonymous.

For the moment because of some PA system glitch he could focus on her just one moment longer. There was always a novel stuffed in with her other books. She read constantly. When he had called her name she'd looked at him with curiosity, not the least bit apprehensive. Complicated, huh? Of course, when he called her name at least a dozen other pairs of eyes had looked at him, too, not the least of them Bianca's, curious, Sheri's, with a jealous glower, and Arlene's, glaring darkly.

"Whatcha reading this week?"

"*Anne of Green Gables*. Have you read it, Mr. Riley?"

"Not yet, but I will."

"You gonna stand around out here all day?" Arlene called out as Robin's class began to move past his back.

Neil smiled at her pleasantly. "Thank you, Arlene. You're absolutely right. We have a lot to do today and if we get started right away we might get out of here before four this afternoon."

There were groans at that remark and from the chief perpetrator, "Oh, gaw."

In Room 6-306: With Pauli finally in his seat and Arlene quiet and Brenda watching Neil's every move—with hatred? fear? —he called the roll. This was a deliberate act, to demonstrate his control, the fascist who could make the trains run on time. They were all there, every single one of them. He knew that when he picked them up in the schoolyard.

"Miss Wallace?"

"Whatcha want?" Sheri snapped.

"'Yes, Mr. Riley,'" Neil said in a high voice. "'How can I help you?' Could you try that?"

"Whoa, pretty flippy," Clyde said, waving his hands on loose wrists.

Neil said, "We'll wait until Clyde stops calling out."

Clyde sighed deeply, but said nothing.

Neil said, "Sheri, just once, let's try to have a polite exchange. You know, I call on you and you don't bite my head off? Want to try?"

With the whole class watching, Sheri smiled widely and said, "I guess."

"Okay, here goes. Miss Wallace?"

Sheri batted her eyelashes. Pauli, then Sammy, whooped in appreciation. There was an, "Oh, my Lord, that girl," from Arlene and laughter and clapping across the room.

Sheri waited until the hubbub died down, then said, "Yes, Mr. Riley, how can I help you?" While she definitely expressed concern, it was laden with the suggestion that this Mr. Riley's demands would be excessive. And, still, she made it clear that they would receive the utmost consideration. But what impressed Neil most about her reply was that she used perfect "school" pronunciation.

It was his turn to wait for the laughter and clapping to end and his timing was not nearly as good as Sheri's. "Would you be so kind as to hand out Tuesday's math homework? And collect the homework for today?"

In a flash she was at his desk.

Softly he said, holding the papers up out of reach, "This may be the last set of papers you give out. Wait, don't fret," he said to the blooming red lower lip and distrustful eyes. "Once everyone's busy correcting their mistakes, I want to have a job interview with you. Okay?"

"Okay," she said, looking up at him uncertainly. She was trying to read his face.

"What's he sayin'?" Arlene called out.

"You mind your own beeswax," Sheri said.

"Don't," Neil said to Bianca, who had turned in her chair, ready to fill in Arlene. "We'll wait while Arlene and Sheri learn not to call out."

Arlene raised her hand. Neil did an exaggerated double-take. He clutched his chest.

"Arlene! Miss Whitman, you had a question?"

"What yawl talkin' about?"

"I'm opening negotiations with Miss Wallace on a very sensitive matter. I'm not ready to divulge the details to the public just yet. Once we've ironed out an agreement I'll allow questions and answer them as best I can."

"That man crazeeee," Arlene said.

Neil stared at her, but chose not to say anything. After all, it was his silliness that had instigated her response.

He handed Sheri the papers. "Except this one. I want to give this one out myself."

Sheri was off. Neil walked over to Charles, clutching a crumpled piece of notebook paper.

Neil heard Sheri say, "Don't you mess with me," and Arlene began some rejoinder and several people from all sides of the room, most notably Bianca and Clyde, said *shush* as Neil put his hand on Charles' shoulder. Charles sat up and let the jacket slide up his head so one eye was visible.

"Thank you, buddy. This was good. Not perfect, but really good. I was so pleased when I saw this. I can't tell you."

Charles had printed his name, ChArles FrNAklin, at the top of the page and then copied the first five problems. His numbers were too large and then too small. At the bottom of the page he had written all the numbers from 1 to 10.

Neil knew this paper was a plea: *Teach me.* He had been tempted to write across the paper: *I don't know how.* What he had actually done was correct FrNAklin underneath in red with *Franklin* and written in bold blue print: *GOOD WORK!* He put the paper down carefully in the middle of Charles' desk and gently pressed it out.

Charles had already disappeared back under his jacket, but Neil knew that when he turned away the boy would peek out again.

Back at his desk, Neil, with just about everyone else in the class, watched Charles lift his head up and with a finger slide the paper closer, then put his whole hand on it, then take a look.

Two weeks ago Neil had given Charles a loose-leaf notebook with a pack of fifty lined pages and slots back and front for hand-outs and long pockets for three pencils, which Neil had filled with sharpened brand new yellow number twos. Neil had shown him that it was wide enough so that if he wanted to take a book he liked home he could slip it under the cover and no one could see it. Charles often secretly hid picture books from the library under his jacket. Now he could put them in his notebook. He hid them because they were picture books for first and second graders. He had by now crisscrossed his notebook with two knotted dirty white elastic bands to hold everything inside.

It was Neil's constant provocateur, Bianca, who had first suggested he give Charles the notebook. "He don't ever have somethin' to write with," she said after Neil gave Charles yet another piece of paper and yet another pencil. "And he ain't ever gonna. You should give him like a workbook or something. I bet he'd keep that."

It was, as usual, an excellent idea. "You may be trying to convey an idea worthy of consideration," Neil said. "It's just that I didn't understand a word you said."

"I'm sayin'…" She paused, studied his smirk and said, with a lift of her head, "I'm saying Charles never has anything to write with and won't unless you give him some sort of workbook." She smiled. "Thass all."

"It's an excellent idea," he said.

"I know," she said, flipping the word at him.

When Neil gave Charles the notebook, the boy, rubbing the cover, was moved to proclaim with near lucidity, "Like your briefcase." It was a glossy white cover with NY Yankees in bold blue letters across the front; nothing, in fact, like Neil's briefcase.

The first day Charles got the notebook he carried it everywhere.

Someone, most likely Clyde, had convinced him no one would dare steal it, because the next day he left it under his desk when the class went to lunch.

Now, even though everyone was watching, he slid the notebook out from the wire holder under his seat and very carefully undid the elastic and clacked open the three hole clasps, put his paper inside and clipped them closed. Then he turned the page and took out one of his pencils and began to write, his exposed head bent in concentration. Meanwhile, if he had done anything last night it would somehow appear on Neil's desk later. He wouldn't give it to Sheri.

"You know what I want you all to do now."

"Correct our mistakes," Pedro said.

"Exactly."

"How come he gets to call out?" Arlene asked.

Neil pointed at Pedro. "She's right. You're supposed to raise your hand like Miss Whitman did not do."

Pedro raised his hand.

"Mr. Rodriguez?"

"We're supposed to correct our mistakes."

"That's right. I've circled them in red, but I haven't corrected them. What happens now?"

Constance, among others, raised her hand.

"Miss Andrews?"

"We can get help from anybody, but then we gonna have to go to the board and explain our problems."

"Then we gonna have another quiz?"

"We'll wait until Arlene stops calling out."

"We'll wait until Arlene stops callin' out," Arlene repeated.

Neil nodded. "That's exactly right. We're waiting. And in the meantime I want to remind you that we're going to have to get through this schedule before we leave today."

He pointed at the corner of the board where he had printed, as usual, the day and the date and beneath that heading the subjects they would cover:

Wednesday, November 19, 1969
Mathematics
Reading
Library
Lunch and Recess
Spelling
Social Studies

Brenda raised her hand.

"Brenda?"

"Mr. Riley, please, I can't leave late anymore."

"Her uncle give her a lickin'," Arlene said.

Brenda turned and stared at Arlene.

"Well, he do," Arlene said to her.

Brenda mumbled something.

"What'd you say, Miss Smarty?" Arlene called out.

"'Does.' I said 'does.' You said, 'Well, he do.' Say, 'Well, he does.'"

"Well, he does," Arlene said compliantly.

Neil was so stunned by Arlene's willingness to be corrected that he had to take a moment to remember what was going on. This was not the first time Brenda had done this, but each time it shocked Neil that Arlene submitted so obediently. The one time he dared correct Arlene's English ("*I have, not I has*") she snarled at him to shut up, then for the rest of the day deliberately repeated *I has* ad nauseam. *I has no paper. Oh, and I has a headache. And I has the ugliest teacha I has eva has.*

"We'll wait for as long as it takes for you two to stop wasting our time."

"How come..." Sheri started, then stopped herself and raised her hand.

"Sheri?"

"How come we all have to stay late just cause *she* always callin' out?"

There was no doubt in anyone's mind who *she* was, but if there were the referent made it clear, saying, "Oh, yeah, and you never call out or jump up outta your seat or knock papers all over the place. You such a good little girl."

"We're waiting," Neil said.

"I raised my hand," Sheri said, anguished at the injustice of it all.

"Time's passing."

Morris raised his hand and said, "It's not fair, though, Mr. Riley. Sheri's right."

"So, if you raise your hand, it's okay to call out? And I disagree. Sheri's not right. You all let it happen. Arlene starts something and Carmen takes out her makeup purse," which she had just done, "Sandra starts to draw." He pointed at Sandra drawing. "Cole says something to Jason and Jason repeats it to Javier and Pauli starts playing with his cars." All of which in fact had just happened. "And if I weren't talking to you you and Pedro would have started playing hangman. Okay? She distracts me and you all figure, 'Break time! He'll be messing with her for a while. Might as well catch some zzzs.'"

Arlene got up and went back to the coat hangers and took her coat and folded it under her arm.

"Arlene," Neil said, "if you leave the room without a pass you will not come back, not until I meet with your mother. Do you understand? Be very clear about this. No one, not Mr. Bernbach, not Mrs. Bane, no one will get you back in this classroom until your mother comes in and explains to me why I should let you disrupt this entire class EVERY MINUTE OF EVERY DAY!" he shouted.

Arlene stood looking at him.

"We'll wait until Arlene hangs up her coat and sits down."

Arlene sat down with her coat in her arms.

"Arlene, we're waiting for you to hang up your coat."

"Gaw."

She marched to the coat hooks and hung up her coat, demonstrating with her stomping feet how unreasonable he was being. When she was back in her seat she said, "I ain't gonna do no math."

"We're waiting."

There was then actually a moment of silence.

"All right," Neil said, "correct your mistakes. Clyde, you and Pedro can wander around the room and help anyone who doesn't understand his mistakes."

"What about me? I got them all right, too. Don't I get to help nobody?" Bianca called out. "Anybody," she corrected herself coyly.

"Brenda, you got them all right, too, didn't you?" Neil asked.

"Yes, Mr. Riley."

"You can go around, too, if you want. Bianca, maybe if you raised your hand instead of calling out, I'd have taken your objection into account."

Bianca, making a face, waved an angry hand at him, then sat with her arms folded, her hands under her armpits, her head held high.

Constance raised her hand.

"Miss Andrews?"

"Please Mr. Riley, I understand the way Bianca explains it."

"Not today," Neil said. "She's got to learn not to call out just like everybody else."

"That's..." Arlene suddenly raised her hand.

"Miss Whitman?"

"That's right. Bianca's got to learn not to call out."

Neil smiled. To Bianca he said, "Good advice."

Bianca stared at him without comment.

Constance raised her hand again.

"Constance?"

"What about Harriet?"

Who was at that moment sitting straight up, her hands folded across her paper, on which as usual was a big blue 100% plus *5% extra credit for Language Arts*. Harriet liked to make teasing comments in the margins of her math homework. On one she had written, in the blue pencil he used to make such comments himself: *note how carefully the student has placed her columns.* On this one she had put a small dash through the staff of all her sevens and written in the margin the first time she did this, *This is how they do sevens in Europe. But of course you know that.* He had replied with the same blue pencil: *Actually I did know it, but just the same am giving you extra credit for reminding me.*

"Harriet," he said.

"Yes, Mr. Riley, how can I help you?"

She was playing with him! Brainy, smart-mouthed little bitch.

"Could you help Constance?"

"Yes, of course," she said.

To the class, he said, "Okay, you have about fifteen minutes. Remember, if you goof off and I call you to the board and you can't explain your mistake then you get a check for your homework, but you don't get a plus. Okay. Sheri? Can I speak with you?"

She streaked over to his desk.

"Before you sit down, could you get the pole and push that upper window closed, the one right where Charles is?"

Neil worried that she couldn't handle the job.

"Yeah," she said.

She got the pole, which was nearly twice as tall as she was, and went back and engaged the hook in the hole in the upper window frame. The window was tilted open at a slant. Sheri pushed it closed.

"Just one more thing," he said, after she leaned the pole back in its place in the corner behind his desk. "Could you close this window?" he asked, indicating the window right at his elbow, which was open about a foot at the bottom.

"Why should I?" Sheri asked, suspicious.

"Because I asked you to."

She slammed the window shut.

"Gaw," Arlene complained.

When Sheri sat back down on the chair next to his desk Neil suddenly noticed how quiet it had become. Normally even as now when the class was being reasonably cooperative there was a buzz, a swirling mix of talk, blown noses, sudden ouches, scraping desks, snapped notebooks, whispers, laughter, all the things each child of thirty-three children might add to the stew. Where was that noise? Both Neil and Sheri looked up: to find everyone watching them.

Neil raised a finger to his lips, telling Sheri to keep quiet. "Mind your own beeswax," he said to the class, catching a laugh, even from Arlene. Then to Sheri he said, "Mac gets really mad when I forget to close the windows at night and I sometimes forget to open them in the morning and then it gets really hot."

"You want me to be the window monitor?" Her tone left no doubt how she felt about taking the job.

"I have some conditions."

"I can't give out no more papers."

"That's one."

"What's the other one?"

"There's more than one."

"What?" Clearly she had begun to realize how much this could cost her.

"You can't make a fuss," he said.

"I know," she said indignantly, as if suggesting that she would make a fuss was utterly baseless; how dare he bring it up. "What else?"

"If we're taking a test and you're not finished and I ask someone who is finished to do the windows or do a window, you won't go berserk."

He waited, suppressing a smile, as she agonized.

"Don't worry, won't nobody do it less he asks," Bianca whispered.

Since this was intended for Sheri Bianca seemed to assume Neil would pretend not to hear her and, too, since she was supporting him she seemed to expect him to let her in on the negotiations.

"What they sayin'?" Arlene asked, knowing Bianca would be fully informed.

"She's gonna be the window monitor." Bianca's loud answer was delivered behind her hand as if she were whispering.

"How come she get to do everything?" Pauli protested.

"Math?" Neil said. "Have you done your math, Pauli? Bianca, could you please just mind your own business?"

"No," both she and Sheri said simultaneously.

"Yes," he said. To Sheri, he said, "What you gonna say to that? She gets to do everything? What am I gonna say to that? Mr. Riley, you always let Sheri do everything?"

"I got to do somethin'. I got to."

"That's the truth," Neil said, thinking how perfect her answer was. "You've got to do something. But let's understand; it's a blatant bribe on my part. I give you a job, your job, and you don't bug me about any other jobs, especially giving out papers."

"What's blatant?" Bianca asked.

"Look it up. Bla-tant," he said. "What's the first three letters?"

"B-l-a."

"Exactly," Neil said, pleased.

"See. She all a time callin' out an' you doan say nothin'," Sheri complained.

"That's right," Arlene said.

"Cause it's about words," Bianca said to Arlene in a yanyan tone.

"Cause you think you so smart," Sheri said in the same tone.

"Okay, cut it out, all of you. Sheri, do we have a deal?"

"Yeah."

"Okay. Every morning first thing starting with my window I want you to open every other window on the bottom. Then with the pole I want you to open the other three from the top. At the end of the day, when we start to get our coats, I want you to close all the windows. If we can get this right, I'll never again have to listen to Mac telling me I left the windows open. And that's essential because he's our source for everything. Books, paper, erasers, everything."

"I'll remind you," Bianca said.

"Bianca, please stop calling out," Neil insisted.

"All right," she said. She held up her hand.

"What?" he asked.

"All right," she said. "I'll stop calling out."

Neil held his hand out to Sheri, who quickly offered hers; they shook on it.

"You've got the job. You're the window monitor."

Before she sat down Sheri went to the window by his elbow and opened it about a foot, then got the pole, opened the top window she had closed before and placed the pole back against the wall behind his desk.

The morning moved on without incident, though Neil didn't quite understand when Clyde gave up on helping Sheri with her math and, moving on to Sammy, called out to Pedro, "She's your problem, not mine."

Then on the way to the library Neil saw Pedro and Sheri furtively brushing hands. They were so fascinated by this transaction it didn't seem to cross their minds that anyone would notice what they were doing. Ruth, right behind Sheri in the girls' line, caught Neil's eye with a knowing smirk. Ruth, Row 2, Seat 1, was a friend of Sheri's

and cared enough for her not to make out loud any of the acid observations Arlene would surely have made. The fact that Ruth had
engaged Neil at all shocked him. Who was Ruth? But more immediately, what was going on between Sheri and Pedro?

Chapter 2:

Talking to the Wall: Sixth Graders in Love

In Neil's apartment: on Friday afternoon he showered and put on fresh underwear, battered jeans, a grey sweat shirt with a coffee stain down the front, his beat up loafers and a jean jacket he got in high school. If he was going to goof off he was damn sure going to dress for it.

He took a booth in the deli and began *The Secret Garden* over dinner. When he worried about the usual mountain of papers waiting to be graded, he reminded himself he only had to prepare for two days. Next week was Thanksgiving, Wednesday was a half day and he would have Thursday and Friday off. Still this whole blasé don't-bother-me attitude would have been inconceivable only two weeks ago when he might find himself standing over the toilet bowl holding a paper with his free hand with a marker between his teeth, because he couldn't stop working long enough to pee.

After dinner when he came home, without quite meaning to, he sat down at his desk and stared at the wall. He picked up the notebook he used to scribble what he had come to think of as *Talking to the Wall*, found the page after his last entry, entered the date and wrote:

I think this week actually went okay. Maybe even, careful now, you don't want to get carried away, you could say it was a good week. There, I've said it. That doesn't mean it was easy. I didn't say easy. I don't know if teaching sixth grade could ever be easy. Aside from the fact that I'm a, what did Clyde call me? a rookie they shouldn't have put in the game, my opinions about teaching change from day to day. How about minute to minute? Anyway, let's get this straight: my credentials qualify me to make no grand statements about teaching.

He stared at the wall for a very long time.

Pedro and Sheri, their hands, small, quick brushings and then those delightful quivers. They're doomed. Sheri knows it. How do you know that? I just do. Okay, because she loves him with her entire being. It's a way he can't understand. He's got his family, his friends, his interests, his future, his life. Yeah, he "likes" her. She loves him. She has made that leap. He is a part of her. But she also knows he's practically white. Spanish. Maybe that's worse. Not black, that's for sure. Not available. End of story.

Just answer the question. How do you know how Sheri feels?

Go back to Wednesday after I turned my class over to Mrs. Worash and could wander, looking. There was Sheri over by the back window all by herself. Sheri all by herself? Pensive, a faraway expression on her face. Gorgeous child, yes, but also the woman she will become. Don't tread on me exterior and inside that passionate drive to be appreciated. "Well, I can give out the papers." Oh, my lovely child, you can give so much more. If only you are allowed.

And so my heart wishes you the best. Well, not always. But, come on, it does, it does.

Right. So where's Pedro? At a table in the back with Morris and Clyde. Morris I understood, but Clyde? My first thought was tits. Not pussy, unless Clyde had a really forbidden stash. Sleazy Riley. Wrong, so, so wrong. I had lent Clyde a book called Math for the Millions, *which has all kinds of information about mathematics: games, the different ways numbers are used, the special language they represent. Clyde was showing the book to Pedro.*

There was so much happening at that table to be excited about. Clyde discovering himself lecturing to the smart kid, *Pedro finding someone as intellectually involved as he was, Morris witnessing minds sorting through information.*

Yeah, yeah, yeah and what did that brilliant educator, that student of the elementary school child, that pissant rookie think? Pedro, why aren't you over there with Sheri?

Once again he stared at the wall, going… long ago and far away.

I'm sorry, Mr. Riley, but you still haven't answered my question. How do you know how Sheri feels?

It's as if I've stepped through some time portal. Because all of a sudden (what a phrase, "all of a sudden," but it's so accurate.) All of a sudden out of the blue unexpectedly here I am drenched in memories of you. And here they come: those moments, that happiness, behind the large oak in the playground at Lake Haven Elementary. It has to be spring because the leaves are out, but a new, light green, the air around us cool. We stand in our own small enclave, a place of wonder. You, my sweet lovely Lurlene, unzip the tan jacket Aunt Connie gave me, pull it open with both hands and step inside, looking into my eyes. Oh. Oh. Yours are blue, large, searching. It's a moment I'll never forget, a location so different from anyplace I had ever been before, and yet we could find it again and again, in our cabin by the lake, on hot days sitting under a tree our bikes leaning together behind us, just by looking at each other. I have never again found such a place anywhere with anyone. Oh, oh, how serious can that be?

He twisted up out of his seat and staggered over to the kitchen, then looked back at the chair angled away from the desk. He imagined it pulled in, himself sitting there, his pen flying across the page, writing that stuff. "Oh, oh," he simpered out loud. *Jesus,* he thought. *That's not me, okay? I don't know who the hell that is, but that's not me.*

Of course he remembered her. When he started sixth grade at Lake Haven Elementary there she was. Lurlene Stumph from Winston-Salem, North Carolina was suddenly there. He learned soon enough that her father had moved to Lake Haven because he had to complete a number of land deals for the tobacco company he worked for, which was definitely of interest to Aunt Connie. They often came into the restaurant, father and daughter. You should have seen the way Connie skipped over to his table to warm up his coffee even if it wasn't her station.

From the moment Neil saw her she became a confusingly radiant presence. The way in school she crossed her legs at her ankles, how her lips closed carefully over a fork, the intense form of her standing out and away from everything around her, everything about her was a torment and a joy. He wanted her to look at him, to notice him, and was terrified that she would. To this day memories of her surfaced the way some dreams do, immediate, real, then gone, unobtainable. He walked over to the desk, peeked at the open page as if eavesdropping, gripped the chair and sat down. He took the pen up gingerly, regarding it with suspicion; then dove right back into his reverie.

This is so ridiculous. We were eleven. As our closed, pathetically uninformed lips pressed together, I was so... I hate this... swept away. It was my first real kiss. And I will never forget it. I keep saying that. I will never forget it. But I did forget it. I forgot you. Or at least I managed to squeeze what happened between us into a tightly wrapped pod and pretend it was too trivial to take seriously.

But you were all that mattered to me. And I believed I was all that mattered to you. How brave you were to take up with that Riley kid, how brazen and, now I see, how exciting. Oh, oh, Lurlene. I still love you, even if, yes, even if I was just a little excitement in your life while you were away from your North Carolina home.

He stood up again. "Fuck this," he said and slammed the copybook closed. But the memories had already broken out and were running like a fever through his body. He paced restlessly back and forth, wanting this to end. Knowing that was impossible, he thought, *Out.* He put on sneakers, grabbed his jacket and took off, down the stairs, south on Lexington, west on 96th, walking, running, south to 59th, across to Broadway, up to 79th, even passing once that bar, *Silhouettes,* up to Riverside Park.

What would that long-haired streetdancer think of a man whose great love came and went when he was eleven years old? He moved when he could, waited for traffic when he had to, playing the lights, until the ripple of the breeze across the water, the magical places they found in the clouds and the bouts of wrestling that ended with them wrapped in each other's arms, until all that slid under a numb weariness and he knew that no matter how unsettled he might be when he woke up tomorrow he would be able to sleep tonight.

The next morning, Saturday, with his first cup of coffee he was back at his desk.

Of course I identify with these children. A guy like me? Living in a place where all the other kids got everything they wanted, while all I got was everybody wanting to take my life away. I remember reading, when? ninth grade, civics, reading The Declaration of Independence, *tears starting up, quick rub of your forehead, pretending you have a headache. Even then I had trouble with that stuff about the savage evil Indians. Kill 'em all. Why? Seemed to me they were just another downtrodden bunch like me. When we got to* The Constitution, *shit, I understood it completely. All the twists and turns. The hold your nose cause that's the way it is, then, fuck it, no we won't hold our nose. Why was I so smart in American history? It was about me. No. It* is *about me. Right here. Right now.*

And it's about Clyde, Bianca, the unknown middle, Javier, Marta, Simon, all of them. They too are created equal, they too have the unalienable right to life, liberty and the pursuit of happiness. Smart lively children with gifts and dreams, The Declaration *is theirs,* The Constitution *is theirs. Those rights belong to them.*

His anxieties won out and he spent the rest of the day grading papers. But after dinner, Chinese takeout, there he was, driven.

Garibaldi Junior High School. It looms eight blocks from Grant

Elementary, wide steps leading up to those two steel doors, opening out to swallow my children into what purportedly will be their seventh grade and in fact will be the beginning of three years in hell. My hope is they can make it to the tenth grade without too many scars. No high school in the city is as bad as Garibaldi.

How dare they call that place a school? How dare they allow it to exist? How do I know what a cesspool it is? Well, chillren, I almost worked there.

My program advisor, Miss Ivealreadyforgottenhername, kept pushing me to interview at junior highs, "where the jobs are." So I went to Garibaldi, headed down a hall that looked like an abandoned battlefield. Papers, bottle tops, crushed soda cans, pieces of clothing, half a watchband—debris— were strewn across the blue concrete floor, locker doors hung open, some dangling on one hinge. Classes were in session, but there were a number of children, mostly boys, sitting on the stairs or leaning against the walls, some looking like casualties, some like predators about to pounce, and as I headed for the office four black boys who looked too large for junior high turned the far corner and came running at me chased by a black man, who was (and remains to this day) the tallest man I'd ever seen.

The boy on the far side of the hall pointed at me, a signal to his blockers, yelling, "Pig, pig, get the pig!" Hey, I've played the game. I saw it coming. It was a simple maneuver. I jumped behind an open locker door and shoved it forward, the slam of knuckles on steel, a kind of crunchy shattering of bones and the scream of pain from the boy who meant to sucker punch me definitely being at that moment the highlight of my job search. The three other boys were pulling at him, "Come on, man, come on," none of them including the injured boy aware yet that probably that hand, that wrist, shit, probably that entire forearm were never going to be the same again.

This was (and is) very confusing to me. I felt really good about what I had done to that kid. He was going to get me. Instead I got him. Still, you know? What did I feel good about? From that sound, that sickening mix of shattering bones, slamming rattling metal and that scream I knew I had done that boy a very bad turn.

The boys were out the huge front doors and gone. I couldn't have described any of them, certainly not the one I injured. If I saw him on the street I wouldn't know him. It's unlikely he'd know me. I'd just given a complete stranger a permanent disability and we would have no other connection. Here's the thing. I didn't have to shove that locker forward. If I'd just stepped behind the door and stood there he would have swung and missed, no harm done.

Now I'm staring at the waist of the man who had been chasing them. I'm exaggerating a bit, but let's remember I'm often the tallest person in the room. Well, pilgrims, not this time. It was definitely a Jack and the Beanstalk moment for me. I was tiny little Jack and the person who introduced himself to me as "Solly," and who was subsequently revealed to be Solomon Davis, one of the first blacks in college basketball history to be named an all-American center, was definitely the giant. He was also revealed to be quite a jovial fellow and, by the way, he was the assistant principal of Garibaldi Junior High School, one of the most notoriously dysfunctional educational institutions in the United States of America. Perhaps more notable than his entire basketball career was the fact that Solly had been at this job for three whole years. When he learned I was there to interview for a slot in the social studies program he hired me on the spot. He said the paperwork was a mere formality. He liked the way I had "messed with those punks," who, he explained, were down from another district trying to muscle in on the Garibaldi drug trade.

I followed him to his office to give him my particulars. But first I listened while he called the police and asked that a patrol car keep an eye out for the four boys. I was impressed by the detailed descriptions he gave of each boy. Clearly, this was all business as usual.

When he turned his attention back to me I had pretty much de-cided this wasn't the best place to avoid a war. So instead of hedg-ing my bets— taking the job and calling to cancel if I got something better—I told him the truth. I had one more interview scheduled that day and I intended to keep it. When you're job hunting, telling the whole truth is seldom recommended, but in this case in a wishy-washy way I was trying to burn my bridges. It didn't work. I got an annoyed, "Well, if you don't get the job, you may not get the same of-fer from me tomorrow." But as we shook hands that mellowed into, "Let me know if you're still interested. I might be able to fit you in."

As he walked me to the door he advised me to take off my tie until I got to Grant. "If those boys are smart they're on the subway and out of here. But just in case they're stupid enough to nose around the neighborhood looking for a lanky teacher type, I can tell you with-out that tie you are definitely not that type." I'm still not sure how to take this, but it was good advice. I took off my tie until I got to Grant.

Where I was interviewed by Assistant Principal Ronald Bernbach, the warm reassuring educator, not the shut up and do what I tell ya prick I've come to know and loathe. Actually, even then I knew I was being given a monumental snow job. I would get the second bright-est group, although actually they were the smartest given the harsh backgrounds they had overcome to reach their level of achievement. If I hadn't been so impressed by the clean orderly halls, white walls, shiny red and black tiled floors, the smell of Clorox and Lysol, I would have known that what he was really saying was these are tough, angry kids who are going to chew you up.

You could say I went with Bernbach on the rebound. (I know, I know. I've never been good at jokes.) Garibaldi made little ole Grant Elementary look like a highly functional educational insti-tution. And while now I would definitely cross out the "highly," I would have to maintain still that Grant is functional. That's why I chose to go there: because I figured hiding out at Grant for two years would be a lot easier than hiding out at Garibaldi. And so, as promised, chillren, that's how I almost taught at Garibaldi and how I came to teach sixth grade at Grant Elementary, a tale you must concede has lots of anti-heroic action and dubious derring-do.

It was well past noon when he stopped his meandering pen and went to work. That evening, there he was again, reading his last entry and continuing:

One thing's perfectly clear; weren't no psychotherapeuticly fatey determined thingy about it. I thought teaching sixth grade was the easiest way to live through the two years they thought I should go die for my country. There was no deep emotional summons. It was dumb chance that heaved me through a twisted warp into a bleak negative of a once upon a time when I was eleven and for almost a year was in Paradise. Now here I am the grownup. Oh, man. In charge of a roomful of eleven-year-olds? Witnessing two of them fall head over heels in love. And where do all my sympathies go? To the one who truly loves with all her heart and soul.

How do I know how Sheri feels? Here's how. I've felt that way myself. The big difference between the two of us is that she, my poor poor baby, knows how it will end even in her moments of ecstasy. I thought my love would last forever. Shame roils through my body. Let it. No one will read this. Might as well be truthful.

She disappeared. One hot August morning I rode my bike over to the huge columned house at the end of town where Lurlene was the reigning female. (Her mother was a sodden wraith who rarely made an appearance. Like my father she started the day with a stiff one: in her case of gin. Daddy preferred bourbon, though gin would do in a pinch. The sound of bottles rattling in the closet was an affliction Lurlene and I shared.) A moving van sat in the driveway and a line of guys, and I mean that, a line, seven, eight guys, were piling furniture, rugs, boxes, and, I distinctly remember, her three-speed "English" bicycle in its cavernous trailer. Vanished.

Later I learned from Aunt Connie Lurlene's mother had "a nervous breakdown" and needed to be rushed back to the comfort of her family. Even later I learned (from the same source, who it turns out had a "friendship," her term, with Mr. Stumph) that only weeks after their return to Winston-Salem Mrs. Stumph ran a red light and was instantly killed by the pickup that slammed into the driver's side of her Cadillac. Lurlene, on the passenger's side, had her left leg shattered and would have bled to death but for the quick actions of a nurse who witnessed the accident. More recently I learned that Lurlene became a nurse, married a doctor and as I write this is expecting her first child.

Is all that supposed to comfort me? She had my address and telephone number. I had no way of reaching her. She could have called, or at least written. I could do neither. Ask me again. How do I know how Sheri feels? And like Sheri, who will be in a few years glad to hear that Pedro is off on his scholarship to the institution that manages to seduce this brainy "disadvantaged minority student" to its program, I think it's true to say I'm glad I know Lurlene is well, has a profession, is suitably married and is enjoying the prospect of motherhood. The bitch.

Who would understand this? Roger? Who wants to play for me the latest rock band he's discovered. Betty? Betty is furious with me for not taking her insane friend off her hands. Mrs. Robin? Are you kidding? I'm her Galatea. A nip here, a tuck there and voila: a sixth grade teacher. She doesn't want to hear about some sick identification with one of my children. Connie's worse. She wants an upstanding member of the community, active in, no, President of, the Lake Haven Chamber of Commerce. Really? That little gutter rat, Neil Riley? Really. Put on your blue suit. A clean white shirt. Nice paisley tie. Funny how I know both Robin and Connie would agree on the blue suit.

I keep thinking of that streetdancer, her eyes always on me.

Okay, so I tell her I'm suffering over my lost eleven-year-old love. And she says? "That was only a few years ago. Give it time. You'll grow out of it."

Neil stood up, stretched and closed the book. *How did you spend your Saturday night, Mr. Riley?* They would all think he'd been with his "movie star."

The next morning, Sunday, he pressed himself to finish his plan book. They'd spend most of Monday reviewing Friday's tests. For Tuesday morning he had an idea of a fun way to introduce measures and weights. Wednesday, he gave out report cards and if he got anything else done before he took them to lunch, which was unlikely, there certainly wouldn't be enough time for a party. So if he was going to do something for them before the break it had to be Tuesday afternoon. He spent the rest of Sunday rummaging through Roger's records and checking out the kinds of treats he might buy at Key Foods. Tired, exhausted really, and worried, no, terrified, that if he gave them a party it might end in chaos, he prepared for bed. He pulled the covers back and then in a rush he went to his desk and wrote.

Oh, God, I'm going to admit it. I care about those kids. I do. I care about those kids. Why else would I be spending every waking minute of my life trying to learn how to do it? The pronoun "it," by the way, stands for teach. Teach. To truly care for them I must learn how to teach.

Is that why Bernbach chose me? With his superhuman assistant principal X-ray vision he gazed right through my armor to my true inner soppy egalitarian eleven-year-old self. That prick, that bastard, he knew he could throw his nasty dust at me and make me do his will.

You can lead a horse to water but you can't make him drink. So here you are, Horse. Whatcha gonna do? I'm gonna let myself care about them.

Chapter 3:

Time to Go Home

In Room 6-306: after recess on Tuesday Neil went quickly to the blackboard to hide his grin as the children discovered the cheese crackers and small containers of orange juice on their desks. When he turned around Arlene was on her feet, eyes searching, probably to make sure no one got more than she did. And of course darling Pauli hid his crackers under his desk and cried that he didn't get any amid calls of "cheater" and "that boy" and "don't you believe him Mr. R." Pauli, smirking, not the least shamed, reached down, got the crackers and opened them. As he put a whole one in his mouth he said, "So?" He lifted his head to keep pieces of cracker from crumbling down his chin.

Neil had brought in a small record player, a hand-me-down from Roger, to play *Peter, Paul and Mary*. Pedro asked that he play it again, and in a surprisingly beautiful voice sang *500 Miles* and *Sorrow* along with the record. Everyone, including Arlene, and yes, Clyde, everyone wanted Neil to play all the songs again. Harriet and Arlene, especially Arlene, sang along with Pedro and the third time around they all joined in. He suddenly had himself an impromptu music class. Who would have thought it? He couldn't read a note of music, he couldn't carry a tune, but he was giving a music class. Another favorite was *Where Have All the Flowers Gone?* How could he build on this? How could he proceed?

Harriet, raising her hand, requested *It's Raining* and sang with Mary that she wouldn't be her father's Jack or her mother's Jill, but would run off and do as she pleased. Harriet, swaying, sang along in a full proud voice. From the corner of his eye Neil caught Clyde pushing himself out of his desk. *To watch Harriet.* Clyde saw Neil's glance and strolled over to the back window where it would seem something of great interest was going on in the playground. This all occurred in a rush and Neil only recorded the incident as a fuzzy conjecture: Harriet singing of her independence, Clyde's amorous interests broadening to include Harriet.

There were more requests for favorites and then the demand that he play the whole record again, and then again, and, yeah, again. No one wanted to end the party, except perhaps after a while, though he refused to admit it, Neil. They sang all the songs, argued over which were best and insisted repeatedly he play them all again. His children, the class of 6-306, groaned in protest when he told them it was time to go home. He kept repeating that to himself as he led them down to the schoolyard: *My kids, they groaned in protest when I told them it was time to go home.*

Chapter 4:

No More Mes, No More Books,
No More Arlene's Dirty Looks

In Neil's apartment: it was Wednesday afternoon. Suddenly there would be no school for four days. Suddenly he had no papers to grade. He threw his briefcase on the floor the minute he walked in the door and left a trail of clothing on his way to bed. In his underwear he slept until sometime in the early evening when the phone rang at least twenty times.

Amy had promised not to call and she didn't have the patience to ring that many times. It was more like her to give up after seven or eight rings and call again the next time her internal pressure to contact him shredded her resolve. In fairness, she had lived up to her promise. Therefore, it was probably...

He called the restaurant first; she picked up immediately.

"It's me," he said.

"Are you coming up?" she asked.

"No."

Silence. She could have said: Can't you bring yourself to show me one small kindness?

She never fought him. She didn't have to. If she had not made it a question, if she had said, "You're coming up," he would have. But then she seldom did that. On one level she always needed him to come and on another level she didn't need him to do anything. Losses can be quickly cauterized. She had taught him that. She was a master at cauterization.

"I'm half-crazy," he said. He didn't like explaining himself, but with her he felt he had to. "I'm so tired I can hardly see straight. I need not to have to do anything."

"I understand," she said.

Do you really? he thought. *For three months I've been standing in the middle of thirty-three demanding egos. I want, I need, gimme, see me, no me, here, me, over here, me, no me, me. No more mes, no more books, no more Arlene's dirty looks. Just me, Neil Riley. Me.*

"Okay, but Christmas is different," she said. It wasn't a question.

"I'll be home for Christmas."

"All right. Christmas. Do you need anything?"

"No. I'm fine."

"You get my checks?"

Of course. She had for years sent him, unasked, two hundred dollars a month so that instead of scraping by he generally had more than he needed. These days a lot of it went for stuff for the kids, but most of it went for pastrami on rye with mustard and roast beef on a roll with lettuce and tomato, light mayo on one side, light mustard on the other. And some small chunk of it actually found its way into savings so that after all his bills were paid he would this month have a balance in his savings account of nearly three hundred dollars. The man was rich beyond his wildest dreams. Never mind that in reality he would never go wanting, that if he had asked she would have given him everything she had.

"You know I do. And you know I appreciate it."

"It's yours. You earned it. All those years bussing for nothing. You earned it."

"I love you, Connie."

"Right. So then you're coming home for Christmas?"

"I promise."

"I'm with someone," she said, as if it were an obvious follow-up to his agreement to come home. "He's nice for a change," she added.

After Uncle Maury died and she started dating there were some painful episodes until the warning, *I'm with someone*, had become her way of indicating: *I'm sleeping with someone*. Even before Connie had become the focus of Neil's erections he had been outraged when some guy she was seeing would put his hands on her. Each time this happened Neil had sulked and pouted until Connie made it a point to warn him about the involvement and to make the *someone* keep his hands to himself when Neil was around.

"I'm glad," he said and he meant it. "Look, I just got home," he lied.

"You have to go."

"Yes, I should." Another lie.

"Do you need anything? Is the money enough?"

"Absolutely. I'm fine. Really. Fine." Was that the ultimate lie?

The basic agreement between them was: She gave; he took. Connie had set that up from the moment when, though she was only seventeen, she had taken him in her arms, a four-year-old whose mother had abandoned him to an alcoholic father. Connie held him for days, fed him, took him to the bathroom when either of them had to go, kept him in her bed at night, kept him with her until he would allow himself to become distracted by something other than that warm embrace because he had actually begun to believe that embrace was always going to be there. And it was, year in and year out, until at last he believed it, unequivocally, emphatically, that embrace would always be there. And it was.

"Now listen to me, Neilly. More than anything I want you to be happy. That's what makes me happy. Your job is to find your way."

Which wasn't exactly a lie because she believed it, but what she really wanted more than anything was for him to find his way back to Lake Haven, something that for reasons he could hardly explain to himself, never mind to Connie, he would never do. Once he left for college he arranged things so that he almost never went home again. He would be there for a week's vacation and for holidays, then be gone, to take summer courses and summer jobs, finding his way. Connie never tried to blackmail him into staying; not once. In fact, it was during this period that his 'monthly allowance' began. Those days it was a hundred a month no questions asked. If he needed more, she sent it.

During the summer before his senior year he prepared for the LSAT, hurried to Hartford in September, right in the middle of sign-up week, to take it and was surprised to find how primed he was. He scored in the ninetieth percentile. His advisor supported his plan to apply for next fall and helped him select five likely schools, including UConn. NYU was an afterthought and Neil expected a quick and decisive rejection. What a strange and wonderful process this admissions business was, because he was not only accepted, but given a full tuition scholarship. All Neil had to do was find a way to live in one of the most expensive cities in the world and buy texts that even secondhand cost more than a closet full of clothes.

Connie had expected him to stay at UConn. But when he chose NYU she put two thousand dollars in his checking account and doubled his monthly stipend. Neil knew she was deeply hurt, that she didn't understand his aversion to Lake Haven, that it was a place where she had found fulfillment and success. But pursuant to her original agreement, regardless of where life took him, she gave; he took.

Chapter 5:

Penelope Unraveling Her Dream

From CC Harp's notebook: Saturday, Oct. 4, 1969. Saturday night and Daddy's safely asleep. Tonight he took his mashed potatoes and ground beef without a struggle. I've browbeaten him into submission? Until the next episode. At least now I'm free to relax, though relaxed is hardly how I would describe my mood. Before I met the wildchild I would have comfortably settled into my big chair with a nice cup of tea and watched the late night movie. No longer. It's Saturday night! How absurd, how positively lowbrow, oh God, how horny.

I cannot believe the way I threw myself at him. Why? I may lie, often, but this is no lie. Never ever before have I been aroused simply because a man was... standing next to me. I've always been the demure restrained excuse me could you please remove your hand? But all he did was look at me. That look:

> *"He was looking at me that way,*
>   *no doubt about it,"*
> *the girl sitting across from me*
>   *told her friend.*
> *The subway pulled off*
>   *and that look*
> *was lost in clatter.*
>   *Still I could think of a few.*
> *My brother when he wants coffee,*
>   *his laundry picked up*
>   *or his favorite glazed chicken*

has this liquid stare
  brewed to dissolve
that obdurate blob
  back into his doting sister
And Juan at LaGuardia
  going back to Puerto Rico
    watching me
      watch him go
Juan turning back in disbelief
  as he was funneled
    onto the plane.
How could I?
Oh, my, I've seen a lot of those.
And I always could.

Then you gave me your offhand look
  And I was stripped down
    to my essential parts.

"*I threw myself at him.*" *What a phrase. Think of it literally. To leap at this boy, young man, long tall wildchild radiating maleness appearing suddenly through a door trailing the dark of the park, the heat of the street. Oh, my dear smitten CC, you reek of longing and bad rhymes. I threw myself at him and what did he say? He said he was too busy.*

November 23rd: Back from Santa Cruz. Another bad mistake and bad dreams on the plane back home. One of the dreams brought this turbulence, which seems to have a graphic component meant to suggest an hourglass continually turning. The dream is verbatim; the first "you," I know, is the wildchild, the second is the flamboyant Maurice, who in another lifetime might have been the important one (not really):

The
recollected
heat of that warm
night flickering cathode
grey voices mumbling secrets
about you I find a window to escape
through and take the bridge that
ends in mid-air use you to fill
the emptiness and at dawn
my heels click down the
busy street
amid...
the
recollected
heat of that warm
night flickering cathode
grey voices mumbling secrets
about you I find a window to escape
through and take the bridge that
ends in mid-air use you to fill
the emptiness and at dawn
my heels click down the
busy street
amid...

Chapter 6:

Here, Now

In Silhouettes: he saw her the moment she came through the door and he knew from the sudden lift of her head, a kind of 'oh,' that she saw him. He had been sitting at the bar; now he was standing.

The bar crowd—about seven or eight of them, an elderly couple had joined them while he waited for her, two men had left—clumped up in the middle of the bar around a red-faced jowly man with a large white walrus mustache. They were, and had been for a while, reminiscing about a certain Davy who, God rest his soul, was no longer with us. Davy had distinguished himself by his prodigious drinking exploits, "Sitting right there in that very stool straight as an arrow, doubles, a fifth an hour I tell ya, and a mug, boilermakers. That was a regular evening. You shoulda seen him on New Year's."

For Neil it had a certain uncanny familiarity. His father, Jack, had for years ended each day of his working life at the center of such a group, arguing whose round was up, urging another, stumbling back to piss only when he absolutely had to because that's when his cohorts found it most convenient to peel away, remembering wives and children, unfed pets, demanding relatives. *Oh, Jesus, it's eight-thirty. I've got to go. My poor sister will kill me.* They disappeared one by one until there was only ole Jack downing just one more. Then around ten o'clock each evening, if it was summer, his son, a good, good boy, would pry him loose and follow him quietly as he weaved his way home. During school ole Jack had to weave his way home alone because blasted Aunt Connie wouldn't let his son out of her sight, even on Friday and Saturday nights. But whatever the night ole Jack would be back and so would the others, telling their stories of Davy or Harry or Mary.

Here now this woman he had called on a whim, CC Harp, was wearing the same camel's-hair coat she had worn the first night they met and slung over her right shoulder was the strap of a large dark brown leather purse. He realized then that that first night she had not been carrying a bag. That night she'd had a wallet stuffed in the inner pocket of her coat like a man. Tonight perhaps because of that shoulder bag she looked even more self-possessed than he had dared remember. What was he doing messing with a woman like this?

Neil was wearing his charcoal grey trousers, a blue oxford button-down, but no tie. After all they were just going to the movies. He had decided on a warm tan windbreaker instead of a jacket and overcoat and on his more comfortable brown loafers, although the black ones were in better shape. All these decisions had been made and remade as if he really cared what she thought of him. It was when he definitely decided he'd wear the windbreaker because carrying an overcoat would be awkward, especially when he'd be fumbling around in a movie seat trying to figure out where to put it, that he realized the obvious: he cared what she thought of him.

Here now he didn't understand exactly how it happened. As she approached she said, "It's been a while." And he agreed, "Yes, it has." But that didn't explain how his hands found their way to her hips. He had wanted his hands on her hips the moment he saw her. And her hands were on his ribcage, caressing him, which gave him permission to caress her. And they were kissing. Then his hands were on her back inside her coat and her hands were on his back and they were as close as clothing would allow, each moving slowly to feel as much as clothing would allow.

Neil felt there were a lot of things wrong with this and he knew by a certain tension and release in her embrace that she too knew there were a lot of things wrong with this. There was the general, oh, God, there's another one of those exhibitionistic couples. Go get a hotel room. Then there was the ghost of Neil's father sitting in the middle of his cronies nudging and pointing and jabbing the forefinger of his right hand through a hole formed by the thumb and forefinger of his left while nine-year-old Neil watched and time jumped back five years through the circle of his father's fingers, wondering where his mother had gone.

Neil was four when she disappeared. She was there when he went to sleep; gone the next morning. "She don't give a shit about us," his father said. "She's gone and she ain't comin' back. Forget about her." Though of course neither of them did any such thing.

Nor could he forget those thirty-three children going oooou and shaving a finger at them. Which was when Neil wondered, *Am I anywhere near prepared for this?*

All of that rushed through him, debris on a cold wind, blown away by this mysterious desire. For whatever reason, this stranger was the person he wanted to be with. And he was kissing her, which was exactly what he wanted to do. All he felt for a very long time was that this was all that mattered. They were here. Now.

Then Neil or CC, both together was how it felt, knew they had to stop and they stopped and stood suddenly in this place where a bartender and a small crowd at the bar were watching them. Their audience suddenly burst into applause. CC hid her head in her hands. Neil put his hand on her arm and turned so that she was shielded from them.

"We could leave," he said.

She stood up and pecked him on the cheek.

"Go, pretty mama," one of the men said.

She leaned past Neil and, with a wide clown's smile, gave them a broad dismissive wave.

"Let's get a booth, shall we?" she said.

"Absolutely."

She took off her coat, threw it onto the bench of a booth and sat down. She was wearing a dark brown skirt that came just above her knees, light brown stockings or pantyhose, a long sleeved tan jersey and a light brown vest. Neil wanted more skin, but what's a poor boy to do when winter's coming on and women's bodies retreat into sleeves and leggings?

A waitress, wearing the standard Silhouettes black minidress with the large white buttons and black tights, came over the moment they sat down. *Not our young Josie,* Neil observed to himself. Her hair was tied back in a red and black checkered kerchief, which emphasized her thin, tight-lipped face. *Piqued,* he thought, consciously using a Robin word.

"After seven the booths are reserved for people ordering dinner," she said.

"That's us," Neil said. "Are those ours?" He pointed at the menus she was carrying.

"Sure." She hesitated a moment. "Sure," she repeated. "Here."

"Thanks," Neil said. "While we're deciding can we order drinks?" He lifted his beer glass, which he had brought with him from the bar.

"Yes, of course. Would you like to see our wine menu?"

"A wine menu?" CC said, making a wide-eyed, oh, my, aren't we fancy face at Neil. "Yes, we'd like that."

When she was gone CC said, "Not Josie."

"Not even close. Of course, we should have waited to be seated by the cashier. Who by the way is not Josie's step-mother. And maybe kissing at the bar isn't allowed after seven either."

"So where's Josie?" CC asked.

"Well, I'd ask the waitress, but frankly I'm scared to death of her."

"Me, too," she said.

"Tell you what. I'll throw you. Loser has to ask."

She edged closer to the table. "You're on," she said. "I'll kill ya."

She put her elbow on the table as if they were going to arm-wrestle.

"Best two out of three?" he asked.

"Not enough time. Sudden death. Live dangerously. Ready? I'll count," she insisted.

"You count, I choose. Odds."

"On three. One two *three*."

They both threw one finger.

"Don't mess wid da champ," she crowed, thumbing her nose. "You ask," she commanded.

"Shit," he said.

"You ask," she repeated.

"I will. I will. Damn."

"Be brave."

"God, I forgot how much I enjoy you," he said.

"Don't start," she said.

"Here's the wine menu," the waitress said. "Have you decided what you want for dinner?"

"We're still working on it," Neil said. "By the way, we used to be regulars. Last summer. And our waitress..."

"Her name was Josie," CC interjected.

"Do you mind?" Neil said to CC. "Her name was Josie," he said to the waitress. "We were wondering..."

"We don't give out that kind of information," the waitress said, cutting him off. "I'll give you time to make up your minds." She sped away.

"What kind of information?" CC asked in a whisper.

"The kind a couple of subversives like us would want to weasel out of her," he whispered back.

CC nodded knowingly.

"Do you think we should hurry up and decide what we want to eat?" Neil asked.

"Not on your life," CC said. "I want to look at this vaunted wine menu, which contains..." She waved it in the air and then looked at it carefully. "Oh my goodness, some real wines. Or so they say. How bout it, my friend? I'm only looking at the reds. There's a Burgundy, but I fear it may not be true to its name. There's a Cab, but again God only knows the wherefore and why. And there's a Beaujolais. At least we can be sure of its provenance. Want to try a glass of Beaujolais? A nice smooth red. At least it should be."

"A smooth red? Sounds good to me."

The waitress was back. "Ready to order yet?"

"No," CC said. "But we'd both like a glass of your Beaujolais?"

When she left, Neil said, "Us shrinking violets do so like to have everything taken care of by strong domineering women."

"I'm sorry," she said. She pulled her chin in. Blushing? It was hard to tell in the dim light. But it was clear she was truly apologetic. "I'm used to being on my own. I travel a lot for my job. It's second nature." She opened her hands out in supplication. "Do you see?"

Neil reached over, took her hands, pulled them together and folded them into his. She exhaled and leaned forward, making it easier for him to hold on.

"You're in charge," he said. "But it's my turn to pay."

She locked his fingers with hers and flipped his hands over. Tugging gently, she asked, "Can you afford this?"

He flipped her hands over and pinned them to the table. "I've been saving up for it."

"I can pay, you know. Or go halves," she added quickly. There was tension in her hands and her eyes were still searching his.

He realized that during these last two months what he remembered most about her wasn't how she looked, but how she looked at him, making eye contact, paying attention. He smiled. "Let's take each other at his word. No means no. Yes means yes. I'll pay means I'll pay. I owe you an evening. I'm paying."

The waitress put their wine down on the table. The glasses were wet and warm to the touch, as if they had just been washed. "Are you ready to order?" she asked Neil.

With a wave of his hand he referred her to CC.

"No, we are not ready to order," CC said slowly, enunciating each word. "When we are, I will come and find you and I will tell you: We are ready to order."

CC and the waitress stared at each other and then the waitress looked at Neil, raising her eyebrows. He stared at her with the same tight look CC had given her.

"She will come and find you," he said.

As the waitress whirled away Neil heard a giggle that could've been Bianca's. It wasn't just that she understood what he had done, she loved what he had done. It was a smitten giggle, and it rushed through him like a trumpet call. He felt larger; the room felt smaller.

She leaned her chin forward with her elbows on the table, lowering her voice, chattering, giddy. "Wine in a warm glass. How could she? Of course, I know exactly what I want. They tell me that the only meal to consider is the cheeseburger with bacon, lettuce and tomato, and with a large side of steak fries."

"That'll be two. When you go and find her," he said.

She sat back. "All in good time."

He was admiring her squared shoulders. It wasn't forced, this perfect posture; it was simply how she held herself.

"Let her stew a while." CC sipped her wine. "Pretty skimpy serving." But the complaint came with a delightful shake of her head, nothing like real annoyance.

"Probably a special order just for you," Neil said. "God only knows what she'll do to our burgers."

At that moment the waitress reappeared, slapped a piece of purple paper on the table and started away.

"Wait!" CC demanded and gave their order.

When she said she wanted her burger medium rare, Neil

suggested she would do better to make it medium "because of the nature of the evening." He offered this opinion with a pompously raised finger.

"Oh, I agree absolutely," CC said. "It has to be medium."

Neil looked at the purple page the waitress had left behind. "I don't believe it! Look at this!" Neil said, fluttering the page back and forth between them. "It's a flyer. Josephine O'Rourke is appearing as Nora in a production of Ibsen's *A Doll's House* at the Actor's Loft, three performances only, Thursday, Friday and Saturday."

CC took the flyer, turned it toward the light and moved her head forward. "Oh, my God. What kind of turnout do you think they had Thanksgiving night?"

"Maybe they figured a holiday, former students home on vacation," he said. "The real problem's that tonight is the last night and it's too late for us to make it."

"But we could contact them and make sure we know what else might be coming up." Then she paused. "Wait. This is getting complicated. Let's file this for the moment." She held the flyer up and shook it. "Do you want to hang on to this?" she asked, offering it to him.

"No, you hold it for now," he said.

She put it in her purse. "One evening at a time."

Neil watched her carefully zip her bag closed. It was closer in size to an attaché case than a purse, with silver studs that fixed the strap ends to the carrier. The dark brown leather had been worked so that on a strip about two inches high along the side there seemed to be a line of slender dancing figures.

"Is that new? I don't remember you with a pocketbook last time."

"Different gear for different situations," she said. "I got this in Santa Cruz at a street fair." She checked to make certain the case was closed then held it up for his inspection. "I was swept away by the figures gamboling along the side; they're all so similar in form, androgynous, yet definitely human. And each one moves so differently. They reminded me of that final scene in Bergman's *The Seventh Seal* when all the characters except the little troubadour and his wife followed Death over the hill. Where are they off to? Why so gaily? I thought these figures were an answer. Don't ask me why."

"Just for the record? I know Bergman directs movies because we're going to see a Bergman film tonight, but I've never seen *The Seventh Seal*. What I really want to know is why Santa Cruz? Is that in Mexico?"

She laughed. "California."

"What were you doing in Santa Cruz... California?"

"I had to run a survey in L.A., so while I was out there I visited my mother. She lives in Santa Cruz."

"What kind of survey?" he asked.

"No, wait. I need to catch up. The last I remember you were going away to? Not Nam, but a job. And I'm not sure. Were you coming back?"

"I'm here," he said.

"Yes, but I'm still trying to recall. Did you say you were coming back?"

He knew her eyes were trained on him, watching as he lifted his glass with his right hand and with the pointer finger of his left traced the faint moist circle where it had been, first clockwise, then counterclockwise.

"No, I didn't," he said. He met her eyes for a moment, then looked back at the wet circles he was tracing on the table. He exhaled and raised his eyes again, met her gaze again. In the dim light her complexion looked dark, ruddy, when in fact he knew her skin was very white. Her face had a strong, edged jawline and her eyes, boring into him, looked black. Her black hair, pulled back in a ponytail, fell loosely around the tops of her ears, leaving her entire face open, unhidden. "Do you think I have something to apologize for?" he asked.

Her eyes flicked away, then back. It was as if he had stung her and she was trying to hide it. The last thing he wanted was to hurt her. Did he know what the first thing was?

"Tell me why you asked that," she said. She waited, very still, watching him. After a moment, she tilted her head and raised her eyebrows, then straightened up, very still again.

"I think… Could we start again? I'm feeling like an idiot. I had your number. And a memory of a very good time. So I called your number. I called to find out if we could spend an evening together, get to know each other, that sort of thing." He shook his head and said, "I dunno," over a forced chuckle. It sounded more like a snort.

With wide eyes, clutching her chest with both hands, she asked, "What was that?"

"Me! having a hard time saying hello, that's all. I owe you an evening. Now…"

"Because I paid for your dinner?" she asked.

While he said, "…here you are and I don't know what to say… What?"

"You said you owed me because I paid for your dinner last time."

She spoke with certainty, as if those were his exact words. Neil thought there was a hint of triumph in her gaze. He was reminded of Bianca, who could one moment be sensitive and astute and in the next a mean little viper.

"I didn't say that."

"You said you owed me for the evening and wanted to repay me."

"Yeah, I said I owe you," he said. "Because you were so… Because you helped me out. It wasn't about money," he insisted. "I was close to a total meltdown…" He took a deep breath. "Okay, this is hard, but I need to say it. I was miserable. Not with you. I don't mean that. With my life, what I had to do. I am embarrassed by this. But you... You came dancing in." He laughed. "Literally. And for a moment, it was just a moment, wasn't it? That evening?"

"Three hours was the allotted time," CC said. "I think we may have exceeded that, give or take a minute or two. But, yes, metaphorically speaking it was a moment. Perhaps even less."

"For one wonderful moment, perhaps even less, three incredible hours plus a minute or two, I stepped away from my pitiful self into a wonderful, sexy... for me, okay? ...speaking strictly for me... sexy place. It was..."

"...among other things sexy for everyone involved. After all, we held hands and I do remember that we kissed goodbye. It was all very sweet and in a manner of speaking sexy."

"Most of all it was extraordinary. Being with you, because of you, I felt I could have a life after all. And that brings me back to hello. Hello, CC, I think it's extraordinary that we're here. I wanted to thank you so much for that evening we had."

"We said hello, didn't we? At the bar?"

"I can't explain that. It just happened."

"It takes two, as they say."

They both spent a long time staring at their wine.

She was the one who broke the silence. "So you called and here we are."

As always she was urging direct eye contact. He expected her to continue, but she didn't. She expected a response.

"I wanted to see you," he said. He looked down at the table and watched himself make wet circles with his finger.

"And I wanted to see you," she said.

"So here we are," he said.

Neil sat now with his eyes cast down, looking at the table top, at his hands, at anything but her. He expected her to still be staring at him, but when he peeked saw that just like him she had her head down. Buried in the same confusion? All through college and law school he had found dating so easy. Keep the attention on her, answer her questions in ways that were reassuring, always be nice, nonthreatening, complimentary. That was how you made out. If it didn't work, which was rare, cross her off your list, move on; she wasn't going to fuck you.

Tonight none of the above applied, not the it was so easy part and definitely not the crossing off part.

"One of us should say something pretty soon," she said.

That's just it, he thought. *She's always on top.* "That's just it," he said, "I don't know how to say what I'm feeling."

"Can you name the feeling?"

"No," he said. *Yes,* he thought. *You scare the hell out of me. I don't want to lose you. But I don't want to lie to you to keep you. Choose one.* "I don't want to say something stupid," he said. He rolled his head back, eyes squeezed shut. "Oh, God, see? That's so *stupid!*"

"I'm feeling the same way," she said.

"What way?"

"Scared."

How did she know? This was all so strange to him and yet, to some deep craving, so familiar. "All right, scared," he said. "But it's not like I'm going to get my head bashed in scared. Right?"

"No, it's worse than that. It's like I'm going to..." She hesitated, took a deep breath, and said, "...lose everything I ever wanted." Her voice, her body pressed forward urgently before she let herself fall back, saying quickly, "Those feelings... I'm not saying you are everything I ever wanted. I don't even know you. I'm just saying... It's just that the way you left me..." She shook her head, no, no, no. "This conversation has gotten out of hand." She actually clasped her hands together on the table. Brenda's: See how good I'm being? "One of the things that I've been thinking is that you're only wearing a jacket and they're predicting that the weather is going to get much colder. Don't you think you should have worn an overcoat?"

"No, wait, don't leave it there." He said this in a whisper, demanding it.

Surprising her, apparently. Her head moved back, her eyes closing, a flicker, and there she was again, her wide, extraordinary face confronting him, her eyes searching, curious. "Tell me what you heard me say."

He rubbed at the hair at his temples, thinking it was definitely time to get a haircut. Wondering then why he couldn't focus. What had he heard her say? What he felt was they kept leaning closer then moving away. And all at once with an awareness that defied all misgivings, he knew exactly what she was saying.

"What I heard you say? That there's some connection..." He waved a finger between them as he said this. "...between us that we need to think about. Wait! That's my interpretation. I don't mean those were your words. It's what I think you meant. That there's some connection."

"Yes, that's exactly what I meant. But you know... the way you... I wonder what's going on with you? For all I know we have a few hours and you'll be gone again."

"Yeah, but... that night I'm pretty sure I told you how up in the air things are with me."

"I know you didn't desert me or anything like that. That's not what happened. It's just the way we separated... said goodbye... I would not want that to happen again."

"Here's the thing. On Wednesday Congress passed the lottery, but according to a guy I know at my board that won't affect me. I'm still job exempt. I'm twenty-four, turning twenty-five in March. The March after that I'll be twenty-six and he says I'll be Four A. Four A, man! That's it. It'll all be over. Forget about Canada. I'll be going to NYU Law."

She stared at the ceiling and shook her head. "I didn't understand a word you just said." Facing him again, she heaved a great self-mocking sigh and said, "But I do remember now that there's a war going on."

"Yeah," he said. "A war. And I've been told it's my war. You can join if you want to, but I'm male and until I'm twenty-six I have no choice. It's called being One A. Without my job exemption that would be me. That's Roman numeral I dash A."

She cocked her head, said, "You know…" then clamped her lips together, then blurted, "I'm so glad I'm out of it. It's not fair, but that's the way I feel."

"That makes perfect sense to me. And if I play my cards right in a year and a half I'll be twenty-six and I'll be out of it too."

"You're only twenty-four." Her voice gave 'only' a slight bite. "Next month I'll be twenty-eight. I'm more than three years older than you."

Neil looked up at the ceiling and counted with his fingers. "December, January, February, March." He looked at his four fingers, nodding and pressing his lips together. "Yes, three years, four months."

"You're just a baby," CC said, leaning back with an incredulous squint.

"You're practically an old maid," Neil said, raising the right side of his upper lip in mock distaste.

The waitress brought their food.

"Saved by the burger," CC said when the woman, demonstrating once again she did not want any chit-chat, laid out their platters and left. "All right, but we have established a few things. We have a vast age divide, a vague hint of a connection and a slight problem in Vietnam. What do we do now?"

"You mentioned a movie," he said.

"I'd rather talk. After dinner let's get coffee and dessert at Four

Brothers. How about it?"

"That would be great," he said.

"Yeah, but right this minute…" She took the catsup bottle from him and, as he had, shook it over her fries and her open burger. Then she closed the burger, leaned forward and took a huge bite, dripping some catsup on her plate and dribbling some of it down the left side of her chin.

This was not the dainty nibble of the calorie-conscious female he was programmed to expect. Still, he envisioned her hurriedly dabbing at her chin with a napkin. Instead she swiped at the dribble with the back of her hand, licked off the mess and took another huge bite. He realized, finally, she was mocking him, but gently, a sort of complicated way of urging him to be himself. That was when he realized that each breath he took had become a hit. His shoulders had come down from high alert and a grin was playing with his jaw.

"Whaa?" she asked, mouth full.

He was besotted and famished. "I'm admiring your impeccable table manners," he said. "I'm sure I can't match your style, but I can certainly try. Watch."

He leaned forward over his plate and took a huge bite of his own burger. They stared at each other as they chewed. Her expression also seemed to have settled into a kind of smile. Did she feel as happy as he did?

He noticed again how unexpectedly blue her eyes were. They should have been dark brown to match her straight black hair and her American Indian face. Instead they were like the puries in your marble collection that you never used as shooters and never ever gave up when you got knocked out of the ring. Her eyes were clear, beckoning, a blue to treasure, to explore. His dick was as hard as an iron rod.

"So tell me about teaching," she said when she had swallowed most of her mouthful.

"You don't know what you're asking," he said with his mouthful still a mouthful and feeling that anything he said about teaching would embarrass him, bore her and ruin the evening. And yet in spite of all that he did want to talk about it; he longed to talk about it.

"Yes means yes and no means no and tell me about teaching means tell me about teaching," she said.

"I don't know where to begin."

"Say the first thing that comes to mind."

"There are so many. And they're all so shameful."

"Then confess." She crossed her arms, laid them on the table and leaned forward with a diabolical sneer. "Talk. Or you won't get any dessert at *Four Brothers*." To his look of alarm. "That's right. No dessert. So talk."

He crossed his arms at the wrists as if they were tied. Then he jerked his head to the left and cried out, "I don't know what I'm doing." His head whipped to the right. "I've never felt so helpless." He suddenly stopped the game. "Did I just say that? Seriously, I've been really shaken up. And I don't even understand it." He rolled his eyes. "That sounds so nebulous. But it's the absolute truth. Three months ago? Less than three months ago?" He let his eyes go out of focus. It was a way of not thinking.

"Three months ago..." she prompted.

When he focused again, it was on her, on the thrill of her watching him. He forgot what he had been saying, simply lost it, which brought him right back to where he had been. He pressed his lips together, a confident smirk. "I knew what I wanted and I knew how to get it. And clearly... I'm really boring you, aren't I?"

"Don't you dare. You can't leave it there. Don't you even try." She leaned forward. "Go on. You knew what you wanted then, but now?"

"Whoa, you're bad," he said.

"Bad. Baaad to the bone. And I listen. And I remember. Three months ago. What did you know then?"

"That I needed to make sure nobody could fuck with me. *Nobody*. In a way I was already there. The trick is to make damn sure you don't need anybody and nobody needs you. They want to draft me? Fuck'em. I'll leave everything. I'll start all over again, find out how to play it in another country. At least they speak the same language. This is totally out of control. Why am I telling you all this?"

"Because you have to."

He sat very still, playing back in his head what he had said to her, things he hadn't quite said even to himself. "I haven't talked to anyone like this... ever. I've never talked to anyone like this." *Not even to myself,* he thought.

He let the situation sink in. In a way this was all so ordinary. He was sitting in the booth of a bar with, well, perhaps not exactly an ordinary woman, but still just sitting with her, eating a hamburger, sipping a half-glass of wine and thinking *this is all so ordinary*. And feeling *this is all so remarkable*. He was a free spirit gliding through a wide blue sky, so glad to be alive. It had been a long time since he had felt so shit-faced stoned. So shit-faced stoned that he welcomed Mrs. Robin's sudden intrusion to demand he find words better suited to the occasion. *Giddy. Elated.*

"You need to talk," she prodded.

Actually what he needed was to keep on watching her watching him. He wouldn't call her expression detached. A bit too much concern for detached. Also, her lips were maybe a little too thick, but otherwise perfect lips, certainly perfect when you thought of running your tongue along the line where they pressed together, forcing them open. What're you gonna do? Sit here and moon all night? Bail outta this. "I need to eat," he said. He speared a steak fry and stuffed it in his mouth.

"Me, too," she said, following his example. They chewed vigorously at each other.

But he couldn't stop himself. He put down his fork. Nothing mattered until he conveyed how confused he was. "Did I just say I don't
want to be pushed around? Ha! I'm nothing but pushed around. I'm
on probation. All first year teachers are. That means my boss, that's
Mr. Bernbach to you, Mr. Riley, can fire me on a moment's notice,
without cause, no union protections apply. I look at him funny? He
can can my ass like *that*." He snapped his fingers. "Of course, I look
at him funny every time I see him, but so what? He tells me what
he's going to do to me and I tell him I won't let him and he does it
anyway. But that's not why he won't fire me. You want to know why
he won't fire me?"

"Tell me."

"He won't fire me. It's even probable he'll keep me on for next
year because, as he's told me more than once, 'You're doing fine,
Mr. Riley. You keep your children out of the halls.' Do you see?"

"I don't, quite. You seem to feel powerless in the situation and
yet as you describe it…"

"You don't understand. If I were to leave now, if I were to just
quit, you know what that would mean? It would mean my kids
would be screwed. They probably couldn't replace me in the middle
of the semester or even at the end of the first semester so they'd have
to bring in substitutes. And that's the end of even the shaky order
I bring to my class. My angry ones would erupt, my scared ones
would stay home, and the majority, the ones who, I swear to God,
like school and want to get on with their day, they would get beaten
to a pulp for speaking out or would join in the general mayhem
just to protect themselves. If I left," he said, falling back, "my kids
would lose a year of school."

"If I understand correctly you're saying that you are effective as
a teacher and that matters to you. Is that right?"

"No. I didn't say that. I'm barely adequate. *Barely.* Effective? I
wish."

"All right. You're saying, and I'm quoting, you're 'barely adequate.'"

Her vest opened as her arms reached up to make the quotes. Her nipples made distinct points on her jersey. The recognition that she wasn't wearing a bra caused him to lose touch with the conversation.

"I'm sorry," he said, "What did you say?" He lifted his glass and looked at the small mouthful of wine he still had left. "I think this stuff's got a special kick to it."

Her eyes did a slight shift as she pulled at her vest, suggesting she knew where that 'special kick' really came from. "I said it sounds like you're improving as a teacher."

"I didn't say that. Don't put words in my mouth. I mean..." He shook his head. The annoyance in his voice worried him.

"You mean, don't put words in your mouth. Okay, I won't. But can I ask you a question?"

"I guess. Sure. Go ahead."

"Are you improving as a teacher?"

He stared over the heads of the people at the bar, trying to think. He grew lush fantasies of CC's nipples. Simultaneously he envisioned the chaos in his class during those first weeks. It wasn't like that now. He was getting better. No, say the situation was getting better. Why did it bother him to think even that? The extent of his hunger to talk about himself in the midst of his (Mrs. Robin would say) tumescence was shocking. The whole group at the bar, eight or nine of them, burst into laughter. As they moved and stood and sat the red face of the man with the large white walrus mustache at the center suddenly emerged, beaming at everyone, then disappeared. *God, I hate that guy,* Neil thought.

She took his right arm and shook it. "Hello, Mister, are you okay?"

The disturbance he felt was from confusion, not pain. He seemed to be trying to stop this conversation and had a pressing need to continue it. "Yes, fine," he said.

"What were you thinking just now?" she asked.

"I'm trying to find the words," he said. And that was true. It seemed urgent for him to tell her how he was feeling. "Okay, suppose you go out to the store. You turn the corner and *presto* everything is different. I mean, *different*. But wait, not really. Nothing's changed. Everything's exactly the same. But you know it's different. Understand? You don't have a *feeling* this is different, you don't *think* this is different. You *know* this is different. Okay, but... and believe me this is a very big but... if everything looks exactly the same where are you? Does that make any sense?"

"You feel yourself changing."

"Yes, changing. But that's just the half of it. Confused. Totally. In constant turmoil. Say it any way you want. I don't know my ass from my elbow."

"Would you say this has to do with your interactions with your children?"

"Interactions with my children," he repeated. The question seemed so studied, as if she were reading from a script. She must be sick of all his talk. And why not? Should he expect her to want to listen to him all night? "I'd say I've talked enough," he said. "Tell me what you were doing in L.A."

"Is the question..." She paused, then asked, "What just happened? One moment you were so animated, and a second later you just collapsed."

"That's funny. You think something happened to me and I think something happened to you. I'm..." He thought for a moment. "No. Something did happen to me. It dawned on me that while I'm sitting here baring my soul you're sitting there thinking how trivial this all sounds."

"But that's not true. Why would you even think it?"

"Well, for one thing, I don't think I've ever bared my soul before to anyone, *ever*, so I'm really embarrassed. Because, I guess... because I've revealed how small I feel... Okay," he said, "and how out of control. And you..." He speared her with his eyes. "The more... yeah, I can say that. The more honest I tried to be the more," and here he pulled his head back, "the more removed you became. Until it was like I was this poor floundering nitwit trying to explain to this very conscious higher being all the profound things that were going on with me and you were thinking, how pathetic."

"I..." She looked down and shook her head. "No, I won't do that." She looked up. "I could just deny... What I mean is... I could just say I don't know what you're talking about. But the truth is you're right... I... When you described how you were feeling, how things seemed the same but everything had changed... that was... that's how I feel. And it all seems so risky. It terrifies me. No, I don't think what you're saying is pathetic. Not at all. I didn't feel removed. I felt threatened, not because..."

"But why?"

"That's too personal."

He made a loud sound. He meant it to be a guffaw, but what came out was more like a howl, apparently surprising her even more than it surprised him.

She clutched at her jersey with a tight fist. Only half joking, she gasped, "Now what was that? You have this whole menagerie lurking in there."

"That was the cry of a sucker who's just been had. I sit here telling you my deep dark secrets and you say you can't tell me something personal?"

She was still pulling at the collar of her jersey. All he could think of was the way the material molded her left breast. He closed his eyes and took a deep breath, thinking, *Jesus, Riley, can't you get your mind off her tits?*

"You're on this amazing adventure," she was saying.

That brought him back to the matter at hand quickly enough. "Amazing adventure! You have got to be kidding."

"It's true. You may not see it that way but all the signals are there, of a challenge, of excitement, of danger." She enumerated each item with the fingers of her right hand, the one that had been pulling at her jersey. "The challenge is exploring a profession you see as noble and demanding. The excitement is because you have fallen desperately in love with these children. The danger, of course, is that you might have to leave in the dead of night for Canada. Oh, yes," she said to the long raspberry that was his response to all this. "You are involved, challenged, committed, *engaged*."

"Wow." His eyes roved over the crowd at the bar, back down to his wine glass, then back to her. "Don't try to change the subject. What's this personal business you can't tell me?" He leaned forward. "If you don't talk you won't ever get any dessert ever again. So fess up. *Now*."

She smiled. "The table's turned. All right, I'm an imposter."

The waitress appeared at that moment, saying, "I know who you are!"

They gaped at her, alarmed. Neil thought that in a snapshot they'd look like shoplifters caught goods in hand.

"You're Josie's groovy lovers," the waitress said. Then pointing to herself she announced, "I'm Josie's mother."

"That's great!" CC said, warmly. There wasn't a hint of her former hostility. "You must be so proud of her."

Neil tried to make his snicker sound as if he were clearing his throat, but CC got it and gave him a quick nasty look before whipping her attention back to Josie's mother. That wrinkle of a smile at the edge of her lips had to be off the same glee he felt. Gloriously silly moments kept bubbling up. Everything that remained the same had suddenly become quite different.

Josie's mother was saying, "It's the same old story. I have to be here holding down the fort while they all go off to her biggest night and the final curtain and the cast party."

CC gripped her hand. "That sounds really hard."

What an operator, Neil thought. His appreciation was not without uneasiness. *Just like that she's completely won the poor woman over.* Who was this imposter and why was he dying to know her? Out loud he said, "Will you tell Josie we had no idea this was happening or we would have been there throwing flowers at the star."

"Oh, I'll tell her, all right. This is so great. The whole thing. The way you walked in," she said to CC. "And the way you grabbed her. This is almost better. Are you back?" she asked Neil.

"Yeah, I think so," Neil said. "Yeah, I'm pretty sure."

"Yes, well, obviously there's still some uncertainty," CC added. "What we would want Josie to know is there's a happy ending. The only sad part is that we didn't get to see her play."

"But you're here!" Josie's mother said. "That's the best part."

"Yes," CC said. "We're definitely here."

Chapter 7:

Penny Wishes

On Broadway: Neil pushed her shoulder and said, quoting, "'That sounds really hard.' I nearly threw up. You were *sooo* empathetic."

"Well, I was. It was hard to miss the final curtain. It was. We don't need to mention she probably ran out on them a long time ago, otherwise she wouldn't have been the one left to hold down the fort. Bitch. And figuring out who we were. It wasn't for Josie that it warmed the cockles of her vengeful heart. It was because *she*, Miss Bitch, had the scoop. So you can all go to the cast party if you want to, but I was there when they kissed. Ask Godfrey."

"Who's Godfrey?"

"The bartender, dummy. Bartenders are always named Godfrey. Everybody knows that."

"I didn't know that."

"Well, I meant everybody who's anybody."

"Oh." After they had walked for a while he took her arm in his and was reminded of Pedro and Sheri shivering, ecstatic.

"What are you thinking?" she asked.

"How much I enjoy being with you."

"Meant for each other," she said and then quickly put her free hand over her mouth. "I did not say that."

He stopped, pulled her into his embrace and put a hand on her cheek. "If I kiss you do you think it will summon our late night friend?"

"Let's find out."

They kissed. They spent a long time at it. At first Neil felt a tentativeness in how their bodies met. Then it seemed every move, all the awkwardness, their bruised lips, his bowed head, her craned neck, their shifts to fit their bodies, were a kind of slow dance, a way of building a place, a place he could not leave.

Apparently she could. "Our friend did not appear," she said, moving her head back.

"No three-ways tonight."

"Two's just about right." Then she said quickly, "Let's talk about pies. I think apple is the best."

"Not me. Blueberry's the only way to go."

"Obviously we're totally incompatible." As she said this she touched his cheek, watching him. Her hand cupped his chin, lingered there. Then with a brusque turn she stepped off again.

After they had walked for a while, brushing hands, holding hands, then locked arm-in-arm, he brought them to a halt, whipped her around and gripped her upper arms. He leaned down and put his forehead on hers. "All right, Miss Imposter, if you're not that woman, CC Harp, then who are you?"

She rolled her forehead back and forth on his. "I'm CC Harp."

"Oh, it's so obvious. How could I not know? You're not CC Harp. You're CC Harp."

"Exactly." She leaned her head back as far as his embrace allowed. "The last time you met CC... actually it was the first time, wasn't it? That other time you met CC? That was definitely not me."

"You mean The Streetdancer wasn't you?"

She snuggled her body against his, giggling, delighted. "The Streetdancer?"

"That's who I met the first last time. She whirled into my life right off the curb. That isn't who you are?" He slipped some of Sheri's indignation into the question.

Though he still held her upper arms she managed to move her hands around to his lower back, slide them onto his buttocks and begin to slowly massage them. "The Streetdancer? I love it. I love *her*. That brazen dancer who picked you up. But she was too alive. This CC, me, the one who's vigorously resisting every effort you make to embrace her, is practically an old maid."

"Oh, right, this CC. The one who practically leapt on me at the bar and... would it be unchivalrous to mention?... has her hands all over my ass."

She pinched him with both hands and let go. "Well, I never... And while I'm at it I can assure you I would never ever throw myself at a man the way that Jezebel threw herself at you. And..." She pulled free from his grasp and backed away. "I've got to say this. You've got to understand. This is serious. I'm boring."

"Wait. Say that again? You're boring?"

"I'm a businesswoman and when I'm not working I spend most of my time looking after my father and my brother. When I have a chance I like to read and I take long walks. I've had one real boyfriend and he was even more boring than me. You have no idea. I was so relieved when he wrote to explain that "the pressures of my double major make it impossible to continue our relationship." That's a quote. And that night we met? You and I? At Roger's party? That was my first night out in over a month. And the way I behaved? And again tonight? The Streetdancer? I don't know where she comes from." She stared at him, lost for words.

"Why are you telling me all this?"

"Because you... You're so involved. Intense. You'd find out." CC put her hands on her cheeks. "And she's gone. I feel... this is all so embarrassing. I'm mortified."

He reached out a hand. "CC, could I, may I, hold your hand?"

She put her hand in his with a slight curtsy and they continued on their way.

"I'm of the opinion," he said, "that we all deserve dessert."

"Even me?"

"Both of you. You, you wanton hussy, of course, but you, too, you prim tedious goody goody. In fact, oh yes, you especially." He licked his lips. "You'll see. In the meantime, to stave off the tedium of our journey, why don't you regale me with stories of L.A. and Santa Cruz and the mother who lives there?"

"There's so little to tell."

"Then it should be easy. Tell me. First L.A."

"L.A. is a sprawling series of cities. I never know where I am when I'm there. I always feel like I'm travelling in circles. Every six blocks or so there's a business district that looks just like the one I left behind. Chandler found it exotic and menacing. I'm not qualified to argue.

"When I'm in L.A. I always stay at a Holiday Inn near the offices of a temp agency. They provide me with potential interviewers. I use a small banquet room in the hotel to screen the applicants and train the hires. For this trip I needed twelve, preferably from the areas where they would be doing their interviews.

"There. That's more than you need to know. What I do in L.A., and in all the other cities I travel to, is stay in a hotel large enough to provide me with a reasonably priced room, a space to work in and an easy way to get my meals. I hire a bunch of people, train them and guide them through their visits. During the rare moments I'm not working, I work out then read, usually just before I go to bed. I seldom leave the hotel, mainly because I don't have the time, but also because I'm a woman alone and not free to just wander around like a man would.

"So, what I really did this trip was try to stay in shape and read Styron's *Lie Down in Darkness* and Levertov's *Oh, Taste and See.* Have you read Styron?"

Neil cleared his throat and said bravely, as if under oath, "I've never heard of either of those guys."

"Business major then law school?"

"I majored in history."

"Where?"

"UConn, okay? Now moving on to Santa Cruz where you stayed with your mother."

"Oh, no, I stayed in a charming little oasis called *La Oceana*, a two-storied hotel built around a courtyard where you took your morning coffee and buttered roll out to squishy chairs and umbrellaed tables under lush palm trees. There was a fountain that shot out of the mouth of a white stone seal and on windy days it sprayed the whole area. The base of the fountain was full of pennies. I never saw anyone throw a single penny in that fountain but there they lay, hundreds of them. And on my last day I threw in mine. I made a wish and thanked the fairies that sweetened that lovely garden."

"What did you wish for?"

"Oh, no, I can't tell you that."

"Just so you know? The person who told me about her little oasis? I think that was The Streetdancer making an impromptu appearance. But go on. Your stay in Santa Cruz was delightful."

"My stay at *La Oceana* was delightful. And my bill for the room and the courtyard and the fairies flitting around my breakfast cost less than half what I paid for my room in L.A. By the way, not to be too pedantic, Levertov is a woman. Denise."

"Ah, yes, Denise. I know her well."

"I bet you'd go for her. She's quite attractive. Though she's even older than I am."

"Oh, then she's ancient. And your mother? She's older than you, too, I suspect."

They walked on another half block.

"Your mother?" he prodded.

"My mother is a consummate bitch. She is also gorgeous, not to put too fine a point on the matter. Even at the ripe old age of fifty-one she manages to capture everyone's attention wherever she goes.

And there are some, even some not beholden to her, who think she is a talented painter. I am none of the above; neither captivated nor beholden nor impressed by her artistry. We met twice, over a very unpleasant dinner and the next day over an icy breakfast. I doubt that we will ever meet again. It's my singular distinction to be the only person in the world she can't manipulate and for that she detests me. The feeling is mutual, by the way, in case you weren't able to detect that from my dispassionate appraisal of her character."

"It's none of my business, but, well, with all that ill-will, why go see her?"

"My brother and I are selling my father's business. We wanted to keep it going until he recovered..."

He felt her shiver and glimpsed down in time to catch her eyes squeezing shut, her mouth twisted.

She gave a fierce shake of her head. "Came back... He's not coming back... from this illness... ever. No one can make sense of it."

She pulled away, walking now as if he were a stranger, which, of course, he was.

"The way I describe it to myself is that a ghoul latched onto him and sucked out his soul and all that's left is the residue, a sort of wandering shell.

"However you want to put it, he's gone. I mean the man I called my father is just gone. And after at least two years of denial both my brother and I have finally allowed ourselves to accept that. But wait..." She pressed a palm out. "How could we even consider such a thing? What about my mother? After all she's paid a biweekly salary and gets a rather substantial annual share of the earnings for?... doing *nothing*. I mean, she does absolutely *nothing*." She stopped and looked at Neil as if he had said something appalling. "Don't you dare think her reasons for opposing the sale are self-interested. It's so obvious she's only concerned with my father's legacy. She told me so herself." CC snickered. "What's most heartwarming for me is that she's the one who insisted on the non-voting shares. She didn't want even the hint of responsibility. But no responsibility, no rights.

"The reason I went to Santa Cruz was to tell my mother the sale was going forward. What I wanted most was to see her kick and scream. Make no mistake; in this case the messenger truly was to blame. And I definitely wanted to assure her that if she tried to sue, we would do our best to take our legal costs out of her earnings. Then, too, well, yes, it was legally prudent to make sure she was given the courtesy of a face-to-face consultation. Otherwise can't you hear her attorney moaning wide-eyed, 'You didn't even have enough respect to present this decision to your mother in person?'"

"Your brother, I take it, is for the sale."

"Oh, more than I am. Though of course he's terrified of her. And for inexplicable reasons he cares for her. I on the other hand am not in the least intimidated by her. And let the record show: I detest her. Best of all I absolutely petrify her. When I was an infant, I could out scream her; when I was a little girl, I could out pout her, and by the time I was a teenager I could bully her. In case you haven't noticed, we are there," she said, waving at the doors of the *Four Brothers Coffee Shop*.

Chapter 8:

Cross Your Heart

In the Four Brothers Coffee Shop: CC put down her tea and said, incredulous, "I don't believe this. She's giving out a set of papers and you ask someone else to give out another set and she goes crazy and knocks the papers out of the other person's hand?"

"In a flash. Faster than a flash. Faster than a speeding bullet. Wham! All the papers go everywhere. It drove me crazy. That's not merely an expression. I was crazed, infuriated, and determined to beat her. So I decided she would never ever give out another set of papers for as long as she was in my class and I started to walk around with each of the other children who I knew were dying to give them out. It was so painful. She was devastated, in tears."

"Oh, poor baby."

"Yeah, but don't forget that poor baby was killing me."

"You said this was one of your biggest success stories? Hurting her? Hurting you, too, it seems. That doesn't sound so successful to me."

"I haven't finished." He took a bite of his pie.

"So?" she insisted.

He sipped his coffee.

"You have exactly one second to tell me what happened."

"I did what any base lily-livered wretch would do. I bribed her. I made her permanent window monitor. It's her job to open the windows in the morning and to close them in the evening. It's not really a bribe. It's a very important job and she's the only one who does it right. It has to be done because the cost of heating the building goes up if the windows are left open at night. Most important it has to be done because the custodian says so. The custodian, Mac, is one of the powers that be in the school. He has control of all the supplies, knows where everything is and fixes lights, repairs doors, cleans up messes, or not, depending on how he feels about you. In my day Mac would have been called a janitor and be low man on the totem pole. Well, Mac ain't no janitor. He's a Custodian, with a capital C. He's a small duchy all to himself, with his own budget, his own employees and his own agenda.

"Anyway, I used to do the windows myself because even though a couple of my kids would do them once in a while, Pedro, Morris and Pauli in particular, all of them would forget, or I would forget, and Mac would have to close the windows. When that happened I got a sweet little note saying, 'Riley, you're expected to close your windows before you leave for the night.' Translated that reads, 'Close your windows or you're gonna get it!'

"Have I made it clear how very important it is not to forget to close the windows before you leave for the night? And Sheri does not forget. Morning and night, she does her job. Believe me, won't anyone else do it now, cause they know they'll die if they even touch that window stick. And believe it or not she doesn't have to give out the papers. And just as important to me—not to Sheri, who could care less—the other children accept this arrangement, in part I think because they're relieved to not have her going nuts over the papers."

"And they must see that she really is the only person who does the job. Didn't you say she's small?"

"Tiny."

"Why would anyone be afraid of her?"

"Ho, ho, ho and a bottle of rum, ain't nobody gonna mess with Sheri less they got a gun. Honestly, she won't back down from anybody. It's not that she's fearless. She knows when to be afraid. She'll run and look for protection and even tell somebody not to mess with her because they too big. She's not fearless, she's brave, and relentless. And slowly I'm learning how to accommodate her craving for attention. Sometimes I can even do it with pleasure. When I can she's happy and I'm happy."

"What's she look like?"

"A flash of lightning. Oh, God, this is hard. I should take pictures."

"Yes, I'd like that, but I'd still want your take. Come on, tell me."

"She's thin and very black. I use that word advisedly. Her skin is a deep beautiful dark color that shades to black. Her hair is black and like all the black girls she straightens it. And then keeps it shoulder length around her face or for another look pulls it back tightly with one of those clips; what do girls call them?"

"Barrettes? Like this?" She turned her head to show him hers. And her long straight black hair cascading down her back from the wooden clasp.

It took Neil a moment to collect himself. Then he said quickly, "Right. Barrette. Sheri. She has a round face and large round brown eyes that look straight out at you. I mean they're not timid or frightened. No way. They can go shifty and when they do watch out. Her features are appealingly symmetrical. She has a broad nose and thick lips. And then there's her smile. Her lips are large and on the outside a very deep very dark reddish black. But just on the inside everything, her lips, her tongue, her gums are a vivid red. Vivid. And she has large even white teeth. So when she smiles it's as if the middle of her face blooms into this incredible red and white flower. It's mesmerizing. She can also pout the best pout I have ever seen pouted. And she can, what's the word. Flirt. But that's not it. Play."

"She sounds wonderful."

"She's a character. If she could only learn how to do her math I'd forgive her all the grief she's ever caused me."

"Math. It's overrated."

"That's what she says. More like, 'How come I got to learn that ole math anyway.' I'll tell you this though. I worry about my kids. I can't help it. You know, I try to look ahead and think what will they do? How will they survive? And I think Sheri will do better than most just because she's so courageously alive. Maybe that's wishful thinking." He looked down at the remains of his coffee, drank the last mouthful and gave out a long guttural protest. "It's so frustrating. Once upon a time she was just a problem. Now I'm worried about *her* problems.

"She's madly in love with Pedro. I mean, I can't stress this enough; she's deeply, truly, head-over-heels in love with Pedro. And he, well, yeah, you could say he loves her, although he would probably say he 'likes' her. Look, there's nothing quite like caring for someone who cares for you, is there? So they have that. Sheri has that. But Pedro has so much outside. A family, younger sisters that he's expected to look after, friends, music, brains. I mean, the kid's about as smart as they come and learning, understanding, exploring everything, it all matters to him. So this year's over, they'll never see each other again, he'll be sad and he'll walk away to whatever comes next. What he doesn't know is what Sheri knows all too well. She's going to lose the love of her life, an experience she's never had before, what she wants most and has and is bound to lose. Do you see?" He looked at his watch and shook his head. "I've been talking for over an hour. I don't do this."

"You need to do this," CC said.

"But it's so insane. Last I remember you were telling me about your mother. Right? And selling the business? The next thing I know I'm talking about my kids. Again." He pointed at her. "You. I know you keep bringing things back to me. But it's so easy isn't it? All you have to do is ask me if I'm thinking about my kids and I'm off again. Because I'm always thinking about my kids. Always. It's pathetic."

"You think it's pathetic because you care about them?"

"Care about them? What a thought. Who do you think I am?"

"Oh, no, that's for you to tell me. Who are you?"

"That's for me to know and you to find out. That's what my kids say. By the way, only The Streetdancer would ask a question like that."

"And only a concerned, soft-hearted teacher would dodge it. A tough guy would snarl out a prickly retort distilled by grim pride."

He laughed. "Oh, my God. All right. I don't know about the tough guy stuff, but I'm going to take a swing at your question. I might even throw out a little grim pride."

"Come on, baseball metaphors. That's pretty tough. But I'm not clear. Are you hitting or pitching?"

"Just wait. We'll get to that." He put the fingers of his right hand on his forehead. "The whole game's right here. This is me. I don't know how I got here. And it's not clear to me where I'm supposed to go. I've sure gotten a helluva lot of advice about that though, not to mention persuasion and out and out indoctrination. One thing's for sure. I can't stand it when anyone tells me who I am or where I'm supposed to go. I hate it so much that even though more than anything else I want to stay alive I'd rather die than let somebody tell me how to live. So there you have it. I'm this egotist encumbered with all sorts of impediments determined to the best of my ability to live my life my way. That's what's basic, that I decide..." He paused. "That's it. I decide. Period."

"Based on my voluminous knowledge of you I'd say that's a pretty credible self-portrait. I was just wondering. What if this..." She tapped her forehead. "...were to disappear. Just suddenly went away."

"I'd be dead."

She took a deep breath. Shook her head. Said nothing. He was so used to having her make eye contact with him, seeming to insist on it, that he was shocked to see her eyes wander up over his head.

He didn't have to guess. He knew. *Instantly.* She was bored. And the sense of loss he felt, the intensity of it, caught him completely off guard. She was just someone he had met at a party, a woman he had invited out to dinner. That she didn't want to be with him wasn't the end of the world. So why did it feel like the end of the world?

"Okay, that's it," he said. "I can stop talking. Really. I've never jabbered on like this before in my life. This is awful."

"I have an annoying observation to make," she said. She was smiling as if everything was all right and she wasn't just aching to get away from him. "I don't think this picture you've painted of yourself would exclude teacherly worries about the kids in your class."

"Sometimes it seems there's no room for anything else," he said. *What a crybaby,* he thought, listening to himself. "Anyway, I'm done." He pushed at his coffee cup. "We can leave anytime you're ready."

Her eyes narrowed. "Yes, of course." She reached over to pick up her bag, which was on one of the empty seats at their table. She put the bag on her lap and opened it, but then she sat staring at the floor. "I should pay for this," she said.

There was a briskness in her voice, a finality, that didn't match the sudden wilted look of her shoulders. Her hands lay loosely on the top of the bag.

"Look," he said, "I know this has been a bad night for you. I mean... I'm sure it wasn't what you expected. To have to listen to me go on and on and on. And no, you shouldn't have to pay anything for what has to have been the most boring night of your life."

"You think I'm bored?"

"Come on. I know you are."

"I peppered you with questions. I... I may not understand all you're going through, but I think I've gotten the gist of it. And I'm definitely interested. What I think is… I think you just want to get rid of me."

She started to cover her face.

At the same moment he opened his arms, pleading. "Not at all. What makes you think that?"

She glanced at him cautiously while her hands leapt out and pulled his tightly together. She tilted her head slightly and said, as if it were a question, "We've got to find a way to check each other out?"

"How?" he said.

She shrugged. "What if we just say, I need to know what you're feeling?"

"Okay, but we've got to answer honestly. I need that."

"I need that too."

"Okay, only…" He had taken his right hand out of her grasp to run his fingers along one side of the thin silver watch on her wrist then with a single finger trace the band back along the other side. It was a very gentle, intimate caress that claimed most of his attention. And, he felt, claimed most of hers. But he remembered the gist of what he had meant to say and managed, "…there might be things you don't want to talk about. You know. Stuff you may not want to say. You know, stuff like that."

She gave a slight shift of her body, her eyes looking up ominously from under her brows. "You mean things like shitting?"

He burst out laughing. "Oh, God, where did you come from?"

"I was conjured up one night out of a drain near 92nd and Broadway by a young prince in desperate need."

"Yes. You were. There you are. I knew I had seen you before."

"Yes, but… Ahem." She cleared her throat, pulled her hands together on the table Brenda fashion and said, "Enough of this frivolity. We have serious matters to attend to. We decided if you need to know how the other person is reacting to you all you have to do is say…"

"…I need to know how you're feeling. And," he added, "you've got answer honestly."

"As honestly as possible," she agreed.

"I swear it. Do you?" he asked.

"I swear it."

"Cross your heart and hope to die?"

"I cross my heart and hope to die," she said, crossing her heart. "Now you."

"I cross my heart and hope to die," he said, crossing his heart. "Okay. So, I need to know how you're feeling."

"Like I need for you to come home with me tonight. Now you."

"I need to go home with you tonight."

Chapter 9:

When Eagles Fly

In CC's bed: she said softly in his ear, "Whitman has a poem in *Songs of Myself* called *The Dalliance of the Eagles* that describes a pair of eagles who make love by flying as high as they can, locking themselves together in a sexual embrace and free-falling until they almost hit the ground. Now I know how that feels."

Neil said nothing. Lying on his side next to her he was working the flat of his hand over her stomach, down her thighs and back to her breasts. Her breasts were the only soft parts of her and they were rather small and set in hard pectorals over a broad ribcage. He took her hand and placed it on his penis.

"For informational purposes," he said then put his mouth on her left nipple, which became as erect as his prick.

"I forgot. You're still a growing boy," she said, working her hand all around his erection.

"It's been a while," he said.

She opened her legs as he rolled on top of her; their bodies sliding together released a cloud of inciting odors. He grunted when she took him in hand and hunched a bit to put him inside her. Immediately the world became exactly as it should be, sending him off on an exquisite soaring voyage far away from words.

After a moment she put her hand on his chest. "Wait," she said. "I want to talk."

"Now?"

"If you go away again I won't want you to come back," she said, then, "No, wait!" She gripped his buttocks to keep him inside her. "Don't go. That's good. Do that. That's very good." Then after a few more moments, the hand was back on his ribcage. "Just let me finish. No, that's too good. Wait. Just a minute."

He put his mouth on her neck and licked it up to her ear. "Speak now or forever hold your peace," he whispered.

"I'm not accusing you of anything," she said. "You were more than forthright. You owe me nothing. It's just that I meant what I said. Whatever happens when I'm with you, I want to explore it. Or let it go. I can't let it hang out there, messing me up."

"I'm not going to stop," he said and did not.

In a fierce rush they tumbled together into a vast awakening, which was suddenly over, leaving them melded together in a bath of lush sweat. Neil remembered that a long time ago as if in a dream she had said he must not go away. Where would he go when he was exactly where he wanted to be?

When he placed some of his weight on his forearms she knocked them out from under him with her elbows and brought his full weight back again across her body and his senses back into their sharp smells. When, if ever, had he felt so satisfied?

"I'm crushing you," he said.

"Yes you are."

"So shouldn't I get off?"

"In a minute."

After a while responding to a tentative hand on his side he rolled over onto the bed next to her.

"I've never felt like this before," he said.

"Do you want to elaborate on that?" she asked when it became clear that was all he had to say on the matter.

"I heard what you said. About my going away. I know what you mean."

She waited. After a while she rose up and lay along his side. "For a man who spent the whole evening talking, you've become strangely taciturn."

"Strangely. You love that word. Is it even a word?"

"An adverb, expressing a quality, in this case of an adjective."

"Uh-oh, an English major. And taciturn? Mrs. Robin would love that one."

"Mrs. Robin? I've heard that name before."

"A sixth grade teacher at school."

"Like you?"

"I wish. No, not like me. Mrs. Robin is a master teacher. She told me she started teaching in Valdosta, Georgia. Could there be such a place? She was nineteen, with two years of college and a certificate that specified she could teach only Negro children. She was, as she put it, still in pigtails and some of the boys in her class were as old as she was and a head taller. Now she teaches me, a white boy from Lake Haven, Connecticut, who's half her age and almost twice as tall."

"There's too much going on here. Still, being a woman, I know how to focus on the most important part. You said you had never felt like this before. Tell me what you mean by that."

"Strangely."

"Oooo. No, that's how you're going to feel..." She grabbed his balls. "...after I castrate you unless you can quickly, an adverb expressing time and modifying a verb, proceed with a real response to my request."

"I want you to understand."

"That's it?"

"You have no idea. For my whole life my aunt has been the only person I wanted to understand me. Actually, I expected her to understand me. Just one person. And suddenly there's two more. Mrs. Robin, though I only just now realized that about her, and you. You probably want to know what I'm talking about."

"Well, yes, come to think of it, yes, that might be helpful. And then maybe we can get to Mrs. Robin. The aunt I'm assuming we can take for granted, the loving relative."

"I mean… Look, we can all die in a second. I start to get out of bed, twist my ankle, fall, hit my head, die. We all live with that; it could happen. But it usually doesn't. But then it does. What happens tomorrow? Everybody, well… most people think about tomorrow. They need to get up, they need to brush their teeth, they need to get dressed, they need to go to work, they need to see their friends. They do all this planning. So do I in the sense that if I'm going to teach those fucking… sorry, I mean… marvelous children I've got to prepare. But that's my only tomorrow. I have no others. Beyond that I can't say this is what I'm going to do tomorrow. I cannot plan because if I lose this job I'm going to have to leave the country. Do you see? I cannot plan. Strangely, strangely, I want you to understand that. Okay, that said… See, you've got me talking again."

"Yes, I see. Go on."

"When I started this teaching gig I thought I'd do the bare minimum. But it isn't working out that way. My kids matter to me. Tonight talking to you I realized how much they matter. They're all like me. Thirty-three doppelgangers I can't ignore. I've never cared this much about anything before. Which is a good thing I guess because it means I'm probably going to keep my job for at least this year. Wow. Did I just say that?

"Then suddenly there's you. I want to see you. I want to say, I want to see you all the time. That would be true, but not all true. Because, you know what, I'm obsessed. I've got to work at this. I want you to understand."

"I understand," she said, "that we will see each other on a catch-as-catch-can basis. Is that the deal?"

"Can you accept that?"

"I have no idea. It's going to be one day at a time. You're off now. This is your Thanksgiving break? It's Saturday night, pushing on toward Sunday morning. How long before you disappear this time?"

"I go back to school on Monday," he said. "I should leave by mid-afternoon tomorrow. But I don't know that I have to disappear. I... I'm making all sorts of wild claims tonight. But I'm going to say it. I think I have a handle on the situation. Oh, God, now the sky's going to open and a burning finger's going to stab me in the chest and a booming voice is going to say, 'Fi fie foe fum, liars rot in hell till kingdom come.'"

"How much time do *we* have?" she asked, pushing a finger into his chest on the *we*. "Right *now*."

"Until tomorrow afternoon. Then I have to go home to prepare for Monday. There's no choice. I have to. But look, maybe we could talk about next weekend."

"Ah, one weekend at a time."

"Well, maybe, you know like Saturday night."

"Ah, one day of one weekend at a time."

Chapter 10:

Hurt

From CC Harp's notebook:
Clay
Your faded blue eyes
worn denim
in a clay face
too dry to throw.
Where is the broad smile
when I turn to you,
the don't-hurt-yourself worry
as I leap into your arms?
Daddy
it's me, CC,
I've just grabbed
your hands.
Can't you see?
I'm hurt.
CC Harp

Chapter 11:

A Noel Coward Moment

In his dream: his father reached down from his barstool and placed the flat of his hand on his chest, preventing him from going to make a weewee. The beers on the counter and the peanut shells on the floor reeked of loneliness and longing and the threat of some terrible loss to come. Behind his father a woman, he couldn't make her out even though he strained and squinted, peeked over his father's shoulder. She stood flickering in black and white, fading, a very old silent movie. Suddenly a face zoomed forward, strange and grotesque with huge painted lips and bulging eyes.

He woke up gasping remembering a morning when through the cracked-open door of his father's bedroom he saw his mother in their bed even though they kept saying she was gone. He ran in and jumped on the bed crying, "Mama!" then nearly peed in his pajamas when she turned, sleepy, annoyed and said, "Get off me, kid. I ain't your mama."

Here now, wherever here was, he winced, then smiled wryly. He didn't have any pajamas to pee in, but he sure as hell had to pee. This place, which was dimly lit by shafts of daylight finding gaps in the huge drapes across the room, had to be a bedroom and for some reason (oh, yeah, over there a dressing table, for one thing, and the smells of creams, lotions; and the drapes themselves; no man would have put up that fancy rig) he knew it was a woman's bedroom, yes, and immediately remembered what woman. He also knew it was morning, not only because of the light, but because of an internal humming like the cat's purr, a hum he only felt after a long deep sleep. That woman. Oh, yeah, that woman. Her bedroom.

He climbed out of bed and found his briefs and pants folded neatly on one of two large stuffed chairs set catty-corner to a table at the window. He couldn't find his tee or button-down. He put on his pants and as he looked around for the door remembered that shortly before he had gone to sleep she had said, "I'll be right back. I have to check on my father," which, of course, had to be wrong because he had seen the whole apartment last night and knew there was no father lurking anywhere.

The brilliant detective Neil Riley deduced the bathroom must not be in this closet full of women's clothes and shoes. He decided it was instead somewhere outside that other door over there. But before opening it he stopped to collect himself.

She had shown him around when they arrived last night. Admittedly he had been in such a state of lust that very little registered. Still, he was fairly certain there was only this bedroom, the living room, a kitchen and a bath. There simply wasn't a room in which to cram a needy father. He was sure of it. It must have been a dream, he decided, then wondered what had provoked a night of father dreads. Did he feel he had wandered into forbidden territory? He opened the door to that unanswered question and was brought blinking into a sun-drenched hall that led past other doors on his left to the one at the end that looked like the entrance to the apartment.

To his right the hall opened into a room where she stood on her head, not naked, but almost, in a tight white translucent leotard. Every muscle of her back shoulders arms and most of all buttocks was clearly, beautifully outlined. Rodin would have been pleased; Neil Riley was transfixed, as she slowly dropped to her knees. Now kneeling with her back to the window, she lifted herself on her arms, spread her legs, twisted her hips and lowered herself into a split. While in this impossible position she stretched her arms to the ceiling and tilted her face upwards. Without pause, but slowly, as she turned toward him she moved one leg, then the other, so that she was sitting with the soles of her feet pressed together, both knees flat on the floor. That's when she saw him and pulled herself into a cross-legged position, from which she stood, using only her legs, her arms stretched out in front of her.

He pointed to his left. "The bathroom?"

"Thataway," she pointed in agreement. "There's coffee when you're ready."

While he relieved himself, staring at the flat white cover to the water tank, a memory popped up of him standing staring at the rim of an iron grey metal desk. Aunt Connie was saying, 'Me! I'm his guardian!' She squeezed his hand, as if to make the point to Neil as well. 'But Connie, you're just a child.' 'Excuse me, mister. My name is Mrs. Maury Riley and this is my nephew; and my husband, who is twenty-one, and I are his legal guardians. I AM HIS GUARDIAN!' 'No need to shout.' 'Really? Seems to me you have trouble hearing.' Registering him for school. If he was six, add thirteen, she was nineteen. The principal was right: she *was* a child. She was right: she *was* his guardian.

Was this a betrayal?

CC was in the kitchen. She had slipped on a floppy tee and a pair of loose grey knit pants. He would have preferred just the leotard. She was still barefoot, with wide long feet. He felt slightly self-conscious without his shirt.

She held up a coffeepot. "How do you take it?"

"Black, no sugar," he said.

Through tight lips she snarled, "Yeaaaah, I shudda known." She swiped at her nose with the back of a hand.

Neil lifted his head to inform her, in what he intended to be his best effete gentleman's manner, "You most certainly should have. To taste the full flavor of the bean, one doesn't want to contaminate it with cows' goo."

"Oh, dear, forgive me." She filled one of those thick white diner mugs to the brim with an "ugh," then filled a mate three-quarters of the way, to which with an "ahhh," she added half-and-half and a large spoonful of sugar.

Neil said, "What strange country is this where the inhabitants make such a mess of perfectly decent coffee?"

"Watch out, Mr. Purist," she warned. "Yours will be really hot."

"Gotcha." He lifted the mug to his nose and took a deep whiff. "Real coffee. Smells delicious. I've been drinking mostly instant for months." Looking up warily, mocking the guilt he actually felt, he asked, "If we tease each other, is that a good sign?"

"It puts us somewhere between polite and affectionate," she said after a sip. "If it goes on too long, though, it gets hostile." Locking eyes with him she took a loud slurp. "Now that's a civilized coffee." She jabbed a finger at her mug. "You see? Slurping and pointing takes us to the edge of hostile. Can you feel that edge up against your cojones?"

"I don't want it to get hostile," he said carefully.

"Me neither," she said. "But you're easy to push."

"Push?"

"Teasing makes you angry," she said.

"Are push and manipulate synonyms?"

"Oookay," she said, stringing the word out. She put her mug on the counter, guided his hands to place his mug next to hers and keeping his hands in hers, moved closer, her head raised so that her lips were close to his chin. "I started this so I guess I have to be the one to try to understand what's going on. On my side anyway."

She studied him. He watched her impassively.

"It looks like you're not going to help me," she said.

She let go of his hands. He folded them across his chest. She let hers drop, defeated. "This is a really good place for me say I need to know what you're feeling."

"I don't know," he said. "Awkward."

"Sounds like we're on the same side. Though I'd probably say scared."

"I should have said scared. Want to know which side I want us to be on?" he asked.

"Which side?"

"The one where we're being empathetic. That side."

"That sounds like exactly the place to go. How do we get there?"

He put his hands on her hips. "Tell me why you're scared. I'm really confused. It will help me... Everything seems different. I hardly know you, but... I mean. Here we are. See? I don't want to be smart."

"Me either." She thought a moment. "Why am I scared? Suppose..." She leaned against him, touched his ribcage, ran her hand along the bottom rib. "Just suppose I was made out of one of your ribs. Wait! Don't say anything." He hadn't shown any sign he was about to, but she covered his mouth with her left hand anyway. Her right was still pressed palm open on his lower left rib, softly caressing it. "It feels like that to me."

For a second he thought this was some reference to his rib, but that wasn't what she meant at all. He stood in a trance, pleased and flattered by her caress, but wary, too, because he was wide open and she was positioned to give him a furious jab.

"That like Eve I was newly sprung from this encounter. Most of the time I'm... among other things I'm not me. I mean... Yes, that's exactly what I mean. Most of the time I'm not me. I'm this person at work, telling people what to do; around here I tell people how to take care of my father. I read books, watch movies, read *The Times*. This is all so stupid. I don't know what you think of me, but most people, a lot of people think I'm some haughty know-it-all. When I'm just... I dunno... waiting. It feels like one way or the other I have a lot to lose. Does that make any sense at all?"

He allowed himself the pleasure of what had become a major

need, to have his hands on her hips. Front or back, that was how he
held her when he was inside her. Now it seemed to have brought
them into the same space. "I'm not sure what you're saying. I need
to ask you. This is hard. I don't trust you. I mean, I don't trust anybody. My aunt, I guess. So this is hard." He closed his eyes, took a
deep breath and said in a rush, "Are you saying this is the beginning
of something?" Then he lifted his head and groaned, "Oh, my God,
that sounds so stupid."

"No, no," she said. Then quickly, "I mean, yes, yes, it is. The
beginning of something, I mean. Not a stupid thing to say."

At that moment they heard a door open and slam shut and quick,
slippered footsteps slapped down the hall.

"Oh, shit, I don't believe this," CC said.

"I smell coffee," a lilting voice sang the way Neil's kids sang,
'You're gonna get it.' A slender male version of CC appeared at
the kitchen door and halted, shocked by Neil's presence. He recovered adroitly with a thoroughly theatrical eye-rolling hand-to-mouth
dismay.

"I don't believe this, a pure Noel Coward moment. Unfortunately
I am not the injured husband, only the poor disillusioned brother.
But still, a half-naked young lothario. My sister has obviously been
despoiled. You," he said to CC, "could have put on something more
appropriate. A negligee, or at least one of those sleazy short night-
ies." He raised himself to his full height. "Still, pray, kind sir, what
are your intentions regarding my poor injured kindred?"

His black silk robe was decorated with golden instruments,
trumpets, trombones, saxophones and flutes emitting golden musical notes. As he placed his hands on his hips the robe fell open on
a smooth well-proportioned white body, his male parts kept private
with a pair of very brief white briefs that were, like women's panties, smooth across the front. A twin. He had the same straight black
hair as CC, his brushed back, cut neatly, expensively; his face had

the same wide American Indian angularity, the same high cheek-bones, but was drawn more sharply. He had the same blue eyes, though they were more mobile, and the same long eyebrows. The big difference between them, other than the obvious one, was that he was pretty. Whatever CC was, handsome, exotic, striking, beautiful, she was not pretty.

"Charles!" CC said, not amused. "Do you mind?"

"Oh, my goodness," Charles said, looking down in not very disturbed dismay. He belted himself back to respectability.

"Charles," Neil said. "One of my kids is named Charles."

"*One* of your kids?" Charles repeated, registering real alarm. He looked to CC to underline his distress.

"He's a teacher," she said, dripping exasperation.

"We've already met," Neil said. "My name is Neil." He held out his hand.

"Oh, no. I would have remembered *that* encounter." He took Neil's hand in both of his, his soft gentle touch suggesting a caress.

"Charles, please be straight," CC pleaded.

"But, my dear, I am so decidedly not." All the same she had apparently gotten through to him for he said, in an entirely different tone, "I'm Charles Harp. And I honestly don't remember ever meeting you." He shook Neil's hand and let him go.

"At Roger's party."

"At Roger's party," he said. Then pointing, "Oh, indeed! You're the one who brought that little hysteric and left with, of all people..." At this CC got a wiggling finger. "You were, if I remember, wearing a shirt that night. Perhaps that's why I didn't recognize you. I'm assuming CC told you what happened after the two of you escaped into the dark of night."

"I didn't bring her. She's Betty's friend. And, no, I don't know what happened after we left."

"She started banging the wall with her fists, screaming, 'Bloody murderers, bloody murderers,' then dripped down into a puddle on the floor of the hall, still pounding away, still screaming. My God, she was magnificent! It did rather spoil the party, though. Betty and Roger got her into the bedroom and we more or less gulped down all the wine, cheese and crackers we could manage before we felt we absolutely had to leave. I mean, with a woman expiring in the next room and all it seemed rather tacky to stand around sizing each other up, so we hurried through the process and went home with whoever we would have gone home with anyway. Sort of like you two. Only with less drama and, I might add, less romance. So. What are you up to now?" He raised his eyebrows suggestively.

"Sweet brother, lovely birth partner," CC said in a soft voice, switching to a harsh rasp, "the answer to the question you should have asked is: Yes, you are interrupting something. Get it? Go away!"

"Are you asking me to leave?"

"No! I'm telling you. Leave! Go! Get out of here!"

"She's such a darling. And so subtle," Charles said to Neil. To CC he said, "Only if you fix me a cup of coffee."

"Blackmail," she muttered as she got down another mug and made him the same heavy on the cream and sugar concoction she had made for herself. Instead of handing it to him she reached around Neil and put it on the counter. "There. Now go!"

"Yes, I guess I'll be on my way." He picked up the cup with both hands and took a careful sip. "Oh, that is perfect. Well, now, where were we?"

"Cut it out, Charles."

"We all know how hard it is to say goodbye…"

"*Please.*"

"Okay."

And just as he seemed to actually be ready to leave she blurted, "Did you check on Dad?" Her tone was urgent, her body braced.

"Comatose at the front window. Maria's doing her nails in the most godawful purple."

"Could you make sure she feeds him? He likes that Familia stuff I got, with just a little milk. Tell her not to drench it."

"Madam, I am, as always, at your command." He straightened up, thumped his slippers together, nodded his head.

"Thank you."

"We aim to please. What I really came up for, aside from the coffee and," to Neil, "our little chat, was to ask about the L.A. data."

"My office, Monday morning, ten o'clock." Her voice now officious, like Bernbach ordering a meeting.

"Your office, Monday afternoon, two o'clock," Charles said using the same tone.

"Goodbye, Charles," CC said.

"It was good to see you again," Neil said, offering his hand, then quickly lifting it apologetically because Charles was holding the mug in his right hand. "Sorry, no need..."

But very deliberately Charles put his mug down and again gripped Neil's hand in both of his, saying, "Oh, yes, there is every need. I wish you the best of luck. She's much too good for you. On the other hand..." He leaned forward and said with a stage whisper, "We all know what a woman really needs."

CC threw up her hands. "Will you just go!"

"Parting is such sweet sorrow," Charles said as he left the kitchen and flip-flopped down the hall.

Neil and CC stood frozen until they heard a door slam, and then just a moment longer to test that he was truly gone.

Neil sipped his coffee. CC sipped hers.

"He's..." CC lowered her head, shaking it. Then spoke firmly, chin up, "He's my brother."

"He looks like you. Well, I mean, you have a lot in common. Not really, but some. Are you a dancer?" he asked quickly.

"I wanted to be. Modern, of course. But I'm too clumsy."

"You're not clumsy," he objected.

"Oh, yes, I am. And I'm so tall. Anyway, I never feel right around other girls."

"You're not too tall," he said. She seemed just about right to him.

"How tall do you think I am?"

"You're just about right," he said.

"Come on, how tall?"

"Five eight? I'm terrible at this. Five nine?"

"I'm five ten and a half in my bare feet. As tall as or taller than sixty percent of the male population in America and a total freak when I go to Paris."

"See? I would have never guessed. You look kinda puny to me." He put his mug on the counter, thinking to somehow use the discussion as an excuse to hold her again.

"Right. Puny. I weigh one forty-five and I haven't weighed less than one thirty since I was fourteen. Do you have a sport? I mean, is there something you're really good at?"

"Nothing. I played football in high school, mostly as a blocking back. But I'm really slow. When I got to college, I went out for a day. It was a joke. I was so embarrassed. I mean there were these huge fat guys running circles around me. Basketball, same story. In high school it was my size that even got me on the team. The one thing I'm really good at is being alone."

"Ah," she said. She took a sip of coffee, then over the rim of her mug, "Your shirt, undershirt, jacket, all that is in my closet if you want to get moving. I'll get them for you if you want."

He stared at her, then straight ahead, not knowing what to say.

She put her mug on the counter. "Do you want to get your stuff or do you want me to get it for you?"

"I dunno. I mean. What just happened? Why are you so angry?"

"You said you wanted to be alone. So go. Be alone."

"I didn't say that."

She was standing in the middle of the kitchen, shaking her head. Neil reached out and grabbed her hips. She pressed her hands against his chest. But the barrier quickly became a caress as her hands moved to his back and pulled him to her; she turned her head down and away as he bent to kiss her, then quickly turned back, reached up and kissed him, pushing her tongue between his teeth and deep into his mouth. When he began to caress one of her breasts she gripped his forearm and guided it to her back as she pressed her face into his chest again. She mumbled something he couldn't understand.

"What? I didn't hear you?"

She mumbled again. It sounded something like, "Momgaydahis."

"I'm sorry. That's not a language I know," he said. "Could you translate?"

She leaned back, holding his arms just above the elbows to keep her balance. "I guess I'm going to do this," she said, sounding annoyed. She poked her lips out in an ugly pucker, her nose and forehead scrunched down toward the middle of her face. "Take that," she said.

"Oh, yeah? Well, how about this?" He gave her Pauli's thick lips, formed by putting his tongue up on his upper lip and turning his lower lip down, so that his lips looked double-sized.

"Oh, God, that's gross! But I've got you!" She opened her mouth as wide as she could and crossed her eyes.

"No fair!" he cried. "I can't cross my eyes."

"It's not my problem if you're seriously impaired. You'd better give up or next time it'll be with a mouth full of something brown and yucky, like chili."

"What if I can't keep my hands off you," he said, running his hands up the hard muscles of her stomach to the small, soft swell of her breasts.

"Just hold me," she said, pulling at his wrists.

He put his arms around her and pulled her in close. "I didn't say I wanted to be alone," he whispered in her ear.

They stood rocking together.

She rubbed her belly against his erection. "You certainly are persistent," she said looking up and smiling. "I need to know who you are. I need to be careful," she said, searching his face.

"Yes," he said. "I need that too." He leaned back, locking his forearms against hers and closing his eyes, trusting her to keep him balanced, not being careful at all.

"We should talk," she said.

"That's for sure." His mind's eye was focused on the vision of her upside down butt, the crack of her ass.

"My brother is…"

"Rather flamboyant."

"…a pain in the ass."

They spoke simultaneously.

Then she tapped her forehead. "Remember telling me about how you lived here? About deciding who you are?"

"Yeah," he said, not quite sure where this was leading.

"My brother decided to be who he is. It hasn't been easy. I know. I see what he goes through. That act. It's an act."

"I don't… I'm not hung up on…" He thought queers, then fags. "…homosexuality. He lives in the building?" he asked, changing the subject.

"In the apartment under mine."

"And your father lives here, too?"

"He has the first floor. My mother keeps a studio on the second, though she's hardly ever here. She comes in for these whirlwind tours. This thing at the Modern and that thing at the Guggenheim and her special galleries, the names of which are so so important and somehow never quite stay in my head."

He had let go of her and stepped back. "You live on the top floor."

"It seems like a small building now. But it was probably once the showcase of the block, maybe the whole neighborhood. The two high-rises squashing us in were probably built on the grounds that used to surround the house. That little road out front was for carriages, not cars. What's wonderful is that given our narrow space this old house will probably stay just the way it is. I can't see some developer wanting to build ten stories of one-bedrooms."

"Your family rents the entire building?" He reached for his coffee.

"In a way. Actually, I've set it up as a co-op. Or rather my accountant has. This is actually owned by Harp Riverside, Inc. and a management company called All Services runs it because otherwise guess who would be responsible for maintenance and the mortgage? Can you see my brother putting out the garbage? This way all the repairs are done properly and our monthly maintenance charges are billed as if I never had any say in the matter. It's perfect."

Neil tested his coffee. It was now just right. He took a large sip. It had the strong dark flavor of the coffee Connie made for the breakfast crowd.

While she spoke CC's eyes never stopped watching him. It was as if he were the one talking while she was listening carefully. "I've made it so I take care of my parents' payments through the company payroll. And when my brother forgets to pay his, which is often, I dock his paycheck and send the money to the management company myself."

They now faced each other, mugs held in both hands level at their chests, mirror images of a driver gripping the steering wheel after hearing a sudden clunk in the front of the car.

"I'm rich," she said.

He nodded, quick bobs, as if to show that he understood the problem and sympathized.

"Very rich," she said. "Not Rockefeller rich, but up there. Since the turn of the century there's been Harp money. No prestige. We have no religious affiliation and the decision makers in the family have *never ever* favored philanthropy."

"I get it," he said. "You're very rich."

"Right. And the more you get it the farther away you move."

He looked at the floor space separating them. He had moved to a place at the edge of the counter closest to the doorframe.

"Harp Research is a sideline of my father's. He's a sociologist with a genius at postulating representative groups and sucking the vital statistics out of them. In academic circles it's called demography. But the family's real money is in trust. I earn more from dividends than I do as President of Harp Enterprises, etc."

"I make about one hundred dollars a week after taxes," he said, looking deep into his coffee mug.

"I can spend a hundred a week on wine. That's three bottles of fairly decent chateau bottled Bordeaux." She walked up to him, unzipped his pants and worked her fingers into the opening in his underwear. "My weekly wine bill is probably bigger than your salary." She pulled out his penis and began to manipulate it with exquisite care, gentle and aware.

His pleasure was heightened by her audacity, the bluntness of it. He was without question in her hands.

"See," she said, rubbing her thumb across the head of his penis, "Things always get sticky."

"I don't know a lot about sticky. Sticky's too… too... profound. Complicated though. I know about complicated. Things have gotten complicated."

"What's complicated?" she asked.

"Letting go when you think you should be holding on. Feeling really good, when maybe you ought to be asking a whole bunch of questions. Don't you think ignoring things you don't understand is looking for trouble?"

"Yes, I think that's true."

"So what are we doing now?" he asked.

"Ignoring things. Looking for trouble."

"Sounds so wise when you put it that way," he said.

In her bed after they made love he found himself once again on top of her, her hands pressed hard against his buttocks to keep him from pulling out. He might not be the most astute lover but he was perceptive enough to understand this was something she found satisfying, perhaps even necessary, and he made a mental note: *If possible end on top and lay there.*

Still, even after dropping maybe ten pounds in the last three months, he must weigh one eighty, one eighty-five. "Aren't I heavy?" he asked.

"Stay!" she ordered, addressing him the way you would a dog in need of training. "Don't move."

"But I must be crushing you."

"Yes. Crushing me. Now, to continue our dialogue. We need to make some structural changes in the way the playing field is laid out."

"Oh, God," he said.

"Be calm. It's okay."

She licked his collarbone. He turned his head so that she could reach his neck and felt her wide wet mouth on the right side of his Adam's apple.

She dropped her head to the bed and said, "I'm not accusing you of anything. You do what you do quite naturally, I think. Without thinking. It's an impressive strategy."

"You know I don't know what you're talking about, don't you?" he whispered in her ear. He licked her earlobe.

"You will. You will." She shrugged to stop his tongue. "I'm talking about how you always build a moated castle at the top of the hill and essentially fight all your battles from up there, while we poor commoners, friends and foes alike, stand exposed and vulnerable in the wide valley below. Even if you do deign to come down it's made perfectly clear that you may at any time run back across that moat, pull up the bridge and glare down at us from the ramparts."

"Of course, you're not accusing me of anything or anything. Just declaring in no uncertain terms that I'm a closed, uptight, unreceptive abomination."

"All I'm saying is that you always maintain a certain position; I suppose most people would perceive it as strength. I rather think it's plain old defensiveness suited up as cool. Either way the message is, 'I don't need you and don't you forget it.' I'm sorry. I want us to start in the same vulnerable place. I want us both to agree that this relationship matters."

"It does matter. I've made that perfectly clear. And that's why I'm so worried that I'll smother you to death."

"Never mind that. Say these words to me: 'CC, I want to see you again.'"

That was the moment his penis chose to drop out of her vagina.

"You shit! That's your answer?"

"Wait. Damn. That's just the vicissitudes of nature. I do want to see you again. I have to see you again."

"When? Next Christmas?"

"Next Saturday."

"What time?"

"Seven."

"Too late. Make it earlier and you can stop crushing me."

He did a quick calculation. "Do you run?" he asked.

"Never. It's bad for your legs. I walk."

"Saturday, three o'clock, we walk, then do dinner and a movie."

"Next Saturday, three o'clock. Now get off me!"

"How'd I do strategically? Coming down from the castle?"

"You were perfect. I got just what I wanted."

She bolted her front door, "Against blackmailers and thugs," she explained.

Still nude they made breakfast. Neil scrambled the eggs and CC buttered the toast while both made sure there were many bumps and slides in the process. They did manage to set up two plates before rushing back to bed. After their dalliance and a ravenously devoured breakfast they shared a shower, toweled each other down and very slowly, reluctantly put on clothes.

In the living room as she was rooting around in her shoulder bag, pulling out various items and placing them on the sofa he asked, "What's in there? It's practically a suitcase."

She shook the bag at him and said, "It is a suitcase. Diaphragm and sperm killer, dummy. And a toothbrush, tissues, pads and clean undies in case I spent the night at a strange man's apartment. Don't you know anything?"

"Apparently not. None of that even crossed my mind. It should have, I guess. But what about not even being sure you were going to stick around? There were moments when you seemed ready to walk away from this whole enterprise."

"Then again, what if the minute we saw each other we couldn't keep our hands off each other and practically engaged in coitus in front of the whole wide world? And you were the kind of naïve child who didn't know enough to carry condoms? Although that's silly since, of course... You do carry around condoms, don't you?"

"Carry around condoms? You mean have them on your person?"

"I mean, you do carry them, right? Surely you don't leave the entire responsibility for birth control to the women you see."

"Well, I have to admit that on occasion..."

She shook her shoulder bag at him. "You see? Diaphragm and

sperm killer. I rest my case. There's just one more thing and I'll let you go." She placed a hand on his chest. "I'll just be a sec."

She came back from her bedroom with a heavy wool turtleneck and insisted he wear it under his jacket. "It's the river," she said. "Look." She led him to her front window, to a view of the choppy, surging Hudson. It was an ugly grey, almost colorless, feeling dangerous even from their safe perspective.

"You can see from the way the wind is coming down the river it must have turned much colder last night. You'll freeze in just that jacket."

In a way he didn't quite understand he wanted the sweater the moment she held it out to him.

"It was a gift from my mother. She got it at Harrods during one of her six thousand trips to London. It's only about four sizes too big. Closer than she usually gets. Less of an insult."

It fit him perfectly. "I'll give it back next week."

"It's yours," she said, "now and forever."

The moment he stepped outside he realized she had been right. It felt like the temperature had dropped a good twenty degrees since yesterday. Walking east on 96th the sweater made all the difference. Buses were few and far between on Sunday, but he thoroughly enjoyed the blustering wind. Weather. If he were ever to try teaching a section of science he would start there. What made the temperature drop twenty degrees in the space of a few hours? What made the wind blow? What made the embrace of this sweater so warm? He would see her again next Saturday, hold her in his arms. Oh, God, what was happening to him? How can things change so rapidly?

Chapter 12:

Diana Unstrung

From CC Harp's notebook: *Three step lines with apologies to Dr. Williams.*

> *Your kind hands*
>   *treacherous wands*
>   *undo me*
>
> *the shell*
>   *it took years to assemble*
>   *falls open*
>
> *knots*
>   *I pulled and tightened*
>   *simply part*
>
> *stripped*
>   *now*
>   *bare*
>
> *a plowed field*
>   *yearning*
>   *for your seed*
>
>   *Let's do it again, a sonnet bleeding even more*
>   *metaphorically.*

Those treacherous wands your hands melting
like that armor forged in a cold crucible.
I can't count the lines, their hands slinking
around: "Just let me, you'll see, it's sooo incredible."

Come on, buddy, I'm Diana, breasts plated,
shield emblazoned with the heads of men
like you so poised cock sure sighted
wait until you get the arrow I send.

Becomes a boomerang in your kind hand,
cuts the taut fierce string that bends my bow,
easing me down, softly, incredibly, a supplicant:
oh, sweet, with your hands feel me now

slide through my (once) protected gate,
my open, luxuriant, fertile, ready fate.

The morning after, Byronic in mood if not manner:

Uh-Oh, Diana, Uh-Oh

How now, fine lass?
faux sonnets in euphemisms?
hot hungry ass
he plays with his exemptions
while you call pregnant
luxuriant?
Ready, aye? Steady,
keep that diaphragm
close at hand, ma'am,
or your wish will come to pass.
Know what I think, missy?
Your ass is grass.

Line four being one of those required obscure personal references: "He plays with his exemptions." I'd have to put an asterisk and a footnote explaining that among his other sterling qualities he's a draft dodger. Nor did I mention that I'm robbing the cradle. Won't Charles have a ball with that? "Remember, Cecilia, child molesting is a felony." Oh, well, what's a girl to do? You know what, CC? Why don't you just take it for what it is? About the most delicious thing that's happened to you since you took the silver in the hundred meter crawl senior year. And look, all of a sudden you're playing with words again. That's worth the price of admission right there. Don't you get it? You're happy. Is that such a trial? One day at a time…

Chapter 13:

Compliments

In the hall: On bad weather days and then every day after Thanksgiving break till spring the children were ushered through the main gates at eight twenty-five and herded up to their classrooms. There the teachers waited in the halls to line them up. Sheri arrived at the door of 6-306 at eight twenty-seven, breathing hard, ready to do her job. While the other children had to form two lines, girls to his left, boys to his right, Sheri was allowed to go in and do the windows; then if the class was still shifting around outside, as was usually the case, she would come back out and take her place at the front of the girls' line. Neil had never had to tell her to come back out. Sheri wasn't about to miss anything.

This morning Neil said, "Don't go in just yet."

"How come?" She looked suspicious. "I got to do the windows."

"Just hang out with me for a little while."

"You feelin' awright?"

"I'm feeling fine. I only want to talk to you, that's all."

"I didn't do nothin'."

"It's okay, it's okay," he said, making a soothing, petting motion with his hand, the same tone and gesture he used to ease the cat when he had moved too quickly. "I just haven't seen you in four days." He had intended to ask her about her Thanksgiving, but it had become obvious casual conversation with a teacher wasn't a favored activity. He shifted to teacher mode and told her, as he had intended to do at some point anyway, "I want to compliment you."

"What for?"

Her defensiveness had turned to full-blown alarm. He saw it in her eyes. This teacha could say it was okay, but he was going to do something, jus' you wait. *Was it possible she didn't know what a compliment was?*

"A compliment is a good thing," he said.

"I know that," she said, huffing up in a way that suggested she didn't.

"It means I want to tell you something good about you."

"Huh? What's that?"

"I want to tell you what a good job you're doing with the windows. Nobody, and I mean nobody, not me or Morris or Pedro, nobody ever really did the windows right. But you always do them right."

She raised her chin up and turned her eyes to look sideways at him, still suspicious, but with a trembling around her lips as if fighting not to smile, or cry; it could have been either.

"Good morning, Mr. Riley," Bianca said, breathless.

She, too, rushed to be early when they lined up inside, so she could do exactly the thing Sheri dreaded: have him all to herself for conversation before anyone else arrived. She had never managed to beat Sheri to the classroom, but this was the first day that posed a problem. Bianca's involuntary sourpuss face showed her displeasure at finding them together. But sensing something unusual she quickly went into what Neil thought of as her awareness overdrive, eyes set, body alert, senses throttled open. "What's going on?" she asked.

The question stopped him cold. *I can't believe how perceptive you are,* he thought. "I was just complimenting Sheri on what a good job she does with the windows," he said, collecting himself.

"That's so rye-iiite," Bianca said, singing the word to emphasize her agreement. "She does that so guoood."

"Thas what I got to do right now," Sheri said.

Neil held up a finger. *Ah, shit, what a teacherly thing to do,* he told himself. "One more thing, then you can go."

"What?" Sheri asked.

"We," he said, moving his finger back and forth between himself and Sheri, "want Bianca to define compliment."

"That's right," Sheri said. "What's compliment?"

"It means, well, you know. I know. But it's hard to say. Like…"

"You said something good about somebody," Sheri said quickly.

"That's right," Bianca said. "He told you."

"I already knew," Sheri said.

"You both knew and I just started trouble. But you see," he said to Sheri, "Bianca complimented you, too. She knows you do the windows better than anybody, too."

"She does," Bianca said.

"I'm going to do them," Sheri said, rushing past Neil and into the room.

They heard her step even before she asked, loudly, "What's happenin'?" Somehow even Arlene's stare was loud. She looked at Neil and then Bianca.

"Not much," Neil said, looking past her to nod at Brenda, who actually smiled at him. The pleasure he felt at that was unexpectedly deep and warm.

"Somethin'," Arlene insisted.

"Well, for one thing," Neil said, "here you are. And early. The third person on the scene."

"Cause Bianca's always first," Arlene said.

"Actually Sheri was first," Neil said.

"Cause she's already doin' them windows."

"Because she's already doing *those* windows," Brenda corrected her.

"Cause she's already doin' *those* windows," Arlene repeated.

In Room 6-306: After he had the children in each row put their coats on the back hooks Neil quickly called the roll. Then in the corner of his plan book under the note *movement* he wrote, *Conversation. How to.* Bianca, who was searching her dictionary, stopped to watch him.

"Does anyone know why Simon's not here today?"

"He's my cousin," Arlene said. "His grand momma's crazeeey. They was a fire or somethin' in the hall up on Eleven and they went knockin' on people's doors and she got scared and won't come out. My mom and Brenda's aunt they look after her. An' Simon he takes care of her. What yo aunt call her?"

"Paranoid," Brenda said.

"Thas right. Paranoided. So I spect he stayin' home to be wid her. He's so nice. Don't nobody mess wid him. They's too many people don't want to see him get hurt."

"Could I ask you and Brenda to take him his homework tonight?"

"I'll do it," Brenda said quickly, effectively heading off any objections from Arlene.

"Okay. Thank you."

Neil had already written the day's schedule on the board. He turned and pointed to the first item. "Everyone take out their math books, please. But first..." He picked up a piece of chalk and went to the board.

He wrote: *compliment*

Then beneath that he wrote: *com pli ment*

"That's what I was looking up," Bianca said.

"Don't call out," Morris said.

Neil acknowledged Morris with a sweep of his hand. "I couldn't have said it better myself. To both of you."

Clyde raised his hand.

"Mr. Johnson."

"You still can't write worth a dang, Mr. Riley."

"We should..." Bianca caught herself and raised her hand.

"We should have that contest," Arlene called out.

"To get somebody who can write to write on the board," Sheri called out.

"We'll wait," Neil said. "Thank you, Brenda," he said because she had immediately sat up and clasped her hands in front of her on her desk. With everyone looking at her she still stared straight ahead. "That is so great," he said. The gratitude in his voice was spontaneous, true, heartfelt. She had become for him the only person in the room. "I know you want to go home on time and you know what? I don't care if the rest of us stay here until midnight, you're going to leave when the three o'clock bell rings."

As if on command everyone, and that included Arlene, Pauli, Clyde, Sheri and Bianca, sat exactly as Brenda was sitting. There wasn't a sound in the room. He turned toward the board, took a deep breath and turned back. They were still sitting quietly, staring straight ahead. Quiet, no one talking, no one scraping a desk, no one secretly poking at someone else, in Room 6-306 was always an event.

"You guys... You guys... I can't compliment you enough. Okay, from now on, if you'll come to order when I say 'we'll wait' and we can get on with the lesson, everyone leaves when the three o'clock bell rings."

Arlene's hand was up.

"Miss Whitman. You have a question?"

"How come you wrote complimint on the board?"

Neil clasped his hands together in glee. "Arlene, you always ask just the right question. It's wonderful."

"Gaw. I hope he's okay," she said to the world in general. Then to him, in a mincing, super polite voice, "Thank you for the compliment, Mr. Riley."

"Why, you are certainly welcome, Miss Whitman." To Sheri, he said, "Waddaya think? Arlene knows what compliment means." To Arlene he said, "But to answer your question I first have to ask Miss

Wallace, since this is actually her word. May I tell the class about our conversation?"

Sheri's head bobbed back and forth and after a glance at Pedro she said, "That would be fine with me."

"I was complimenting Sheri on how well she does her job as window monitor."

"She does," Pedro said.

"Actually, Pedro, that's what Bianca said," Neil told him. "When I told her about the compliment I paid to Sheri she complimented her, too. Everybody seems to agree, she's a wonderful window monitor."

"She's the best," Pedro said.

"Pedro likes Sheri," Pauli teased in a sing-song voice.

"You mind your own beeswax," Sheri snapped.

"What of it?" Pedro said. "Since it's true."

"Yawl better not be walkin' out on the street. They cut you up good, on both sides," Pauli said.

"We ain't gonna be walkin' out on no street," Sheri said.

"It ain't that bad," Pedro insisted.

"Yes it is," Clyde said, urgently. "You can't be out there together."

"We ain't gonna be walkin' on no street," Sheri said, near tears.

"I know," Pedro said, speaking directly to her.

"Wait a minute," Neil said to Pedro. "What about when you and Morris walk home together?"

"Thas different," Arlene said.

"No it ain't," Clyde said. "They jus goin' home. What if they go to the movies? Or walk over to the park?"

"Thas true," Arlene said.

Bianca was shaking her head.

"What're you thinking, Bianca?" Neil asked her.

"It's so crazy," she said.

"This ain't about school," Clyde said.

"It's not?" Neil said. "How come?"

"What you gonna do?" Clyde asked him. "Make *Los Fuertes* sit up straight? Tell the *Black Blades* 'we're waiting?'"

Harriet had her hand up.

"Miss Wilson, you wanted to add something?"

"I have a compliment for Arlene and Bianca," she said.

"Go ahead."

"I want to compliment Arlene and Bianca for getting all the girls to play together. The boys get one side of the court and the girls get the other. But we didn't play together so half the time the girls had these nothing little games or people just dribbling around and stuff and the boys started saying why can't we play full court? So they—I mean Arlene and Bianca—said, 'No, the girls will play together just like the boys,' and now they do. They always pick sides because they're the best. But they don't just pick their friends."

"Thas right, Mr. Riley," Arlene said.

"Let me finish, Arlene."

Pauli went, "uuuooo."

Harriet, undaunted, continued. "Because it was you and Bianca who did this. Everything has changed in the gym because of you two. The girls play basketball and they love it. But you," she pointed at Neil, "try to get one of them to tell the other how good she is and I can tell you you'll wait until doomsday. And what I want," she said to him, "is for you to ask them why? Why can't one of them compliment the other?"

Quiet. A long, very long quiet invaded 6-306. Skinny, brainy, *nice* Harriet, who had probably never had a fight in her life, had just challenged three of the most powerful people in the room. It was one of those catch your breath quiets, an uh-oh now what? quiet, a thrilling something's got to happen quiet.

Arlene's hand was up.

"Miss Whitman?" Neil said.

"Bianca shoots better than me, but I'm better under the basket."

Again, quiet. The siren and blat of a fire truck rushing by made no impression on the people in the room.

"She is," Bianca said. "She gets that ball…" Bianca shook her head for emphasis.

"If we played anybody else," Arlene said.

"Them smarties in Mrs. Robin's class?" Bianca agreed.

"We'd whip they pants off," Arlene insisted.

"Yeah, well, with me and Clyde our best boys would take you down," Morris said.

"Who sez?" Arlene asked.

Neil wrote in his plan book, *Tobin, basketball. Teams. Class vs class? Boys vs girls?*

"He's thinking something," Bianca said.

Neil looked at her. As always unnerved by how aware of him she was.

"I'm thinking it's time to get on with math."

Marta had her hand up.

"Marta?"

"Sandra's the best writer. She should put the schedule on the board."

"Thas right," Sheri said.

"I think so, too," Pauli said.

"She has to be better than him," Clyde said.

"Anyone want to challenge Sandra?" Neil asked.

No one raised a hand.

"Sandra, would you like to erase the schedule and copy from my book?"

Chubby Sandra was beaming. "That's all right, Mr. Riley. I already copied it. I can erase it and write it again."

"You've already copied it?"

"I do that in my notebook every day. For practice."

"Please get out your math books," he said. Meanwhile, he jotted another note in his plan book. *Can't walk together? That ain't about school?*

Sheri had her hand up. Will wonders never cease? *Sheri had her hand up.*

"Miss Wallace?"

"You should put compliment on the spelling test."

"That's an excellent idea," he said.

Chapter 14:

Paranoided

In Neil's apartment:

"Is this Mrs. Wolf?"

"Who wants to know?"

"This is Neil Riley. Simon's teacher?"

"Simon ain't feelin' too well."

"I thought that was the case. He's been out two days. I was worried about him. Is this Simon's grandmother?"

"Thas right."

"I tried to call you the night we agreed, but your phone was busy."

"What of it?"

"I, uh… I said I would call. And I wanted to tell you some things about Simon."

"You cane tell me nothing about Simon."

"That's true. But as his teacher I know you want me to report on his progress."

"He sez you ain't too bad."

"So I'm making progress," Neil said, with a nervous chuckle. "But he's making progress, too. In the last three weeks or so since I spoke to you he's shown a marked improvement in all his subject areas." This was the absolute truth. From the very next day after Parents' Night Simon's math, reading and spelling grades had jumped from their usual 70s to 80 and 85 and in spelling even an occasional 90 percent. It was as if Simon had woken up. Or maybe it was as if he had realized his teacher cared about him.

"Thas what he says."

"And it's true. If I were to draw a line graphing Simon's…" *(Ah, shit, shut up, Riley.)* "Simon's grades have jumped up to all B's," he said.

"He should be gettin' A's."

"Yes, he should, but he's not there yet."

"Are you finished?"

"Yes, ma'am, except it's a pleasure to have Simon in my class. He's very well-behaved."

"He better be."

"Well, he is."

"You done now?"

"Yes, ma'am, unless you have something you want to say to me."

"Simon will be in school tomorrow."

"I look forward to seeing him."

"Goodbye."

"Good…" But she had already hung up.

He sat lost in the immensely complicated position he had stumbled into, like a man who had stepped out for a breath of air and found himself in a hailstorm. Wolf. Same as Simon's so she must be his paternal grandmother. Where were his mother and father? He would probably never know. Paranoided or no, her fierce commitment to her grandson was evident if only in the courage it took for her to make her appearance in 6-306 on Parents' Night.

Chapter 15:

Goodnight

She said: "Hi."

"Hi, it's me. Neil Riley?"

"Hi, Neil Riley. I knew it was you from your ring."

"Oh, did you now?"

"Yeap. It had Neil Riley rung all over it."

"Did I get you at a bad time? Can you talk?"

"I had just settled down with a cup of peppermint tea and sent out my order for you." After a moment, "Hello? Are you there?"

"You're so much faster than I am. It's kinda hard on the fragile male ego."

"You'll learn." There was a sipping sound. "That's so good."

"What are you wearing?" he asked. "On top first."

"A sweat shirt."

"What color?"

"Grey."

"And underneath?"

"Just me. And my not very ample mes."

"Hmmm. Pretty good mes. Moving on to the lower body."

"I call 'em floppies. They're officially sold as sweats, but they're floppies to me. You get them at dance places."

"I remember those," he said. "They pretty much hide everything. What about underneath?"

"Full-cut comfortable old lady underpants. Don't dare think panties. That would be like calling pajamas a negligee. Nothing could be quite as unsexy as these underpants."

"That's not your call."

"I guess. Okay, your turn. On top?"

"A T-shirt. With a long we'll say brown stain I think is tomato sauce down the front. It was one of those cheapies that came back from the wash two sizes smaller so I can only wear it around the house so I end up wearing it all the time. Underneath is me and I'm not nearly so ample as some."

"Rather skimpy, actually. Lower body, please."

"My funky running jeans, one of two pairs. These are clean. The others are pretty much standing up in the clothes hamper."

"And those Jockey briefs?"

"Yes. Also…"

"Also?"

"Well, I don't want to brag."

"Go ahead."

"Thinking about your unsexy full-cut old lady underpants has given me an ample moment here. Pretty large, I'd say."

"That's the thing about you tall skinny fellows. You tend to long deliberations waiting to be sucked into the mouth of the infinite. It's profoundly... Words fail me."

"Procreative."

"Exactly. I, on the other hand, have discerned certain lava-like responses simply from hearing your voice. Speaking of which, did you have some specific reason for calling?"

"Well, you made me, as you have already acknowledged. But there may have been other reasons, as well."

"Tell me."

"I don't know where to start."

"That's usually how our conversations begin. What's the first thing that comes to mind?"

"Sheri. On Monday I told Sheri I wanted to compliment her on the good job she was doing with the windows and I could tell she wasn't sure what I meant. For once, I was cagey. I didn't say,

'*Compliment*? You don't know what *compliment* means?'"

"Come on, Neil, you would never do that to her."

"I know. But I was cagey. I immediately gave her the definition as if, of course, she knew what it meant. But then I wrote the word on the board and… I started to say, all hell broke loose. But really all heaven broke loose. Who started it? I don't remember. I'll have to think how it happened, but there was a conversation about race, how black and Spanish kids can't be friends outside, and Harriet… Oh, Jesus, I just remembered. It was about how Pedro and Sheri could never walk together out on the street. You had to be there to see how frightened Sheri got when Pedro got all puffed up and said it wasn't so bad. Sheri knows it's bad, that one or both of them would get killed if they got caught together out on the street. Pedro knows it, too, but he ain't about to admit it in front of the whole class. And then Harriet brought the conversation around one hundred and eighty degrees. This was such a brave, perceptive thing to do. She complimented Arlene and Bianca for getting the black and Spanish girls to play together in the gym. But more than that, and this had to be deliberate, which is what makes it so amazing to me; she brought the whole class together. It was the best day I've had so far. I kept waiting for things to fall apart and they didn't. It was incredible. I'm sorry, this must be really boring. I'll stop. It's just that sometimes this job has me so jacked up I can't sit still. It's pretty clear now I called you so I could unload."

"This is not boring. Please don't stop. I know there's more."

"Okay. It's about Arlene. You know how I think of her. As this monster, this colossal blight. My vision of her has epic proportions. She's like a Fury out of a Greek myth." He whispered into the phone. "I wish she were dead. No. That wouldn't be enough. I want to kill her. Slowly." He took a deep breath, blew it all out. "And I worry about her. Because she wants to be small and pretty and charming and smart. Not smart smart, you know like Harriet or Bianca, but smart enough to know the answer if she's called on, smart enough not to look stupid if she has to read or go to the board, smart enough just to be still and know what's going on." He took another deep breath; blew it out. "She's *big*." He growled the word. "She's *ugly*." He caught his breath. "Nobody likes her. She knows it. Worst of all? She's *dumb*." Since he knew CC couldn't see him he allowed the pain this caused him full possession of his face. "I don't think she's dumb. I think there's so much noise about so much in her life she can't possibly make real decisions. She just reacts. You know what I mean?"

"She's constantly reacting to misconceptions of events because of her image of herself."

"Constantly. Always. It's so clear. So now I worry about Arlene. I mean, I ache for this kid I hate."

"She really makes you angry."

"I could kill her. But I see her. I don't want to, but I do. Today, again, she let Brenda correct her English. It happens all the time. I don't know how this got started, but she must have told Brenda to do it, or they must have discussed talking, you know, school talk, not real talk. Oh, man, I'd love to have been a fly on the wall when they had that conversation." He glanced at his clock. "We need to stop. It's after ten. I know you get up at some crazy hour to do your father and take your dance class."

"It keeps me sane. But you have to tell me how Arlene and Bianca reacted."

"Oh, no I don't. I'm getting wise to you. You know just what to ask to keep me talking. This is amazing, by the way. I've never talked to anyone like this in my entire life. I guess to my aunt. Some. And to Mrs. Robin. Some. Only with both of them I have to censor huge chunks of material or I'll set off all kinds of noise."

"Give me an example of noise."

"Just stuff I don't need to hear."

"What kind of things do you have to censor with your aunt?"

"Anything that would suggest I was stressed. I can't tell her…" He stopped mid-sentence. "You did it again. Come on, CC, tell me something about yourself. Tell me the most important thing that's happening in your life right now."

She didn't say anything. He waited a long time. She still didn't say anything.

"CC? Are you there?"

"I'm here," she said.

"What did I do? I'm confused. I just want to know what's going on with you. I just want to know who you are."

She laughed. "I have several responses to that."

"Let me have it. Them. Go ahead. Several responses. Scattershot."

"How can I let you know who I am when I don't know myself? I'm not sure you really want to know who I am. I'm not sure I want you to know who I am. And most of all I don't think you want to hear what's happening to me right now."

He stared at the wall.

"Neil?"

"Yes?"

"Say something."

"I want to know what's going on with you means I want to know what's going on with you. I want to know who you are means I want to know who you are. If you don't trust me, if this is about my unreliability, say so. Also, if you've had it with me and my constant jabbering, better just go ahead and say that too."

"I'm not sick of you. I can't begin to tell you how not sick of you I am. And unreliable? The appalling thing about you, it's remarkable actually, is that to my knowledge you've never tried to con me. You are who you say you are. If it turns out you are someone other than who you say you are, well, you've got me totally hoodwinked. No, you are, you prick, perfectly, reliably straightforward. And far too self-reliant, if you ask me. I mean, not to put too fine a point on it, you could be a bit more needy. A woman, especially the insecure, uncertain creatures you seem to favor would prefer, once in a while, to give soothing advice, to feel, if not absolutely essential, at least reasonably desirable."

"CC…"

"No. Wait. You wanted me to talk. I'm going to do this no matter what it costs me. Are you listening?"

"I'm listening."

"My father's going away. He's disappearing before my eyes. My daddy."

She paused. He waited. He heard nothing but the buzz of the telephone line.

"My daddy doesn't know me," she said finally. "Do you understand? My daddy does not know who I am. Sometimes he thinks I'm Fiona. Only guess what? I don't know who Fiona is. My mother's name is Pamela. For the last couple of weeks he doesn't get up even to go to the bathroom. He goes in his pants. And last month he disappeared. I mean, his caretaker went to the bathroom and poof, he was gone. We called the police. You know what they did? They made a note. To be fair, what could they do? The policeman who answered the phone didn't put me on hold. He probably put his hand over the speaker part, but I heard him say, you know, yell, 'Hey, Joe, we got another 'wanderer.'' He was calling my daddy a *wanderer*. It infuriated me, but I loved it, too. I could hear my daddy saying, 'See, Sweetie, I'm a demographic.' The policeman who took the information told me, 'They usually turn up.' And sure enough, he did. He turned up. Just for the hell of it after about two days I looked in my mother's studio. She had left the door unlocked and he was sitting in there on the floor in his own mess.

"The doctors, psychiatrists, nutritionists, physical therapists, neurosurgeons, that I've consulted all basically say the same thing.

'We can't do anything. Give him constant care. Twenty-four hours a day.' I've hired a nurse. And home care aides. Three of them. A whole damn nursing staff. The neurosurgeon gave his condition a name. It's the name of the German doctor who first described it. His possible condition. They're not even sure that's what's got him. It doesn't matter. Say dementia to the nth degree. And it's getting worse. Sooner or later his nervous system won't be able to make his organs function, his body will reach a general state of disrepair, he'll catch something and he'll die. I know it's the care he's getting that keeps him going.

"When I visited my mother in Santa Cruz she said, 'Put him away.' Just like that, with a wave of her bad fairy hand. She didn't bat an eye. I needed to talk about what to do. She may be right. But she wasn't thinking about Daddy. 'Put him away.' You know, like 'off with his head.' God, what a consummate bitch. All that bothers her is that Charles and I plan to close down the company. You know, auction off the keypunch machines and whatever other crap anyone wants, and walk away. She wants us to keep it going. Never mind that it's destroying our lives. Or sell it, as if it were an ongoing enterprise. The whole operation depended on my father's ability to set up representative groups and get them to respond to his questionnaires. Basically he had our clients buy these groups. People would be solicited to allow us to study their television habits. They'd receive a small monthly stipend. Twenty-five bucks, to be precise. Their television habits. That isn't even half of it. They're questioned six ways to Sunday. When my dad started this some caught on and sent him packing, but most of them, some five thousand representative souls, seem willing to go along forever. The whole scheme is based on daddy's expertise. I keep updating his questionnaires then go out and train a group of interviewers to revisit our subjects. This has been going on for years and if daddy were…" She gave a kind of guttural *huh*? "…I started to say alive. If daddy were okay, you know, not sick, he'd be fascinated with the evolving interests, in the questions and the answers.

"Meanwhile, Charles and I knew nothing about market research when we got started and though we may have learned a lot you wouldn't want to get the idea either of us are… hmmm… the truth? …even mildly interested. We got involved because… because about eight years ago… It was just about the time I began my second year at Barnard. My father started slipping. Forgetting dates, misplacing things.

"The point is my mother has nothing to do with the business. No interest. Nada. And she doesn't care what happens to us. She just wants us to increase his estate. And she certainly doesn't want to lay out the money it will take to buy this building from the company."

After a silence, "Neil? Are you listening?"

"Yes. I wanted to ask about your mother."

"It's getting late. I want to stop."

"It sounds to me like you're just getting started."

"As you said, it's after ten. We both have to work tomorrow. Did you eat?"

"Jesus. Everybody's always worried about my eating."

"Because you're so skinny! Did you eat? Don't lie."

"I ate. I had a salad and a Reuben washed down with a glass of milk and just before I called the paranoid grandmother of one of my children I had a Knickerbocker's ale. Then I called you."

"When did you do your prep?"

"This afternoon."

"Who's the other person who worries about your eating?"

"Mrs. Robin. Why are you doing this?"

After a pause, she said, "The problem's out there now, isn't it? I'll have to keep telling you what's happening, won't I?"

"Yes you will."

"There's no one else I can talk to. 'He'll snap out of it,' Charles says. I mean, what a dreamer. Part of it is he's terrified because his daddy was the only other person in the world besides me he could rely on. And part of it, frankly, is that he doesn't want the trouble. If there's nothing to worry about, then there's nothing he has to do."

"Oh, yeah, I'm pretty good at that myself. It's called avoiding responsibility. Sounds like that's not something you're very good at."

"Is that a compliment?" she asked.

"I think it's just what I think," he said.

"Can I tell you something?"

He laughed. "Yes, please. I want you to talk to me. I want to know you."

"That's what I'm afraid of. That you'll get to know me and realize, 'Oh, God, she's just like all the other needy, insecure women I've known.'"

"I haven't known so many women. And…"

"And?"

"I've never been in a give and take like this."

"Does that scare you?" she asked.

It took him a while to say, "Yes."

It took her longer to say, "Your silence speaks volumes."

He let his silence babble on for a while. Then he said, "CC…" And after a little while, "You know?…"

"Neil?…" He heard her take a deep breath. "I ask some pretty dumb questions sometimes, don't I?"

"Not that I've noticed. It's just that I…" He took a deep breath or two of his own. "Okay, here we go. My first reaction to your question was to huff and puff. Wadda ya mean scared? I ain't scared a nothin'. Even asking the question shows you know better. The point with you is always: what's going on?

"Yes, I'm scared and I don't know why. But a lot of it has to do with the fact that I don't want to lie. At all. I especially don't want to do the dating lie I always did before. For years. Make up a cool scenario. You know, this is me and that's you and this movie will be over in about three months."

"Was that fun?"

"Yeah, come to think of it," he said with a snicker. "Though I only just realized it."

"Why? I mean both. Why did you do that? You know, the scenario? And why did you just come to realize it? Scenario first."

He laughed out loud. "Right there. Nailed. Okay, quickly, because I know I'm keeping you up. You said it. You want to see where this will go. Me too. And that's a first. I mean, usually one date and I know, yeah, I want to get laid and, no, I don't want to go anywhere else. Why did I come to realize that? Because this is so different. Even if it's a game, I don't make all the rules. And I definitely want to see where it's going."

"Wow, there are layers and layers to be unearthed in that little presentation. But you're saved by the bell. It's very late. We have to quit," she said.

"Oh, no, not just yet. Your turn. Are you scared?"

"Yes," she said.

There was a long pause.

"Come on, silence don't do it," he said. "What're you afraid of?"

"Losing you," she said.

He caught his breath. "Not a chance."

She took her time. Being careful? Smug? "So you're not going to run away?"

"No," he said. "Not unless I'm forced to. Only then."

She yawned. He heard the aah that went with a stretch. He imagined her arm reaching up, envisioned that line from her armpit to her waist. Remembered how it felt to run his hand along her body. Remembered how muscular she was.

"I've got to get some sleep," she said.

"Me, too. See you Saturday."

"Around two?" she asked.

"I think we said three. I may have to get some stuff done. I'll call before I leave."

"Oh, Neil, that's so perfectly you. No dame's gonna manipulate you, huh? Listen, I've got a fix on our scenario. It's so completely nondirective. Can I try it out on you?"

"Of course."

"Are you ready?"

"I'm ready."

"You will do what you will do and I will do what I will do. Does that sound right to you?"

He shivered. "Say it again."

"You will do what you will do and I will do what I will do."

"That's exactly right," he said. "Although… it sounds like there could be more to it."

"Yes, and it might take a lot longer than three months to figure out what that is. But right now… I was wondering how we could say goodnight without saying goodnight."

He glanced anxiously at the clock. "We could say it as if we were already in bed and getting ready to go to sleep."

"I like that. Let's do it," she said. "Only I need to be the one to go last. And then I need to be the one to hang up first."

"Why?" he asked.

"Because tonight I get to make the rules. Okay?"

"Okay," he said. "Here goes. Goodnight."

"Goodnight." She hung up.

He suddenly found himself in the kitchen holding one of the cabinet doors open, his heart racing. The next thing he knew he was in the bathroom without being quite certain why. Had he just brushed his teeth? If so he was brushing them again. He kept wondering about that Beatles song playing everywhere, saying he had to let her under his skin to make it better. What did that mean? He repeated her phrase: *There's no one else I can talk to,* hearing a new significance in the words. And he said, *I've never been in a give and take like this before.* That was the absolute truth. After a while he was stretched out in bed with his head resting in his arms. She said, *I need to be the one to go last.* And he said, nobly, *Okay,* because tonight she needed to make the rules. Then he said, easy, a smooth kind of guy, *Goodnight.* Then it got even better because she said, oh, God, then she said, *Goodnight.*

Chapter 16:

Love Walked In

On Riverside Drive: she asked, "Can I trust you?"

His head whipped around. He stared at her with what he intended to be a *what kind of question is that?* look.

They were on the sidewalk near the 79th Street entrance to Riverside Park. CC had insisted they walk first then decide on the rest of the evening. She had even insisted he meet her outside "because if you come up before we get out we probably won't." Neil had conceded that possibility, but wondered why that would be a problem. "If we're going to fuck like eagles we need to stay in shape," she told him.

So here they were, strolling, heading downtown, and here she was suddenly bursting into laughter, grabbing his right arm and wrapping both of hers around it, pulling it tight against her chest and leaning her cheek on his shoulder.

"What's so funny?" he asked.

She stepped away, but still gripped his arm tightly, her left hand at his triceps, her right on his wrist. He wasn't going to get away. "You don't know how disturbed you look. You are definitely the proverbial deer caught in the headlights."

He put his free arm around her waist and pulled her in close and whispered, "You have a way of making a guy feel like... I don't know... words fail me... no, I know exactly... a deer caught in the headlights."

He pushed his hand up between them and began to knead her left breast.

She rubbed her body against his erection. "Is that all you can think about?" she asked.

"Oh, God, if you only knew. Night and day."

"Come on," she said, pushing him away. "Let's walk."

She set off at a brisk pace and Neil had to step out smartly to catch up.

When he did he said, breathing hard, "Of course you can trust me."

For answer, she waved her hand, dismissing the question for now.

They turned into the park and headed north on the trail closest to the Drive.

It was one of those crisp cloudless fall days that beckon to all but the most serious night owls. The dog walkers were certainly there in force, leashes strung across the way. Young couples with strollers moved along slowly, aware that the future was in their hands. Runners occasionally passed them, setting off a competitive tightening in Neil's stride. Near 82nd she led them on a path that curled above a playground and sent them up to the promenade with its own diverse spread of lovers, forlorn wanderers, slow seniors, many different kinds of dog owners with many different kinds of dogs, a man with a monkey on his shoulder and on a wide turnaround an ancient Asian man, probably Chinese, executing his perfect Tai Chi. Through it all CC, looking neither left nor right, kept up a brisk pace, barking as she went along, "On your left! Watch your back! Coming by, please!" And she was able to move all but the most dedicated trail-hogs aside for them to squeeze by just as they were forced to do for the occasional runner. They followed the trail north of the promenade to 95th then turned and headed back to the promenade, then down and through the playground where a large number of young couples with their swaddled offspring were enjoying the sunshine.

CC slowed down and even stopped as several children went

racing in front of them. The minute they were through the playground she revved up the pace again.

Once they were back in quickstep mode Neil asked, "What were you looking at?"

"What do you mean?"

"Come on, you know what I mean. In the playground. You scanned every inch of the place."

"Was I that obvious?"

"You looked like one of those heavies in the movies who's supposed to be reading his newspaper and's really watching that hapless dope who's got the whole audience yelling at him, 'Look out for that goon with the newspaper.'"

He slowed down as he barked this, demonstrating how everyone would have used their hands as megaphones. She didn't slow down.

When he caught up with her he said, "Just because that goon's disguised as a beautiful woman in a pair of tight jeans and a sweatshirt that says..." He peered around to look and read: "'When You're Thirsty, Budweiser'. Across your breasts?"

She ignored this. "The fathers. On Saturdays you get a pretty good father turnout. It's a motley crew. Occasionally I've been able to do this walk on a weekday. The same mothers are out there every day. They hang out together. They've formed a sort of community even though I suspect they're from very different environments. That interests me."

"Really? Why?"

"Well, I am my father's daughter after all. How could the offspring of a sociologist ignore an obvious urban phenomenon? I've been in playgrounds on the East Side and in Central Park where everybody is split off, young mothers, obvious nannies, grandmothers. They sit separately or play with their kids separately. It's a lonely enterprise. It doesn't seem to me these women are lonely. How did it get going? Is it a particular person who starts it? Does it happen that often in other playgrounds? I'd like to know."

"What makes you think they come from different backgrounds?"

"Well, the clothing the women wear, for one thing. Even in winter the coats they choose tell a story. Now today you saw the fathers."

They were well past the playground by now.

"I guess. I wasn't particularly paying attention."

"In the summer I bet you'd pay attention to the mothers. There are some real knockouts in that crowd. Naturally, the ones with the best bodies tend to wear the least clothing."

"Actually I might look that way now and then for sociological purposes."

"I bet you might."

"I never claimed to be a eunuch."

"Thank God," she said.

They had made it back to 79th with neither of them particularly winded. They wandered slowly up the sidewalk next to the Drive.

"Okay, Miss Smarty, but what makes you think they're from such different backgrounds? You've got a bunch of young couples with young children living on the Upper West Side. They all looked white to me, they must all have pretty good apartments and if they're out there every day the mothers don't work, so the men must all do fairly well."

"Not bad," she said. "Assumptions we would need to examine. Including mine. I assume they're from, you said different backgrounds, I prefer to say environments only because that might generate questions about the future as well as the past. In any case, among the fathers there was a smattering of men stamping around in their upscale outdoor gear, several long-haired bearded types and one or two obviously older than the rest. One of whom, you failed to notice, was a black gentleman. I would hypothesize that under any other circumstances they would not be a very likely group. In the summers, by the way... Did you notice the picnic benches?"

"Uh, not really," Neil said.

"The whole group, some ten couples, twenty or more adults and a passel of preschoolers from just born to can't stop moving around and making trouble, the whole bunch of them are there milling around almost every Saturday evening having a potluck."

"You really have studied the situation," he said.

"As I said, I am my father's daughter. Another circuit?" she asked and without waiting for an answer led them back to the entrance to the park and was off again.

It wasn't exactly to his credit, but it pleased Neil that as they wound back down past the playground this time around she began to struggle, her pace a trace slower, her breath a tad ragged. She might be in better overall shape than he was, but he had the aerobic edge. It wasn't all macho competitiveness, he insisted to himself. Some of it, surely, was that he didn't want her to think he was a sissy. *When was the last time he worried a girl would think he was a sissy? Lurlene? You know you're smitten,* he thought, *when you feel like you're eleven and everything is happening for the first time.* Had she been testing him? What was more frightening? Wondering that she would do that? Or worrying that he hadn't passed the test. And another thing. She might not have wanted to look like a sissy either.

"Let's just stroll," she said when they reached 79th again.

"Want to head home?"

He ran his hand up her spine and kept it on her back as they left the park. He remembered how The Carver had held on to Junebug. *Men are all alike,* he conceded to all womankind.

"No, I want to stay out a while. Actually, I'd like for us to have tea; you know, like the British? That's sort of a mid-afternoon thing, isn't it? We could get some sort of pastry to stand in for crumpets." She took his hand and swung it back and forth like a schoolgirl.

"Tea sounds fine, but coffee would be better."

"Four Brothers has fairly clean bathrooms and at this time of day we can sit for a while without getting in the way."

"Back to Four Brothers," he said.

Using her hand to jerk him to a stop she suddenly faced him. "Are you seeing anyone else? You know, am I just a treat?"

He let go of her hand. "CC. Damn. You know? No, I am not seeing anyone else." He said this slowly, with emphasis on each word. "I'm not like that! Why did you ask me that?" The pain in his voice shocked him. It was embarrassingly close to a cry.

"It came out wrong, I think. I didn't mean I thought you were dishonest... I'm not sure what I meant." She put her arm around his waist, her elbow resting on his butt. "I don't know."

"That really clears it up," he said.

She tapped him lightly with her elbow. "Don't get smart." She chuckled. "Anyway, I certainly got a rise out of you. You should have seen your face."

"That startled deer thing I do?"

"Exactly. Like you were cornered with two seconds to live."

"Did it ever occur to you I might be worried about your mental state? Sort of, you know, what is this woman smoking?"

She grabbed both his arms and pulled him around to face her. "I wanted to tell you something, but I didn't have the courage, so I chickened out and asked a stupid question. I wanted to tell you that I would never intentionally hurt you." She thought about this. "What a load of crap. If you were really shitty to me... Let's suppose I found out you're engaged to be married and getting a little last minute nooky on the side? Man, I'd cut your heart out. But first I'd get your balls."

"And you wonder why I might look a little scared?"

She smiled and shook her head, then shook him, her expression tight, almost angry. "No, wait, this is serious." She made direct eye contact. "I love you." She threw herself at him, burying her face in his chest. "I'm in love with you." She said this as a confession, as if she had committed a sin of atrocious proportions. "I've never been in love before. It's awful." She looked up at him; to gauge his reaction? "Well, maybe not awful, but not easy. I'm worse than your little nut case, aren't I? I'm afraid you'll run off. I don't know what to do. Oh, God, I'm so embarrassed. I could just die," she said burying her face in his chest again.

He kissed the top of her head, which smelled faintly of coconuts. "Don't die," he said. "I would be very upset."

"Don't be smug, you crappy male beat-you-at-anything," she said. "I can't help it. It's all or nothing. I mean it. All or nothing."

He was too rattled to hold anything back. *All or nothing at all,* he thought. "I love you, too," he said. "And I don't know what to do about it either."

They kissed and he wondered at this blessing that had descended on him when she started pushing him away, suddenly all elbows.

"We can't do this," she said. "That's the whole point. Damnit, I don't believe in love at first sight. It's capitalist propaganda. They made it up so everybody would buy kitchens and dining room sets."

"But you own a business that depends on that stuff. It's your job to fall in love."

"You know, nobody likes a smartass. In the first place I ought to know better. And in the second place you should stop being so in charge of it all."

"Could we do that tea thing? I mean, I could really use some coffee."

Chapter 17:

All or Nothing at All (Sort of)

In the Four Brothers Coffee Shop: she blew on her tea then took a careful sip, all the while staring at him over the rim of her cup. Her eyes, blue, clear, sparkling, were startling enough in themselves, but even more so hinting at the sly smile she was savoring back there behind her cup. She was so often not where he expected her to be, so often not behaving the way he thought she would, that he had begun to anticipate it; there would always be some tricky English on her emotional cue ball. Her usual expression, alert, attentive, was simply gone. She was all blush and stagger, her whole body swaying in a sort of press and retreat. Neil realized this was how she was when they made love, childlike, delighted, impish.

"I really have to confront this," she said. "Well... I want to do this, but it's... Okay. All or nothing."

"Let's do it," he said. "All or nothing. Or as the song goes, *all or nothing at all.*"

She sipped her tea, eyes wandering over his face, over the wool sweater she had given him. She reached out with her free hand and pulled at the sleeve. "I hated that sweater," she said. "Now I love it. The colors are perfect for you." The sweater, all wool, was a thick weave of browns with a single strand of black throughout. "That bit of black, the dark side, the hidden... worry. Yes, worry." She turned his hand palm up and caressed it with hers. "I feel something bothers you. Not about us in particular. About..." She waved an arm around, "...all of us. I won't try to pin it down. I can't." After more scrutiny she said, "You're so good-looking. Yeah, but not... not smooth. Rough. That's the first impression and then you turn out to be so...

considerate is too easygoing. You aren't easygoing. But thought-ful. You are thoughtful. Willing and able to think about a question from many angles. That's you, for sure. That's why I go so..." She shivered. "That's how everyone reacts to you, I bet, expecting this savage and finding instead an innately empathetic being who under-stands suffering."

He hid the raspberry he would normally have made. He was thinking of the way she could listen to him, holding back her jan-gling barbs, letting him have his say. He knew she wanted that now and he wanted to give it to her if he could.

She put her tea down and took his outstretched hand in both of hers. He felt again, as he often did when he was with her, how ex-traordinary it was to be exactly where he wanted to be.

"It's absurd," she said. "That night. You know, that night?"

"When we went to *Silhouettes*?"

"When you walked in the door at Roger's party, red-cheeked, gorged—interesting choice of words, huh? —with pee and good health and animal energy, before you said a word, I... what? Felt? Fell. I fell. I fell in love." She laughed. "Oh, God, did I really say that? Think of Sleeping Beauty. Fantastic fairy tale? Well guess what, it's perfectly true. Of course, they always neglect to mention that she was a shameless wanton who woke up so horny she couldn't keep her legs closed. I can still see you, long tall underfed coyote, beat-up old jeans and your scruffy warmup jacket." She took her hands away, which, irrational as all hell, felt like a rejection. She bowed her head and began to massage her forehead. "I see you. Before you said a word... I fell for you." She peeked at him. "This is excruciating. The way you're looking at me. You look so scared."

"Scared? Ever heard of the cat who ate the canary?"

"Smug. I knew it. You're gloating. Sexist pig!"

He pressed his lips together and shook his head. He wanted to quip, *Poor me, falsely accused, can't win for losing*, but he didn't.

She glared at him. "That night just looking at you. I woke up the next morning from a long sleep and carefully reviewed the whole evening. It was very painful. The evening had been so much fun. At least for me. I'm only speaking for myself."

"Me, too," he insisted.

"Yeah, but you walked away! Don't react!" she commanded. "Let me do this!"

He gripped the edge of the table with both hands, hanging on. He stared at her, lifted his eyebrows, asked in a whiny voice, violating his resolution to be a good listener, "I'm not to react? Even if you're totally wrong?"

"That's exactly right," she said, jabbing a finger at him. She dropped her head and shook it. "No, wait, this is not banter." She straightened her shoulders, looked him squarely in the eye. "Poor guy," she said, suddenly softening.

"I'm listening. Truly." *Anyway, I'm trying,* he thought.

"Yes, but this is so desperate. I'm throwing myself at you. You hate that… And I'm going to get hurt. I know it." She squeezed her eyes closed, took a deep breath, exhaled and stared at him. "You walked away." She waved away any objections. "Never mind all the extenuating circumstances. You could walk away. And did. I couldn't. I didn't. We were together, let's say three hours, and I was *happy*." She put her curled hands out as if trying to grip some elusive object, rasping the word like a protest. "*Happy*! And then it was over and I was miserable. *Miserable*," she barked. She brought her hands in across her breasts, clutching her shoulders. "Miserable," she repeated in a subdued voice. "It was wonderful." She crooned the word. Then sat back, alert, catching his eye. "Remember Josie? Our little cupid?"

"How could I ever forget Josie."

"Remember here here. We're *here here*."

"Yes," he said. "I remember."

She took his right hand in both of hers again. "Well that was the first time in a very long time I was *here here*. Happy, miserable, you name it, I felt it. And I wanted to feel it. I had to go back a long way to remember feeling like that, even wanting to feel like that." She watched herself slowly stroke his hand. "*Here*," she said. "Right here, right now." She lowered her head and looked up at him coyly. "I keep expecting you to do something drastic. Pull your hands back in horror and start yelling, 'What are you? Crazy? I didn't ask for this.' I keep expecting you to get up and run away."

"I'm still here," he said.

"Nobody said you could talk."

"Sorry."

She leaned forward. "Just in case you're wondering if this will ever be over, I'm just getting started." Then she leaned away and tilted her head back, taking the long view. "I did try to forget you. In spite of what you may think, I'm not very experienced, you know, sexually. I'd slept with three boys before I met you and one doesn't even count. Really," she said emphatically to his wide-eyed head shake (which he immediately regretted). "Then boom, boom." She pounded her right fist into her left palm. "Like that I slept with two men after we saw each other. I rather think I thought… What a silly thing to say. I didn't rather think anything. I was pretending and I knew it. I was pretending my complaint was sexual frustration so I slept with the man who delivers our punch cards, a complete jerk, I might add, and with a man I met in Santa Cruz. A very attractive man. A painter. He shows in my mother's gallery. He teaches set design at UC Santa Cruz. I said goodbye to him under circumstances similar to those in which you said goodbye to me. I got to be you. I told him that where he lives would make the relationship impossible. The difference, of course, is that my painter friend and I had started something that you and I had not. What I was doing was—what would be the right word? trashing, shredding, pulverizing, all of the above?—a commitment that had already been made." Suddenly tears were running down her cheeks.

"That sounds hard," he said.

"Yeah, well." She shrugged. She got a napkin and wiped her cheeks. "Think of it this way. I could easily go to Santa Cruz three, maybe four times a year. So if my painter professor is impossible, what the hell are you? The boy next door? Always been there, waiting for me to finally recognize your dependable charms?" She cocked her head to one side, as if listening to what she had been saying. "Women are not supposed to talk this way with men, you know, especially with the man involved. What you're getting is pure, unexpurgated girlfriend talk." She wiped her cheeks again. "The point is this, pure and simple. You can't leave me."

"Yeah, but…"

"No, no buts. You can leave me, but do it now. Right now. Get up and walk out. You'll be free and clear. I'll pay the bill. I won't bother you again. I promise."

"No, wait, you have to let me hem and haw. Seriously."

"Soft talk me? Equivocate?"

"Tell you the truth."

Her gaze, looking back at him from her averted face, was not sympathetic.

"I won't leave you unless I have to. Can I continue?"

"Maybe." She waited.

"I think you're being unfair. Will you go with me to Canada? Right now. No questions asked. Will you?"

Her body slumped, stung by the question. "I can't." The minute she said this she put her hand over her mouth.

"Can I continue?"

She nodded.

"You have to say, 'yes, you can continue.'" he said.

"Yes, you can continue."

"I have a job that exempts me from the draft. A job," he said through a kind of chortle. "Okay, I don't know what it is, but I'm managing to do it well enough so I don't think I'll be fired." He looked up at the ceiling. "Whenever I say anything like that I have to wait a minute to see if lightning's gonna shoot down and strike me dead." He waited. "But there, I've said it and I'm still here. Okay, so I expect to be able to keep this job until I'm exempt from the draft. And as long as that is the case I won't walk out on you. I promise. Unless we really screw it up. We'll both know if we've done that. If I lose this job I lose the exemption. Then I either go to Vietnam, Leavenworth or Canada. I won't leave you, I'll be dragged away. So that's the situation. I won't leave you unless I'm dragged away."

"Well, I guess that's all or nothing at all," she said. "Sort of."

"Deal?"

"Deal," she said.

"Now tell me about the set designer from San Jose."

"The *painter* from *Santa Cruz*. That was over the minute it began. What we need to do right now is plan how we're going to do dinner. Then I will tell you every sad detail, including the wish I made to the fountain fairies just before I checked out of the *Hotel La Oceana*."

"The penny wish you wouldn't tell me? You're not afraid to spoil it?"

"I can't spoil it. It's come true. The two of us, we're *here here*, you know what I mean?"

Chapter 18:

Pirouettes

In Room 6-306: the card was leaning against the tissue box. He knew immediately how it got there. Sheri snuck it in when she did the windows. And one glance at the art work and he knew who had made it. Across the top in Sandra's beautiful block lettering was written *Merry Christmas* and centered neatly underneath that, *Mr. Riley.* It was on regular 8 1/2 by 11 vanilla construction paper folded in half. The letters were alternately red and green and a string of multicolored lights was intricately woven through the letters. The picture was of him, standing next to his desk facing forward, but pointing at the blackboard on which was scribbled in a pretty good imitation of his messy scrawl: *Merry Christmas.* He was wearing his blue suit, the jacket buttoned over a white shirt and his striped red and blue tie. She had put something in his stance, a kind of pugnacious tension. Was that true? Well, she had certainly gotten the unruly hair, brown shading to black, which was usually too long because he seldom had time to get a haircut. His face was a formula eyebrows, eyes and mouth, and for some reason she had made his brown eyes blue, but the prominent nose was perfect. The drawing had the feel of a quick study; the colors, even though they were done with crayons, were sharp and tasteful. How did she manage to string those lights through the letters? His appreciation was immediate and unfeigned, and layered with an aching sense that this talent would never find its complete expression.

He looked up then, sensing that unnerving change in the air. Silence. They were all watching him. He opened the card and quickly turned toward the blackboard to hide his dismay at the power of his response. At the top of the card Sandra had printed in bold black letters: **FROM 6-306:** and then thirty-three signatures were scrawled or printed or carefully lettered or, particularly in the case of Marta's, painstakingly scripted.

Just as he had no doubt who had drawn the card, he had no doubt who had planned the project: conceived the card, commissioned the artist, gotten all the signatures and orchestrated its appearance on his desk. He just couldn't believe he could have been so unaware. She must have managed most of this yesterday when they were making Christmas cards.

He had given everyone a box of crayons. "To keep?" Pauli asked. "Yes, to keep, to take home for Christmas." The policy regarding presents was that students shouldn't give them to each other or their teachers. Neil approved wholeheartedly. A dollar was a fortune for most of his kids. To do even the traditional draw-a-name would have created a painful situation, not an exciting activity. On the other hand, giving his students supplies he wanted them to have and that the school would not supply was not only acceptable, but expected.

Yesterday he had given them two hours at the end of the day to make Christmas cards to decorate the classroom. It was a free period and everyone could share their ideas and look at what others were doing. Neil remembered now that Bianca seemed to share and look more than the others. Of course. That's when she got the signatures. Even when she stopped to talk to Charles—no one ever stopped to talk to Charles—he hadn't suspected anything. After all, it was Bianca. She would go anywhere.

He held the card up. "I'm sure you all saw it, but still…" He looked at Sandra. "It's beautiful. I mean it."

"I need to work on faces," Sandra said.

"What I'd like is for you to take up each person's card and spread them all out on the window sill so that when you're ready we can go, *one* row at a time," he said, emphasis on the *one*, "and look at them. And while Sandra is doing that…" He reached down and lifted up the stash of Oreos he had put under his desk yesterday afternoon and placed them on top of the desk. Then the napkins. Then out of the corner he took the grocery bag containing the six half-gallon orange juices he had lugged across town this morning. Next to all this he placed a fifty-pack of small paper cups. "I brought in a little treat. Now. No one gets seconds until everyone has had firsts. Is that clear?"

He got a, "Yes, Mr. Riley," from several quarters, but it was clear to Neil that it wasn't clear to everyone.

"You should get somebody like Clyde to give them out. Won't nobody take more than one from him," Bianca suggested.

Clyde heard this. "Me? I ain't givin' out no cookies."

"Arlene," Bianca whispered, loudly.

"Me. I ain't givin' out no cookies neither."

"Why?" Neil asked. "I'm not saying you should give them out. I'd just like to know why you're so against it."

"Her mother makes her do everything," Brenda said.

"You hush up," Arlene snapped.

This was Arlene's I'm-not-kidding-around voice, but Brenda just smiled back at her sweetly. Brenda snagging Arlene. Brenda smiling. *Holy shit!*

"It's okay," Neil said, laughing.

"Why you laughing at me?" Arlene was clearly, deeply upset.

"No, wait, don't," Neil said, sending a surrender signal with his waving hands. "I was laughing at myself."

"How come?" Bianca asked.

"I practically grew up in my aunt's restaurant."

Suddenly he had everyone's attention. It was always like that these days. Any mention of his outside life and immediately they were all ears. If only he could get this kind of rapt interest in long division with decimals. Dream on.

"It isn't a fancy you know white tablecloths and folded napkins kind of place. It's more like the *China Moon*. Only there are booths on both sides and against the window looking out on the street with tables in the middle. The *China Moon* is all tables. They probably have about the same stations, you know, tables. And that's about where the similarities end. And that's about where this story ends."

There were loud groans, particularly from Arlene and Bianca, but also from Pauli and Clyde and Pedro and Morris. Harriet raised her hand.

"Harriet?"

"You said you were laughing at yourself. You should at least explain that."

"And tell us what your aunt's restaurant is called," Bianca demanded.

"*Connie's Corner.* And stop calling out." To Harriet he said, "Thank you for raising your hand, Miss Wilson."

"Oh, you're quite welcome, Mr. Riley."

"Oh, la de da," Arlene said.

"Arlene deserves an explanation," Harriet said.

"Not if she's going to make fun of me," Neil said, making a pouty face.

"Come on, Mr. Riley, tell us the story," Clyde insisted.

"No story," Neil said, "just an ironic twist."

"Oh, gaw, whatever that is," Arlene commented.

"Ire-on-nee," he said to Bianca, who was already flipping through her dictionary.

"I-r," she replied.

"Then on," he said.

"*Mr. Riley,*" Harriet insisted impatiently.

"*Miss Wilson,*" he replied in the same exasperated tone. "Okay. Here's what I was thinking. I used to spend a lot of time in my aunt's restaurant and I always wanted to you know bus the tables or wait on the customers and she wouldn't let me. I had to finish my homework first and then she'd let me work. So working became like a special treat. Whereas Arlene probably sees it the other way around. She'd probably rather do her homework."

"Yeah, right," Clyde said. "That's Arlene, for sure. She'd rather do her homework than almost anything."

"Nobody ast you," Arlene said.

"Nobody didn't neither," Clyde responded.

"Could we go back to the original question?" Neil asked.

"What was that, Mr. Riley?" Pedro asked.

"Who's going to give out the cookies?"

"Not me," Arlene insisted. "Anybody want to make something of it?"

Given the silence that followed her question it seemed apparent that nobody did.

Sheri sat with her head turned away from him, her hands locked under her armpits.

"Won't nobody mess with Sheri, either."

Bianca! She always seemed to know what he was thinking before he did.

"Sheri? Would you?..."

She was at his desk before he finished.

"...give out the...?"

"Won't nobody get more than one," she said.

"Just take one box at a time and come back for the next one. If there are twelve cookies in a box, how many cookies, Mr. Johnson?"

"Yeah, well, forty-eight, but what's left over, Mr. R.?"

"And everybody gets a napkin," Neil told Sheri.

"I know," she said impatiently.

"Fifteen. Only not if Pauli tries one of his tricks. Wait," he said. "We should give out the cups first."

Sheri stood looking at Pedro while he asked, "Who wants to give out the cups?"

Pauli, Sammy, Marta and Maria, one from each row. Perfect.

"Pauli, you first. Just take the cups you need for your row." And so it went, row by row.

Then he said, "All right, Arlene, you've got to help me. Please. I need someone strong to pour the orange juice." Yes, he was pushing her, but it seemed to be an anything is possible kind of day.

"I told you. I ain't gonna pour no orange juice. I doan do nothin' for no teacha."

Brenda raised her hand.

"Brenda?"

"I could do it. I'm pretty strong." Brenda stood up and turned toward Arlene. "You should say, 'I'm not going to pour any orange juice. I won't do anything for a teacher.'"

"How come you... Why are you going to pour it?" Arlene asked her.

"I think it will be fun. We could do it together."

And that, oh, my God, is exactly what happened. Arlene held the cup and Brenda poured. Neil knew better than to make any comment. His chest felt so tight with emotion he wouldn't have been able to say anything anyway.

"You should wait to drink it till everybody has theirs," Arlene ordered each time.

And behind them came Sheri, giving out one Oreo at a time. Neil watched this unfold with something just short of disbelief. He looked at Bianca, whose quick pleased nod, eyebrows lifted, mouth tight with satisfaction, wrung from him an agreement too full, a happiness too rich for his thin view of what was possible. He turned away, feeling exposed, then turned quickly back, pointing at her, smiling broadly.

"You did this," he said.

At that moment Sandra called out to him, "Mr. Riley, could you help me, please?"

"What's the problem?"

"Charles won't give me his card. Look at it. It's beautiful!"

"Is it for your mom?" Neil asked moving between the rows.

Charles shook his head, no. His jacket fell away from his head, but he bent quickly and covered himself back up. With his head down, his nose almost touching the desk, he held the card up in his right hand. Neil grabbed it and after a token resistance Charles let it go. Like most of the others, the card was on vanilla construction paper folded in half. In the middle of the picture on the front was a green triangle. A solid blue surrounded the triangle and the space over the point. It rested on a solid red that covered the bottom of the page. Its conception was immediately, radiantly apparent. It was an abstract of a Christmas tree using only three basic colors. Neil peeked inside the card and saw that on one side Charles had written in large shaky letters

FOR

and on the other side

MR R

"Oh, man, this is great! This is really great! Can I let Sandra put it on the window sill with the others? It will make me really proud."

Charles nodded yes.

"It's really good," Sandra said, speaking beyond Neil to Bianca.

"Let me see," Bianca said.

"No," Neil told Sandra firmly. "We'll let everyone look at the cards after you arrange them." While this was going on his distribution crew was now winding its way up rows 3 and 4. Neil said, "Save your juice. I want to propose a toast."

"I drank mines!" Pauli wailed.

"I told you," Arlene snarled.

Neil said, "Pauli, what would your grandmother do?"

Pauli looked at him sad-eyed and with a straight-faced, earnest insistence said, "She'd give me some more."

"Oh, really?"

Pauli smiled. "Really."

"You know that ain't true," Sammy said.

"She'd swat him upside the head," Arlene opined. "Thas what I oughta do."

Pauli gave the look of one deeply wronged, with a smile suddenly breaking through.

"Can I give him some of mines?" Sammy asked.

"Yes, you may. Just enough so he can drink with us, okay? Sammy, you're a good buddy. And you're proof of what I'm about to say." Neil raised his cup to the class. "I want to propose a toast to the most wonderful group of students a teacher could ever have. And I want to wish you all a Merry Christmas and a Happy New Year. *And...* this is the most important part... after the holidays I want you all to come back home safe and sound."

They all drank with him and gobbled up their cookies; then began the begging for more and the complaints that it wasn't fair, nobody should get seconds if everybody didn't. Neil sorted it out by insisting on a show of hands by those who really wanted seconds. He made sure there were enough, then sent his crew to dole out what remained. But he kept one and gave it to Charles wrapped in a napkin.

"For your mother, if that's all right. And wish her a Merry Christmas for me?"

Charles stashed the cookie away in the pocket of his jacket. Neil winced inwardly, wondering if this wasn't a stupid, condescending impulse. What shape would that Oreo be in if it reached its destination? And if it did how would it be received? Why, Neil wondered, couldn't he ever feel he was doing the right thing? Do the best you can and move on, he told himself, as he organized the viewing of the

Christmas cards. When that began to drift into a milling uncertainty he knew it was time to bring them back to order.

He clapped his hands and spoke up loudly. "Okay, we still have almost two hours before I take you to the cafeteria. Here's our schedule for the rest of the day."

Which read in Sandra's incredible hand:

Social Studies

Reading

"Ah, Mr. Riley," Clyde protested, "take a break."

Neil raised his eyebrows. He tapped the board. "I'm going to let you decide. If it's social studies I have a game in mind. If it's reading, I'll continue with *The Secret Garden*."

"What kind of game?" Sheri asked, ever suspicious. "Somethin' about math, I bet. You cane fool me."

"No, it's not about math," Neil sniped back, craning his neck forward the way she did. Then in a normal voice he asked, "How many of you have ever played *Red Light/Green Light*?"

"What's that?" Pedro asked.

"The person who gets to control the lights, he's the Traffic Cop, stands in front of everybody else. He turns his back and shouts 'Green Light' and counts to five, and it has to be a clear count—one, two, three, four, five—not—unoureeourive—and while his back is turned everybody can move forward, but when he turns around…"

"*Freeze*," Clyde called out. "It's called *Freeze*."

"That's it," Pedro said.

"Nobody ever called it 'Red or Green' or what you said," Arlene told him.

"Thas what they call it where he comes from," Sheri said.

Was Sheri defending him? Better just let it ride. "Okay, then, *Freeze*. I don't care what we call it as long as we can agree on the rules."

"How we gonna play with the desks in the way?" David asked.

Neil had already worked this out in his mind. "We'll push rows one and two against that wall and three and four against the windows. Everybody starts at the back of the room. The person who calls the lights... what do you call out?" Neil asked Pedro.

"You say, 'Go,' and count like you said."

"Okay, the caller..."

"He's called the Snowman," Clyde informed him.

"Okay, the Snowman turns and says go and counts to five before he can turn around."

Everyone was already up and moving their desks. Everyone. It began as one spontaneous movement.

"Wait a minute! Wait a minute! Do you want to play the game?"

Some people paused for a split second to look at him, as if wondering what he was asking. Simon smiled. David shook his head back and forth: *poor teacha, doan he get it?*

Harriet said, "Mr. Riley, I'd say we want to play the game."

And while they were still moving the desks he said to Bianca, who kept looking at him and smiling. "What's so funny?"

"Nothin'," she said, still smiling.

"Come on, Bianca. What devious plot is working its way through that smart little noggin of yours?"

"You said 'home,'" she said.

"What? I don't understand."

"You said after the holidays we'd come back home."

"I said home?"

"So who gets to be up first?" Arlene asked.

Fair question. A teacher can't just announce a game with thirty-three players and expect it to evolve into perfectly organized play, especially when only one person is to be in charge. *So, Miss Smarty, didn't believe the teacha could think it through, didja?* He could crow to himself now, but it had taken him several anxious hours to work through all the logistics and he still wasn't certain he could pull this off.

"Everybody will pick a number." He quickly scribbled "22" on a piece of notebook paper and folded it into a small tight rectangle. "Here's the winning number."

People started calling out numbers.

"Wait, wait!" Neil shouted, making the stop motion. "Let me finish. Sandra, would you please copy the roster on the board."

Sandra took his precious Seating Roster, once the side of a cardboard box that held fifths of Johnny Walker Red. He had folded it in half and on each side cut two rows of slots with a razor. He had used the flexible cardboard bottle separators to make nametags that could be inserted into the slots. This was not one of the many typed sheets he used each day to call the roll, jot notes on and treat as a daily anecdotal record. This was the one and only *Seating Roster*, an essential tool when he moved his students around. The fact that he handed it so casually to Sandra indicated how much he trusted her.

Sandra held the roster open and looked up at the class, checking its accuracy. "Could you stand still for a minute," she asked. Everyone stood still for her. "And you know be in your row." The four rows formed on command. She checked each row against the roster. "Okay," she said, and turned back to her task. Just like that.

Neil had watched this in amazement. *Did you see what just happened?* he scribbled on today's roll. *You want to see them cooperate? Give them something they want to do.* Tonight when he glanced at this he might scratch his head, wondering what lame-brained idea had inspired this notation. Or if he were lucky he would remember the incident, describe it in his *Staring at the Wall* journal and even come up with other activities that would encourage this much enthusiasm.

Back in the real world the scraping desks grated on Neil's nerves like the squeak of chalk on the blackboard. "Could you guys lift those desks? 4-206 is going to think we're killing each other." Then wily shit that he was, thinking, *if they really want to do this...* he added, "And Mrs. Stables complains and we may not get to play the game."

Suddenly some people, Pedro and Morris, and Sheri on her side, *Sheri*, began to lift their desks and stare disapprovingly at those who didn't. Then Neil noticed that a number of students, particularly the quiet ones, Simon, Steven, Maria and Karen, had begun to watch Sandra at the board. But Neil's attention was diverted by the concern of some for their desks. It was their safe haven. For many, Marta, Carmen, Charles, Norbert and Brenda, for example, it was perhaps one of the few safe places to be in the world. So while Clyde was comfortable slinging his desk up against the side of the room, Carmen took her jacket off the back of her chair and put it on, bent and made certain her books and pocketbook were carefully stacked on the bottom rack and then and only then gently lifted her desk and moved it the two feet to the wall under the windows. Charles hurried his to the rear corner and dove into it with his jacket again up over his head. Neil didn't have time to see what others did.

"Okay," Neil said, "you should be getting a number in your head. From one to one hundred. I'm going to call the roll, only this time from the bottom up, z to a, since we always do a to z. We'll switch it to the middle next time."

"What if somebody gets your number before you do?" Morris asked.

"Then you'll have to get another one."

"What if you doan wanna get another one?" Sheri asked.

"Then I guess you doan get to play," Neil told her.

"Look what she's doing," Maria said to Bianca.

"She's got practically the whole class up there," Marta said.

Others began now to watch Sandra at the board. She was wearing a navy dress made of soft, supple cotton that had a sash that tied in the back. The skirt and blouse outfits she occasionally wore tended to draw attention to her round tummy and to her inability to keep multiple pieces of clothing in order. Her mother (mercifully, lovingly, Neil suspected) had made her a series of these dresses, which allowed her freedom of movement—she was an active, well-coordinated child—and which still remained neat and unruffled looking in the face of her indifference to her clothing. Also, miraculously, the bow of the sash remained tied, perhaps because it was sewn tied?

With her back to them, she had deftly laid out her lists. She had written the row numbers on the board first, as high as she could reach, and then instead of writing each name in each row from top to bottom she wrote them from left to right. The names were so evenly lined up that it was as if she were using a straightedge as a guide.

"Sandra's almost done. Once she's written all the names on the board…"

Neil paused and with the rest of the class watched her as she finished the last two lines. She was so involved that she didn't know they were watching. As for her audience, they seemed to feel as Neil felt. A magician was performing one of her marvelous tricks. She knew exactly how much space she needed; and the names came up perfectly as if from a typesetting machine. How did she do that?

Not only did Neil appreciate how special this child was, but he was filled with pride that his class, all of them it seemed, were able to allow Sandra to have her special talent. This admiration couldn't have occurred so openly a month ago. Why? Would it have threatened their place in the group? Would it have robbed them of their standing? Had something in his behavior made them feel more secure? Neil knew these questions were important, but too much was going on for him to take the time to make note of them. Bianca had exchanged a look with Harriet and nodded her head back at him, with a knowing smile from both. What was that all about? Why?

Why? And never enough time to ponder the question. That was a given.

When Sandra was done and, suddenly aware of the silence, turned to look, together, spontaneously, Clyde, Harriet, Bianca, Pauli, and then Neil and then everyone began clapping. Sandra's round pale face turned crimson and she lowered her head to one side as she rushed back toward her desk, saw in confusion it was now against the window and simply turned and stood, backed up against the wall, head down, hands clasped in front of her.

"Sandra, that was amazing," Harriet said.

"She's the best," Marta said.

"It's not just names," Clyde said.

"Like a picture," Sheri said.

"It's so organized, that's why," Clyde said.

"Who's going to erase it?" Pauli said.

"Me," Sandra said. "I will."

"All right," Neil said, "you can erase it before we go home, but right now you still have a job to do."

She looked at him, perplexed.

"You have to write the numbers next to the names. When I call the names people have to tell us their number and you have to write it down. Nobody else would dare."

Sandra hurried back to the board and Neil called the roll, z (or to be accurate, w) to a. And, yes, there were several disputes because that was my number and there were a few hurt silences by the ones who had their numbers taken but would never call out and when it evolved that Sheri had chosen twenty-two and was the only person to have chosen twenty-two and twenty-two was in fact the number written on the folded-up paper you cheated Mr. Riley, you told her the number, he did not, then how come you got it, I just did.

"She just got it!" Neil shouted.

"He wouldn't never cheat," Bianca insisted.

"Oh, my Lord, that girl…" Arlene gasped, with no need to explain what it was about that girl.

"Can we just play the game?" Neil asked.

And, yes, that turned out to be possible. The person Neil knew as the Traffic Cop and that the children knew as The Snowman and who was in any case Sheri, chosen fair and square regardless of what anyone said, was ready to take her place at the front of the class and the game actually began. Neil's job, of course, was to settle disputes because even though he cheated to give Sheri first up he was the only person who would be fair.

Once the game was under way Neil became fascinated by the different styles of the players. Some stepped out quickly, others cautiously. Both Arlene and Bianca were amazingly fast, and seemed instinctively to know just when Sheri's one-two-three-four-FIVE *FREEZE!* was coming. They were determined to win. And they quickly took the lead, neck and neck. But watch out, because another competitor, David, stepped out just behind them, using them for cover, playing a waiting game. Clyde, on the other hand, went out of his way to demonstrate that he could care less. He took a couple of cool steps then stopped well before the count was ended. Sandra always took a quick mini-step and stopped, then seemed to take the time left to observe her fellow students. Scrutinize them. *Fascinating,* Neil thought. *No time to think about it.* Charles, of course, didn't play. He stayed in his desk in the back corner but made no attempt to hide the fact that he was watching. He sat up, his jacket held with both hands at his forehead, his face visible from his eyes to his chin. Harriet, too, didn't play. She stood with her back to the table that had been pushed against the rear wall.

Pauli was another matter. His first steps were with a swimming motion of his arms, his face haughty and indifferent. When he froze his right arm was crooked over his head, his left stretched out indolently. Neil's attention had to be on the game. Was Sheri playing fair? Were the calls justified? But he was also captivated by Pauli's grace and creativity. This was a cut-throat game for most, and yet Pauli by choreographing a new dance each turn took it in an entirely different direction.

"Carmen, you moved," Sheri announced. "Back to The Freezer."

Carmen had fluffed her hair. It was such a habitual movement she probably didn't even know she was doing it.

Sheri put her hand on her mouth. "Look at Pauli!"

And Pedro, Javier, Maria and Simon did. And were immediately sent back to The Freezer for their gullibility. Sheri's quick tender glance at Pedro didn't change the reality. You move you melt.

Meanwhile, Harriet too had watched Pauli with marked interest. The next round she took off on tippy toes, freezing with her hands lifted daintily next to her head, a prissy look on her face. Pauli had caught her movement and...

"Pauli, you looked at Harriet," Sheri said. "And so did Clyde and Morris. Back to The Freezer."

But Arlene and Bianca were both advancing inexorably to the front, indifferent to any foolishness around them. They were the enemy and Sheri knew it.

"Bianca's ahead of Arlene," Sheri said.

It didn't work. Neither of them budged. Sheri didn't seem to be aware of David.

The next round Pauli had no interest in Harriet. He wound his hands toward the ceiling, reaching, searching, and when the FREEZE came his arms were stretched toward the sky, his face in torment. Harriet had made sure she was slightly ahead of him and at the FREEZE was in an appreciative curtsy.

The list of those who looked at Pauli and Harriet grew longer. But it did not include Arlene or Bianca or, for that matter, the cagey David. Pedro, who seemed to have no real interest in winning, was no longer looking at Pauli and Harriet. He only had eyes for Sheri.

Meanwhile, next turn Harriet moved forward with a fancy wave of her hands at each step, then froze with the pointer finger of her left hand under her chin, eyes raised so soulfully, her right hand out to ward off any rude advance. Pauli was in a gentleman's bow. And so now you had most of the class back at The Freezer, the two dance performers, Harriet and Pauli, taking up much of the room in the middle, and three uncompromisingly aggressive stalkers, Bianca, Arlene and David, bearing down on The Snowman. Sheri now saw David's game. Pedro longed for Sheri.

Neil was entranced, not only that Pauli had been able to turn this competitive, winner-take-all game into a dance, but that Harriet, of all people, had joined him. For good or ill Neil had been aware of Pauli's inclination to dramatize situations, but he had not been aware of the underpinning of grace and imagination that impelled him. Then what to make of his quiet one: shy, brilliant Harriet stepping out, as gracefully as Pauli? Who was she?

"David's trying to sneak up behind Arlene," Sheri said.

But it didn't matter because next turn Arlene with her tenacious athleticism and long reach beat Bianca and David, and tapped The Snowman before she could even get to four.

"Everybody back! Arlene is up!" Neil shouted.

The game continued in its strange bifurcated fashion with David, Bianca, Sheri and, who knew? Norbert focused on winning. There were others who were trying too, Sammy, Morris, Carmen, but the killer instinct just wasn't there. They were too cautious, too self-conscious, too easily distracted by the dance being performed by Pauli and Harriet. Taking turns, now Pauli whirled around and ended in a drunken slump, his tongue hanging from his mouth, with Harriet waving a competitor's esteemed appreciation. Now Harriet was a windup doll tilting this way and that, wide-eyed, arms up and down, winding down, with Pauli equally appreciative. But when Pauli finished a torturous journey through a terrible terrain standing on his right leg, leaning forward, his right arm pointing straight out in front of him, his left leg stretched straight out behind him, perfectly balanced, perfectly still, Harriet conceded defeat in full view of The Snowman with a shake of her head, a low humble bow and a silent clapping of her hands.

"Harriet, you moved. Back to The Freezer!"

But Pauli wasn't going to let her go down alone. He stood and raised his right arm to her in the black power salute. She returned it, bolstered and defiant, and, comrades-in-arms, they went back to The Freezer together.

This Snowman was tricky. The rule was she could stare at her stalkers for up to ten seconds to see if they moved before she had to turn around and count again and she took full advantage of this. More than once Neil, who was keeping track with his second hand, had to remind her, "Okay, Mr. Snowman, time to start counting." People unconsciously rub their noses, scratch, stretch, nod, look down, look up, move, well within a ten second period. Arlene caught half her melters just by taking her time. Also, she would vary her count. Go slow for one to three, speed up four to five, then change it all the next time.

"No fair, Mr. Riley," Morris complained, when he misjudged Arlene's count.

"Why?" Neil asked. "She's counting to five. She says each number. She's just a wily Snowman, that's all."

"Bianca," Arlene said, "what's that word? You should look that word up. Whiley."

Bianca didn't budge.

"Come on Snowman, ten seconds are up," Neil insisted.

"Awright! Awright!"

This time Pauli and Harriet, as if on cue, twirled once, then faced each other and bowed. Next turn they stepped sideways, advancing by crossing the right leg behind the left, then the left behind the right, the ole football walk, ending again facing each other both with their arms extended, right foot behind the left.

Bianca won a round, then lost to David. Meanwhile, Harriet was a sad clown, a cheerleader, a waitress. Pauli was Superman, a fish feeding in the water, a swordsman fighting off his attackers.

"It's eleven forty-five!" Neil shouted, suddenly coming back to his teacher senses. "Lunch is at noon! We've got to stop."

"One more turn," David said. "Arlene moved!"

"Don't count," she shouted.

"Does."

"Don't."

"WE'LL BE LATE!" Neil shouted.

"It don't matter. Won't nobody take our tables," Arlene said.

"We'll walk in proud," Bianca said.

"6-306," Pedro said.

"Put your desks back, please."

Sheri was already doing the windows. Sandra was erasing the board.

"Mr. Riley!" Clyde called out. And when he had Neil's attention, he made a clapping motion with his hands. "Pauli and Harriet," he said.

"Absolutely," Neil said, waving him five. "Pauli! Harriet!" he said, starting to clap. "You guys were wonderful!"

"They were!" Clyde said, clapping. "An' Sandra, too."

And the whole class joined in, to Pauli's bow, and then at his insistence, Harriet's curtsy. Sandra just kept on erasing. The gamers, particularly Arlene, Bianca and David, didn't fully appreciate what this was about, but they clapped along politely with the rest. Norbert had moved quickly to the rear, standing near Charles.

The windows down, the leftovers wrapped to be dumped in the trash by Morris and Pedro, Neil's briefcase full, the board clean, lights off, the door shut and locked, 6-306 left their classroom until after the Christmas-New Year's break.

Chapter 19:

A Promise Is a Promise

At the double doors of the gym: Clyde said, "Come on now, we're 6-306. Walk tall. Doan look at nobody. We the best."

And indeed as Neil lead his class into the chaos that was the gym turned cafeteria a noticeable quiet moved across the room. There were four large empty folding tables, their tables, waiting for them, and they marched in straight lines, girls first, to the sandwich table.

Inez, the aide giving out the sandwiches, looked at him with a you're late tilt of her head. Coming late was more than an inconvenience since the two aides with Mac and his assistant would have to fold the chairs, break down the tables, stack them against the back wall and mop the floor before they could leave. On normal days they would have to move even more quickly to clear the floor for the next gym class. Betty, next to Inez, giving out the chocolate milk, kept her head down and refused to look at him. She clearly wanted him to know she was furious. Unlike Inez she didn't have a son in fourth grade who might very well have the notorious Mr. Riley in two years.

Neil put his arm on Charles' shoulder as he said loudly, "Everybody! Listen!" When he had their attention he said, quietly, "Have a wonderful Christmas and a happy New Year and come back safe and sound. I'll see you all after the break."

"Come back home," Bianca said.

"Merry Christmas, Mr. Riley," Harriet said.

"I won!" Arlene shouted.

"So did I," the other three winners shouted.

"Yes you did," Neil agreed, pointing at each of them. "And you two," he said, pointing at Pauli and Harriet.

He hung back for a moment, stepping behind the table with Inez. The sandwiches were, as always, ham and cheese on white, turkey and cheese on white or tuna and cheese on white, each with somewhere a limp sliver of iceberg lettuce, you only get one sandwich, and a container of chocolate milk. To Betty he said, "I'm sorry. It was entirely my fault. They were as good as good can be. I just kept them too long."

"You shoulda paid attention," Betty said, not looking at him.

Neil watched as his class filed by in pretty damn good order.

"They really settled down though," Inez said. The "though" to let him know he wasn't entirely off the hook.

Still he knew they were at least moderately mollified. He had taken the trouble to apologize, which was more than some teachers would have done. But what really mattered to Neil were all the small dramas, some obvious, some nearly invisible, he saw unfolding at this very moment. Little things, yes, but glorious to him.

Neil knew that even though Norbert brought his own lunch he would not only get a chocolate milk for himself, but also a sandwich, the ham and cheese because it kept longer, for Charles to carry home. He knew that Charles would sit slumped down at the head of the first table near the wall with Norbert next to him on one side and Clyde on the other, with Pedro next to Clyde and Morris opposite Pedro. Somehow, even though this was mostly a boys' table, Sheri ended up sitting next to Pedro. And somehow containers and wrappers got moved so that their hands frequently, just by chance, touched. Their straws were often surreptitiously (they thought) exchanged.

Harriet was sitting with her back to Clyde. Gone were the days when Clyde's eyes drifted forlornly to the beautiful dark-eyed Carmen. These days he seemed fascinated by the skinny spikey-haired Harriet. On one pretext or another they would find reasons to lean back and make comments to each other, their faces close together, their searching eyes saying much more than their mouths. Today surely Clyde would compliment her for snagging Mr. R. when she made him tell everybody about working in that restaurant.

Las Senoritas had broken up. Carmen spent more and more of her time with Maria. Maria was fine with this, but Neil worried about Carmen. How painful was it for her that these days Bianca and Sandra were almost always with Harriet? And it was intriguing that often Brenda and Arlene, at Bianca's invitation, would join them. Arlene kept an uneasy, watchful eye out for any sign of disrespect, especially from Bianca, and looked for opportunities to snipe at her 'cause she was gaga for that teacha.' Brenda stayed close to Harriet, but was acutely aware of anything Bianca said. Bianca didn't seem to notice any of this. She kept things lively with questions like didja watch *Get Smart* last night? or today, surely, whadja think of that game?

In fact he knew the conversation across all four tables would be about the game, and how come Sheri knew it was 22? and remember Sandra writing the names on the board? and I was the Snowman the longest, no you wasn't, I was, and more than anything what Pauli and Harriet did. What did they do? the gamers would ask disparagingly. They didn't play the game. They just messed up. Messed up? They was the best thing. And there would be the telling and then the calling for a demonstration and meanwhile all the other upper grades, four through six, especially those smarties in Mrs. Robin's class, would be watching those crazies in 6-306. *Because,* Neil said emphatically to himself, *that's the place to be.*

Thinking this he turned on his heel and left the gym. As he passed through the door he heard her calling him. She caught him in the hall.

"Are you taking the bus?" she asked. She was breathless from running.

"Not today. I'm visiting a friend."

"That movie star lady?"

"No, not that movie star lady."

"Who then?"

"Bianca!" he said in his best exasperated teacher's voice.

"It's none of my business," she said with her prune face to show how stupid that was.

"That's exactly right. Here in school I'm your teacher. Out there I'm a grownup with a life and you're a…" He started to say "little," but heard how insulting that would be. "…a girl with your own life. Why should you care about mine?" Immediately from the way she crumpled her shoulders and looked away he saw how utterly tactless the question was.

"Because," she said. Then with determination she pulled herself up. This was a visible effort, a straightening of shoulders, a lifting of head, a tightening of stomach muscles. She put a pleasant smile on her face. "Today was great, wasn't it?"

"It was wonderful," he said. "Bianca, I know who thought up the Christmas card. I'll treasure it for the rest of my life. I mean it." He tried with his earnestness to tell her how important she was to him, how sorry he was to have hurt her.

She lowered her head, eyes shut, teeth clenched. She shivered. Then out of the blue, "You're coming back, aren't you?"

He froze, while her head tilted up, her eyes poring over his face, giving him longer than a ten count. "Bianca… Why are you asking that?" The question was a diversion and a desperate need to know.

"Because… Some mothers, not from our class. Sharon told Brenda you weren't going to stay," she said quickly, biting her lip, probably thinking she had revealed too much.

"I'm coming back." He pulled his head back in wonder that anyone could suggest otherwise. "You tell everybody I'm coming back," he said, jabbing a finger emphatically.

"Do you promise?" She held his eyes with hers. He was not to look away.

"I promise." He made a determined nod of his head.

"A promise is a promise," she said, her lower lip trembling.

"I promise." He took a deep breath. "Cross my heart and hope to die, I promise," he said, accepting the full gravity of the vow, pledging to her the fidelity she deserved.

She smiled. "I knew it. Well, so, Merry Christmas, Mr. Riley. And a Happy New Year," and she turned and skipped back into the gym-turned-cafeteria.

When he got to Amsterdam, he started over to Broadway. It was early, CC wouldn't be home until six-thirty and he would have time to go for a long run up Riverside before he started dinner. Chicken, a garden salad, asparagus, vanilla and chocolate Häagen-Dazs for dessert. She was surprised he could cook. CC, basting, adding herbs, making a mess, was good in the kitchen in an inefficient way. But not tonight. This was his show. She would set the table, pour the wine and let him serve her. Then they would pack for their trip to Connecticut: presents for Aunt Connie, three days' clothing. My God, my God, it was true, what he had told Bianca was absolutely true. *Out here I'm a grownup with a life.*

But instead of continuing on to Broadway he turned north and walked a half block so he could look across the schoolyard at the windows of his classroom. In his mind he heard Sheri say, pouting, *I did the windows.* To which he replied, *Of course you did. You think I don't know that?* To her, *Then how come you lookin' at them?* he would give her Bianca's incontrovertible reply. *Because.*

6-306 Roster as of November 3, 1969

North

Blackboards   Blackboards   Blackboards   Blackboards   Bulletin Board

W   Neil Riley
    Teacher's Desk   Door

	Row 4	Row 3	Row 2	Row 1	
I					B
					U
	Bianca Maldonado	Sandra Ortiz	Ruth Baker	Pauli Cross	L
					L
	Carmen Torres	Marta Albanez	Samuel Holder	Sheri Wallace	E
N					T
	Maria Rivera	Gloria Santiago	Raul Calderon	Joanna Mills	I
					N
	Pedro Rodriguez	Morris Carter	Hector Viera	Doreen Sampson	
D	West			East	B
	Joseph Rice	Cole Nelson	Javier Alvarez	Eva Martin	O
					A
	Karen Mathews	Harriet Wilson	Constance Andrews	Brenda Hardy	R
O					D
	Norberto Rosado	Alicia Barca	Steven Hood	Arlene Whitman	S
	Empty Desk	David Wade	Simon Wolf	Empty Desk	
W					
	Charles Franklin	Empty Desk	Clyde Johnson	Alvin Edwards	

Table and Four Chairs   Cabinets

                                                            Cabinets

<<<<<Coat Hooks >>>>>

South

ACKNOWLEDGMENTS

My greatest debt is to Barbara Lariar, my wife, my editor, my dearest friend. She was the first to declaim, "You will do what you will do and I will do what I will do." We have often had occasion to remind each other of that declaration. Withal we are still together. She is definitely not responsible for my many lapses, but she has certainly saved me from many others. Her work on this book was essential. Her contribution to my life is immeasurable. She understands me and stays anyhow. I adore her.

Thanks to Steven Schnur, author, photographer, cyclist and, most importantly for me, teacher. Speaking softly, with respect and concern, he guided my rough hand back from many a messy page, helped me to focus *again* and gave me the support and confidence I needed to do it. More, he provided a place for me to grow as a writer. He's done that for countless others. He's a teacher. I dare say he's also a friend.

Thanks, too, to Judy Richter, equestrian, horse trader, memoirist and great friend. With her strong grounding in Frost, adventurous spirit and love of a good story, she has been a special reader from the day Neil Riley first made his appearance in the schoolyard of Grant Elementary. And she has been there ever since. Because she has taught all her working life, early on as an English teacher, then as a trainer of world class riders, she knows the demanding skills required of a teacher. She understood immediately the enormity of the task proud ignorant callow Riley was undertaking; the shock that was in store for him up in Room 6-306.

Special thanks to Peter Gilman who has spent more than forty years in the New York City School System, first as a teacher, now as a psychologist. He's still doing it! He graciously lent Neil his birthday and his place in the draft lottery for 1970. And he shared with me some of the experiences he had in the many different settings in which he taught. That, by the way, is not to suggest that he is in any way responsible for the stories I tell, but he definitely confirmed my determination to tell them.

I'm grateful to Chloë Obara for accepting my request to interpret the work of Sandra Ortiz. Chloë taught me how immediate and compelling the work of a young artist can be. Her creations will continue to inform Riley's adventures in a future book. This was an unexpected gift. The moment I saw Chloë's picture of Neil and Charles sitting against the schoolyard fence I knew I had my cover.

Everyone should have a sister like Jane D'Arista. Economist, poet, serious gardener, she has offered me the benefits of unconditional positive regard through many years of friendship. Best of all, she tells great stories, whether about growing up female in Jacksonville, Florida or working as a ranking staffer for the Chairman of the House Banking Committee.

Off and on for some years now I have been a student at the Sarah Lawrence College Writing Institute, mostly in Schnur's workshops. From the first I was amazed that such a place existed. Suddenly I wasn't working in isolation any more. I had access to perceptive readers, the work of many fine writers to review. I know I'd leave too many writers out if I tried to list you, so I won't. But I remember your striking voices, the gorgeous singers, the ones with lines that cut like knives, the laugh-out-loud wits, those who quietly, so easily it seemed, got that exquisite moment just right. Though I'm sure I said this at the time, or tried to, I'll say it again here. Thank you. Truly. Thank you.

CPSIA information can be obtained at www.ICGtesting.com
Printed in the USA
BVOW05s1530260215

389255BV00012B/197/P